RaeAnne Thayne

THE PINES OF WINDER RANCH

HQN™

HQN™

ISBN-13: 978-1-335-01653-9

The Pines of Winder Ranch

Copyright © 2017 by Harlequin Books S.A.

The publisher acknowledges the copyright holder of the individual works as follows:

A Cold Creek Homecoming
Copyright © 2009 by RaeAnne Thayne

A Cold Creek Reunion
Copyright © 2012 by RaeAnne Thayne

Recycling programs for this product may not exist in your area.

This edition published by arrangement with Harlequin Books S.A.

For questions and comments about the quality of this book, please contact us at CustomerService@Harlequin.com.

® and TM are trademarks of Harlequin Enterprises Limited or its corporate affiliates. Trademarks indicated with ® are registered in the United States Patent and Trademark Office, the Canadian Intellectual Property Office and in other countries.

www.HQNBooks.com

Printed in U.S.A.

CONTENTS

A COLD CREEK
HOMECOMING

CHAPTER ONE

"YOU'RE HOME!"

The thin, reedy voice whispering from the frail woman on the bed was nothing like Quinn Southerland remembered.

Though she was small in stature, Jo Winder's voice had always been firm and commanding, just like the rest of her personality. When she used to call them in for supper, he and the others could hear her voice ringing out loud and clear from one end of the ranch to the other. No matter where they were, they knew the moment they heard that voice, it was time to go back to the house.

Now the woman who had done so much to raise him—the toughest woman he had ever known —seemed a tiny, withered husk of herself, her skin papery and pale and her voice barely audible.

The cracks in his heart from watching her endure the long months and years of her illness widened a little more. To his great shame, he had a sudden impulse to run away, to escape back to Seattle and his business and the comfortable life he had created for himself there, where he could pretend this was all some kind of bad dream and she was immortal, as he had always imagined.

Instead, he forced himself to step forward to the edge

of the bed, where he carefully folded her bony fingers in his own much larger ones, cursing the cancer that was taking away this woman he loved so dearly.

He gave her his most charming smile, the one that never failed to sway any woman in his path, whether in the boardroom or the bedroom.

"Where else would I be but right here, darling?"

The smile she offered in return was rueful and she lifted their entwined fingers to her cheek. "You shouldn't have come. You're so busy in Seattle."

"Never too busy for my best girl."

Her laugh was small but wryly amused, as it always used to be when he would try to charm his way out of trouble with her.

Jo wasn't the sort who could be easily charmed but she never failed to appreciate the effort.

"I'm sorry to drag you down here," she said. "I…only wanted to see all of my boys one last time."

He wanted to protest that his foster mother would be around for years to come, that she was too tough and ornery to let a little thing like cancer stop her, but he couldn't deny the evidence in front of him.

She was dying, was much closer to it than any of them had feared.

"I'm here, as long as you need me," he vowed.

"You're a good boy, Quinn. You always have been."

He snorted at that—both of them knew better about that, as well. "Easton didn't tell me you've been hitting the weed as part of your treatment."

The blankets rustled softly as her laugh shook her slight frame. "You know better than that. No marijuana here."

"Then what are you smoking?"

"Nothing. I meant what I said. You were always a good boy on the inside, even when you were dragging the others into trouble."

"It still means the world that you thought so." He kissed her forehead. "Now I can see you're tired. You get some rest and we can catch up later."

"I would give anything for just a little of my old energy."

Her voice trailed off on the last word and he could tell she had already drifted off, just like that, in mid-sentence. As he stood beside her bed, still holding her fingers, she winced twice in her sleep.

He frowned, hating the idea of her hurting. He slowly, carefully, released her fingers as if they would shatter at his touch and laid them with gentle care on the bed then turned just as Easton Springhill, his distant cousin by marriage and the closest thing he had to a sister, appeared in the doorway of the bedroom.

He moved away from the bed and followed Easton outside the room.

"She seems in pain," he said, his voice low with distress.

"She is," Easton answered. "She doesn't say much about it but I can tell it's worse the past week or so."

"Isn't there something we can do?"

"We have a few options. None of them last very long. The hospice nurse should be here any minute. She can give her something for the pain." She tilted her head. "When was the last time you ate?"

He tried to remember. He had been in Tokyo when he got the message from Easton that Jo was asking for him to come home. Though he had had two more days of meetings scheduled for a new shipping route he was negotiating, he knew he had no choice but to drop everything. Jo would never have asked if the situation hadn't been dire.

So he had rescheduled everything and ordered his plane back to Pine Gulch. Counting several flight delays from bad weather over the Pacific, he had been traveling for nearly eighteen hours and had been awake for eighteen before that.

"I had something on the plane, but it's been a few hours."

"Let me make you a sandwich, then you can catch a few z's."

"You don't have to wait on me." He followed her down the long hall and into the cheery white-and-red kitchen. "You've got enough to do, running the ranch and taking care of Jo. I've been making my own sandwiches for a long time now."

"Don't you have people who do that for you?"

"Sometimes," he admitted. "That doesn't mean I've forgotten how."

"Sit down," she ordered him. "I know where everything is here."

He thought about pushing her. But lovely as she was with her delicate features and long sweep of blond hair, Easton could be as stubborn and ornery as Jo and he was just too damn tired for another battle.

Instead, he eased into one of the scarred pine chairs snugged up against the old table and let her fuss over him for a few moments. "Why didn't you tell me how things were, East? She's withered away in the three months since I've been home. Chester probably weighs more than she does."

At the sound of his name, Easton's retired old cow

dog that followed her or Jo everywhere lifted his grizzled gray muzzle and thumped his black-and-white tail against the floor.

Easton's sigh held exhaustion and discouragement and no small measure of guilt. "I wanted to. I swear. I threatened to call you all back weeks ago but she begged me not to say anything. She said she didn't want you to know how things were until…"

Her voice trailed off and her mouth trembled a little. He didn't need her to finish. Jo wouldn't have wanted them to know until close to the end.

This was it. For three long years, Jo had been fighting breast cancer and now it seemed her battle was almost over.

He *hated* this. He wanted to escape back to his own world where he could at least pretend he had some semblance of control. But she wanted him here in Cold Creek, so here he would damn well stay.

"Truth time, East. How long does she have?"

Easton's features tightened with a deep sorrow. She had lost so much, this girl he had thought of as a sister since the day he arrived at Winder Ranch two decades ago, an angry, bitter fourteen-year-old with nothing but attitude. Easton had lived in the foreman's house then with her parents and they had been friends almost from the moment he arrived.

"Three weeks or so," she said. "Maybe less. Maybe a little more."

He wanted to rant at the unfairness of it all that somebody like Jo would be taken from the earth with such cruelty when she had spent just about every moment of her entire seventy-two years of life giving back to others.

"I'll stay until then."

She stared at him, the butter knife she was using to spread mustard on his sandwich frozen in her hand. "How can you possibly be away from Southerland Shipping that long?"

He shrugged. "I might need to make a few short trips back to Seattle here and there but most of my work can be done long-distance through email and conference calls. It shouldn't be a problem. And I have good people working for me who can handle most of the complications that might come up."

"That's not what she wanted when she asked you to come home one more time," Easton protested.

"Maybe not. But she isn't making the decisions about this, as much as she might think she's the one in charge. This is what I want. I should have come home when things first starting spiraling down. It wasn't fair for us to leave her care completely in your hands."

"You didn't know how bad things were."

If he had visited more, he would have seen for himself. But like Brant and Cisco, the other two foster sons Jo and her husband, Guff, had made a home for, life had taken him away from the safety and peace he had always found at Winder Ranch.

"I'm staying," he said firmly. "I can certainly spare a few weeks to help you out on the ranch and with Jo's care and whatever else you need, after all she and Guff did for me. Don't argue with me on this because you won't win."

"I wasn't going to argue," she said. "You can't know how happy she'll be to have you here. Thank you, Quinn."

The relief in her eyes told him with stark clarity how difficult it must have been for Easton to watch Jo dying, especially after she had lost her own parents at a young age and then her beloved uncle who had taken her in after their deaths.

He squeezed her fingers when she handed him a sandwich with thick slices of homemade bread and hearty roast beef. "Thanks. This looks delicious."

She slid across from him with an apple and a glass of milk. As he looked at her slim wrists curved around her glass, he worried that, like Jo, she hadn't been eating enough and was withering away.

"What about the others?" he asked, after one fantastic bite. "Have you let Brant and Cisco know how things stand?"

Jo had always called them her Four Winds, the three foster boys she and Guff had taken in and Easton, her niece who had been their little shadow.

"We talk to Brant over the computer every couple weeks when he can call us from Afghanistan. Our webcam's not the greatest but I suppose he still had front-row seats as her condition has deteriorated over the past month. He's working on swinging leave and is trying to get here as soon as he can."

Quinn winced as guilt pinched at him. His best friend was halfway around the world and had done a better job of keeping track of things here at the ranch than Quinn had when he was only a few states away.

"What about Cisco?"

She looked down at her apple. "Have you heard from him?"

"No. Not for a while. I got a vague email in the spring but nothing since."

"Neither had we. It's been months. I've tried everything I can think of to reach him but I have no idea even where he is. Last I heard, he was in El Salvador or somewhere like that but I'm not having any luck turning up any information about him."

Cisco worried him, Quinn had to admit. The rest of them had gone on to do something productive with their lives. Quinn had started Southerland Shipping after a stint in the Air Force, Brant Western was an honorable Army officer serving his third tour of duty in the Middle East and Easton had the ranch, which she loved more than just about anything.

Cisco Del Norte, on the other hand, had taken a very different turn. Quinn had only seen him a few times in the past five or six years and he seemed more and more jaded as the years passed.

What started as a quick trip to Mexico to visit relatives after a stint in the Army had turned into years of Cisco bouncing around Central and South America.

Quinn had no idea what he did down there. He suspected that few of Cisco's activities were legal and none of them were good. He had decided several years ago that he was probably better off not knowing for sure.

But he *did* know Jo would want one more chance to see Cisco, whatever he was up to south of the border.

He swallowed another bite of sandwich. "I'll put some resources on it and see what I can find out. My assistant is frighteningly efficient. If anyone can find the man and drag him out of whatever cantina he calls home these days, it's Kathleen."

Easton's smile didn't quite reach her eyes. "I've met the redoubtable Kathleen. She scares me."

"That makes two of us. It's all part of her charm."

He tried to hide his sudden jaw-popping yawn behind a sip of water, but few things slipped past Easton.

"Get some sleep," she ordered in a tone that didn't leave room for arguments. "Your old room is ready for you. Clean sheets and everything."

"I don't need to sleep. I'll stay up with Jo."

"I've got it. She's got my cell on speed dial and only has to hit a couple of buttons to reach me all the time. Besides, the hospice nurse will be here to take care of things during the night."

"That's good. I was about to ask what sort of medical care she receives."

"Every three hours, we have a home-care nurse check in to adjust medication and take care of any other needs she might have. Jo doesn't think it's necessary to have that level of care, but it's what her doctors and I think is best."

That relieved his mind considerably. At least Easton didn't have to carry every burden by herself. He rose from the table and folded her into a hug.

"I'm glad you're here," she murmured. "It helps."

"This is where I have to be. Wake me up if you or Jo need anything."

"Right."

He headed up the stairs in the old log house, noting the fourth step from the top still creaked, just like always. He had hated that step. More than once it had been the architect of his downfall when he and one of the others tried to sneak in after curfew. They would always try so hard to be quiet but then that blasted stair would always give them away. By the time they would reach the top of the staircase, there would be Guff, waiting for them with those bushy white eyebrows raised and a judgment-day look on his features.

He almost expected to see his foster father waiting

for him on the landing. Instead, only memories hovered there as he pushed open his bedroom door, remembering how suspicious and belligerent he had been to the Winders when he first arrived.

He had viewed Winder Ranch as just another prison, one more stop on the misery train that had become his life after his parents' murder-suicide.

Instead, he had found only love here.

Jo and Guff Winder had loved him. They had welcomed him into their home and their hearts, and then made more room for first Brant and then Cisco.

Their love hadn't stopped him from his share of trouble through high school but he knew that without them, he probably would have nurtured that bitterness and hate festering inside him and ended up in prison or dead by now.

This was where he needed to be. As long as Jo hung in, he would be here—for her and for Easton. It was the right thing—the *only* thing—to do.

HE COMPLETELY SLEPT through the discreet alarm on his Patek Philippe, something he *never* did.

When he finally emerged from his exhausted slumber three hours later, Quinn was disoriented at first. The sight of his familiar bedroom ceiling left him wondering if he was stuck in some kind of weird flashback about his teenage years, the kind of dream where some sexy, tight-bodied cheerleader was going to skip through the door any minute now.

No. That wasn't it. Something bleak tapped at his memory bank and the cheerleader fantasy bounced back through the door.

Jo.

He was at the ranch and Jo was dying. He sat up and scrubbed at his face. Daylight was still several hours away but he was on Tokyo time and doubted he could go back to sleep anyway.

He needed a shower, but he supposed it could wait for a few more moments, until he checked on her. Since Jo had always expressed strongly negative feelings about the boys going shirtless around her ranch even when they were mowing the lawn, he took a moment to shrug back into his travel-wrinkled shirt and headed down the stairs, careful this time to skip over the noisy step so he didn't wake Easton.

When he was a kid, Jo and Guff had shared a big master suite on the second floor. She had moved out of it after Guff's death five years ago from an unexpected heart attack, saying she couldn't bear sleeping there anymore without him. She had taken one of the two bedrooms on the main floor, the one closest to the kitchen.

When he reached it, he saw a woman backing out of the room, closing the door quietly behind her.

For an instant, he assumed it was Easton, but then he saw the coloring was wrong. Easton wore her waterfall of straight honey-blond hair in a ponytail most of the time but this woman had short, wavy auburn hair that just passed her chin.

She was smaller than Easton, too, though definitely curvy in all the right places. He felt a little thrum of masculine interest at the sight of a delectably curved derriere easing from the room—as unexpected as it was out of place, under the circumstances.

He was just doing his best to tamp his inappropriate interest back down when the woman turned just enough that he could see her features and any fledgling attraction disappeared like he'd just jumped naked into Windy Lake.

"What the hell are you doing here?" he growled out of the darkness.

CHAPTER TWO

THE WOMAN WHIRLED and grabbed at her chest, her eyes wide in the dimly lit hallway. "My word! You scared the life out of me!"

Quinn considered himself a pretty easygoing guy and he had despised very few people in his life—his father came immediately to mind as an exception.

But if he had to make a list, Tess Jamison would be right there at the top.

He was about to ask her again what she thought she was doing creeping around Winder Ranch when his sleep-deprived synapses finally clicked in and he made the connection as he realized that curvy rear end he had been unknowingly admiring was encased in deep blue flowered surgical scrubs.

She carried a basket of medical supplies in one hand and had an official-looking clipboard tucked under her arm.

"*You're* the hospice nurse?" His voice rose with incredulity.

She fingered the silver stethoscope around her neck with her free hand. "That's what they tell me. Hey, Quinn. How have you been?"

He must still be upstairs in his bed, having one of those infinitely disturbing dreams of high school, the kind where he shows up to an advanced placement class and discovers he hasn't read a single page of the text-book, knows absolutely none of the subject matter, and is expected to sit down and ace the final.

This couldn't be real. It was too bizarre, too surreal, that someone he hadn't seen since graduation night—and would have been quite content never to have to see again—would suddenly be standing in the hallway of Winder Ranch looking much the same as she had fifteen years earlier.

He blinked but, damn it all, she didn't disappear and he wished he could just wake up, already.

"Tess," he said gruffly, unable to think of another thing to say.

"Right."

"How long have you been coming here to take care of Jo?"

"Two weeks now," she answered, and he wondered if her voice had always had that husky note to it or if it was a new development. "There are several of us, actually. I usually handle the nights. I stop in about every three or four hours to check vitals and help Jo manage her pain. I juggle four other patients with varying degrees of need but she's my favorite."

As she spoke, she moved away from Jo's bedroom door and headed toward him. He held his breath and fought the instinct to cover his groin, just as a precaution.

Not that she had ever physically hurt him in their turbulent past, but Tess Jamison—Homecoming Queen, valedictorian, and all-around Queen Bee, probably for Bitch—had a way of emasculating a man with just a look.

She smelled not like the sulfur and brimstone he

might have expected, but a pleasant combination of vanilla and peaches that made him think of hot summer evenings out on the wide porch of the ranch with a bowl of ice cream and Jo's divine cobbler.

She headed down the hall toward the kitchen, where she flipped on a small light over the sink.

For the first time, he saw her in full light. She was as lovely as when she wore the Homecoming Queen crown, with high cheekbones, a delicate nose and the same lush, kissable mouth he remembered.

Her eyes were still her most striking feature, green and vivid, almond-shaped, with thick, dark lashes.

But fifteen years had passed and nothing stayed the same except his memories. She had lost that fresh-faced innocent look that had been so misleading. He saw tiny, faint lines fanning out at the edges of her eyes and she wore a bare minimum of makeup.

"I didn't know you were back," she finally said when he continued to stare. "Easton didn't mention it before she went to bed."

Apparently there were several things Easton was keeping close to her sneaky little vest. "I only arrived this evening." Somehow he managed to answer her without snarling, but it was a chore. "Jo wanted to see all of us one more time."

He couldn't quite bring himself to say *last* instead of *more* but those huge green eyes still softened.

She was a hospice nurse, he reminded himself, as tough as he found that to believe. She was probably well-trained to pretend sympathy. The real Tess Jamison didn't care about another soul on the planet except herself.

"Are you here for the weekend?" she asked.

"Longer," he answered, his voice curt. It was none of her business that he planned to stay at Winder Ranch as long as Jo needed him, which he hoped was much longer than the doctors seemed to believe.

She nodded once, her eyes solemn, and he knew she understood all he hadn't said. The soft compassion in those eyes—and his inexplicable urge to soak it in—turned him conversely hostile.

"I can't believe you've stuck around Pine Gulch all these years," he drawled. "I would have thought Tess Jamison couldn't wait to shake the dust of podunk eastern Idaho off her designer boots."

She smiled a little. "It's Tess Claybourne now. And plans have a way of changing, don't they?"

"I'm starting to figure that out."

Curiosity stirred inside him. What had she been doing the past fifteen years? Why that hint of sadness in her eyes?

This was Tess, he reminded himself. He didn't give a damn what she'd been up to, even if she looked hauntingly lovely in the low light of the kitchen.

"So you married old Scott, huh? What's he up to? All that quarterback muscle probably turned to flab, right? Is he ranching with his dad?"

She pressed her lips into a thin line for just a moment, then gave him another of those tiny smiles, this one little more than a taut stretch of her mouth. "None of those things, I'm afraid. He died almost two years ago."

Quinn gave an inward wince at his own tactlessness. Apparently nothing had changed. She had *always* brought out the worst in him.

"How?"

She didn't answer for a moment, instead crossing to

the coffeemaker he had assumed Easton must have forgotten to turn off. Now he realized she must have left
a fresh pot for the hospice worker, since Tess seemed
completely comfortable reaching in the cabinet for a
cup and pouring.

"Pneumonia," she finally answered as she added two
packets of sweetener. "Scott died of pneumonia."

"Really?" That seemed odd. He thought only old
people and little kids could get that sick from pneumonia.

"He was...ill for a long time before that. His immune
system was compromised and he couldn't fight it off."

Quinn wasn't a *complete* ass, even when it came to
this woman he despised so much. He forced himself
to offer the appropriate condolences. "That must have
been rough for you. Any kids?"

"No."

This time she didn't even bother to offer a tight
smile, only stared into the murky liquid swirling in
her cup and he thought again how surreal this was,
standing in the Winder Ranch kitchen in the middle of
the night having a conversation with her, when he had
to fight down every impulse to snarl and yell and order
her out of the house.

"Jo tells me you run some big shipping company in
the Pacific Northwest," she said after a moment.

"That's right." The third biggest in the region, but he
was hoping that with the new batch of contracts he was
negotiating Southerland Shipping would soon slide into
the number two spot and move up from there.

"She's so proud of you boys and Easton. She talks
about you all the time."

"Does she?" He wasn't at all thrilled to think about Jo sharing with Tess any details of his life.

"Oh, yes. I'm sure she's thrilled to have you home. That must be why she was sleeping so peacefully. She didn't even wake when I checked her vitals, which is unusual. Jo's usually a light sleeper."

"How are they?"

"Excuse me?"

"Her vitals. How is she?"

He hated to ask, especially of Tess, but he was a man who dealt best with challenges when he gathered as much information as possible.

She took another sip of coffee then poured the rest down the sink and turned on the water to wash it down.

"Her blood pressure is still lower than we'd like to see and she's needing oxygen more and more often. She tries to hide it but she's in pain most of the time. I'm sorry. I wish I had something better to offer you."

"It's not your fault," he said, even as he wished he could somehow figure out a way to blame her for it.

"That's funny. It feels that way sometimes. It's my job to make her as comfortable as possible but she doesn't want to spend her last days in a drugged haze, she says. So we're limited in some of our options. But we still do our best."

He couldn't imagine *anyone* deliberately choosing this for a career. Why on earth would a woman like Tess Jamison—Claybourne now, he reminded himself— have chosen to stick around tiny Pine Gulch and become a hospice nurse? He couldn't quite get past the incongruity of it.

"I'd better go," she said. "I've got three more patients to check on tonight. I'll be back in a few hours, though, and Easton knows she can call me anytime if she needs me. It's…good to see you again, Quinn."

He wouldn't have believed her words, even if he didn't see the lie in her vivid green eyes. She wasn't any happier to see him than he had been to find her wandering the halls of Winder Ranch.

Still, courtesy drilled into him by Jo demanded he walk her to the door. He stood on the porch and watched through the darkness until she reached her car, then he walked back inside, shaking his head.

Tess Jamison Claybourne.

As if he needed one more miserable thing to face here in Pine Gulch.

QUINN SOUTHERLAND.

Lord have mercy.

Tess sat for a moment outside Winder Ranch in the little sedan she had bought after selling Scott's wheelchair van. Her mind was a jumble of impressions, all of them sharp and hard and ugly.

He despised her. His rancor radiated from him like spokes on a bicycle wheel. Though he had conversed with at least some degree of civility throughout their short encounter, every word, every sentence, had been underscored by his contempt. His silvery-blue eyes had never once lost that sheen of scorn when he looked at her.

Tess let out a breath, more disconcerted by the brief meeting than she should be. She had a thick enough skin to withstand a little animosity. Or at least she had always assumed she did, up to this point.

How would she know, though? She had never had

much opportunity to find out. Most of the good citizens of Pine Gulch treated her far differently.

Alone in the quiet darkness of her car, she gave a humorless laugh. How many times over the years had she thought how heartily sick she was of being treated like some kind of venerated saint around Pine Gulch? She wanted people to see her as she really was—someone with hopes and dreams and faults. Not only as the tireless caretaker who had dedicated long years of her life to caring for her husband.

She shook her head with another rough laugh. A little middle ground would be nice. Quinn Southerland's outright vilification of her was a little more harsh than she really wanted to face.

He had a right to despise her. She understood his feelings and couldn't blame him for them. She had treated him shamefully in high school. Just the memory, being confronted with the worst part of herself when she hadn't really thought about those things in years, made her squirm as she started her car.

Her treatment of Quinn Southerland had been reprehensible, beyond cruel, and she wanted to cringe away from remembering it. But seeing him again after all these years seemed to set the fragmented, half-forgotten memories shifting and sliding through her mind like jagged plates of glass.

She remembered all of it. The unpleasant rumors she had spread about him; her small, snide comments, delivered at moments when he was quite certain to overhear; the friends and teachers she had turned against him, without even really trying very hard.

She had been a spoiled, petulant bitch, and the memory of it wasn't easy to live with now that she had much more wisdom and maturity and could look back on her terrible behavior through the uncomfortable prism of age and experience.

She fully deserved his contempt, but that knowledge didn't make it much easier to stomach as she drove down the long, winding Winder Ranch driveway and turned onto Cold Creek Road, her headlights gleaming off the leaves that rustled across the road in the October wind.

She loved Jo Winder dearly and had since she was a little girl, when Jo had been patient and kind with the worst piano student any teacher ever had. Tess had promised the woman just the evening before that she would remain one of her hospice caregivers until the end. How on earth was she supposed to keep that vow if it meant being regularly confronted with her own poor actions when she was a silly girl too heedless to care about anyone else's feelings?

The roads were dark and quiet as she drove down Cold Creek Canyon toward her next patient, across town on the west side of Pine Gulch.

Usually she didn't mind the quiet or the solitude, this sense in the still hours of the night that she was the only one around. Even when she was on her way to her most difficult patient, she could find enjoyment in these few moments of peace.

Ed Hardy was a cantankerous eighty-year-old man whose kidneys were failing after years of battling diabetes. He wasn't facing his impending passing with the same dignity or grace as Jo Winder but continued to fight it every step of the way. He was mean-spirited and belligerent, lashing out at anyone who dared remind him he wasn't a twenty-five-year-old wrangler anymore who could rope and ride with the best of them.

Despite his bitterness, she loved the old coot. She loved *all* her home-care patients, even the most difficult. She would miss them, even Ed, when she moved away from Pine Gulch in a month.

She sighed as she drove down Main Street with its darkened businesses and the historic Old West lamp-posts somebody in the chamber of commerce had talked the town into putting up for the tourists a few years ago.

Except for the years she went to nursing school in Boise and those first brief halcyon months after her marriage, she had lived in this small Idaho town in the west shadow of the Tetons her entire life.

She and Scott had never planned to stay here. Their dreams had been much bigger than a rural community like Pine Gulch could hold.

They had married a month after she graduated from nursing school. He had been a first-year med student, excited about helping people, making a difference in the world. They had talked about opening a clinic in some undeveloped country somewhere, about travel and all the rich buffet of possibilities spreading out ahead of them.

But as she said to Quinn Southerland earlier, sometimes life didn't work out the way one planned. Instead of exotic locales and changing the world, she had brought her husband home to Pine Gulch where she had a support network—friends and family and neighbors who rallied around them.

She pulled into the Hardy driveway, noting the leaves that needed to be raked and the small flower garden that should be put to bed for the winter. Mrs. Hardy had her hands full caring for her husband and his many medical needs. She had a grandson in Idaho Falls who helped a bit with the yard but now that school was back in session, he didn't come as often as he had in the summer.

Tess turned off her engine, shuffling through her mental calendar to see if she could find time in the next few days to come over with a rake.

Her job had never been only about pain management and end-of-life decisions. At least not to her. She knew what it was like to be on the other side of the equation and how very much it could warm the heart when someone showed up unexpectedly with a smile and a cloth and window spray to wash the winter grime she hadn't had time to clean off because her life revolved around caretaking someone else.

That experience as the recipient of service had taught her well that her job was to lift the burdens of the families as much as of her patients.

Even hostile, antagonistic family members like Quinn Southerland.

The wind swirled leaves across the Hardys' cracked driveway as she stepped out of her car. Tess shivered, but she knew it wasn't at the prospect of winter just around the corner or that wind bare-knuckling its way under her jacket, but from remembering the icy cold blue of Quinn's eyes.

Though she wasn't at all eager to encounter him again– -or to face the bitter truth of the spoiled brat she had been once—she adored Jo Winder. She couldn't let Quinn's forbidding presence distract her from giving Jo the care she deserved.

CHAPTER THREE

APPARENTLY PINE GULCH'S time machine was in fine working order.

Quinn walked into The Gulch and was quite certain he had traveled back twenty years to the first time he walked into the café with his new foster parents. He could clearly remember that day, the smell of frying potatoes and meat, the row of round swivel seats at the old-fashioned soda fountain, the craning necks in the place and the hot gazes as people tried to figure out the identity of the surly, scowling dark-haired kid with Jo and Guff.

Not much had changed. From the tin-stamped ceiling to the long, gleaming mirror that ran the length of the soda fountain to the smell of fried food that seemed to send triglycerides shooting through his veins just from walking in the door.

Even the faces were the same. He could swear the same old-timers still sat in the booth in the corner being served by Donna Archuleta, whose husband, Lou, had always manned the kitchen with great skill and joy. He recognized Mick Malone, Jesse Redbear and Sal Martinez.

And, of course, Donna. She stood by the booth with a pot of coffee in her hand but she just about dropped it all over the floor when she looked up at the sound of the jangling bells on the door to spy him walking into her café.

"Quinn Southerland," she exclaimed, her smoker-husky voice delighted. "As I live and breathe."

"Hey, Donna."

One of Jo's closest friends, Donna had always gone out of her way to be kind to him and to Brant and Cisco. They hadn't always made it easy. The three of them had been the town's resident bad boys back in the day. Well, maybe not Brant, he acknowledged, but he was usually guilty by association, if nothing else.

"I didn't know you were back in town." Donna set the pot down in an empty booth to fold her scrawny arms around him. He hugged her back, wondering when she had gotten frail like Jo.

"Just came in yesterday," he said.

"Why the hell didn't anybody tell me?"

He opened his mouth to answer but she cut him off.

"Oh, no. Jo. Is she…" Her voice trailed off but he could see the anxiety suddenly brim in her eyes, as if she dreaded his response.

He shook his head and forced a smile. "She woke up this morning feistier than ever, craving one of Lou's sweet rolls. Nothing else will do, she told me in no uncertain terms, so she sent me down here first thing so I could pick one up and take it back for her. Since according to East, she hasn't been hungry for much of anything else, I figured I had better hurry right in and grab her one."

Donna's lined and worn features brightened like a gorgeous June morning breaking over the mountains. "You're in luck, hon. I think he's just pullin' a new batch out of the oven. You wait right here and have yourself some coffee while I go back and wrap a half-dozen up for her."

Before he could say a word, she turned a cup over from the setting in the booth and poured him a cup. He laughed at this further evidence that not much had changed, around The Gulch at least.

"I think one, maybe two sweet rolls, are probably enough. Like I said, she hasn't had much of an appetite."

"Well, this way she can warm another up later or save one for the morning, and there will be extras for you and Easton. Now don't you argue with me. I'm doing this, so just sit down and drink your coffee, there's a good boy."

He had to smile in the face of such determination, such eagerness to do something nice for someone she cared about. There were few things he missed about living in Pine Gulch, but that sense of community, belonging to something bigger than yourself, was definitely one of them.

He took a seat at the long bar, joining a few other solo customers who eyed him with curiosity.

Again, he had the strange sense of stepping back into his past. He could still see the small chip in the bottom corner of the mirror where he and Cisco had been roughhousing and accidentally sent a salt shaker flying.

That long-ago afternoon was as clear as his flight in from Japan the day before—the sick feeling in the pit of his gut as he had faced the wrath of Lou and Donna and the even worse fear when he had to fess up to Guff and Jo. He had only been with them a year, twelve tumultuous months, and had been quite sure they would toss him back into the foster-care system after one mess-up too many.

But Guff hadn't yelled or ordered him to pack his

things. Instead, he just sat him down and told one of his rambling stories about a time he had been a young ranch hand with a little too much juice in him and had taken his .22 and shot out the back windows of what he thought was an old abandoned pickup truck, only to find out later it belonged to his boss's brother.

"A man steps up and takes responsibility for his actions," Guff had told him solemnly. That was all he said, but the trust in his brown eyes had completely overwhelmed Quinn. So of course he had returned to The Gulch and offered to work off the cost of replacing the mirror for the Archuletas.

He smiled a little, remembering Lou and Donna's response. "Think we'll just keep that little nick there as a reminder," Lou had said. "But there are always dishes around here to be washed."

He and Cisco had spent about three months of Saturdays and a couple afternoons a week after school in the kitchen with their hands full of soapy water. More than he cared to admit, he had enjoyed those days listening to the banter of the café, all the juicy small-town gossip.

He only had about three or four minutes to replay the memory in his head before Lou Archuleta walked out of the kitchen, his bald head just as shiny as always and his thick salt-and-pepper mustache a bold contrast. The delight on his rough features matched Donna's, warming Quinn somewhere deep inside.

Lou wiped his hand on his white apron before holding it out for a solemn handshake. "Been too long," he said, in that same gruff, no-nonsense way. "Hear Seattle's been pretty good to you."

Quinn shook his hand firmly, aware as he did that much of his success in business derived from watching the integrity and goodness of people like Lou and Donna and the respect with which they had always treated their customers.

"I've done all right," he answered.

"Better than all right. Jo says you've got a big fancy house on the shore and your own private jet."

Technically it was the company's corporate jet. But since he owned the company, he supposed he couldn't debate semantics. "How about you? How's Rick?"

Their son had gone to school with him and graduated a year after him. Tess Jamison's year, actually.

"Good. Good. He's up in Boise these days. He's a plumbing contractor, has himself a real good business. He and his wife gave us our first granddaughter earlier this year." The pride on Lou's work-hardened features was obvious.

"Congratulations."

"Yep, after four boys, they finally got a girl."

Quinn choked on the sip of coffee he'd just taken. "Rick has five kids?"

His mind fairly boggled at the very idea of even one. He couldn't contemplate having enough for a basketball team.

Lou chuckled. "Yep. Started young and threw in a set of twins in there. He's a fine dad, too."

The door chimed, heralding another customer, but Quinn was still reeling at the idea of his old friend raising a gaggle of kids and cleaning out toilets.

Still, an odd little prickle slid down his spine, especially when he heard the old-timers in their regular booth hoot with delight and usher the newcomer over.

"About time you got here," one of the old-timers in

the corner called out. "Mick here was sure you was goin' to bail on us today."

"Are you kidding?" an alto female voice answered. "This is my favorite part of working graveyard, the chance to come in here for breakfast and have you all give me a hard time every morning. I don't know what I'll do without it."

Quinn stiffened on the stool. He didn't need to turn to know just who was now sliding into the booth near the regulars. He had last heard that voice at 3:00 a.m. in the dark quiet of the Winder Ranch kitchen.

"Hey, Miss Tess." Lou turned his attention away from bragging about his grandkids to greet the newcomer, confirming what Quinn had already known deep in his bones. "You want your usual?"

"You got it, Lou. I've been dreaming of your veggie omelet all night long. I'm absolutely starving."

"Girl, you need to get yourself something more interesting to fill your nights if all you can dream about is Lou's veggie omelet," called out one of the women from a nearby booth and everybody within earshot laughed.

Everybody but Quinn. She was a regular here, just like the others, he realized. She was part of the community, and he, once more, was the outsider.

She had always been excellent at reminding him of that.

He couldn't put it off any longer, he knew. With some trepidation, he turned around from the counter to the dining room to face her gaze.

Despite the mirror right in front of him, she must not have been paying attention to the other patrons in the restaurant. He could tell she hadn't known he was there until he turned. He saw the little flash of surprise in her eyes, the slight rise and fall of her slim chest as her breathing hitched.

She covered it quickly with a tight smile and the briefest of waves.

She wasn't pleased to see him. He didn't miss the sudden tension in her posture or the dismay that quickly followed that initial surprise.

Join the club, he thought. Bumping into his worst nightmare two times in less than six hours was twice too many, as far as he was concerned.

He thought he saw something strangely vulnerable flash in those brilliant green eyes for just an instant, then she turned back to the old-timers at the booth with some bright, laughing comment that sounded forced to him.

As he listened to their interaction, it was quickly apparent to him that Tess was a favorite of all of them. No surprise there. She excelled at twisting everybody around her little finger. She had probably been doing the very same thing since she was the age of Lou Archuleta's new granddaughter.

The more the teasing conversation continued, the more sour his mood turned. She sounded vivacious and funny and charming. Why couldn't anybody but him manage to see past the act to the vicious streak lurking beneath?

When he had just about had all he could stomach, Donna returned with two white bakery bags and a disposable coffee cup with steam curling out the top.

"Here you go, hon. Didn't mean to keep you waiting until Christmas but I got tied up in the back with a phone call from a distributor. There's plenty of extra sweet rolls for you and here's a little joe for the road."

He put away his irritation at Tess and took the offerings from Donna with an affectionate smile, his heart warmer than the cup in his hand at her concern. "Thanks."

"You give that girl a big old kiss from everybody down here at The Gulch. Tell her to hang in there and we're all prayin' for her."

"I'll do that."

"And come back, why don't you, while you're in town. We'll fix you up your favorite chicken-fried steak and have a coze."

"It's a date." He kissed her cheek and headed for the door. Just as he reached it, he heard Tess call his name.

"Wait a minute, will you?" she said.

He schooled his features into a mask of indifference as he turned, loathe for any of the other customers to see how it rankled to see her here still acting like the Pine Gulch Homecoming Queen deigning to have breakfast with her all of her hordes of loyal, adoring subjects.

He didn't want to talk to her. He didn't want to be forced to see how lovely and perky she looked, even in surgical scrubs and even after he knew she had been working all night at a difficult job.

She smelled of vanilla and peaches and he didn't want to notice that she looked as bright as the morning, how her auburn curls trailed against her slender jawline or the light sprinkle of freckles across her nose or the way her green eyes had that little rim of gold around the edge you only saw if you were looking closely.

He didn't want to see Tess at all, he didn't want to feel like an outsider again in Pine Gulch, and he especially didn't want to have to stand by and do nothing while a woman he loved slipped away, little by little.

"How's Jo this morning?" she asked. "She seemed restless at six when I came to check on her."

As far as he remembered, Tess had never been involved in the high-school drama club. So either she had become a really fabulous actress in the intervening years or her concern for Jo was genuine.

He let out a breath, tamping down his antagonism in light of their shared worry for Jo. "I don't know. To me, she seems better this morning than she was last night when I arrived. But I don't really have a baseline to say what's normal and what's not."

He held up the bakery bag. "She at least had enough energy to ask for Lou's sweet rolls this morning."

"That's excellent. Eating has been hard for her the past few weeks. Seeing you must be giving her a fresh burst of strength."

Was she implying he should have come sooner? He frowned, disliking the guilt swirling around in his gut along with the coffee.

Yeah, he should have come home sooner. If Easton and Jo had been forthright about what was going on, he would have been here weeks ago. They had hid the truth from him but he should have been more intuitive and figured it out.

That didn't mean he appreciated Tess pointing out his negligence. He scowled but she either didn't notice or didn't particularly care.

"It's important that you make sure she doesn't overdo things," Tess said. "I know that's hard to do during those times when she's feeling better. On her good days, she has a tendency to do much more than she really has the strength to tackle. You just have to be careful to ensure she doesn't go overboard."

Her bossy tone brought his dislike simmering to the surface. "Don't try to manage me like you do everybody else in town," he snapped. "I'm not one of your devoted worshippers. We both know I never have been."

For just an instant, hurt flared in her eyes but she quickly blinked it away and tilted that damn perky chin up, her eyes a sudden murky, wintry green.

"This has nothing to do with me," she replied coolly. "It's about Jo. Part of my job as her hospice nurse is to advise her family regarding her care. I can certainly reserve those conversations with Easton if that's what you prefer."

He bristled for just a moment, but the bitter truth of it was, he knew she was right. He needed to put aside how much he disliked this woman for things long in the distant past to focus on his foster mother, who needed him right now.

Tess appeared to genuinely care about Jo. And while he wasn't quite buying such a radical transformation, people could change. He saw it all the time.

Hell, he was a completely different person than he'd been in high school. He wasn't the angry, belligerent hothead with a chip the size of the Tetons on his shoulder anymore, though he was certainly acting like it right now.

It wasn't wholly inconceivable that this caring nurse act was the real thing.

"You're right." He forced the words out, though they scraped his throat raw. "I appreciate the advice. I'm... still struggling with seeing her this way. In my mind, she should still be out on the ranch hurtling fences and rounding up strays."

Her defensive expression softened and she lifted a

hand just a little. For one insane moment, he thought she meant to touch his arm in a sympathetic gesture, but she dropped her arm back to her side.

"Wouldn't we all love that?" she said softly. "I'm afraid those days are gone. Right now, we just have to savor every moment with her, even if it's quietly sitting beside her while she sleeps."

She stepped away from him and he was rather horrified at the regret suddenly churning through him. All these conflicting feelings were making him a little crazy.

"I'm off until tonight," she said, "but you'll find Cindy, the day nurse, is wonderful. Even so, tell Easton to call me if she needs anything."

He nodded and pushed past the door into the sunshine.

That imaginary time machine had a few little glitches in it, he thought as he pulled out of the parking lot and headed back toward Cold Creek Canyon.

He had just exchanged several almost civil words with Tess Jamison Claybourne, something that a dozen years ago would have seemed just as impossible as imagining that someday he would be able to move past the ugliness in his past to run his own very successful company.

CHAPTER FOUR

"DO YOU REMEMBER that time you boys stayed out with the Walker sisters an hour past curfew?"

"I'm going to plead the fifth on that one," Quinn said lazily, though he did indeed remember Sheila Walker and some of her more acrobatic skills.

"I remember it," Jo said. "The door was locked and you couldn't get back in so you rascals tried to sneak in a window, remember that? Guff heard a noise downstairs and since he was half-asleep and didn't realize you boys hadn't come home yet, he thought it might be burglars."

Jo chuckled. "He took the baseball bat he kept by the side of the bed and went down and nearly beaned the three of you as you were trying to sneak in the window."

He smiled at the memory of Brant's guilt and Cisco's smart-aleck comments and Guff's stern reprimand to all of them.

"I can't believe Guff told you about that. It was supposed to be a secret between us males."

Her mouth lifted a little at the edges. "Guff didn't keep secrets from me. Don't you know better than that? He used to say whatever he couldn't tell me, he would rather not know himself."

Jo's voice changed when she talked about her late

husband. The tone was softer, more rounded, and her love sounded in every word.

He squeezed her fingers. What a blessing for both Guff and Jo that they had found each other, even if it had been too late in life for the children they had both always wanted. Though they married in their forties, they had figured out a way to build the family they wanted by taking in foster children who had nowhere else to go.

"I suppose that's as good a philosophy for a marriage as any," he said.

"Yes. That and the advice of Lyndon B. Johnson. Only two things are necessary to keep one's wife happy, Guff used to say. One is to let her think she is having her own way. The other, to let her have it."

He laughed, just as he knew she intended. Jo smiled along with him and lifted her face to the late-morning sunshine. He checked to make sure the colorful throw was still tucked across her lap, though it was a beautiful autumn day, warmer than usual for October.

They sat on Adirondack chairs canted just so in the back garden of Winder Ranch for a spectacular view of the west slope of the Tetons. Surrounding them were mums and yarrow and a few other hardy plants still hanging on. Most of the trees were nearly bare but a few still clung tightly to their leaves. As he remembered, the stubborn elms liked to hang on to theirs until the most messy, inconvenient time, like just before the first hard snowfall, when it became a nightmare trying to rake them up.

Mindful of Tess's advice, he was keeping a careful eye on Jo and her stamina level. So far, she seemed to be managing her pain. She seemed content to sit in her garden and bask in the unusual warmth.

He wasn't used to merely sitting. In Seattle, he always had someone clamoring for his attention. His assistant, his board of directors, his top-level executives. Someone always wanted a slice of his time.

Quinn couldn't quite ascertain whether he found a few hours of enforced inactivity soothing or frustrating. But he did know he savored this chance to store away a few more precious memories of Jo.

She lifted her thin face to the sunshine. "We won't have too many more days like this, will we? Before we know it, winter will be knocking on the door."

That latent awareness that she probably wouldn't make it even to Thanksgiving—her favorite holiday— pierced him.

He tried to hide his reaction but Jo had eyes like a red-tailed hawk and was twice as focused.

"Stop that," she ordered, her mouth suddenly stern.

"What?"

"Feeling sorry for me, son."

He folded her hand in his, struck again by the frailty of it, the pale skin and the thin bones and the tiny blue veins pulsing beneath the papery surface.

"You want the truth, I'm feeling more sorry for myself than you."

Her laugh startled a couple of sparrows from the bird feeder hanging in the aspens. "You always did have a bit of a selfish streak, didn't you?"

"Damn right." He managed a tiny grin in response to her teasing. "And I'm selfish enough to wish you could stick around forever."

"For your sake and the others, I'm sorry for that. But

don't be sad on my account, my dear. I have missed my husband sorely every single, solitary moment of the past five years. Soon I'll be with him again and won't have to miss him anymore. Why would anyone possibly pity me?"

He would have given a great deal for even a tiny measure of her faith. He hadn't believed much in a just and loving God since the nightmare day his parents died.

"I only have one regret," Jo went on.

He made a face. "Only one?" He could have come up with a couple dozen of his own regrets, sitting here in the sunshine on a quiet Cold Creek morning.

"Yes. I'm sorry my children—and that's what you all are, you know—have never found the kind of joy and love Guff and I had."

"I don't think many people have," he answered. "What is it they say? Often imitated, never duplicated? What the two of you had was something special. Unique."

"Special, yes. Unique, not at all. A good marriage just takes lots of effort on both parts." She tilted her head and studied him carefully. "You've never even been serious about a woman, have you? I know you date plenty of beautiful women up there in Seattle. What's wrong with them all?"

He gave a rough laugh. "Not a thing, other than I have no desire to get married."

"Ever?"

"Marriage isn't for me, Jo. Not with my family history."

"Oh, poof."

He laughed at the unexpectedness of the word.

"Poof?"

"You heard me. You're just making excuses. Never thought I raised any of my boys to be cowards."

"I'm not a coward," he exclaimed.

"What else would you call it?"

He didn't answer, though a couple of words that came immediately to mind were more along the lines of *smart* and *self-protective*.

"Yes, you had things rough," Jo said after a moment. "I'm not saying you didn't. It breaks my heart what some people do to their families in the name of love. But plenty of other people have things rough and it doesn't stop them from living their life. Why, take Tess, for instance."

He gave a mental groan. Bad enough that he couldn't seem to stop thinking about her all morning. He didn't need Jo bringing her up now. Just the sound of her name stirred up those weird, conflicting emotions inside him all over again. Anger and that subtle, insistent, frustrating attraction.

He pushed them all away. "What do you mean, *take Tess*?"

"That girl. Now *she* has an excuse to lock her heart away and mope around feeling sorry for herself for the rest of her life. But does she? No. You'll never find a happier soul in all your days. Why, what she's been through would have crushed most women. Not our Tess."

What could she possibly have been through that Jo deemed so traumatic? She was a pampered princess, daughter of one of the wealthiest men in town, the town's bank president, apparently adored by everyone.

She couldn't know what it was like to have to call

the police on your own father or hold your mother as she breathed her last.

Before he could ask Jo to explain, she began to cough—raspy, wet hacking that made his own chest hurt just listening to it.

She covered her mouth with a folded handkerchief from her pocket as the coughing fit went on for what seemed an eon. When she pulled the cloth away, he didn't miss the red spots speckling the white linen.

"I'm going to carry you inside and call Easton."

Jo shook her head. "No," she choked out. "Will pass. Just…minute."

He gave her thirty more seconds, then reached for his cell phone. He started to hit Redial to reach Easton when he realized Jo's coughs were dwindling.

"Told you…would pass," she said after a moment. During the coughing attack, what little color there was in her features had seeped out and she looked as if she might blow away if the wind picked up even a knot or two.

"Let's get you inside."

She shook her head. "I like the sunshine."

He sat helplessly beside her while she coughed a few more times, then folded the handkerchief and stuck it back into her pocket.

"Sorry about that," she murmured after a painful moment. "I so wish you didn't have to see me like this."

He wrapped an arm around her frail shoulders and pulled her close to him, planting a kiss on her springy gray curls.

"We don't have to talk. Just rest. We can stay for a few more moments and enjoy the sunshine."

She smiled and settled against him and they sat in contented silence.

For those few moments, he was deeply grateful he had come. As difficult as it had been to rearrange his schedule and delegate as many responsibilities as he could to the other executives at Southerland, he wouldn't have missed this moment for anything.

With his own mother, he hadn't been given the luxury of saying goodbye. She had been unconscious by the time he could reach her.

He supposed that played some small part in his insistence that he stay here to the end with Jo, as difficult as it was to face, as if he could atone in some small way for all he hadn't been able to do for his own mother as a frightened kid.

Her love of sunshine notwithstanding, Jo lasted outside only another fifteen minutes before she had a coughing fit so intense it left her pale and shaken. He didn't give her a choice this time, simply scooped her into his arms and carried her inside to her bedroom.

"Rest there and I'll find Easton to help you."

"Bother. She…has enough…to do. Just need water and…minute to catch my breath."

He went for a glass of water and returned to Jo's bedroom with it, then sent a quick text to Easton explaining the situation.

"I can see you sending out an SOS over there," Jo muttered with a dark look at the phone in his hand.

"Who, me? I was just getting in a quick game of solitaire while I wait for you to stop coughing."

She snorted at the lie and shook her head. "You didn't need to call her. I hate being so much of a nuisance to everyone."

He finished the text and covered her hand with his. "Serves us right for all the bother we gave you."

"I think you boys used to stay up nights just thinking about new ways to get into trouble, didn't you?"

"We had regular meetings every afternoon, just to brainstorm."

"I don't doubt it." She smiled weakly. "At least by the middle of high school you settled down some. Though there was that time senior year you got kicked off the baseball team. That nonsense about cheating, which I know you would never do, and so I tried to tell the coach but he wouldn't listen. You never did tell us what that was really all about."

He frowned. He could have told her what it had been about. Tess Jamison and more of her lies about him. If anyone had stayed up nights trying to come up with ways to make someone else's life harder, it would have been Tess. She had made as much trouble as she could for him, for reasons he still didn't understand.

"High school was a long time ago. Why don't I tell you about my latest trip to Cambodia when I visited Angkor Wat?"

He described the ancient temple complex that had been unknown to the outside world until 1860, when a French botanist stumbled upon it. He was describing the nearby city of Angkor Thom when he looked down and saw her eyes were closed, her breathing regular.

He arranged a knit throw over her and slipped off her shoes, which didn't elicit even a hint of a stir out of her. That she could fall asleep so instantaneously worried him and he hoped their short excursion outside hadn't been too much for her.

He closed the door behind him just as he heard the

bang of the screen door off the kitchen, then the thud of Easton's boots on the tile.

Chester rose from his spot in a sunbeam and greeted her with delight, his tired old body wiggling with glee.

She stripped off her work gloves and patted him. "Sorry it took me a while. We were up repairing a fence in the west pasture."

"I'm sorry I called you in for nothing. She seems to be resting now. But she was coughing like crazy earlier, leaving blood specks behind."

Easton blew out a breath and swiped a strand of hair that had fallen out of her long ponytail. "She's been doing that lately. Tess says it's to be expected."

"I'm sorry I bugged you for no reason."

"I was ready to break for lunch. I would have been here in about fifteen minutes anyway. I can't tell you what a relief it is to have you here so I know someone is with her. I'm always within five minutes of the house but I can't be here all the time. I hate when I have to leave her, but sometimes I can't help it. The ranch doesn't run itself."

Though Winder Ranch wasn't as huge an operation as the Daltons up the canyon a ways, it was still a big undertaking for one woman still in her twenties, even if she did have a couple ranch hands and a ranch foreman who had been with the Winders since Easton's father died in a car accident that also killed his wife.

"Why don't I fix you some lunch while you're here?" he offered. "It's my turn after last night, isn't it?"

She sent him a sidelong look. "The CEO of Southerland Shipping making me a bologna sandwich? How can I resist an offer like that?"

"Turkey is my specialty but I suppose I can swing bologna."

"Either one would be great. I'll go check on Jo and be right back."

She returned before he had even found all the ingredients.

"Still asleep?" he asked.

"Yes. She was smiling in her sleep and looked so at peace, I didn't have the heart to wake her."

"Sit down. I'll be done here in a moment."

She sat at the kitchen table with a tall glass of Pepsi and they chatted about the ranch and the upcoming roundup in the high country and the cost of beef futures while he fixed sandwiches for both of them.

He presented hers with a flourish and she accepted it gratefully.

"What time does the day nurse come again?" he asked.

"Depends on the nurse, but usually about 1:00 p.m. and then again at five or six o'clock."

"And there are three nurses who rotate?"

"Yes. They're all wonderful but Tess is Jo's favorite."

He paused to swallow a bite of his sandwich then tried to make his voice sound casual and uninterested. "What's her story?" he asked.

"Who? Tess?"

"Jo said something about her that made me curious. She said Tess had it rough."

"You could say that."

He waited for Easton to elucidate but she remained frustratingly silent and he had to take a sip of soda to keep from grinding his back teeth together. The Winder women—and he definitely counted Easton among that number since her mother had been Guff's sister—could drive him crazy with their reticence that they seemed to invoke only at the most inconvenient times.

"What's been so rough?" he pressed. "When I knew Tess, she had everything a woman could want. Brains, beauty, money."

"None of that helped her very much with everything that came after, did it?" Easton asked quietly.

"I have no idea. You haven't told me what that was."

He waited while Easton took another bite of her sandwich before continuing. "I guess you figured out she married Scott, right?"

He shrugged. "That was a foregone conclusion, wasn't it? They dated all through high school."

He had actually always liked Scott Claybourne. Tall and blond and athletic, Scott had been amiable to Quinn if not particularly friendly—until their senior year, when Scott had inexplicably beat the crap out of Quinn one warm April night, with veiled references to some supposed misconduct of Quinn's toward Tess.

More of her lies, he had assumed, and had pitied the bastard for being so completely taken in by her.

"They were only married three or four months, still newlyweds, really," Easton went on, "when he was in a bad car accident."

He frowned. "Car accident? I thought Tess told me he died of pneumonia."

"Technically, he did, just a couple of years ago. But he lived for several years after the accident, though he was permanently disabled from it. He had a brain injury and was in a pretty bad way."

He stared at Easton, trying to make the jaggedly formed pieces of the puzzle fit together. Tess had stuck around Pine Gulch for *years* to deal with her husband's brain injury? He couldn't believe it, not of her.

"She cared for him tirelessly, all that time," Easton said quietly. "From what I understand, he required total care. She had to feed him, dress him, bathe him. He was almost more like her kid than her husband, you know."

"He never recovered from the brain injury?"

"A little but not completely. He was in a wheelchair and lost the ability to talk from the injury. It was so sad. I just remember how nice he used to be to us younger kids. I don't know how much was going on inside his head but Tess talked to him just like normal and she seemed to understand what sounded like grunts and moans to me."

The girl he had known in high school had been only interested in wearing her makeup just so and buying the latest fashion accessories. And making his life miserable, of course.

He couldn't quite make sense of what Easton was telling him.

"I saw them once at the grocery store when he had a seizure, right there in frozen foods," Easton went on. "It scared the daylights out of me, let me tell you, but Tess just acted like it was a normal thing. She was so calm and collected through the whole thing."

"That's rough."

She nodded. "A lot of women might have shoved away from the table when they saw the lousy hand they'd been dealt, would have just walked away right then. Tess was young, just out of nursing school. She had enough medical experience that I have to think she could guess perfectly well what was ahead for them, but she stuck it out all those years."

He didn't like the compassion trickling through him for her. Somehow things seemed more safe, more ordered, before he had learned that perhaps she hadn't spent the past dozen years figuring out more ways to make him loathe her.

"People in town grew to respect and admire her for the loving care she gave Scott, even up to the end. When she moves to Portland in a few weeks, she's going to leave a real void in Pine Gulch. I'm not the only one who will miss her."

"She's leaving?"

He again tried to be casual with the question, but Easton had known him since he was fourteen. She sent him a quick, sidelong look.

"She's selling her house and taking a job at a hospital there. I can't blame her. Around here, she'll always be the sweet girl who took care of her sick husband for so long. Saint Tess. That's what people call her."

He nearly fell off his chair at that one. Tess Jamison Claybourne was a saint like he played center field for the Mariners.

Easton pushed back from the table. "I'd better check on Jo one more time, then get back to work." She paused. "You know, if you have more questions about Tess, you could ask her. She should be back tonight."

He didn't want to know more about Tess. He didn't want anything to do with her. He wanted to go back to the safety of ignorance. Despising her was much easier when he could keep her frozen in his mind as the manipulative little witch she had been at seventeen.

CHAPTER FIVE

"YOU HAVEN'T HEARD a single word I've said for the past ten minutes, have you?"

Tess jerked her attention back to her mother as they worked side by side in Ed Hardy's yard. Her mother knelt in the mulchy layer of fallen leaves, snipping and digging to ready Dorothy Hardy's flower garden for the winter, while Tess was theoretically supposed to be raking leaves. Her pile hadn't grown much, she had to admit.

"I heard some of it." She managed a rueful smile. "The occasional word here and there."

Maura Jamison raised one delicately shaped eyebrow beneath her floppy gardening hat. "I'm sorry my stories are so dull. I can go back to telling them to the cat, when he'll deign to listen."

She winced. "It's not your story that's to blame. I'm just…distracted today. But I'll listen now. Sorry about that."

Her mother gave her a careful look. "I think it's my turn to listen. What's on your mind, honey? Scott?"

Tess blinked at the realization that except for those few moments when Quinn had asked her about Scott the night before, she hadn't thought about her husband in several days.

A tiny measure of guilt niggled at her but she pushed

it away. She refused to feel guilty for that. Scott would have wanted her to move on with her life and she had no guilt for her dealings with her husband.

Still, she didn't think she could tell her mother she was obsessing about Quinn Southerland.

"Mom, was I a terrible person in high school?" she asked instead.

Maura's eyes widened with surprise and Tess sent a tiny prayer to heaven, not for the first time, that she could age as gracefully as her mother. At sixty-five, Maura was active and vibrant and still as lovely as ever, even in gardening clothes and her floppy hat. The auburn curls Tess had inherited were shot through with gray but it didn't make Maura look old, only exotic and interesting, somehow.

Maura pursed her lips. "As I remember, you were a very good person. Not perfect, certainly, but who is, at that age?"

"I thought I was. Perfect, I mean. I thought I was doing everything right. Why wouldn't I? I had 4.0 grades, I was the head cheerleader, the student body president. I volunteered at the hospital in Idaho Falls and went to church on Sundays and was generally kind to children and small pets."

"What's happened to make you think about those days?"

She sighed, remembering the antipathy in a certain pair of silvery blue eyes. "Quinn Southerland is back in town."

Her mother's brow furrowed for a moment, then smoothed again. "Oh, right. He was one of Jo and Guff's foster boys, wasn't he? Which one is he?"

"Not the army officer or the adventurer. He's the

businessman. The one who runs a shipping company out of Seattle."

"Oh, yes. I remember him. He was the dark, brooding, cute one, right?"

"Mother!"

Maura gave her an innocent sort of look. "What did I say? He *was* cute, wasn't he? I always thought he looked a little like James Dean around the eyes. Something in that smoldering look of his."

Oh, yes, Tess remembered it well.

After leaning the rake against a tree, she knelt beside her mother and began pulling up the dead stalks of cosmos. Every time she worked with her hands in the dirt, she couldn't help thinking how very much her existence the past eight years was like a flower garden in winter, waiting, waiting, for life to spring forth.

"I was horrible to him, Mom. Really awful."

"You? I can't believe that."

"Believe it. He just… He brought out the absolute worst in me."

Her mother sat back on her heels, the gardening forgotten. "Whatever did you do to the poor boy?"

She didn't want to correct her mother, but to her mind Quinn had never seemed like a boy. At least not like the other boys in Pine Gulch.

"I don't even like to think about it all," she admitted. "Basically I did whatever I could to set him down a peg or two. I did my best to turn people against him. I would make snide comments to him and about him and started unsubstantiated rumors about him. I played devil's advocate, just for the sake of argument, whenever he would express any kind of opinion in a class."

Her mother looked baffled. "What on earth did he do to you to make you act in such a way?"

"Nothing. That's the worst part. I thought he was arrogant and disrespectful and I didn't like him but I was...fascinated by him."

Which quite accurately summed up her interaction with him in the early hours of the morning, but she decided not to tell her mother that.

"He was a handsome boy," Maura said. "I imagine many of the girls at school had the same fascination."

"They did." She grabbed the garden shears and started cutting back Dorothy's day lily foliage. "You know how it is whenever someone new moves into town. He seems infinitely better-looking, more interesting, more *everything* than the boys around town that you've grown up with since kindergarten."

She had been just as intrigued as the other girls, fascinated by this surly, angry, rough-edged boy. Rumors had swirled around when he first arrived that he had been involved in some kind of murder investigation. She still didn't know if any of them were true—she really couldn't credit Jo and Guff bringing someone with that kind of a past into their home.

But back then, that hint of danger only made him seem more appealing. She just knew Quinn made her feel different than any other boy in town.

Tess had tried to charm him, as she had been effortlessly doing with every male who entered her orbit since she was old enough to bat her eyelashes. He had at first ignored her efforts and then actively rebuffed them.

She hadn't taken with grace and dignity his rejection or his grim amusement at her continued efforts to draw his attention. She flushed, remembering.

"He wasn't interested in any of us, especially not me. I couldn't understand why he had to be so contrary. I hated it. You know how I was. I wanted everything in my life to go exactly how I arranged it."

"You're like your father that way," Maura said with a soft smile for her husband of thirty-five years whom they both missed dearly.

"I guess. I just know I was petty and spiteful to Quinn when he wouldn't fall into line with the way I wanted things to go. I was awful to him. Really awful. Whenever I was around him, I felt like this alien life force had invaded my body, this manipulative, conniving witch. Scarlett O'Hara with pom-poms."

Her mother laughed. "You're much prettier than that Vivien Leigh ever was."

"But every bit as vindictive and self-absorbed as her character in the movie."

For several moments, she busied herself with garden shears. Maura seemed content with the silence and her introspection, which had always been one of the things Tess loved best about her mother.

"I don't even want to tell you all the things I did," she finally said. "The worst thing is, I got him kicked off the baseball team when he was a senior and I was a junior."

"Tessa Marie. What on earth did you do?"

She burned with shame at the memory. "We had advanced placement history together. Amaryllis Wentworth."

"Oh, I remember her," her mother exclaimed. "Bitter and mean and suspicious old bat. I don't know why the school board didn't fire her twenty-five years before you were even in school. You would think someone who chooses teaching as an avocation would at least enjoy the company of young people."

"Right. And the only thing she hated worse than teenage girls was teenage boys."

"What happened?"

She wished she could block the memory out but it was depressingly clear, from the chalkboard smell in Wentworth's room to the afternoon spring sunlight filtering through the tall school windows.

"We both happened to have missed school on the same day, which happened to be one of her brutal pop quizzes, so we had to take a makeup. We were the only ones in the classroom except for Miss Wentworth."

Careful to avoid her mother's gaze, she picked up an armload of garden refuse and carried it to the wheelbarrow. "I knew the material but I was curious about whether Quinn did so I looked at his test answers. He got everything right except a question about the Teapot Dome scandal. I don't know why I did it. Pure maliciousness on my part. But I changed my answer, which I knew was right, to the same wrong one he had put down."

"Honey!"

"I know, right? It was awful of me. One of the worst things I've ever done. Of course, Miss Wentworth accused him of cheating. It was his word against mine. The juvenile delinquent with the questionable attitude or the student body president, a junior who already had offers of a full-ride scholarship to nursing school. Who do you think everybody wanted to believe?"

"Oh, Tess."

"My only defense is that I never expected things to go that far. I thought maybe Miss Wentworth would just yell at him, but when she went right to the principal, I didn't know how to make it right. I should have stepped forward when he was kicked off the baseball team but I…was too much of a coward."

She couldn't tell her mother the worst of it. Even she couldn't quite believe the depths to which she had sunk in her teenage narcissism, but she remembered it all vividly.

A few days later, prompted by guilt and shame, she had tried to talk to him and managed to corner him in an empty classroom. They had argued and he had called her a few bad names, justifiably so.

She still didn't know what she'd been thinking—why this time would be any different—but she thought she saw a little spark of attraction in his eyes when they were arguing. She had been hopelessly, mortifyingly foolish enough to try to kiss him and he had pushed her away, so hard she knocked over a couple of chairs as she stumbled backward.

Humiliated and outraged, she had then made things much, much worse and twisted the story, telling her boyfriend Scott that Quinn had come on to her, that he had been so angry at being kicked off the baseball team that he had come for revenge and tried to force himself on her.

She screwed her eyes shut. Scott had reacted just as she had expected, with teenage bluster and bravado and his own twisted sense of chivalry. He and several friends from the basketball team had somehow separated Quinn from Brant and Cisco and taken him beneath the football bleachers, then proceeded to beat the tar out of him.

No wonder he despised her. She loathed that selfish, manipulative girl just as much.

"So he's back," Maura said. "Is he staying at the ranch?"

She nodded. "I hate seeing him. He makes me feel sixteen and stupid all over again. If I didn't love Jo so much, I would try to assign her to another hospice nurse."

Maura sat back on her heels, showing her surprise at her daughter's vehemence. "Our Saint Tess making a selfish decision? That doesn't sound like you."

Tess made a face. "You know I hate that nickname."

Her mother touched her arm, leaving a little spot of dirt on her work shirt. "I know you do, dear. And I'll be honest, as a mother who is nothing but proud of the woman you've become and what you have done with your life, it's a bit refreshing to find out you're subject to the occasional human folly just like the rest of us."

Everyone in town saw her as some kind of martyr for staying with Scott all those years, but they didn't know the real her. The woman who had indulged in bouts of self-pity, who had cried out her fear and frustration, who had felt trapped in a marriage that never even had a chance to start.

She had stayed with Scott because she loved him and because he needed her, not because she was some saintly, perfect, flawless angel.

No one knew her. Not her mother or her friends or the morning crowd at The Gulch.

She didn't like to think that Quinn Southerland might just have the most honest perspective around of the real Tess Jamison Claybourne.

THAT EVENING, TESS kept her fingers crossed the entire drive to Winder Ranch, praying she wouldn't encounter him.

She had fretted about him all day, worrying what she

might say when she saw him again. She considered it a huge advantage, at least in this case, that she worked the graveyard shift. Most of her visits were in the dead of night, when Quinn by rights should be sleeping. She would have a much better chance of avoiding him than if she stopped by during daylight hours.

The greatest risk she faced of bumping into him was probably now at the start of her shift than, say, 4:00 a.m.

Wouldn't it be lovely if he were away from the ranch or busy helping Easton with something or tied up with some kind of conference call to Seattle?

She could only dream, she supposed. More than likely, he would be right there waiting for her, ready to impale her with that suspicious, bad-tempered glare the moment she stepped out of the car.

She let out a breath as she turned onto the long Winder Ranch access drive and headed up toward the house. She could at least be calm and collected, even if he tried to goad her or made any derogatory comments. He certainly didn't need to discover he possessed such power to upset her.

He wasn't waiting for her on the porch, but it was a near thing. The instant she rang the doorbell of Winder Ranch, the door jerked open and Quinn stood inside looking frazzled, his dark hair disheveled slightly, his navy blue twill shirt untucked, a hint of afternoon shadow on his cheeks.

He looked a little disreputable and entirely yummy.

"It's about time!" he exclaimed, an odd note of relief in his voice. "I've been watching for you for the past half hour."

"You...have?"

She almost looked behind her to see if someone a little more sure of a welcome had wandered in behind her.

"I thought you were supposed to be here at eight."

She checked her watch and saw it was only eight-thirty. "I made another stop first. What's wrong?"

He raked a hand through his hair, messing it further. "I don't know the hell I'm supposed to do. Easton had to run to Idaho Falls to meet with the ranch accountant. She was supposed to be back an hour ago but she just called and said she'd been delayed and won't be back for another couple of hours."

"What's going on? Is Jo having another of her breathing episodes? Or is it the coughing?"

Tess hurried out of her jacket and started to rush toward her patient's room but Quinn grabbed her arm at the elbow.

Despite her worry for Jo, heat scorched her nerve endings at the contact, at the feel of his warm hand against her skin.

"She's not there. She's in the kitchen."

At her alarmed look, he shook his head. "It's none of those things. She's fine, physically, anyway. But she won't listen to reason. I never realized the woman could be so blasted stubborn."

"A trait she obviously does not share with anyone else here," she murmured.

He gave her a dark look. "She's being completely ridiculous. She suddenly has this harebrained idea. Absolute insanity. She wants to go out for a moonlight ride on one of the horses and it's suddenly all she can talk about."

She stared, nonplussed. "A horseback ride?"

"Yeah. Do you think the cancer has affected her rational thinking? I mean, what's gotten into her? It's after eight, for heaven's sake."

"It's a bit difficult to go on a moonlit ride in the middle of the afternoon," she pointed out.

"Don't you take her side!" He sounded frustrated and on edge and more than a little frazzled.

She hid her smile that the urbane, sophisticated executive could change so dramatically over one simple request. "I'm not taking anyone's side. Why does she suddenly want to go tonight?"

"Her window faces east."

That was all he said, as if everything was now crystal clear. "And?" she finally prompted.

"And she happened to see that huge full moon coming up an hour or so ago. She says it's her favorite kind of night. She and Guff used to ride up to Windy Lake during the full moon whenever they could. It can be clear as day up in the mountains on full moons like this."

"Windy Lake?"

"It's above the ranch, about half a mile into the forest service land. Takes about forty minutes to ride there."

"And Tess is determined to go?"

"She says she can't miss the chance, since it's her last harvest moon."

The sudden bleakness in the silver-blue of his eyes tugged at her sympathy and she was astonished by the impulse to touch his arm and offer whatever small comfort she could.

She curled her fingers into a fist, knowing he wouldn't welcome the gesture. Not from her.

"She's not strong enough for that," he went on. "I *know* she's not. We were sitting out in the garden today and she lasted less than an hour before she had to lie down, and then she slept for the rest of the day. I can't see any way in hell she has the strength to sit on a horse, even for ten minutes."

Her job as a hospice nurse often required using a little creative problem-solving. Clients who were dying could have some very tricky wishes toward the end. But her philosophy was that if what they wanted was at all within reach, it was up to her and their family members to make it happen.

"What if you rode together on horseback?" she suggested. "You could help her. Support her weight, make sure she's not overdoing."

He stared at her as if she'd suddenly stepped into her old cheerleader skirt and started yelling, "We've got spirit, yes we do."

"Tell me you're not honestly thinking she could handle this!" he exclaimed. "It's completely insane."

"Not completely, Quinn. Not if she wants to do it. Jo is right. This is her last harvest moon and if she wants to enjoy it from Windy Lake, I think she ought to have that opportunity. It seems a small enough thing to give her."

He opened his mouth to object, then closed it again. In his eyes, she saw worry and sorrow for the woman who had taken him in, given him a home, loved him.

"It might be good for her," Tess said gently.

"And it might finish her off." He said the words tightly, as if he didn't want to let them out.

"That's her choice, though, isn't it?"

He took several deep breaths and she could see his struggle, something she faced often providing end-of-life care. On the one hand, he loved his foster mother and wanted to do everything he could to make her happy and comfortable and fulfill all her last wishes.

On the other, he wanted to protect her and keep her around as long as he could.

The effort to hold back her fierce urge to touch him, console him, almost overwhelmed her. She supposed she shouldn't find it so surprising. She was a nurturer, which was why she went into nursing in the first place, long before she ever knew that Scott's accident would test her caregiving skills and instincts to the limit.

"You don't have to take her, though, especially if you don't feel it's the right thing for her. I'll see if I can talk her out of it," she offered. She took a step toward the kitchen, but his voice stopped her.

"Wait."

She turned back to find him pinching the skin at the bridge of his nose.

"You're right," he said after a long moment, dropping his hand. "It's her choice. She's a grown woman, not a child. I can't treat her like one, even if I do want to protect her from…the inevitable. If she wants this, I'll find a way to make it happen."

The determination in his voice arrowed right to her heart and she smiled. "You're a good son, Quinn. You're just what Jo needs right now."

"You're coming with us, to make sure she's not overdoing things."

"Me?"

"The only way I can agree to this insanity is if we have a medical expert close at hand, just in case."

"I don't think that's a good idea."

"Why not? Can't your other patients spare you?"

That would have been a convenient excuse, but unfortunately in this case, she faced a slow night, with only Tess and two other patients, one who only required one quick check in the night, several hours away.

"That's not the issue," she admitted.

"What is it, then? Don't you think she would be better off to have a nurse along?"

"Maybe. Probably. But not necessarily this particular nurse."

"Why not?"

"I'm not really much of a rider," she confessed, with the same sense of shame as if she were admitting stealing heart medicine from little old ladies. Around Pine Gulch, she supposed the two crimes were roughly parallel in magnitude.

"Really?"

"My family lived in town and we never had horses," she said, despising the defensive note in her voice. "I haven't had a lot of experience."

She didn't add that she had an irrational fear of them after being bucked off at a cousin's house when she was seven, then later that summer she had seen a cowboy badly injured in a fall at an Independence Day rodeo. Since then, she had done her best to avoid equines whenever possible.

"This is a pretty easy trail that takes less than an hour. You should be okay, don't you think?"

How could she possibly tell him she was terrified, especially after she had worked to persuade him it would be all right for Jo? She couldn't, she decided. Better to take one for the team, for Jo's sake.

"Fine. You saddle the horses and I'll get Jo ready."

Heaven help them all.

CHAPTER SIX

"LET ME KNOW if you need me to slow down," Quinn said half an hour later to the frail woman who sat in front of him astride one of the biggest horses in the pasture, a rawboned roan gelding named Russ.

She felt angular and thin in his arms, all pointed elbows and bony shoulders. But Tess had been right, she was ecstatic about being on horseback again, about being outside in the cold October night under the pines. Jo practically quivered with excitement, more alive and joyful than he had seen her since his return to Cold Creek.

It smelled of fall in the mountains, of sun-warmed dirt, of smoke from a distant neighbor's fire, of layers of fallen leaves from the scrub oak and aspens that dotted the mountainside.

The moon hung heavy and full overhead, huge and glowing in the night and Suzy and Jack, Easton's younger cow dogs, raced ahead of them. Chester probably would have enjoyed the adventure but Quinn had worried that, just like Jo, his old bones weren't quite up to the journey.

"This is perfect. Oh, Quinn, thank you, my dear. You have no idea the gift you've given me."

"You're welcome," he said gruffly, warmed despite his lingering worry.

In truth, he didn't know who was receiving the greater gift. This seemed a rare and precious time with Jo and he was certain he would remember forever the scents and the sounds of the night—of tack jingling on the horses and a great northern owl hooting somewhere in the forest and the night creatures that peeped and chattered around them.

He glanced over his shoulder to where Tess rode behind them.

Among the three of them, she seemed to be the one *least* enjoying the ride. She bounced along on one of the ranch's most placid mares. Every once in a while, he looked back and the moonlight would illuminate a look of grave discomfort on her features. If he could see her hands in the darkness, he was quite certain they would be white-knuckled on the reins.

He should be enjoying her misery, given his general dislike for the woman. Mostly he just felt guilty for dragging her along, though he had to admit to a small measure of glee to discover something she hadn't completely mastered.

In school, Tess had been the consummate perfectionist. She always had to be the first one finished with tests and assignments, she hated showing up anywhere with a hair out of place and she delighted in being the kind of annoying classmate who tended to screw up the curve for everybody else.

Knowing she wasn't an expert at everything made her seem a little more human, a little more approachable.

He glanced back again and saw her shifting in the saddle, her body tight and uncomfortable.

"How are you doing back there?" he asked.

In the pale glow of the full moon, he could just make out the slit of her eyes as she glared. "Fine. Swell. If I break my neck and die, I'm blaming you."

He laughed out loud, which earned him a frown from Jo.

"You didn't need to drag poor Tess up here with us," she reprimanded in the same tone of voice she had used when he was fifteen and she caught him teasing Easton for something or other. He could still vividly remember the figurative welts on his hide as she had verbally taken a strip off him.

"She's a big girl," Quinn said in a voice too low for Tess to overhear. "She didn't have to come."

"You're a hard man to say no to."

"If anyone could do it, Tess would find a way. Anyway, we'll be there in a few more moments."

Jo looked over his shoulder at Tess, then shook her head. "Poor thing. She obviously hasn't had as much experience riding as you and Easton and the boys. She's a good sport to come anyway."

He risked another look behind him and thought he heard her mumbling something under her breath involving creative ways she intended to make him pay for this.

Despite the lingering sadness in knowing he was fulfilling a last wish for someone he loved so dearly, Quinn couldn't help his smile.

He definitely wouldn't forget this night anytime soon.

"She's doing all right," he said to Jo.

"You're a rascal, Quinn Southerland," she chided. "You always have been."

He couldn't disagree. He couldn't have been an easy kid to love when he had been so belligerent and angry, lashing out at everyone in his pain. He hugged Jo a little more tightly for just a moment until they reached the trailhead for Windy Lake, really just a clearing where they could leave the horses before taking the narrow twenty-yard trail to the lakeshore.

"This might get a little bit tricky," he said. "Let me dismount first and then I'll help you down."

"I can still get down from a horse by myself," she protested. "I'm not a complete invalid."

He just shook his head in exasperation and slid off the horse. He grabbed the extra rolled blankets tied to the saddle and slung them over his shoulder, then reached up to lift her from the horse.

He didn't set her on her feet, though. "I'll carry you to Guff's bench," he said, without giving her an opportunity to argue.

She pursed her lips but didn't complain, which made him suspect she was probably more tired than she wanted to let on.

"Okay, but then you'd better come back here to help Tess."

He glanced over and saw that Tess's horse had stopped alongside his big gelding but Tess made no move to climb out of the saddle; she just gazed down at the ground with a nervous kind of look.

"Hang on a minute," he told her. "Just wait there in the saddle while I settle Jo on the bench and then I'll come back to help you down."

"I'm sorry," she said, sounding more disgruntled than apologetic.

"No problem."

He carried Jo along the trail, grateful again for the

pale moonlight that filtered through the fringy pines and the bare branches of the aspens.

Windy Lake was a small stream-fed lake, probably no more than two hundred yards across. As a convenient watering hole, it attracted moose and mule deer and even the occasional elk. The water was always ice cold, as he and the others could all attest. That didn't stop him and Brant and Cisco—and Easton, when she could manage to get away—from sneaking out to come up here on summer nights.

Guff always used to keep a small canoe on the shore and they loved any chance to paddle out in the moonlight on July nights and fish for the native rainbow trout and arctic grayling that inhabited it.

Some of his most treasured memories of his teen years centered around trips to this very place.

The trail ended at the lakeshore. He carried Jo to the bench Guff built here, which had been situated in the perfect place to take in the pristine, shimmering lake and the granite mountains surrounding it.

He set Jo on her feet for just a moment so he could brush pine needles and twigs off the bench. Contrary to what he expected, the bench didn't have months worth of debris covering it, which made him think Easton probably found the occasional chance to make good use of it.

He covered the seat with a plastic garbage bag he had shoved into his pocket earlier in case the bench was damp.

"There you go. Your throne awaits."

She shook her head at his silliness but sat down gingerly, as if the movement pained her. He unrolled one of the blankets and spread it around her shoulders then tucked the other across her lap.

In the moonlight, he saw lines of pain bracketing her mouth and he worried again that this ride into the mountains had been too much for her. Along with the pain, though, he could see undeniable delight at being in this place she loved, one last time.

He supposed sometimes a little pain might be worthwhile in the short-term if it yielded such joy.

As he fussed over the blankets, she reached a thin hand to cover his. "Thank you, my dear. I'm fine now, I promise. Go rescue poor Tess and let me sit here for a moment with my memories."

"Call out if you need help. We won't be far."

"Don't fuss over me," she ordered. "Go help Tess."

Though he was reluctant to leave her here alone, he decided she was safe with the dogs who sat by her side, their ears cocked forward as if listening for any threat.

Back at the trailhead, he found Tess exactly where he had left her, still astride the mare, who was placidly grazing on the last of the autumn grasses.

"I tried to get down," she told him when he emerged from the trees. "Honestly, I did. But my blasted shoe is caught in the stirrups and I couldn't work it loose, no matter how hard I tried. This is so embarrassing."

"I guess that's the price you pay when you go horseback riding in comfortable nurse's shoes instead of boots."

"If I had known I was going to be roped into this, I would have pulled out my only pair of Tony Lamas for the occasion."

Despite her attempt at a light tone, he caught something in her stiff posture, in the rigid set of her jaw.

This was more than inexperience with horses, he realized as he worked her shoe free of the tight stirrup. Had he really been so overbearing and arrogant in insisting she come along that he refused to see she had a deep aversion to horses?

"I'm sorry I dragged you along."

"It's not all bad." She gazed up at the stars. "It's a lovely night."

"Tell me, how many moonlit rides have you been on into the mountains around Pine Gulch?"

She summoned a smile. "Counting tonight? Exactly one."

He finally worked her shoe free. "Let me help you down," he said.

She released the reins and swiveled her left leg over the saddle horn so she could dismount. The mare moved at just that moment and suddenly his arms were full of warm, delicious curves.

She smelled of vanilla and peaches and much to his dismay, his recalcitrant body stirred to life.

He released her abruptly and she wobbled a little when her feet met solid ground. Out of instinct, he reached to steady her and his hand brushed the curve of her breast when he grabbed her arm. Her gaze flashed to his and in the moonlight, he thought he felt the silky cord of sexual awareness tug between them.

"Okay now?"

"I…think so."

That low, breathy note in her voice had to be his imagination. He was almost certain of it.

He couldn't possibly be attracted to her. Sure, she was still a beautiful woman on the outside, but she was still Tess Claybourne, for heaven's sake.

He noticed she moved a considerable distance away but he wasn't sure if she was avoiding him or the horses. Probably both.

"I'm sorry I dragged you up here," he said again. "I didn't realize how uncomfortable riding would be for you."

She made a face. "It shouldn't be. I'm embarrassed that it is. I grew up around horses—how could I help it in Pine Gulch? Though my family never had them, all my friends did, but I've had an…irrational fear of them since breaking my arm after being bucked off when I was seven."

"And I made you come anyway."

She mustered a smile. "I survived this far. We're halfway done now."

He remembered Jo's words suddenly. *You'll never find a happier soul in all your days. Why, what she's been through would have crushed most women. Not our Tess.*

Jo thought Tess was a survivor. If she weren't, could she be looking at this trip with such calm acceptance, even when she was obviously terrified?

"That's one way of looking at it, I guess."

She didn't meet his gaze. "It's not so bad. After the way I treated you in high school, I guess I'm surprised you didn't tie me onto the back of your horse and drag me behind you for a few miles."

His gaze narrowed. What game was this? He never, in a million years, would have expected her to refer to her behavior in their shared past, especially when she struck exactly the right note of self-deprecation.

For several awkward seconds, he couldn't think how to respond. Did he shrug it off? Act like he didn't know what she was talking about? Tell her she ought to have *bitch* tattooed across her forehead and he would be happy to pay for it?

"High school seems a long time ago right now," he finally said.

"Surely not so long that you've forgotten."

He couldn't lie to her. "You always made an impression."

Her laughter was short and unamused. "That's one way of phrasing it, I suppose."

"What would you call it?"

"Unconscionable."

At that single, low-voiced word, he studied her in the moonlight—her long-lashed green eyes contrite, that mouth set in a frown, the auburn curls that were a little disheveled from the ride.

How the hell did she do it? Lord knew, he didn't want to be. But against his will, Quinn found himself drawn to this woman who was willing to confront her fears for his aunt's sake, who could make fun of herself, who seemed genuinely contrite about past bad behavior.

He liked her and, worse, was uncomfortably aware of a fierce physical attraction to her soft curves and classical features that seemed so serene and lovely in the moonlight.

He pushed away the insane attraction, just as he pushed away the compelling urge to ask her what he had ever done back then to make her hate him so much. Instead, he did his best to turn the subject away.

"Easton told me about Scott. About the accident."

She shoved her hands in the pocket of her jacket and looked off through the darkened trees toward the direction of the lake. "Did she?"

"She said you had only been married a few months at the time, so most of your marriage you were more of a caregiver than a wife."

"Everybody says that like I made some grand, noble sacrifice."

He didn't want to think so. He much preferred thinking of her as the self-absorbed teenage girl trying to ruin his life.

"What would you consider it?"

"I didn't do anything unusual. He was my husband," she said simply. "I loved him and I took vows. I couldn't just abandon him to some impersonal care center for the rest of his life and blithely go on with my own as if he didn't exist."

Many people he knew wouldn't have blinked twice at responding exactly that way to the situation. Hell, the Tess he thought she had been would have done exactly that.

"Do you regret those years?"

She stared at him for a long moment, her eyes wide with surprise, as if no one had ever asked her that before.

"Sometimes," she admitted, her voice so low he could barely hear it. "I don't regret that I had that extra time with him. I could never regret that. By all rights, he should have died in that accident. A weaker man probably would have. Scott didn't and I have to think God had some purpose in that, something larger than my understanding."

She paused, her expression pensive. "I do regret that we never had the chance to build the life we talked about those first few months of our marriage. Children, a mortgage, a couple of dogs. We missed all that."

Not much of a sacrifice, he thought. He would be quite happy not to have that sort of trouble in his life.

"I'll probably always regret that," she went on. "Unfortunately, I can't change the past. I can only look forward and try to make the best of everything that comes next."

They lapsed into a silence broken only by the horses stamping and snorting behind them and the distant lapping of the water.

She was the first to break the temporary peace. "We'd better go check on Jo, don't you think?"

He jerked his mind away from how very much he wanted to kiss her right this moment, with the moonlight gleaming through the trees and the night creatures singing an accompaniment. "Right. Will you be okay without a flashlight?"

"I'll manage. Just lead the way."

He headed up the trail toward Jo, astonished that his most pressing regret right now was the end of their brief interlude in the moonlight.

Though Tess loved living in the Mountain West for the people and the scenery and the generally slower pace of life, she had never really considered herself a nature girl.

As a bank manager and accountant, her father hadn't been the sort to take her camping and fishing when she was younger. Later, she'd been too busy, first in college and then taking care of Scott, to find much time to enjoy the backcountry.

But she had to admit she found something serene and peaceful about being here with the glittery stars overhead and that huge glowing moon filtering through the trees and the night alive with sounds and smells.

Well, it would have been serene if she weren't so intensely aware of Quinn walking just ahead of her, moving with long-limbed confidence through the darkness.

The man exuded sensuality. She sighed, wishing she could ignore his effect on her. She disliked the way her heart picked up a beat or two, the little churn of her blood, the way she couldn't seem to keep herself from stealing secret little glances at him as they made their way toward the lake and Jo.

She hadn't missed that moment of awareness in his eyes back there, the heat that suddenly shivered through the air like fireflies on a summer night.

He was attracted to her, though she had a strong sense he found the idea more than appalling.

Her gaze skidded to his powerful shoulders under his denim jacket, to the dark hair that brushed his collar under his Stetson, and her insides trembled.

For a moment there, she had been quite certain he wanted to kiss her, though she couldn't quite fathom it. How long had it been since she knew the heady, exhilarating impact of desire in a man's eyes? Longer than she cared to remember. The men in town didn't tend to look at her as a woman with the very real and human hunger to be cherished and touched.

In the eyes of most people in Pine Gulch, that woman had been somehow absorbed into the loving, dutiful caretaker, leaving no room for more. Even after Scott's death, people still seemed to see her as a nurturer, not the flirty, sexy, fun-loving Tess she thought might still be buried somewhere deep inside her.

Seeing that heat kindle in his eyes, replacing his

typical animosity, had been both flattering and disconcerting and for a moment, she had been mortified at her little spurt of panic, the fear that she had no idea how to respond.

She just needed practice, she assured herself. That's why she was moving to Portland, so she could be around people who saw her as more than just Pine Gulch's version of Mother Teresa.

They walked the short distance through the pines and aspens, their trail lit only by pale moonlight and the glow of a small flashlight he produced from the pocket of his denim jacket. When they reached the lake a few moments later, Tess saw Jo on a bench on the shore, the dogs at her feet. She sat unmoving, so still that for a moment, Tess feared the worst.

But Quinn's boot snapped a twig at that moment and Jo turned her head. Though they were still a few yards away, Tess could see the glow on her features shining through clearly, even in the moonlight. Her friend smiled at them and for one precious instant, she looked younger, happier. Whole.

"There you are. I was afraid the two of you were lost."

Quinn slanted Tess a sidelong look before turning his attention back to his foster mother. "No. I thought you might like a few moments to yourself up here."

Jo smiled at him as she reached a hand out to Tess to draw her down beside her on the bench. When she saw the blankets tucked around Jo's shoulders and across her lap, everything inside her went a little gooey that Quinn had taken such great care to ensure his foster mother's comfort.

"Isn't it lovely, my dear?"

"Breathtaking," Tess assured her, her hand still enclosed around Jo's thin fingers.

They sat like that for a moment with Quinn standing beside them. The moon glowed off the rocky face of the mountains ringing the lake, reflecting in water that seethed and bubbled as if it was some sort of hot springs. After several moments of watching it, Tess realized the percolating effect was achieved by dozens of fish rising to the surface for night-flying insects.

"It's enchanting," she said to Jo, squeezing her fingers. She didn't add that this moment, this shared beauty, was almost worth that miserable horseback ride up the mountainside.

"This is such a gift. I cannot tell you how deeply it touches me. I have missed these mountains so much these past weeks while I've been stuck at home. Thank you both so very much."

Jo's smile was wide and genuine but Tess didn't miss the lines of pain beneath it that radiated from her mouth.

Quinn must have noticed them as well. "I'd love to stay here longer," he said after a moment, "but we had better get you back. Tess has other patients."

Jo nodded, a little sadly, Tess thought. A lump rose in her throat as the other woman rose, her face tilted to the huge full moon. Jo closed her eyes, inhaled a deep breath of mountain air, then let it out slowly before turning back to Quinn.

"I'm ready."

Her chest felt achy and tight with unshed tears watching Jo say this private goodbye to a place she loved. It didn't help her emotions at all when Quinn carefully and tenderly scooped Jo into his arms and carried her back toward the waiting horses.

She pushed back the tears as she awkwardly mounted her horse, knowing Jo wouldn't welcome them at all. The older woman accepted her impending passing with grace and acceptance, something Tess could only wish on all her patients.

The ride down was slightly easier than the way up had been, though she wouldn't have expected it. In her limited experience on the back of a horse, gravity hadn't always been her friend.

Perhaps she was a tiny bit more loose and relaxed than she had been on the way up. At least she didn't grip the reins quite so tightly and her body seemed to more readily pick up the rhythm of the horse's gait.

She had heard somewhere that horses were sensitive creatures who picked up on those sorts of things like anxiety and apprehension. Maybe the little mare was just giving her the benefit of the doubt.

As she had on the way up the trail, she rode in the rear of their little group, behind the two black and white dogs and Quinn and Jo, which gave her the opportunity to watch his gentle solicitude toward her.

She found something unbearably sweet—disarming, even—at the sight of his tender care, such a vivid contrast to his reputation as a ruthless businessman who had built his vast shipping company from the ground up.

That treacherous softness fluttered inside her. Even after she forced herself to look away—to focus instead on the rare beauty of the night settling in more deeply across the mountainside—she couldn't ignore that tangled mix of fierce attraction and dawning respect.

As they descended the trail, Winder Ranch came into view, sprawling and solid in the night.

"Home," Jo said in a sleepy-sounding voice that carried across the darkness.

"We're nearly there," he assured her.

When they arrived at the ranch house, Quinn dismounted and then reached for Jo, who winced with the movement.

Worry spasmed across his handsome features but she watched him quickly conceal it from Jo. "Tess, do you mind holding the horses for a few moments while I carry Jo inside and settle her back in her bedroom?"

This time, she was pleased that she could dismount on her own. "Of course not," she answered as her feet hit the dirt.

"Thank you. I'll trade places with you in a few moments so that you can get Jo settled for bed while I take care of the horses."

"Good plan."

She gave him a hesitant smile and was a little astonished when he returned it. Something significant had changed between them as a result of one simple horseback ride into the mountains. They were working together, a team, at least for the moment. He seemed warmer, more approachable. Less antagonistic.

They hadn't really cleared any air between them, other than those few moments she had tried to offer an oblique apology for their history. But she wanted to think perhaps he might eventually come to accept that she had become a better person.

CHAPTER SEVEN

AFTER QUINN CARRIED Jo inside, Tess stood patting the mare, savoring the night before she went inside to take care of Jo's medical needs. Quiet moments of reflection were a rare commodity in her world.

She had gotten out of the habit when she had genuinely had no time to spare with all of Scott's medical needs. Perhaps she needed to work at meditation when she moved to Portland, she thought. Maybe yoga or tai chi.

She was considering her options and talking softly to the horses when Quinn hurried down the porch steps a few moments later.

"How's Jo?"

"Ready for pain meds, I think, but she's not complaining."

"You gave her a great gift tonight, Quinn."

He smiled a little. "I hope so. She loves the mountains. I have to admit, I do as well. I forget that sometimes. Seattle is beautiful with the water and the volcanic mountains but it's not the same as home."

"Is it? Home, I mean?"

"Always."

He spoke with no trace of hesitation and she wondered again at the circumstances that had led him to Winder Ranch. Those rumors about his violent past swirled through her memory and she quickly dismissed them as ridiculous.

"I'm sorry. Let me take the horses." He reached for the reins of both horses and as she handed them over, their hands brushed.

He flashed her a quick look and grabbed her fingers with his other hand. "Your fingers are freezing!"

"I should have worn gloves."

"I should have thought to get you some before we left." He paused. "This was a crazy idea, wasn't it? I apologize again for dragging you up there."

"Not a crazy idea at all," she insisted. "Jo loved it."

"She's half-asleep in there and I know she's in pain, but she's also happier than I've seen her since I arrived."

She smiled at him, intensely conscious of the hard strength of his hand still curled around her fingers. Her hands might still be cold from the night air but they were just about the only thing not heating up right about now.

He gazed at her mouth for several long seconds, his eyes silvery-blue in the moonlight, and for one effervescent moment, she thought again that he might kiss her. He even angled his head ever so slightly and her gaze tangled with his.

Her pulse seemed abnormally loud in her ears and her insides jumped and fluttered like a baby bird trying its first awkward flight.

He eased forward slightly and her body instinctively rose to meet his. She caught her breath, waiting for the brush of his mouth against hers, but he suddenly jerked back, his expression thunderstruck.

Tess blinked as if awakening from a long, lovely nap

as cold reality splashed over her. Of course he wouldn't kiss her. He despised her, with very good reason.

With ruthless determination, she shoved down the disappointment and ridiculous sense of hurt shivering through her. So what if he found the idea of kissing her so abhorrent? She didn't have time for this anyway. She was supposed to be working, not going for moonlit rides and sharing confidences in the dark and fantasizing about finally kissing her teenage crush.

Since he now held the horses' reins, she shoved her hands in the pocket of her jacket to hide their trembling and forced her voice to sound cool and unaffected.

"I'd better go take care of Jo's meds."

"Right." He continued to watch her out of those seductive but veiled eyes.

"Um, good night, if I don't see you again before I leave."

"Good night."

She hurried up the porch steps, feeling the heat of his gaze following her. Inside, she closed the door and leaned against it for just a moment, willing her heart to settle down once more.

Blast the man for stirring up all these hormones she tried so hard to keep contained. She *so* did not want to be attracted to Quinn. What a colossal waste of energy on her part. Oh, he might have softened toward her a little in the course of their ride with Jo, but she couldn't delude herself into thinking he was willing to forgive and forget everything she had done to him years ago.

She had work to do, she reminded herself. People who needed her. She didn't have time to be obsessing over the past or the person she used to be or a man like Quinn Southerland, who could never see her as anything else.

SHE DID HER best the rest of the night to focus on her patients and not on the little thrum of desire she hadn't been able to shake since that almost-kiss with Quinn.

Still, she approached Winder Ranch for her midnight check on Jo with a certain amount of trepidation. To her relief, when she unlocked the door with the key Easton had given her and walked inside, the house was dark. Quinn was nowhere in sight, but she could still sense his presence in the house.

Jo didn't stir when Tess entered her room, which worried her for a moment until she saw the steady rise and fall of the blankets by the glow of the small light in the attached bathroom that Jo and Easton left on for the hospice nurses.

The ride up to the lake must have completely exhausted her. She didn't even wake when Tess checked her vitals and gave her medicine through the central IV line that had been placed after her last hospitalization.

When she was done with the visit, she closed the door quietly behind her and turned to go, then became aware that someone else was in the darkened hallway. Her heart gave a quick, hard kick, then she realized it was Easton.

She wasn't sure if that sensation coursing through her was more disappointment or relief.

"I hope I didn't wake you," Tess said.

The other woman's sleek blond ponytail moved as she shook her head. "I've still got some pesky accounts to finish. I was in the office working on the computer and heard the door open."

"I tried to be quiet. Sorry about that." She smiled at her friend. "But then, Jo didn't even wake up so I couldn't have been *too* loud."

"You weren't. I'm just restless tonight."

"I'm sorry."

Easton shrugged. "It sometimes knocks me on my butt if I think about what things will be like in a month or so. I'm trying to get as much done now on ranch paperwork so I have time to…to grieve."

Tess placed a comforting hand on her arm and Easton smiled, making a visible effort to push away her sadness. "Quinn told me about your adventure tonight," she said.

Tess made a rueful face. "I'm nowhere near the horsewoman you are. I felt like an idiot up there, but at least I didn't fall off."

"Jo was so happy when I checked on her earlier. I haven't seen her like that in a long time."

"Then I suppose my mortification was all for a good cause."

Easton laughed a little but her laughter quickly faded. "It won't be much longer, will it?"

Tess's heart ached at the question but she didn't pretend to misunderstand. "A week, maybe a little more. You know I can't say exactly."

Her friend's blue eyes filled with a sorrow that was raw and real. "I don't want to lose her, Tess. I'm not ready. What will I do?"

Tess set her bag on the floor and hurried forward to pull Easton into her arms. She knew that ache, that deep, gnawing fear and loss.

"You'll go on. That's all you can do. All any of us can do."

"First my parents, then Guff and now Jo. I can't bear it. She's all I have left."

"I know, sweetheart."

Easton didn't cry aloud, though Tess could feel the quiet shuddering of her shoulders. After a moment, the other woman pulled away.

"I'm sorry. I'm just tired."

"You need to sleep, honey. Everything will seem a little better in the morning, I promise. Midnight is the time when our fears all grow stronger and more vicious."

Easton drew in a heavy breath, then stepped away, swiping at her eyes. "Brant called from Germany earlier. He's hoping to get a flight any time now."

She remembered Brant Western as a tall, serious-minded boy who had always seemed an odd fit to be best friends with both Quinn, the rebellious kid with the surly attitude, and Cisco Del Norte, the wild, slightly dangerous troublemaker.

"Jo will be thrilled to have him home. What about Cisco?"

Easton's mouth compressed into a tight line and she focused on a spot somewhere over Tess's shoulder. "No word yet. We think he's somewhere in El Salvador but we can't seem to find anything out for sure. He's moving around a lot. Seems like everywhere we try, we just keep missing him by a day or even a few hours. It's so aggravating. Quinn has his assistant in Seattle trying to pull some strings with the embassy down there to find him."

"I hope it doesn't take much longer."

Easton nodded, her features troubled. "Even if we find him, there's no guarantee he can make it back in time. Quinn has promised to send a plane down to bring him home, even if he's in the middle of the jungle, but we have to find him first."

Her stomach gave a strange little quiver at the idea of Quinn having planes at his disposal.

"I'll keep my fingers crossed," she said, then picked up her bag and headed for the front door. Easton followed to let her out.

"Get some rest, honey," she said again. "I'll be back for the next round of meds around three. You'd better be asleep when I get back!"

"Yes, Nurse Ratched."

"I mean it."

Easton smiled a little, even past the lingering sadness in her eyes. "Thanks, Tess. For everything."

"Go to sleep," she ordered again, then walked out into the night, with that same curious mix of relief and disappointment that she had avoided Quinn, at least for a few more hours.

HE AWOKE TO the sound of a door snicking softly closed and the dimmer switch in the bathroom being turned up just enough to jar him out of dreams he had no business entertaining.

In a rather surreal paradigm shift, he went from dreaming about a heated embrace on a warm blanket under starry skies near the lake to the stark reality of a sickroom, where his foster mother lay dying.

Oddly, the same woman appeared in both scenes. Tess stepped out of the bathroom, looking brisk and professional in her flowered surgical scrubs.

He feigned sleep and watched her through his lashes as she donned a pair of latex-free gloves.

He could pinpoint the instant she saw him sprawled in the recliner, purportedly asleep. Her steps faltered and she froze.

Probably the decent thing would be to open his eyes and go through the motions of pretending to awaken. But he wasn't always crazy about doing the decent thing. Instead, he gave a heavy-sounding breath and continued to spy on her under his lashes.

She gazed at him for several seconds as if trying to ascertain his level of sleep, then she finally turned away from him and back to her patient with a small, barely perceptible sigh he wondered about.

For the next few minutes, he watched her draw medicine out into syringes, then she quietly began checking Jo's blood pressure and temperature.

Though her movements were slow and careful, Jo still opened her eyes when Tess put the blood pressure cuff on her leg.

"I'm so sorry to wake you. I wish I didn't have to," Tess murmured.

"Oh, poof," Jo whispered back. "Don't you worry for a single moment about doing your job."

"How is your pain level?"

Jo was silent. "I'm not going to tell you," she finally said. "You'll just write it down in your little chart and the next thing I know, Jake Dalton will be increasing my meds and I'll be so drugged out I won't be able to think straight. My Brant is coming home. Should be any day now."

As Jo whispered to her, Tess continued to slant careful looks in his direction.

"Easton told me earlier that he was on his way," she said in an undertone.

"They'll be good for Easton. The four of them, why, they were thicker than thieves. I can't tell you how glad I am they'll still have each other."

Quinn swallowed hard, hating this whole situation all over again.

Tess smiled, relentlessly cheerful. "It's a blessing, all right. For all of them and especially for your peace of mind."

He listened to their quiet conversation as Tess continued to take care of Jo's medical needs. He was still trying to figure out how much of her demeanor he was buying. She seemed to be everything that was patient and calm, a serene island in the middle of a stormy emotional mess. Was it truly possible that this dramatic change in her could be genuine?

He supposed he was a cynical bastard but he couldn't quite believe it. This could all be one big show she was putting on. He had only been here a few days. If he stuck around long enough, she was likely to revert to her true colors.

On the other hand, people could change. He was living testimony to that. He was worlds away from the bitter, hot-tempered punk he'd been when he arrived at the Winders' doorstep after a year in foster care and the misery that came before.

He pushed away the past, preferring instead to focus on today.

Tess finished with Jo a few moments later. After fluffing her pillow and tucking the blankets up around her, she dimmed the light in the bathroom again and moved quietly toward the door out into the hallway.

He rose and followed her, careful not to disturb Jo, who seemed to have easily slipped into sleep again.

"I'll walk you out," he said, his voice low, just as she reached the door.

She whirled and splayed a hand across her chest. She

glared at him as she moved out of the room to the hallway. He followed her and closed the door behind him.

"Don't do that! That's the second time you've nearly scared the life out of me. How long have you been awake?"

"Not long. Here, let me help you with your coat."

He took it off the chair in the hallway where she had tossed it and stood behind her. Her scent teased him, that delectable peach and vanilla, that somehow seemed sweet and sultry at the same time, like a hot Southern night.

She paused for a moment, then extended her arm through the sleeve. "Thank you," she said and he wondered if he was imagining the slightly husky note to her voice.

"You're welcome."

"You really don't need to walk me out, though. I'm sure I can find the way to my car by myself."

"I could use the fresh air, to be honest with you."

She looked as if she wanted to argue but she only shrugged and turned toward the door. He held it open for her and again smelled that seductive scent as she moved past him on her way out.

The scent seemed to curl through him, twisting and tugging an unwelcome response out of him, which he did his best to ignore as they walked out into the night.

The moon hung huge over the western mountains now, the stars a bright glitter out here unlike anything to be found in the city.

The October night wasn't just cool now in the early morning hours, it was downright cold. This time of year, temperatures in these high mountain valleys could show a wide range in the course of a single day. Nights were invariably cool, even in summer. In spring and fall, the temperature dropped quickly once the sun went down.

His morning spent in the garden soaking up sunshine with Jo seemed only another distant memory.

"Gorgeous night, isn't it?" Tess said. "I don't ever get tired of the view out here."

He nodded. "I've lived without it since I left Cold Creek Canyon, but something about it stays inside me even when I'm back in Seattle."

She smiled a little. "I know I'm going to miss these mountains when I move to Portland in a few weeks."

"What's in Portland?" he asked, curious as to why she would pick up and leave after her lifetime spent here.

"A pretty good basketball team," she answered. "Lots of trees and flowers. Nice people, from what I hear."

"You know what I mean. Why are you leaving?"

She was silent for a moment, the only sound the wind whispering through the trees. "A whole truck-load of reasons. Mostly, I guess, because I'm ready for a new start."

He could understand that. He had sought the same thing in the Air Force after leaving Pine Gulch, hadn't he? A place where no one knew his history in the foster-care system or as the rough-edged punk who had found a home here with Jo and Guff.

"Will you be doing the same thing? Providing end-of-life care?"

She smiled and in the moonlight, she looked fresh and lovely and very much like the teenage cheerleader who had tangled the hormones of every boy who walked the halls of Pine Gulch High School.

"Just the opposite, actually. I took a job in labor and delivery at one of the Portland hospitals."

"Bringing life into the world instead of comforting those who are leaving it. There's a certain symmetry to that."

"I think so, too. It's all part of my brand-new start."

"I suppose everybody could use that once in a while."

"True enough," she murmured, with an unreadable look in her eyes.

"Will you miss this?"

"Pine Gulch?"

"I was thinking more of the work you do. You seem... very good at it. Do you give this same level to all your patients as you have to Jo?"

She looked startled at the question, though he wasn't sure if was because she had never thought about it before or that she was surprised he had noticed.

"I try. Everyone deserves to spend his or her last days with dignity and respect. But Jo is special. I can't deny that. She used to give me piano lessons when I was young and I've always adored her."

Now it was his turn to be surprised. Jo taught piano lessons for many years to most of the young people in Pine Gulch but he had never realized Tess had once had the privilege of being one of her students.

"Do you still play?"

She laughed. "I hardly played then. I was awful. Probably the worst student Jo ever had, though she tried her best, believe me. But yes, I still play a little. I enjoy it much more as an adult than I did when I was ten."

She paused for a moment, then gave a rueful smile. "When he was...upset or having a bad day, Scott used

to enjoy when I would play for him. It calmed him. I've
had more practice than I ever expected over the years."

"You should play for Jo sometime when you come
out to the house. She gets a real kick out of hearing her
old students play. Especially the hard ones."

"Maybe. I'm worried her hearing is a little too fragile
for my fumbling attempts." She smiled. "What about
you? Did Jo give you lessons after you moved here?"

He gave a short laugh at the memory. "She tried.
I'm sure I could have taught you a thing or two about
being difficult."

"I don't doubt that for a moment," she murmured.

She gazed at him for a moment, then she shifted her
gaze up and he could swear he saw a million constel-
lations reflected in her eyes.

"Look!" she exclaimed. "A shooting star, right over
the top of Windy Peak. Quick, make a wish."

He tilted his neck to look in the direction she pointed.
"Probably just a satellite."

She glared at him. "Don't ruin it. I'm making a wish
anyway."

With her eyes screwed closed, she pursed her mouth
in concentration. "There," she said after a moment.
"That should do it."

She opened her eyes and smiled softly at him and he
forgot all about the cold night air. All he could focus on
was that smile, that mouth, and the sudden wild hunger
inside him to taste it.

"What did you wish?" he asked, a gruff note to his
voice.

She made a face. "If I tell you, it won't come true.
Don't you know anything about wishes?"

Right now, he could tell her a thing or two about

wanting something he shouldn't. That sensuous heat wrapped tighter around his insides. "I know enough. I know sometimes wishes can be completely ridiculous and make no sense. For instance, right now, I wish I could kiss you. Don't ask me why. I don't even like you."

Her eyes looked huge and green in her delicate face as she stared at him. "Okay," she said, her voice breathy.

"Okay, I can kiss you? Or, okay, you won't ask why I want to?"

She let out a ragged-sounding breath. "Either. Both."

He didn't need much more of an invitation than that. Without allowing himself to stop and think through the insanity of kissing a woman he had detested twenty-four hours earlier, Quinn stepped forward and covered her mouth with his.

CHAPTER EIGHT

SHE GAVE A little gasp of shock but her mouth was warm and inviting in the cold air and he was vaguely aware through the haze of his own desire that she didn't pull away, as he might have expected.

Instead, she wrapped her arm around his waist and leaned into his kiss for more.

A low clamor in his brain warned him this was a crazy idea, that he would have a much harder time keeping a safe distance between them after he had known the silky softness of her mouth, but he ignored it.

How could he possibly step away now, when she tasted like coffee and peaches and Tess, a delectable combination that sizzled through him like heat lightning?

Her lips parted slightly, all the invitation he needed to deepen the kiss. She moaned a little against his mouth and he could feel the tremble of her body against him, the confused desire in the slide of her tongue against his.

The night disappeared until it was only the two of them, until he was lost in the unexpected hunger for this woman in his arms. Her kiss offered solace and surrender, a chance to put away for a moment his sadness and embrace the wonder of life in all its tragedy and glory.

He lost track of time there in the moonlight. He forgot about Jo and about his efforts to find his recalcitrant foster brother and his worries for Easton. He especially refused to let himself remember all the reasons he shouldn't be kissing her—how, as he'd told her, he wasn't even sure he liked her, how he still didn't trust that she wasn't hiding a knife behind her back, ready to gut him with it at the first chance.

The only thing that mattered for this instant was Tess and how very perfect she felt in his arms, with her mouth eager and warm against his.

A coyote howled from far off in the distance, long and mournful. He heard it on the edge of his consciousness but he knew the instant the spell between them shattered and Tess returned to reality. In the space between one ragged breath and the next, she went from kissing him with heat and passion to freezing in his arms like Windy Lake in a January blizzard.

Her arms fluttered away from around his neck and he sensed she would have backed farther away from him if she hadn't been pressed up against her car door.

Though he wanted nothing more than to crush her to him again and slide into that stunning heat once more, he forced himself to step back to give them both a little necessary space.

Her breathing was as rough and quick as his own and he could see the rapid rise and fall of her chest.

Despite the chill in the air, the night seemed to wrap around them in a sultry embrace. From the trees whispering in the wind to the carpet of stars overhead, they seemed alone here in the darkness.

Part of him wanted to step toward her and sweep her into his arms again, but shock and dismay began to seep through his desire. What kind of magic did she wield against him that he could so easily succumb to his attraction and kiss her, despite all his best instincts?

He shouldn't have done it. In the first place, their relationship was a tangled mess and had been for years. Sure, she had been great with Jo tonight and he had been grateful for her help on the horseback ride into the mountains. But one night couldn't completely transform so much animosity into fuzzy warmth.

In the second place, he had enough on his plate right now. His emotions were scraped raw by Jo's condition. He had nothing left inside to give anything else right now, especially not an unwanted attraction to Tess.

Maybe that's why he had kissed her. He needed the distraction, a few moments of oblivion. Either way, it had been a monumentally stupid impulse, one he was quite certain he would come to regret the moment she climbed into her little sedan and drove down Cold Creek Canyon.

She continued to gaze at him out of those huge green eyes, as if she expected him to say something. He would be damned if he would apologize for kissing her. Not when she had responded with such fierce enthusiasm.

He had to say something, though. He scrambled for words and said the first thing that came to his head.

"If I had known you were such an enthusiastic kisser, I wouldn't have worked so hard to fight you off in high school."

The moment he said the words, he wished he could call them back. The comment had been unnecessarily cruel and made him sound like an ass. Beyond that, he didn't like revealing he remembered anything that had happened in their long-ago past. Apparently she still tended to bring out the worst in him.

He couldn't be certain in the darkness but he thought she paled a little. She grabbed her car door and yanked it open.

"That's funny," she retorted. "If I had known you would turn out to be such a jerk, I wouldn't have spent a moment since you returned to Pine Gulch regretting the way I treated you back then."

He deserved that, he supposed. *Now* he wanted to apologize—for his words at least, not the kiss—but the words seemed to clog in his throat.

She slid into her driver's seat, avoiding his gaze. "It would probably be better for both our sakes if we just pretended the past few moments never happened."

He raised an eyebrow. "You think you can do that? Because I'm not at all sure I have that much imagination."

She cranked the key in her ignition with just a little more force than strictly necessary and he felt a moment's pity that she was taking out her anger against him on her hapless engine.

"Absolutely," she snapped. "It shouldn't be hard at all. Especially since I'm sorry to report the reality didn't come close to measuring up to all my ridiculous teenage fantasies about what it might be like to kiss the bad boy of Cold Creek."

Before he could come up with any kind of rejoinder—sharp or otherwise—she thrust her car into gear and shot around the circular driveway.

He stared after her, wondering why the cold night only now seemed to pierce the haze of desire still wrapped around him.

Her words about teenage fantasies seemed to echo through his head. He supposed on some level, he must have known she had wanted to kiss him all those years ago. She had tried it, after all. He could still remember that day in the empty algebra classroom when he had been so furious with her over the false cheating allegations and then she had made everything much worse by thinking she could reel him in with a few flirtatious words.

He had always assumed her fleeting interest in him, her attempts to draw his attention, were only a spoiled fit of pique that he didn't fall at her feet like every other boy in school. Now he had to wonder if there might have been something more to it.

Trust him to make a mess out of everything, as usual. She had been kind to Jo and he had responded by taking completely inappropriate advantage. Then he had compounded his sins by making a stupid, mocking comment for no good reason.

She was furious with him, and she had every right to be, but he couldn't help thinking it was probably better this way. He didn't like having these soft, warm feelings for her.

Better to remember her as that manipulative little cheerleader looking so sweet-faced and innocent as she lied through her teeth to their history teacher and the principal than as the gentle caregiver who could suppress her own fears about horseback riding to help a dying woman find a little peace.

TESS WAITED UNTIL she drove under the arch at the entrance to Winder Ranch and had turned back onto the main Cold Creek road, out of view of the ranch house, before pulling her car over to the side and shifting into Park with hands that still trembled.

She was such an idiot.

Her face burned and she covered her hot cheeks with her hands.

She couldn't believe her response to him, that she had kissed him with such heat and enthusiasm. The moment his mouth touched hers, she had tossed every ounce of good sense she possessed into the air and had fallen into his kiss like some love-starved teenage girl with a fierce crush.

Oh, mercy. What must he think of her?

Probably that she was a love-starved thirty-two-year-old who hadn't known a man's touch in more years than she cared to remember.

How had she forgotten that incredible rush of sensations churning through her body? The delicious heat and lassitude that turned her brain to mush and her bones to rubber?

She had nearly burst into tears at how absolutely perfect it had felt to have his arms around her, his mouth sure and confident on hers. Wouldn't *that* have been humiliating? Thank the Lord she at least had retained some tiny modicum of dignity. But she had wanted to lose herself inside that kiss, to become so tangled up in him that she could forget the hundreds of reasons she shouldn't be kissing Quinn Southerland on a cold October night outside Winder Ranch.

If I had known you were such an enthusiastic kisser, I wouldn't have worked so hard to fight you off in high school.

His words seemed to echo through her car and she wanted to sink through the floorboards in complete mortification.

What was she thinking? Quinn Southerland, for

heaven's sake! The man despised her, rightfully so. If she wanted to jump feetfirst into the whole sexual attraction thing, shouldn't she *try* to have the sense God gave a goose and pick somebody who could at least stand to be in the same room with her?

The unpalatable truth was, she hadn't been thinking at all. From the first instant his mouth had touched hers with such stunning impact, she felt like that shooting star she had wished upon, bursting through the atmosphere.

She had been rocked to her core by the wild onrush of sensations, his hands sure and masculine, his rough, late-evening shadow against her skin, his scent—of sleepy male and the faint lingering hint of some expensive aftershave—subtle and sexy at the same time.

To her great shame, she had wanted to forget everything sensible and sound and just surrender to the heat of his kiss. Who knew how long she would have let him continue things if she hadn't heard the lonely sound of a coyote?

Blast the man. She had everything planned out so perfectly. Her new job, relocating to Portland. It wasn't fair that he should come back now and stir up her insides like a tornado touching down. She didn't need this sort of complication just as she was finally on the brink of moving on with her life.

She scrubbed at her cheeks for another moment, then dropped her hands and took a deep, cleansing breath. The tragic truth was, he wouldn't be around much longer and she wouldn't have to deal with him. Jo was clinging by her fingernails but she couldn't hold on much longer. When she passed, Quinn would return to Seattle and she would be starting her new life.

For a few weeks, she would just have to do her best to deal with this insane reaction, to conceal it from him.

He didn't like her and she would be damned if she would pant after him like she was still that teenage girl with a crush.

"THANKS A MILLION for taking a look at the Beast," Easton said. "I really didn't want to have to haul it to the repair place in town."

Four days after his startling encounter with Tess, Quinn stood with his hands inside Easton's temperamental tractor, trying to replace the clutch. "No problem," he answered. "It's good to know I can still find my way around the insides of a John Deere."

"If Southerland Shipping ever hits the skids, you can always come back home and be my grease monkey."

He grinned. "It's always good to have options, isn't it?"

She returned his smile, but it faded quickly. "Guff wanted you to stay and do just that, didn't he? You could always find your way around any kind of combustion engine."

True enough. He never minded other ranch work—roundup and moving the cattle and even hauling hay. But he had always been happiest when he was up to his elbows in grease, tinkering with this or that machine.

"Remember that old '66 Chevy pickup truck you used to work on? The blue one with the white top and all those curves?"

"Oh, yeah. She was a sweet ride. I imagine Cisco drove her into the ground after I left for the Air Force."

Something strange flashed in her mind for a moment, before she blinked it away. "You could have stayed. You would have been more than welcome," Easton said after a moment. "But I knew all along you never would."

He raised an eyebrow. Had he been so transparent? "Pine Gulch is a nice place and I love the ranch. Why were you so certain I wouldn't stick around? I might have been happy running a little place of my own nearby."

She shook her head. "Not you. Brant, maybe. He loves his ranch, though you would have to use that crowbar in the toolbox over there to get him to admit it. But you and Cisco had wanderlust running through your veins even when we were kids."

Maybe Cisco, Quinn thought. He had always talked about all the places he wanted to see when he left Idaho. Sun-drenched beaches and glittering cities and beautiful, exotic women who would drop their clothes if you so much as smiled at them.

That had been Francisco Del Norte's teenage dream. Quinn had no idea how close he had come to reaching it, since the man was wickedly skillful at evading any questions about his wandering life.

Quinn had his suspicions about what Cisco might be involved with, but he preferred to keep them to himself, especially around Easton. While she might love him and Brant like brothers, he had always sensed her feelings for Cisco were far different.

"I haven't wandered that far," he protested, instead of dwelling on Cisco and his suitcase full of secrets. "Not since I left the Air Force, anyway. I've been settled in Seattle for eight years now."

"Your dreams were always bigger than a little town like Pine Gulch could hold. I think deep down, Guff and Jo knew that, even if they were disappointed you didn't come home after you were discharged."

"They didn't need me here. They always had you to run the ranch." He sent her a careful look. "I always figured you were just fine with that. Was I wrong? You left for a while there, but you came back."

She had that strange look in her eyes again when he mentioned the eight months she had moved away from the ranch after Guff died. She didn't like to talk about it much, other than to say she had needed a change for a while. He supposed, like Cisco, she had her share of secrets, too.

"Yes. I came back," she said.

"Do you regret that?"

She raised her eyebrows. "You mean do I feel stuck here while the rest of you went off and conquered the world?"

He made a face. "I haven't *completely* conquered it. Still have a ways to go there but I'm working on it."

She smiled, though her expression was pensive. "I can't deny that sometimes I wonder if there's something more out there for me than a cattle ranch in Pine Gulch, Idaho. But I'm happy here, for the most part. I can't bear the thought of selling the ranch and leaving. Where would I go?"

"You could always come to Seattle. The company could always use somebody with your organizational skills."

"That world's not for me. You know that. I'm happy here."

Even as she said it, he caught the wistful note in her voice and he wondered at it. It wouldn't be easy to just pick up and make a new start somewhere. As had been the case more often than he cared to admit, he couldn't help thinking about Tess. In a few weeks, she was off to make a new start somewhere away from Pine Gulch.

As he worked on the clutch, his mind replayed that stunning kiss a few days earlier: the taste of her, like coffee and cinnamon, the sweet scent of her surrounding him, the imprint of her soft curves burning through layers of clothing.

He could go for long stretches of time without thinking about it as he went about the routine of visiting with Jo, helping Easton with odd jobs and trying to run Southerland Shipping from hundreds of miles away.

But then something would spark a memory and he would find himself once more caught up in reliving every moment of that heated embrace.

He let out a breath, grateful he had seen Tess just a few times since, when she came out to take care of Jo—and then only briefly, in the buffering presence of Easton or Jo. He had wanted to apologize but hadn't been alone with her to do it and hadn't wanted to bring up the kiss in the presence of either of the other women.

That hadn't stopped him from obsessing more than he should have about her when she wasn't around, wondering which was the real Tess—the selfish girl he remembered or the soft, caring woman she appeared to be now.

The sound of an approaching vehicle drew his attention from either the mystery of Tess or the tractor's insides.

"Looks like company." Through the wide doors of the ranch's equipment shed, he watched a small white SUV approach the house. "Isn't it too early in the afternoon for any caregivers? The nurse was just here."

Easton followed his gaze outside. "I don't recognize the vehicle. Maybe it's one of Jo's friends."

They watched for a moment from their vantage point of a hundred yards away as the door opened, then a tall, brown-haired man in uniform stepped out.

"Brant!" Easton exclaimed, her delicate features alight with joy.

With a resounding thud that echoed through the building, she dropped the wrench to the concrete equipment shed floor and ran full tilt toward the new arrival.

Quinn followed at an easier pace and arrived just as Brant Western scooped East into his arms for a tight hug.

"I'll get grease all over your pretty uniform," she warned.

"I don't care. You are a sight, Blondie."

"Back at you." She kissed his cheek and Quinn watched her dash tears away with a surreptitious finger swipe. He remembered again the little towheaded preteen who used to follow them around everywhere. He couldn't believe her parents had let them drag her along on all their adventures but she had always been a plucky little thing and they had all adored her.

After another tight hug, Brant set her down, then turned to Quinn with a long, considering glance.

"Look at you. A few days back on the ranch and Easton has you doing all the grunt work."

He looked down at the oil and grime that covered his shirt. "I don't mind getting my hands a little dirty."

"You never did." Brant smiled, though his eyes were red-rimmed with exhaustion. He looked not just fatigued but emotionally wrung-out.

Quinn considered Brant and Cisco his best friends,

his brothers in every way that mattered. And though they had never been particularly demonstrative with each other, he was compelled now to step forward and pound the other man's back.

"Welcome home, Major."

"Thanks, man."

"Now I'm the one who's going to get grease all over your uniform."

"It will wash." Brant stepped away and Quinn was happy to see he seemed a little brighter, not quite as utterly exhausted. "On the flight over, I was trying to remember how long it's been since we've been together like this."

"Four years ago January," Easton said promptly.

Quinn combed through his memory bank and realized that must have been when Guff had died of a heart attack that had shocked all of them. By some miracle, they had all made it back from the various corners of the world for his funeral.

"Too damn long, that's for sure," he said.

Brant smiled for a moment but quickly sobered. "Like the last one, I wish this reunion could be under happier circumstances. How is she?"

"Eager to see you." Easton slipped her arm through his. "She'll be so happy you could make it home."

"I can't stay long. I was able to swing only a week. I'll have my regular leave in January and will have a couple more weeks home then if I can make it back."

Jo wouldn't be around for that and all of them knew it.

Easton forced a smile. "A day or a week, it won't matter to Jo. She'll just be so happy she had a chance to see you one last time. Come on, I'll take you inside. I want to see her face when she gets a load of you."

"You two go ahead," Quinn said. "I'm almost done out here. Since I'm already dirty, think I'll finish up out here first and come inside in a few."

Brant and Easton both nodded and headed for the house while Quinn returned to the tractor. A few minutes later, he was just tightening the last nut on the job when he heard the front door to the house bang shut.

"Quinn! Come quick!"

He jerked his gaze toward the ranch house at the urgency in Easton's voice and his blood ran cold.

He dropped the wrench and raced toward the house. Not yet, he prayed as he ran. Not when Brant had only just arrived at Winder Ranch and when his people hadn't managed to find Cisco yet.

His heart pounded frantically as he thrust open the door to Jo's room. The IV pump was beeping and the alarm was going off on the oxygen saturation monitor.

He frowned. Jo was lying against her pillow but wild relief pulsed through him that her eyes were open and alert, though her features were pale and drawn.

Just now, Easton looked in worse shape than Jo. She stood by the bedside, the phone in her hand.

"I don't care what you say. I'm calling Dr. Dalton. You were unconscious!"

"All this bother and fuss," Jo muttered. "You're making me feel like a foolish old woman."

Despite her effort to downplay her condition, he could see the concern in the expressions of both Brant and Easton.

"She was out cold for five solid minutes," Easton explained to Quinn. "She was hugging Brant one moment, then she fell back against her pillows the next and wouldn't wake up no matter what we tried."

"I should have called to let you know I was on my way." Brant's voice was tight with self-disgust. "It wasn't right to rush in like that and surprise you."

"I wasn't expecting you today, that's all," Jo insisted. "Maybe I got a little excited but I'm fine now."

Despite her protestations, Jo was as pale as her pillow.

"The clinic's line is busy. I'm calling Tess," Easton declared and walked from the room to make the call.

"Tess?" Brant asked.

Just when his heart rate started to slow from the adrenaline rush, simply the mention of Tess's name kicked it right back up again.

"Tess Claybourne. Used to be Jamison. She's one of the hospice nurses."

The best one, he had to admit. After several days here, he knew all three of the home-care nurses who took turns seeing to Jo. They were all good caregivers and compassionate women but as tough as it was for him to swallow, Tess had a knack for easing Jo's worst moments and calming everybody else in the house.

Brant's blue eyes widened. "Tess Jamison. Pom-pom Tess? Homecoming Queen? That Tess?"

Okay, already. "Yeah. That Tess."

"You're yanking my chain."

"Not this time." He couldn't keep the grimness out of his voice.

"She still hotter than a two-dollar pistol?"

"Brant Western," Jo chided him from her bed. "She's a lovely young woman, not some…some pin-up poster off your Internet."

When they were randy teenagers, Jo had frequently lectured them not to objectify women. Brant must have remembered the familiar refrain as well, Quinn thought, as the deep dimples Quinn despised flashed for just a moment with his smile.

"Sorry, Jo. But she was always the prettiest girl at PG High. I used to get tongue-tied if she only walked past me in the hall."

She was still the prettiest thing Quinn had seen in a long time. And he didn't even want to think about how delectable she tasted or the sexy little sounds she made when his mouth covered hers....

Easton walked in, jarring him from yet another damn flashback.

"I reached Tess on her cell phone. She's off today but she's going to come over anyway. And I talked to Jake Dalton and he's stopping by on his way up to Cold Creek."

Pine Gulch's doctor had been raised on a huge cattle ranch at the head of Cold Creek Canyon, Quinn knew.

"Shouldn't we take her to the hospital or something?" Brant asked.

Quinn and Easton exchanged glances since they had frequently brought up the subject, but Jo spoke before he could answer.

"No hospital." Jo's voice was firm, stronger than he had heard it since he arrived. "I'm done with them. I'm dying and no doctor or hospital can change that. I want to go right here, in the house I shared with Guff, surrounded by those I love."

Brant blinked at her bluntness and Quinn sympathized with him. It was one thing to understand intellectually that her condition was terminal. It was quite another to hear her speak in such stark, uncompromising terms about it. He at least had had a few days to get used to the hard reality.

"But it's not going to happen today or even tomorrow," she went on. "I won't let it. Not until Cisco comes home. I just need to rest for a while and then I want to have a good long talk with you about what you've been doing for the army."

Brant released a heavy breath, his tired features still looking as if he had just been run over by a Humvee.

Quinn could completely sympathize with him. He could only hope Jo held out long enough so his people could track down the last of the Four Winds.

CHAPTER NINE

"WHAT'S THE VERDICT?" Jo asked. "Is my heart still beating?"

Tess pulled the stethoscope away from Jo's brachial artery and pulled the blood pressure cuff off with a loud ripping sound.

She related Jo's blood pressure aloud to Jake Dalton, who frowned at the low diastolic and systolic numbers.

"Let's take a listen to your ticker," Pine Gulch's only doctor said, pulling out his own stethoscope.

Jo responded by glaring at Tess. "Dirty trick, bringing Jake along with you."

"I told you I called him," Easton said from the doorway of the room, where she stood with Quinn and the very solemn-looking Major Western. Tess purposely avoided looking at any of them, especially Quinn.

It was a darn good thing Jake wasn't checking her heart rate right about now. She had a feeling it would be galloping along faster than one of the Winder Ranch horses in an open pasture on a sunny afternoon.

Knowing Quinn was only a few feet away watching her out of those silver-blue eyes was enough to tangle her insides and make her palms itch with nerves.

"And I told you I don't need a doctor," Jo replied.

"Be careful or you'll hurt my feelings," Jake teased.

"Oh, poof. Your skin is thicker than rawhide."

"Yet you can still manage to break my heart again and again."

Jo laughed and Tess smiled along with her. Jake Dalton was one of her favorite people. He had been a rock to her after she moved back to Pine Gulch with Scott. Though her husband had a vast team of specialists in Idaho Falls, Jake had always been her first line of defense whenever she needed a medical opinion about something.

He was a good, old-fashioned small-town doctor, willing to make house calls and take worried phone calls at all hours of the day and night and treat all his patients like family.

She had been thrilled four years earlier when he married Maggie Cruz, a nurse practitioner who often volunteered with hospice. She now considered both of them among her dearest friends.

"This is all a lot of nonsense for nothing," Jo insisted. "I was a little overexcited when Brant arrived, that's all."

Jake said nothing, only examined her chart carefully. He asked Jo several questions about her pain level and whether she had passed out any other times she had neglected to tell them all about.

When he was finished, he smoothed a gentle hand over her hair. "I'm going to make a few changes in your meds. Why don't you get some rest and I'll explain what I want to do with Tess, okay?"

Tess knew it was an indication of Jo's weakened condition that she didn't argue, only nodded and closed her eyes.

Jake led the way out into the hall where the others waited. He closed the door behind him and headed for the kitchen, which Tess had learned long ago was really Command Central of Winder Ranch.

"What's happening?" Easton was the first to speak.

Jake's mouth tightened and his eyes looked bleak. "Her organs are starting to shut down. I'm sorry."

Even though Tess had been expecting it for days now, she was still saddened by the stark diagnosis.

"Which means what?" Brant asked. He looked very much the quintessential soldier with his close-cropped brown hair, strong jaw and sheer physical presence.

"It won't be long now," Jake said. "A couple of days, maybe."

Easton let out a long breath that wasn't quite a sob but probably would have been if she had allowed it.

Tess reached out and gripped her hand and Easton clutched her fingers tightly.

"I think it's time to think about round-the-clock nursing," Jake said. "I'm thinking more of her comfort and, to be honest, yours as well."

"Of course," Quinn said. "Absolutely. Whatever she needs."

Tess's chest ached at his unhesitating devotion to Jo.

Dr. Dalton nodded his approval. "I'll talk to hospice and see what they can provide."

Tess knew what the answer would be. Hospice was overburdened right now. She knew the agency didn't have the resources for that level of care.

"I'll do it. If you'll let me."

"You?" Brant asked, and she gave an inward flinch at the shock in his voice. Here was yet another person who only saw her as the silly girl she had been and she wondered if she would ever be able to escape her past.

"Right now the agency is understaffed," she answered. "I know they don't have the resources to have someone here all the time, as much as they would like to. They're going to recommend hospitalization in Idaho Falls for her last few days."

"She so wants to be here." Easton's voice trembled on the words.

"Barring that, they're going to tell you you'll have to hire a private nurse. I'd like to be that private nurse. I won't let you pay me but I want to do this for Jo. I'll make arrangements for the others to cover all my shifts and stay here, if that's acceptable to you all."

Tess refused to look at Quinn as she made the offer, though she could feel the heat of his gaze on her.

Part of her wondered at the insanity of offering to put herself in even closer proximity with him, but she knew he would be far too preoccupied to spend an instant thinking about a few regrettable moments of shared passion.

"I think it's a wonderful idea, if you're sure you're up to it," Brant said, surprising her. "Quinn and Easton both tell me you're the best of her nurses."

"Are you sure?" Easton asked with a searching look.

"Absolutely. Let me do this for her and for you," she said to her friend.

"What do you think?" Easton turned to Quinn, and Tess finally risked a glance in his direction. She found him watching the scene with an unreadable expression in his silver-blue eyes.

"It seems a good solution if Tess is willing. Better than bringing in some stranger. But we *will* pay you."

She didn't argue with him, though she determined she would donate anything the family insisted on back to hospice, which had been one of Jo's favorite charities even before she had need of their services.

"I'll need a little time to make all the arrangements but I should be back in a few hours," she said.

"Thank you." Easton squeezed her fingers. "I don't know how we'll ever repay you."

"I'll see you in a few hours."

She said goodbye to Dr. Dalton and headed for the door. To her shock, Quinn followed her.

"I'll walk you out," he said gruffly, and her mind instantly filled with images from the last time he had walked her outside, when they had given into the intimacy of the night and the heat simmering between them.

She wanted to tell him she didn't need any more of his escorts, thanks very much, but she didn't want to remind him of those few moments.

"Why?" Quinn asked when they were outside.

She didn't need to ask what he meant. "I love her," she said simply.

His gaze narrowed and she could tell he wasn't convinced.

"Have you done this before? Round-the-clock nursing?"

She arched an eyebrow. "You mean besides the six years I cared for my husband?"

"I keep forgetting that."

She sighed, knowing he was only concerned for his foster mother. "I won't lie to you, it's always difficult at the end. The work is demanding and the emotional toll can be great. But if I can bring Jo a little bit of comfort and peace, I don't care about that."

"I don't get you," he muttered.

"I'm not that complicated."

He made a rough sound of disbelief low in his throat. He looked as if he wanted to say more but he finally just shook his head and opened the car door for her.

Two hours later, Tess set her small suitcase down in the guest room on the first floor, right next door to Jo's sickroom.

"This should work out fine," she said to Easton. It was a lovely room, one she hadn't seen before, filled with antiques and decorated in sage and pale peach.

She found it restful and calm and inherently feminine, with the lacy counterpane on the bed and the scrollwork on the bed frame and the light pine dresser.

Where did the others sleep? she wondered. Her insides trembled a little at the thought of Quinn somewhere in the house.

Why did sharing a house with him feel so different, so much more intimate, than all those other days when she had come in and out at various hours to care for Jo?

"I hope I'm not kicking someone else out of a bed."

"Not at all." Easton smiled, though she wore the shadow of her grief like a black lace veil. "No worries. We've got room to spare. There are plenty of beds in this place, plus the bunkhouse and the foreman's house, which are empty right now since my foreman has his own place down the canyon."

"That's where you were raised, wasn't it? The foreman's house?"

Easton nodded. "Until I was sixteen, when my parents were killed in a car accident and I moved here with Aunt Jo and Uncle Guff. The boys were all gone by then and it was only me."

"You must have missed them."

Easton smiled as she settled on the bed, wrapping her arms around her knees. "The house always seemed too empty without them. I adored them and missed them like crazy. Even though I was so much younger—Quinn was five years older, Brant four and Cisco three—they were always kind to me. I still don't know why but they never seemed to mind me tagging along. Three instant older cousins who felt more like brothers was heady stuff for an only child like me."

"I was always jealous of my friends who had older brothers to look out for them," Tess said.

"I loved it. One time, Quinn found out an older boy at school was teasing me because I had braces and glasses. Roy Hargrove. Did you ever know him? He would have been a couple years younger than you."

"Oh, right. Greasy hair. Big hands."

Easton laughed. "That's the one. He used to call me some terrible names and one day Quinn found me crying about it. To this day, I have no idea what the boys said to him. But not only did Roy stop calling me names, he went out of his way to completely avoid me and always got this scared look in his eyes when he saw me, until his family moved away a few years later."

Easton smiled a little at the memory. "Anyway, there's plenty of room here at the house. Eight bedrooms, counting the two down here."

Tess stared at her friend. "Eight? I've never been upstairs but I had no idea the house was that big!"

"Guff and Jo wanted to fill them all with children but it wasn't to be. Jo was almost forty when they met and married and she'd already had cancer once and had to have a hysterectomy because of it. I think they thought about adopting but they ended up opening the ranch to foster children instead, especially after Quinn came. His mother and Jo were cousins, did you know that? So we're cousins by marriage, somehow."

"I had no idea," she exclaimed.

"Jo and his mother were good friends when they were younger but then they lost track of each other. From what I understand, it took Jo a long time to get custody of him after his parents died."

"How old were you when they moved here?"

"I was almost ten when Quinn came. He would have been fourteen."

Tess remembered him, all rough-edged and full of attitude. He had been dark and gorgeous and dangerous, even back then.

"Brant moved in after Quinn had been here about four months, but you probably already knew him from school."

She knew Brant used to live on a small ranch in the canyon with his family. He had been in her grade and Tess always remembered him as wearing rather raggedy clothes and a few times he had come to school with an arm in a sling or bruises on his arms. Just like Quinn, Brant Western hadn't been like the other boys, either. He had been solemn and quiet, smart but not pushy about it.

She had been so self-absorbed as a girl that she hadn't known until years later that the Winders had taken Brant away from his abusive home life, though she had noticed around middle school that he started dressing better and seemed more relaxed.

"And then Cisco moved in a few months after Brant." Easton spoke the words briskly and rose from the bed, but not before Tess caught a certain something in her eyes. Tess had noticed it before whenever Easton mentioned the other man's name but she sensed Easton didn't want to discuss it.

"Jo and Guff had other foster children over the years, didn't they?"

"A few here and there but usually only as a temporary stopping point." She shrugged. "I think they would have had more but…after my parents died, I was pretty shattered for a while and I think they were concerned about subdividing their attention among others when I was grieving and needed them."

Her heart squeezed with sympathy for Easton's loss. She couldn't imagine losing both parents at the same time. Her father's death a few years after Scott's accident had been tough enough. She didn't know how she would have survived if her mother had died, too.

"They have always been there for me," Easton said quietly.

Tess instinctively reached out and hugged her friend. Easton returned the embrace for only a moment before she stepped away.

"Thank you again for agreeing to stay." Her voice wobbled only a little. "Let me know if you need anything."

"I will. Right back at you. Even just a shoulder to cry on. I might be here as Jo's nurse but I'm your friend, too."

Easton pulled open the door. "I know. That's why I love you. You're just the kind of person I want to be when I grow up, Tess."

Her laugh was abrupt. "You need to set your sights a little higher than me. Now Jo, that's another story. There's something for both of us to shoot for."

"I think if I tried the rest of my life, I wouldn't be able to measure up to her. She's an original."

CHAPTER TEN

THE ENTIRE RANCH seemed to be holding its collective breath.

Day-to-day life at the ranch went on as usual. The stock needed to be watered, the human inhabitants needed food and sleep, laundry still piled up.

But everyone was mechanically going through the motions, caught up in the larger human drama taking place in this room.

Forty-eight hours later, Tess sat by the window in Jo's sickroom, her hands busy with the knitting needles she had learned to wield during the long years of caring for Scott. She had made countless baby blankets and afghans during those years, donating most of them to the hospital in Idaho Falls or to the regional pediatric center in Salt Lake City.

Jo coughed, raspy and dry, and Tess set the unfinished blanket aside and rose to lift the water bottle from the side of the bed and hold the straw to Jo's mouth.

Her patient sipped a little, then turned her head away.

"Thank you," she murmured.

"What else can I get you?" Tess asked.

"Cisco. Only Cisco."

Her heart ached for Jo. The woman was in severe pain, her organs failing, but she clung to life, determined to see her other foster son one more time. Tess wanted desperately to give her that final gift so she could at last say goodbye.

A few moments later, Jo rested back against the pillow and closed her eyes. She didn't open them when Easton pushed open the door.

Tess pressed a finger to her mouth and moved out into the hall.

"I came to relieve you for a few moments. Why don't you go outside and stretch your legs for a while? Go get some fresh air."

She nodded, grateful Easton could spell her for a few moments, though she had no intention of going outside yet. "Thanks. I'll be back in a few moments."

"Take your time. I'm done with the morning chores and have a couple hours."

When Easton closed Jo's door behind her, Tess turned toward the foyer. Instead of going outside, though, she headed up the stairs toward the empty bedroom Quinn had taken over for an office while he was in Pine Gulch.

She approached the open doorway, mortified that her heart was pounding from more than just the fast climb up the stairs.

She heard Quinn's raised voice before she reached the doorway, sounding more heated than she had heard him since that long-ago day she had accused him of cheating.

He sat with his back to the door at a long writing desk near the window. From the angle of the doorway, she could see a laptop in front of him with files strewn across the surface of the desk.

He wore a soft gray shirt with the sleeves rolled up and she could see his strong, muscled forearm flex. His dark hair looked a little tousled, as if he had run his fingers through it recently, which she had learned was his habit.

She wasn't sure which version of the man she found more appealing. The rugged cowboy who had ridden to Windy Lake, his hands sure and confident on the reins and his black Stetson pulled low over his face. The loving, devoted son who sat beside Jo's bedside for long hours, reading to her from the newspaper or the Bible or whatever Jo asked of him.

Or this one, driven and committed, forcing himself to put aside the crisis in his personal life to focus on business and the employees and customers who depended on him.

She gave an inaudible sigh. The truth was, she was drawn to every facet of the dratted man and was more fascinated by him with every passing hour.

Jo. She was here for Jo, she reminded herself.

"Look, whatever it takes," he said into the phone. "I'm tired of this garbage. Find him! I don't care what you have to do!"

After pressing a button on the phone, he threw it onto the desk with such force that she couldn't contain a little gasp.

He turned at the sound and something flared in his eyes, something raw and intense, before he quickly banked it. "What is it? Is she…"

"No. Nothing like that. Was that phone call about Cisco?"

"Supposed to be. But as you can probably tell, I'm hitting walls everywhere I turn. That was the consulate in El Salvador. He was there a few weeks ago but nobody knows where he is now. I have tried every contact I have and I can't manage to find one expatriate American in Latin America."

She walked into the room, picking her words carefully. "I don't think she's going to be able to hang on until he gets here, though she's trying her best."

"I hate that I can't give her this."

"It's not your fault, Quinn." She curled her fingers to her palm in an effort to fight the impulse to touch his arm in comfort, as she would have done to Easton and even Brant, who, except for those first few moments when he arrived, had treated her with nothing but kindness and respect.

Quinn was different. Somehow she couldn't relax in his company, not with their shared past and the more recent heat that unfurled inside her whenever he was near.

She let out a breath, wishing she could regard him the same as she did everyone else.

"Sometimes you have to accept you've tried your best," she said.

"Have I?" The frustration in his voice reached something deep inside her and this time she couldn't resist the urge to touch his arm.

"What else can you do? You can't go after him."

He looked down at her pale fingers against the darker skin of his arm for a long moment. When he lifted his gaze, she swallowed at the sudden intensity in his silver-blue gaze.

She pulled her hand away and tucked it into the pocket of her scrubs. "When you've done all you can, sometimes you have no choice but to put your problems in God's hands."

His expression turned hard, cynical. "A lovely sentiment. Did that help you sleep at night when you were caring for your husband?"

She drew in a sharp breath then let it out quickly,

reminding herself he was responding from a place of pain she was entirely familiar with.

"As a matter of fact, it did," she answered evenly.

"Sorry." He raked a hand through his hair again, messing it further. "That was unnecessarily harsh."

"You want to fix everything. That's understandable. It's what you do, isn't it?"

"Not this time. I can't fix this."

The bleakness in his voice tore at her heart and she couldn't help herself, she rested her fingers on his warm arm again. "I'm sorry. I know how terribly hard this is for you."

He looked anguished and before she quite realized what he was doing, he pulled her into his arms and clung tightly to her. He didn't kiss her, only held her. She froze in shock for just a moment then she wrapped her arms around him and let him draw whatever small comfort she could offer from the physical connection with another person. Sometimes a single quiet embrace could offer more comfort than a hundred condolences, she knew.

They stood for several moments in silence with his arms around her, his breath a whisper against her hair. Something sweet and intangible—and even tender— passed between them. She was afraid to move or even breathe for fear of ruining this moment, this chance to provide him a small measure of peace.

All too soon, he exhaled a long breath and dropped his arms, moving away a little, and she felt curiously bereft.

He looked astonished and more than a little embarrassed.

"I... Sorry. I don't know what that was about. Sorry."

She smiled gently. "You're doing your best," she repeated. "Jo understands that."

He opened his mouth to answer but before he could, Brant's voice sounded from downstairs, loud and irate.

"It's about damn time you showed up."

Tess blinked. In her limited experience, the officer was invariably patient with everyone, a sea of calm in the emotional tumult of Winder Ranch. She had never heard that sort of harshness from him.

In response, she heard another man's voice, one she didn't recognize.

"I'm not too late, am I?"

Quinn's expression reflected her own shock as both of them realized Francisco Del Norte had at last arrived.

Quinn took the stairs two at a time. She followed with the same urgency, a little concerned the men might come to blows—at least judging by Brant's anger and that hot expression in Quinn's eyes as he had rushed past her.

In the foyer, she found Brant and Quinn facing off against a hard-eyed, rough-looking Latino who bore little resemblance to the laughing, mischievous boy she remembered from school.

"Where the hell have you been?" Quinn snapped.

Fatigue clouded the other man's dark eyes. Tess wasn't sure she had ever seen anyone look so completely exhausted.

"Long story. I could tell you, but you know the drill. Then I'd have to kill you and I'm too damn tired right now to take on both your sorry asses at the same time."

The three men eyed each other for another moment and Tess held her breath, wondering if she ought to step in. Then, as if by some unspoken signal, they all moved together and gave that shoulder-slap thing men did instead of hugging.

"Tell me I'm not too late." Cisco's voice was taut with anguish.

"Not yet. But she's barely hanging on, man. She was just waiting to say goodbye to you."

Tears filled Cisco's eyes as he uttered a quick prayer of gratitude in Spanish.

She was inclined to dislike the man for the worry he had put everyone through these past few days and for Jo's heartache. But she couldn't help feeling compassion for the undisguised sorrow in his eyes.

"They didn't... I didn't get the message until three days ago. I was in the middle of something big and it took me a while to squeeze my way out."

Brant and Quinn didn't look appeased by the explanation but they didn't seem inclined to push him either.

"Can I see her?"

Both Brant and Quinn turned to look at Tess, still standing on the stairs, as if she was Jo's guardian and gatekeeper.

"Easton's in with her. I'll go see if she's awake."

She turned away, but not before she caught an odd expression flicker across his features at the mention of Easton's name.

She left the three men and walked down the hall to Jo's bedroom. When she carefully eased open the door, emotions clogged her throat at the scene she found inside.

Easton was the one asleep now, with her head resting on the bed beside her aunt. Jo's frail, gnarled hand rested on her niece's hair.

Jo pressed a finger to her mouth. Though she tried to shake her head, she was so weak she barely moved against the pillow.

"It's not time for more meds, is it?" she murmured, her voice thready.

Though Tess could barely hear the woman's whisper, Easton still opened her eyes and jerked her head up.

"Sorry. I must have just dozed off."

Jo smiled. "Just a few minutes ago, dear. Not long enough."

"It's not time for meds," Tess answered her. "I was only checking to see if you were awake and up for a visitor."

Though she thought she spoke calmly enough, some clue in her demeanor must have alerted them something had happened. Both women looked at her carefully.

"What is it?" Easton asked.

Before she could answer, she heard a noise in the doorway and knew without turning around that Cisco had followed her.

Easton's features paled and she scrambled to her feet. Tess registered her reaction for only an instant, then she was completely disarmed when the hard, dangerous-looking man hurried to Jo's bedside, his eyes still wet with emotion.

The joy in Jo's features was breathtakingly beautiful as she reached a hand to caress his cheek. "You're here. Oh, my dear boy, you're here at last."

Quinn and Brant followed Cisco into the room. Tess watched their reunion for a moment, then she quietly slipped from the room to give them the time and space they needed together.

CHAPTER ELEVEN

THE WOMAN QUINN loved as a mother took her last breath twelve hours after Cisco Del Norte returned to Winder Ranch.

With all four of them around her bedside and Tess standing watchfully on the edge of the room, Jo succumbed to the ravages cancer had wrought on her frail body.

Quinn had had plenty of time to prepare. He had known weeks ago her condition was terminal and he had been at the ranch for nearly ten days to spend these last days with her and watch her inexorable decline.

He had known it was coming. That didn't make it any easier to watch her draw one ragged breath into her lungs, let it out with a sigh and then nothing more.

Beside him, Easton exhaled a soft, choked sob. He wrapped an arm around her shoulder and pulled her close, aware that Cisco, on her other side, had made the same move but had checked it when Quinn reached her first.

"I'll call Dr. Dalton and let him know," Tess murmured after a few moments of leaving them to their shared sorrow.

He met her gaze, deeply grateful for her quiet calm. "Thank you."

She held his gaze for a moment, her own filled with an echo of his grief, then she smiled. "You're welcome."

He had fully expected the loss, this vast chasm of pain. But he hadn't anticipated the odd sense of peace that seemed to have settled over all of them to know Jo's suffering was finally over.

A big part of that was due to Tess and her steady, unexpected strength, he admitted over the next hour as they worked with the doctor and the funeral home to make arrangements.

She seemed to know exactly what to say, what to do, and he was grateful to turn these final responsibilities over to her.

If he found comfort in anything right now, it was in the knowledge that Jo had spent her last days surrounded by those she loved and by the tender care Tess had provided.

He couldn't help remembering that embrace with Tess upstairs in his office. Those few moments with her arms around him and her cheek resting against his chest had been the most peaceful he had known since he arrived at the ranch.

He had found them profoundly moving, for reasons he couldn't explain, anymore than he could explain how the person he thought he despised most in the world ended up being the one he turned to in his greatest need.

He was lousy at doing nothing.

The evening after Jo's funeral, Quinn sat at the kitchen table at the ranch with a heaping plate of left-overs in front of him and an aching restlessness twisting through him.

The past three days since Jo's death had been a blur

of condolence visits from neighbors, of making plans with Southerland Shipping for the corporate jet to return for him by the end of the week, of seeing to the few details Jo hadn't covered in the very specific funeral arrangements she made before her death.

Most of those details fell on his shoulders by default, simply because nobody else was around much.

He might have expected them to all come together in their shared grief but each of Jo's Four Winds seemed to be dealing with her death in a unique way.

Easton took refuge out on the ranch, with her horses and her cattle and hard, punishing work. Brant had left the night Jo died for his own ranch, a mile or so up the canyon and had only been back a few times and for the funeral earlier. Cisco slept for a full thirty-six hours as if it had been months since he closed his eyes. As soon as the funeral was over earlier that day, he had taken one of the ranch horses and a bedroll and said he needed to sleep under the stars.

As for Quinn, he focused on what work he could do long-distance and on these last few details for Jo. Staying busy helped push the pain away a little.

He sipped at his beer as the old house creaked and settled around him and the furnace kicked in with a low whoosh against the late October cold. Forlorn sounds, he thought. Lonely, even.

Maybe Cisco had the right idea. Maybe he ought to just get the hell out of Dodge, grab one of the horses and ride hard and fast into the mountains.

The thought did have a certain appeal.

Or maybe he ought to just call his pilot and move up his departure. He could be home by midnight.

What would be the difference between sitting alone

at his house in Seattle or sitting alone here at Winder Ranch? This aching emptiness would follow him everywhere for a while, he was afraid, until that inevitable day when the loss would begin to fade a little.

Hovering on the edge of his mind was the awareness that once left Winder Ranch this time, he would have very few reasons to return. With Jo and Guff gone, his anchor to the place had been lifted.

Easton would always be here. He could still come back to visit her, but with Brant in the military and Cisco off doing whatever mysterious things occupied his time, nothing would ever be the same.

The Four Winds would be scattered once more.

Jo had been their true north, their center. Without her, a chapter in his life was ending and the realization left him more than a little bereft.

He rose suddenly as that restlessness sharpened, intensified. He couldn't just sit here. He didn't really feel like spending the night on the hard ground, but at least he could take one of the horses out for a hard moonlit ride to work off some of this energy.

The thought inevitably touched off memories of the other ride he had taken into the mountains just days ago—and of the woman he had been doing his best not to think about for the past few days.

Tess had packed up all the medical equipment in Jo's room and had left the ranch the night Jo died. He had seen her briefly at the funeral, a slim, lovely presence in a bright yellow dress amid all the traditionally dark mourning clothes. Jo would have approved, he remembered thinking. She would have wanted bright colors and light and sunshine at her funeral. He only wished he'd been the one to think of it and had put on a vibrant tie instead of the muted, conservative one he had worn with his suit.

To his regret, Tess had slipped away from the service before he had a chance to talk to her. Now he found himself remembering again those stunning few moments they had shared upstairs in his office bedroom, when she had simply held him, offering whatever solace he could draw from her calm embrace.

He missed her.

Quinn let out a breath. Several times over the past days, as he dealt with details, he had found himself wanting to turn to her for her unique perspective on something, for some of her no-nonsense advice, or just to see her smile at some absurdity.

Ridiculous. How had she become so important to him in just a matter of days? It was only the stress of the circumstances, he assured himself.

But right now as he stood in the Winder Ranch kitchen with this emptiness yawning inside him, he had a desperate ache to see her again.

She would know just the right thing to say to ease his spirit. Somehow he knew it.

If he just showed up on her doorstep for no reason, she would probably think he was an idiot. He couldn't say he only wanted her to hold him again, to ease the restlessness of his spirit.

His gaze fell on a hook by the door and fate smiled on him when he recognized her jacket hanging next to his own denim ranch coat. He had noticed it the day before and remembered her wearing it a few nights when she had come to the ranch, before she moved into the spare room, but he had forgotten about it until just this moment.

If he gave it a moment's thought, he knew he would talk himself out of seeing her while his heart was still raw and aching.

So he decided not to think about it.

He shrugged into his own jacket, then grabbed hers off the hook by the door and headed into the night.

THE NATURE OF hospice work meant she had to face death on a fairly consistent basis but it never grew any easier—and some losses hit much harder than others.

Tess had learned early, though, that it was best to throw herself into a project, preferably something physical and demanding, while the pain was still raw and fresh. When she could exhaust her body as much as her spirit, she had half a chance of sleeping at night without dreams, tangled-up nightmares of all those she had loved and lost.

The evening of Jo's funeral, she stood on a stepladder in the room that once had been Scott's, scraping layers of paint off the wide wooden molding that encircled the high ceiling of the room.

Stripping the trim in this room down and refinishing the natural wood had always been in her plans when she bought the house after Scott's accident but she had never gotten around to it, too busy with his day-to-day care.

She supposed it was ironic that she was only getting around to doing the work she wanted on the room now that the house was for sale. She ought to leave the redecorating for the new owners to apply their own tastes, but it seemed the perfect project to keep her mind and body occupied as best she could.

The muscles of her arms ached from reaching above her head but that didn't stop her from scraping in rhythm to the loud honky-tonk music coming from her iPod dock in the corner of the empty room.

She was singing along about a two-timin' man so loudly she nearly missed the low musical chime of her doorbell over the wails.

Though she wasn't at all in the mood to talk to anyone, she used any excuse to drop her arms to give her aching muscles a rest.

She thought about ignoring the doorbell, certain it must be her mother dropping by to check on her. She knew Maura was concerned that Jo's death would hit her hard and she wasn't sure she was in the mood to deal with her maternal worry.

Her mother would have seen the lights and her car in the driveway and Tess knew she would just keep stubbornly ringing the bell until her daughter answered.

She sighed and stepped down from the ladder.

"Coming," she called out. "Hang on."

She took a second before she pulled open the door to tuck in a stray curl slipping from the folded bandanna that held her unruly hair away from her face while she worked.

"Sorry, I was up on the ladder and it took me a minute…"

Her voice trailed off and she stared in shock. That definitely wasn't her mother standing on her small porch. Her heart picked up a beat.

"Quinn! Hello."

"Hi. May I come in?" he prompted, when she continued to stare at him, baffled as to why he might be standing on her doorstep.

"Oh. Of course."

She stepped back to allow him inside, fervently wishing she was wearing something a little more presentable than her scruffiest pair of jeans and the disreputable faded cropped T-shirt she used for gardening.

"Were you expecting someone else?"

"I thought you might be my mother. She still lives in town, though my father died a few years back. He had a heart attack on the golf course. Shocked us all. Friends have tried to talk my mother into moving somewhere warmer but she claims she likes it here. I think she's really been sticking around to keep an eye on me. Maybe she'll finally move south when I take off for Portland."

She clamped her mouth shut when she realized she was babbling, something she rarely did. She also registered the rowdy music coming from down the hall.

"Sorry. Let me grab that music."

She hurried back to the bedroom and turned off the iPod, then returned to her living room, where she saw him looking at the picture frames clustered across the top of her upright piano.

He looked gorgeous, she thought, in a Stetson and a denim jacket that made him look masculine and rough.

Her insides did a long, slow roll but she quickly pushed back her reaction, especially when she saw the slightly lost expression in his eyes.

"I'm sorry," she said. "I was stripping paint off the wall trim in my spare bedroom. I…needed the distraction. What can I do for you?"

He held out his arm, along with something folded and blue. "You left your coat at the ranch. I thought you might need it."

She took it from him and didn't miss the tiny flicker of static that jumped from his skin to hers. Something just as electric sparked in his eyes at the touch.

"You didn't need to drive all the way into town to return it. I could have picked it up from Easton some other time."

He shrugged. "I guess you're not the only one who needed a distraction. Everybody else took off tonight in different directions and I just didn't feel like hanging around the ranch by myself."

He didn't look at her when he spoke, but she recognized the edgy restlessness in his silver-blue eyes. She wanted to reach out to him, as she might have done with anyone else, but she didn't trust herself around him and she didn't know if he would welcome her touch. Though he had that day at the ranch, she remembered.

"How are you at scraping paint?" she asked on impulse, then wanted to yank the words back when she realized the absurdity of putting him to work in her spare room just hours after his foster mother's funeral.

He didn't look upset by the question. "I've scraped the Winder Ranch barn and outbuildings in my day but never done room trim. Is this any different?"

"Harder," she said frankly. "This house has been through ten owners in its seventy-five years of existence and I swear every single one of them except me has left three or four layers of paint. It's sweaty, hard, frustrating work."

"In that case, bring it on."

She laughed and shook her head. "You don't know what you're getting into, but if you're sure you're willing to help, I would welcome the company."

It wasn't a lie, she thought as she led him back to the bedroom after he left his jacket and hat on the living-room couch. She had to admit she was grateful to have someone to talk to and for one last opportunity to see him again before he left Pine Gulch.

"You don't really have to do this," she said when they reached the room. "You're welcome to stay, even if you don't want to work."

Odd how what she had always considered a good-size space seemed to shrink in an instant. She could smell him, sexy and masculine, and she wished again that she wasn't dressed in work clothes.

"Where can I start?"

"I was up on the ladder working on the ceiling trim. If you would like to start around the windows, that would be great."

"Deal."

pensive and tailored sleeves of his shirt that looked ex-men's clothes—and grabbed a paint scraper. Without another word, he set immediately to work.

Tess watched him for a moment, then turned the music on again, switching to a little more mellow music.

For a long time, they worked without speaking. She didn't find the silence awkward in the slightest, merely contemplative on both their parts.

Quinn seemed just as content not to make aimless conversation and though she was intensely aware of him on the other side of the room, she wasn't sure he even remembered she was in the room until eight or nine songs into the playlist.

"My father killed my mother when I was thirteen years old."

He said the abrupt words almost dispassionately but she heard the echo of a deep, vast pain in his voice.

She set down her scraper, her heart aching for him

even as she held her breath that he felt he could share something so painful with her now, out of the blue like this.

"Oh, Quinn. I'm so sorry."

He released a long, slow breath, like air escaping from a leaky valve, and she wondered how long he had kept the memories bottled deep inside him.

"It happened twenty years ago but every moment of that night is as clear in my mind as the ride we took to Windy Lake last week. Clearer, even."

She climbed down the ladder. "You were there?"

He continued moving the scraper across the wood and tiny multicolored flakes of paint fluttered to the floor. "I was there. But I couldn't stop it."

She leaned against the wall beside him, hesitant to say the wrong word that mi~~~~ ~~~~ing this part of his past with her.

"What happened?" she murmured, sensing he needed to share it. Perhaps this was all part of his grieving process for Jo, the woman who had taken him in and helped him heal from his ugly, painful past.

"They were fighting, as usual. My parents' marriage was...difficult. My father was an attorney who worked long hours. When he returned home, he always insisted on a three-course dinner on the table, no matter what hour of the day or night, and he wanted the house completely spotless."

"That must have been hard for a young boy."

"I guess I was lucky. He didn't take his bad moods out on me. Only on her."

She held her breath, waiting for the rest.

"Their fighting woke me up," Quinn said after a moment, "and I heard my dad start to get a little rough.

Also usual. I went down to stop it. That didn't always work but sometimes a little diversion did the trick. Not this time."

He scraped harder and she wanted to urge him to spare himself the anguish of retelling the story, but again, she had that odd sense that he needed to share this, for reasons she didn't understand.

"My dad was in a rage, accusing her of sleeping with one of the other attorneys in his firm."

"Was she?"

He shrugged. "I don't know. Maybe. My father was a bastard but she seemed to delight in finding and hitting every one of his hot buttons. She laughed at him. I'll never forget the sound of her laughing, with her face still bruised and red where he had slapped her. She said she was having a torrid affair with the other man, that he was much better in bed than my father."

She drew in a sharp breath, hating the thought of a thirteen-year-old version of Quinn witnessing such ugliness between his parents.

"I don't know," he went on. "She might have been lying. Theirs was not a healthy relationship, in any sense of the word. He needed to be in control of everything and she needed to be constantly adored."

She thought of Quinn being caught in the middle of it all and her chest ached for him and she had to curl her fingers into her palms to keep from reaching for him.

"My father said he wasn't going to let her make a fool out of him any longer. He walked out of the room and I thought for sure he was going to pack a suitcase and leave. I was happy, you know. For those few moments, I was thinking how much better things would be without him. No more yelling, no more fights."

"But he didn't leave."

He gave a rough laugh and set the scraper down and sat beside her on the floor, his back against the wall and their elbows touching. "He didn't leave. He came out of the bedroom with the .38 he kept locked in a box by the side of his bed. He shot her three times. Twice in the heart and then once more in the head. And then he turned the gun on himself."

"Oh, dear God."

"I couldn't stop it. For a long time, I kept asking myself if I could have done something. Said something. I just stood there."

She couldn't help herself, she covered his hand with hers. After a long moment, he turned his hand and twisted his fingers with hers, holding tight. They sat that way, shoulders brushing while the music on her playlist shifted to a slow, jazzy ballad.

She kept envisioning that rough-edged, angry boy he had been when he first came to Pine Gulch. He must have been consumed with pain and guilt over his parents' murder-suicide. She could see it so clearly, just as she saw in grim detail her own awful behavior toward him, simply because he had refused to pay any attention to her.

"I am so, so sorry, Quinn," she murmured, for everything he had survived and for her own part in making life harder for him here.

"The first year after was…hellish," he said, his voice low. "That's the only word that fits. I was thrown into the foster-care system and spent several months bouncing from placement to placement."

"None of them stuck?"

"I wasn't an easy kid to love," he said. "You knew

me when I first came to Pine Gulch. I was angry and hurting and hated the world. Jo and Guff saw past all that. They saw whatever tiny spark of good might still be buried deep inside me and didn't stop until they helped me see it, too."

"I'm so happy you found each other."

"Same here." He paused, looking a little baffled. "I don't know why I'm telling you this. I didn't come here to dump it all on you. The truth is, I don't talk about it much. I don't think I've ever shared it with anybody but Brant and Cisco and Easton."

"It's natural to think about the circumstances that brought you into Jo's world. I imagine it's all connected for you."

"I was on a path to nowhere when Jo finally found me up in Boise and petitioned for custody. I was only the kid of a cousin. I'd never even met her but she and Guff still took me on, with all that baggage. She was a hell of a woman."

"I'm going to miss her dearly," Tess said quietly. "But I keep trying to focus on how much better a person I am because I knew her."

Their hands were still entwined between them and she could feel the heat of his skin and the hard strength of his fingers.

"I don't know what to make of you," he finally said.

She gave a small laugh. "Why's that?"

"You baffle me. I don't know which version of you is real."

"All of it. I'm like every other woman. A mass of contradictions, most of which I don't even understand myself. Sometimes I'm a saint, sometimes I'm a bitch. Sometimes I'm the life of the party, sometimes I just want everybody to leave me alone. But mostly, I'm just a woman."

"That part I get."

The low timbre of his voice and the sudden light in his eyes sent a shower of sparks arcing through her. She was suddenly intensely aware of him—the breadth of his shoulder nudging hers, the glitter of silvery-blue eyes watching her, the scent of him, of sage and bergamot and something else that was indefinable.

Her insides quivered and her pulse seemed to accelerate. "I don't regret many things in my life," she said, her voice breathy and low. "But I wish I could go back and change the way I treated you when we were younger. I hate that I gave you even a moment's unhappiness when you had already been through so much with your parents."

His shoulder shrugged beside her. "It was a long time ago, Tess. In the grand scheme of life, it didn't really mean anything."

"I was so awful to you."

"I wasn't exactly an easy person to like."

"That wasn't the problem. The opposite, actually. I…liked you too much," she confessed. "I hated that you thought I was some silly, brainless cheerleader. I wanted desperately for you to notice me."

His mouth quirked a little. "How could I help it?"

"You mean, when I was getting you kicked off the baseball team for cheating and then lying to my boyfriend and telling him you did something I only *wanted* you to do?"

"That's why Scott and his buddies beat me up that night? I had no idea."

"I'm so sorry, Quinn. I was despicable to you."

"Why?" he asked. "I still don't quite understand what I ever did to turn your wrath against me."

She sighed. "Every girl in school had a crush on you, but for me, it went way past crush. I didn't know your story but I could tell you were in pain. Maybe that's why you fascinated me, more than anyone I had ever known in my sheltered little life. I guess I was something of a healer, even then."

He gazed at her as the music shifted again, something low and sultry.

"I was fiercely attracted to you," she finally admitted. "But you made it clear you weren't interested. My pride was hurt. But I have to say, I think my heart was a little bruised, too. And so I turned mean. I wanted you to hurt, too. It was terrible and small of me and I'm so, so sorry."

"It was a long time ago," he said again. "We're both different people."

She smiled a little, her pulse pounding loudly in her ears. "Not so different," she murmured, still holding his hand. "I'm still fiercely attracted to you."

CHAPTER TWELVE

HER BREATH SNAGGED in her throat as she waited for him to break the sudden silence between them that seemed to drag on forever, though it was probably only several endless, excruciating seconds.

She braced herself, not sure she could survive another rejection. Nerves shivered through her as she waited for him to move, to speak, to do *anything*.

Just when she thought she couldn't endure the uncertainty another moment and was about to scramble away and tell him to ignore every single thing she had just said, he groaned her name and then his mouth captured hers in a wild kiss.

At that first stunning brush of his lips, the slick texture of his mouth, heat exploded between them like an August lightning storm on dry tinder. She returned his kiss, pouring everything into her response—her regret for the hurt she had caused him, her compassion for his loss, the soft tenderness blooming inside her.

And especially this urgent attraction pulsing to every corner of her body with each beat of her heart.

This was right. Inevitable, even. From the moment she heard him ring the doorbell earlier, some part of her had known they would end up here, with his arms around her and his heartbeat strong and steady under her fingers.

She wanted to help him, to heal him. To soak his pain inside her and ease his heart, if only for a moment.

She wrapped her arms more tightly around his neck, relishing the contrast between her curves and his immovable strength, between the cool wall at her back and all the glorious heat of his arms.

"While we're apologizing," he murmured against her mouth, "I'm sorry I was such an idiot the last time I kissed you. I don't have any excuse, other than fear."

She blinked at him, wondering why she had never noticed those dark blue speckles in his eyes. "Of what?"

"This. You." His mouth danced across hers again and everything feminine inside her sighed with delight.

"I want you." His voice was little more than a low rasp that sent every nerve ending firing madly. "I want you more than I've ever wanted another woman in my life and it scares the hell out of me."

"I'm just a woman. What's to be scared about?"

He laughed roughly. "That's like a saber-toothed tiger saying I'm just a nice little kitty. You are no ordinary woman, Tess."

Before she could figure out whether he meant the words as a compliment, he deepened the kiss and she decided she didn't care, as long as he continued this delicious assault on her senses.

He lowered her to the floor and she held him tightly as all the sleepy desires she had buried deep inside for years bubbled to the surface. It had been so long—so very, very long—since she had been held and cherished like this and she wanted to savor every second.

The taste of him, the scent of him, the implacable strength of his arms around her. It all felt perfect. *He* felt perfect.

She supposed that was silly, given the slightly unro-
mantic circumstances. Instead of candlelight and rose
petals and soft pillows, they were on the hard floor of
her spare room with bright fluorescent lights gleaming.

But she wouldn't have changed any of it, especially
at the risk of shattering this hazy, delicious cocoon of
desire wrapped around them.

Okay, she might wish she were wearing something a
little more sensual, especially when his hands went to
the buttons of her old work shirt. But he didn't seem to
mind her clothing, judging by the heavy-lidded hunger
in his eyes after he had worked the buttons free and the
plackets of her shirt fell away.

She should have felt exposed here in the unforgiving
light of the room. Instead, she felt feminine and emi-
nently desirable as his eyes darkened.

"You're gorgeous," he murmured. "The most beautiful thing I've ever seen."

"I'm afraid I'm not the tight-bodied cheerleader I
was at sixteen."

"Who wants some silly cheerleader when he could
have a saber-toothed tiger of a woman in his arms?"

She laughed but it turned into a ragged gasp when
he slowly caressed her through the fabric of her bra, his
fingers hard and masculine against her breast.

He groaned, low in his throat, and his thumb deftly
traced the skin just above the lacy cup. Everything tightened inside her, a lovely swell of tension as he worked
the clasp free, and she nearly arched off the floor when
his fingers covered her skin.

He teased and explored her body while his mouth
tantalized hers with deep, silky tastes and her hands

explored the hard muscles of his back and the thick softness of his hair.

"This is crazy," he said after long, delirious moments. "It's not what I came here for, I swear."

"Don't think about it," she advised him, nipping little kisses down the warm column of his neck. "I know I'm not."

His laugh turned into a groan as she feathered more kisses along his jawline. "Well, when you put it that way..."

She smiled, then gasped when he began trailing kisses down the side of her throat. Every coherent thought skittered out of her head when his mouth found her breast. She tangled her hands in his hair, arching into his mouth as he tasted and teased.

Oh, heaven. She felt as if she had been waiting years just for this, just for him, as if everything inside her had been frozen away until he came back to Pine Gulch to thaw all those lonely, forgotten little corners of her heart.

She thought again how very perfect, inevitable, this was as he pulled her shirt off and then removed his own.

He was beautiful. The rough-edged, rebellious boy had grown into a hard, dangerous man, all powerful muscles and masculine hollows and strength. She wanted to explore every single inch of that smooth skin.

She would, she vowed. Even if it took all night. Or several nights. It was a sacrifice she was fully willing to make.

Again she had that sense of inescapable destiny. They had been moving toward this moment since that first night he had startled her in the hallway of Winder Ranch. Longer, even. Maybe all that dancing around each other they had done in high school had just been a prelude to this.

A few moments later, no clothing barriers remained between them and she exulted in the sheer delicious wonder of his skin brushing hers, his strength surrounding her softness.

He kissed her and a restless need started deep inside her and expanded out in hot, hungry waves. She couldn't get enough of this, of him. She traced a hand over his pectoral muscles, feeling the leashed strength in him.

And then she forgot everything when he reached a hand between their bodies to the aching core of her hunger. She gasped his name, shifting restlessly against his fingers, and everything inside her coiled with a sweet, urgent ache of anticipation.

She felt edgy, panicky suddenly, as if the room were spinning too fast for her to ride along, but his kiss kept her centered in the midst of the tornado of sensation. She wrapped her arms around his neck, her breathing ragged.

He kissed her then, his mouth hot, insistent, demanding. That was all it took. With a sharp cry, she let go of what tiny tendrils of control remained and flung herself into the whirling, breathtaking maelstrom.

Even before the last delicious tremors had faded, he produced a condom from his wallet and entered her with one swift movement.

Long unused muscles stretched to welcome him and he groaned, pressing his forehead to hers.

"So tight," he murmured.

"I'm sorry."

His laugh was rough and tickled her skin. "I don't believe I was complaining."

He kissed her fiercely, possessively, and just like that, she could feel her body rise to meet his again.

With her hands gripped tightly in his, he moved inside her and she arched restlessly against him, her body seeking more, burning for completion. And then she could sense a change in him, feel the taut edginess in every touch. Her mouth tangled with his and at the slick brush of his tongue against hers, she climaxed again, with a core-deep sigh of delight.

He froze above her, his muscles corded, and then he groaned and joined her in the storm.

HE CAME BACK to earth with a powerful sense of the surreal. None of this seemed to be truly happening. Not the hard floor beneath his shoulders or the soft, warm curves in his arms or this unaccustomed contentment stealing through him.

It was definitely genuine, though. He could feel her pulse against his arm where her head lay nestled and smell that delectable scent of her.

"How could I have forgotten?" she murmured.

He angled his head to better see her expression. "Forgotten what?"

She smiled and he was struck again by her breathtaking beauty. She was like some rare, exquisite flower that bloomed in secret just for him.

"This radiant feeling. Total contentment. As if for a few short moments, everything is perfect in the world."

He smiled, enchanted by her. "You don't think everything would be a tad more perfect if we happened to be in a soft bed somewhere instead of on the bare floor of your ripped-apart spare room? I think I've got paint chips in places I'm not sure I should mention."

She made a face, though he saw laughter dancing in her eyes. "Go ahead. Ruin the moment for me."

"Sorry. It's just been a long time since I've been so… carried away."

"I know exactly what you mean."

He studied her. "How long?"

Her lovely green-eyed gaze met his, then flickered away. "Since the night before Scott's accident. So that would be eight years, if anyone's counting."

"In all that time, not once?"

As soon as his shocked words escaped, he realized they weren't very tactful, but she didn't seem offended.

"I loved my husband," she said solemnly. "Even if he wasn't quite the man I expected to spend the rest of my life with when I married him, I loved him and I honored my wedding vows."

He pulled her closer, stunned at her loyalty and devotion. She had put her life, her future, completely on hold for years to care for a man who could never be the sort of husband a young woman needed.

Most women he knew would have felt perfectly justified in resuming their own lives after such a tragic accident. They might have mourned their husband for a while but would have been quick to put the past behind them.

He thought of his own mother, selfish and feckless, who wasn't happy unless she was the center of attention. She wouldn't have had the first idea how to cope after such a tragedy.

Not Tess. She had stayed, had sacrificed her youth for her husband.

"Scott was an incredibly fortunate man to have you."

Her eyes softened. "Thank you, Quinn." She kissed

him gently, her mouth warm and soft, and he was astonished at the fragile tenderness that fluttered through him like dry leaves on the autumn wind.

"Can I stay?" he asked. "It's…harder than I expected to hang out at the ranch right now."

She smiled against his mouth and her kiss left no question in his mind about what her answer would be.

"Of course. I would love you to stay. And I even have a bed in the other room, believe it or not."

He rose and pulled her to her feet, stunned all over again at the peace welling inside him. He didn't think he had come here for this on a conscious level, but perhaps some part of him knew she would welcome him, would soothe the ache in his heart with that easy nurturing that was such a part of her.

"Show me," he murmured.

Her smile was brilliant and took his breath away as she took him by the hand and led him from the room.

SHE WAS HAVING a torrid affair.

Two days later, Tess could hardly believe it, even when the evidence was sprawled beside her, wide shoulders propped against her headboard, looking rugged and masculine against the dainty yellow frills and flowers of her bedroom.

The fluffy comforter on her bed covered him to the waist and she found the contrast between the feminine fabric and the hard planes and hollows of his muscled chest infinitely arousing.

She sighed softly, wondering if she would ever get tired of looking at him, touching him, laughing with him.

For two days, they hadn't left her house, except for

sneaking in one quick trip to Winder Ranch in the middle of the night for him to grab some extra clothes and toiletries.

What would the rest of the town think if news spread that the sainted Tess Claybourne was engaged in a wild, torrid relationship with Quinn Southerland, the former bad boy of Pine Gulch?

Enthusiastically engaged, no less. She flushed at the memory of her response to him, of the heat and magic and connection they had shared the past few days. The sensual, passionate woman she had become in his arms seemed like a stranger, as if she had stored up all these feelings and desires inside her through the past eight years.

She didn't know whether to be embarrassed or thrilled that she had discovered this part of herself with him.

"You're blushing," he said now with an interested look. "What are you thinking about?"

"You. This. I was thinking about how I had no idea I could...that we could..."

Her voice trailed off as she struggled with words to finish the sentence. Her own discomfort astounded her. How could she possibly possess even a hint of awkwardness after everything they had done together within these walls, all the secrets they had shared?

He didn't seem to need any explanation.

"You absolutely can. And we absolutely have."

He grinned, looking male and gorgeous and so completely content with the world that she couldn't help laughing.

This was the other thing that shocked her, that she could have such fun with him. He wasn't at all the intense, brooding rebel she had thought when they were younger. Quinn had a sly sense of humor and a keen sense of the ridiculous.

They laughed about everything from a silly horror movie they watched on TV in the middle of the night to the paint flecks in her hair after they made one half-hearted attempt to continue working on the trim in the guest room to a phone call from Easton the day before, wondering if Tess had kidnapped him.

And they had talked, endlessly. About his memories of the other Four Winds, about growing up on the ranch, about her friends and family and the miracle of how she had been led to become a nurse long before Scott's accident when those skills would become so vital.

They had also talked a great deal about his foster mother and also about Guff. He seemed to find great comfort in sharing memories with her. That he would trust her with those memories touched and warmed her, more than she could ever express. She hoped his sorrow eased a little as he brought those events and people to life for her.

"I wish it didn't have to end," she murmured now, then wished she could recall the words.

No regrets, she had promised herself that first night. She intended only to seize every ounce of happiness she could with him and then let him go with a glad heart that she had this chance to share a few wonderful days with him.

He traced a hand along her bare arm. "I wish I could put off my return to Seattle. But I've been away too long as it is. My plane's coming tomorrow."

"I know."

Her smile felt tight, forced, as she fought to hide

the sadness hovering just out of reach at his impending departure.

How had he become so very important to her in just a few short weeks? Even the idea of moving to Portland, starting over with new friends and different employment challenges, had lost much of its luster.

Ridiculous, she told herself. She couldn't let herself fall into a funk over the inevitable end of a passionate, albeit brief, affair, even one with the man who had fascinated her for two decades.

"We should do something," he said suddenly.

She took in the rumpled bedclothes and the hard muscles of his bare chest. "I thought we *had* been doing something."

His sensual smile just about took her breath away. "I meant go to dinner or something. It's not fair for me to keep you chained up in the bedroom for two days without even offering to feed you."

"We haven't tried the chained-up thing."

"Yet."

Her insides shivered at the single word in that low growl of a voice.

"We could go to The Gulch," he suggested, apparently unaffected by the same sudden vivid fantasies that flashed across her mind.

She pushed them away, wondering what the regulars or Lou and Donna Archuleta would think if she showed up in the café with Quinn looking rumpled and well-loved. What did she care? she thought. She deserved some happiness and fun in her life and if she found that with Quinn, it was nobody's damn business but theirs.

"What about the others?" she asked. "Easton and

Brant and Cisco? Don't you think you ought to spend your last night in town with them?"

He made a face, though she thought he looked struck by the reminder of his friends and the shared loss that had brought them all together.

"I should," he finally admitted. "I stayed an extra few days after the funeral to spend time with them but I ended up a little…distracted."

She pulled away from him and slipped her arms through her robe. "I should never have monopolized all your time."

"It was a mutual monopoly. I wanted to be here."

"If you want to spend your last evening at the ranch with them, please don't feel you can't because of me. Because of this."

"Why do I have to choose? We should all go to dinner together."

She frowned. "I'm not one of you, Quinn."

"After the past two weeks, you feel as much a part of the family as any of us."

She wanted to argue that the others would probably want him to themselves and she couldn't blame them. But she had discovered she had a selfish streak hiding inside her. She couldn't give up the chance to spend at least a few more hours with him.

CHAPTER THIRTEEN

IN HER HEART, Tess knew she didn't belong here with the others but she couldn't remember an evening she had enjoyed more.

Several hours later, she sat at the table in the Winder Ranch dining room and sipped at her wine, listening to the flow of conversation eddy around her.

When they weren't teasing Easton about something, they were reminiscing about some camping trip Guff took them on into Yellowstone or the moose that chased them once along the shores of Hayden Lake or snow-mobiling into the high country.

In every word and gesture, it was obvious they loved each other deeply, despite a few rough moments in the conversation.

Most notably, something was definitely up between Easton and Cisco, Tess thought. Though outwardly Easton treated him just as she did Brant and Quinn, with a sisterly sort of affection, Tess could sense braided ropes of tension tugging between the two of them.

They sat on opposite sides of the table and Easton was careful to avoid looking at him for very long.

What was it? she wondered. Had they fought about something? She had a feeling this wasn't something recent in origin as she remembered Easton's strange reaction whenever Cisco's name had been mentioned, before he made it back to the ranch. Obviously, her feelings were different for him than for Brant and Quinn and Tess wondered if anybody else but her was aware of it.

They all seemed so different to her and yet it was obvious they were a unit. Easton, who loved the ranch and was the only one of the Four Winds not to wander away from it. Brant, the solemn, honorable soldier who seemed to be struggling with internal demons she couldn't begin to guess at. Cisco, who by his demeanor appeared to be a thrill-seeking adventurer type, though she sensed there was much more to him than he revealed.

And then there was Quinn.

Around the others, these three people who were his closest friends and the only family he had left, he was warm and affectionate as they laughed and talked and shared memories and she was enthralled by him all over again.

She was the odd person out but Quinn had insisted she join them, even after Easton suggested they grill steaks at the ranch instead of going out to dinner.

The ranch house seemed empty without Jo. She wondered how Easton endured it—and how her friend would cope when she was alone here at the ranch after the men went their respective ways once more.

"Do you remember that snow prank?" Cisco said with a laugh. "That was classic, man. A masterpiece."

"I still can't believe you guys drove all the way into Idaho Falls just to rent a fake snow machine," Easton said, still not looking at Cisco.

"Hey, I tried to talk them out of it," Brant defended himself.

Quinn gave a rough laugh. "But you still drove the getaway car after we broke into the gymnasium and sprayed the Sweetheart Dance decorations with six inches of fake snow."

Tess set down her fork and narrowed her gaze at the men. "Wait a minute. That was you?"

"Uh-oh. You are so busted." Easton grinned at Quinn.

"I worked on that dance planning committee for weeks! I can't believe you would be so blatantly destructive."

"We were just trying to help out with the theme," Quinn said. "Wasn't it something about snuggling in with your sweetheart for Valentine's Day? What better time to snuggle than in the middle of a blizzard and six inches of snow?"

She gave him a mock glare. "Nice try."

"It was a long time ago. I say we all forgive and forget," Brant said, winking at Tess.

"Do you have any idea how long it takes to clean up six inches of snow from a high-school gymnasium?"

"Hey, blame it all on Quinn. I was an innocent sophomore he dragged along for the ride," Cisco said with a grin.

"You were never innocent," Easton muttered.

He sent her a quick look out of hooded dark eyes. "True enough."

Tess could feel the tension sizzle between them, though the other two men seemed oblivious to it. She wondered if any of them saw the anguished expression in Easton's eyes as she watched Cisco.

The other woman suddenly shoved her chair away from the table. "Anybody up for dessert?" she asked, a falsely bright note to her voice. "Jenna McRaven owed me a favor so I talked her into making some of her famous turtle cheesecake."

"That would be great," Brant said. "Thank you."

"Quinn? Cisco?"

Both men readily agreed and Easton headed for the kitchen.

"I'll help," Tess offered, sliding her chair away from the table. "But don't think I've forgotten the snow prank. As to forgiving, I don't believe there's a statute of limitations on prosecution for breaking the spirit of the high-school dance committee."

All three of the men laughed as she left the room, apparently unfazed by her empty threat.

In the kitchen, she found Easton reaching into the refrigerator. She emerged holding a delectable-looking dessert drizzled in chocolate and caramel and chopped nuts.

"All right, out with it," Easton said as she set the cheesecake on the counter, and Tess realized this was the first chance they'd had all evening to speak privately.

"With what?" Tess asked in as innocent a voice as she could muster, though she had a feeling she sounded no more innocent than Cisco had.

"You and Quinn. He's been gone from the ranch for two entire days! What's going on with you two?"

She turned pink, remembering the passion and fun of the past two days.

"Nothing. Not really. We're just… He's just…"

"You're right. It's none of my business," Easton said as she sliced the cheesecake and began transferring it to serving plates. "Sorry I asked."

"It's not that, I just… I can't really explain it."

Easton was silent for a long moment. "Are you sure you know what you're dealing with when it comes to Quinn?" she finally asked with a searching look. "I wouldn't be a friend if I didn't ask."

"He's leaving tomorrow. I completely understand that."

"Do you?"

Tess nodded, even as her heart gave a sad little twist. "Of course. These past few days have been…magical, but I know it's only temporary. His life is in Seattle. Mine is here, at least for the next few weeks until I move to Portland."

"Seattle and Portland aren't so far apart that you couldn't connect if you wanted to," Easton pointed out.

She wouldn't think about that, especially after she had worked so hard to convince herself their relationship was only temporary, born out of shared grief and stunning, surprising hunger.

"I care about you," Easton said when Tess didn't answer. "We owe you so much for these past weeks with Aunt Jo. You carried all of us through it. I mean that, Tess. You always knew exactly what to say and what to do, no matter what was happening, and I'll be forever grateful to you for all you did for her. That's why I'll be absolutely furious if Quinn takes advantage of your natural compassion and ends up hurting you."

"He won't. I promise."

Easton didn't look convinced. Not surprising, she supposed, since Tess couldn't even manage to convince herself.

"It's just…he doesn't have a great track record when it comes to women," her friend said quietly.

Tess tried hard to make her sudden fierce interest in that particular subject seem casual. "Really?"

"I love him like a brother and have since he came to the ranch. But I'm not blind to his faults, especially when it comes to women. I don't think Quinn has ever had a relationship that has lasted longer than a few weeks. To be honest, I'm not sure he's capable of it."

"Never?"

"I can't be certain, I suppose. He's been away for a long time. But every time I ask about his social life when we talk on the phone or email, he mentions he's dating someone new."

"Maybe he just hasn't met anyone he wants to get serious with. There's nothing wrong with that."

"I think it's more than that, Tess. If I had to guess, I would assume it has something to do with his parents' marriage. He didn't have an easy childhood and I think it's made him gun-shy about relationships and commitment."

"I'm sure it did. He told me about his parents and his messed-up home life."

Surprise flashed in her blue eyes. "He did?"

She nodded. "It can't be easy getting past something like that."

"When we were kids, he vowed over and over that he was never going to get married. To be honest, judging by his track record, I don't think he's changed his mind one bit. It broke Jo's heart, if you want the truth. She wanted to see us all settled before she died, but that didn't happen, did it?"

Tess forced a smile, though the cracks in her own heart widened a little more. "Easton, it's okay. I'm not interested in something long-term right now with Quinn or anyone else. We both needed…peace for a while after Jo's death and we enjoy each other's company. That's all there is to it."

Easton didn't look at all convinced and Tess decided to change the uncomfortable subject.

"What time does Cisco leave tomorrow?" she asked.

The diversion worked exactly as she hoped. Easton's

expression of concern slid into something else entirely, something stark and painful.

"A few hours." Her hand shook a little as she set the last slice of cheesecake on a small serving plate. "He's catching a plane out of Salt Lake City to Central America at noon tomorrow, so he'll be leaving in the early hours of the morning."

Tess covered her hand and Easton gave her an anguished look.

"Without Jo here, I don't know if he'll ever come back. Or Quinn, for that matter. Brant at least has his own ranch up the canyon so I'm sure I'll at least see him occasionally. But the other two…." Her voice trailed off. "Nothing will be the same without Aunt Jo."

Tess pulled Easton into a hug. "It won't be the same," she agreed. "But you're still here. They'll come back for you."

"I don't know about that."

"They will." Tess gave her friend a little shake. "Anyway, Jo would be the first one to tell you to seize every moment. They might not be back for a while but they're here now. Don't sour the joy you can find tonight with them by stewing about what might be coming tomorrow."

"You must be channeling Jo now. I can almost hear her in my head saying exactly those same words."

"Then you'd better listen." Tess smiled.

Easton sighed. "We'd better get this cheesecake out there before they come looking for us."

"Can you give me a minute? I need some water, but I'll be right out."

Easton gave her a searching look. "Are you sure you're all right?"

Tess forced a smile. "Of course. You've got three men waiting for dessert out there. You'd better hurry."

After a pause, Easton nodded and carried the tray with the cheesecake slices out to the dining room.

When she was alone in the bright, cheery kitchen, Tess leaned against the counter and fought the urge to cover her face with her hands and weep.

She was a terrible liar. Lucky for her, Easton was too wrapped up in her own troubles to pay close attention.

She absolutely *wasn't* okay, and she had a sinking feeling she wouldn't be for a long, long time.

I'm not interested in something long-term right now with Quinn or anyone else.

It was a wonder Jo didn't rise up and smite her for telling such a blatant fib in the middle of her kitchen.

Finally, she admitted to herself the truth she had been fighting for two days. Longer, probably. The truth that had been hovering just on the edges of her subconscious.

She was in love with him.

With Quinn Southerland, who planned to blow out of her life like the south wind in the morning.

She loved the way his mouth quirked up at the edges when he teased her about something. She loved his tender care of Jo in her final days and his deep appreciation of the family and home he had found here. She loved the strength and honor that had carried him through incredible trauma as a boy.

She loved the way he made her feel, cherished and beautiful and *wanted*, and the heat and abandon she experienced in his arms.

And she especially loved that he knew the very worst parts of her and wanted to spend time with her anyway.

Whatever was she going to do without him in her world? Just the thought of going through the motions after he returned to Seattle left her achy and heartsore.

She knew she would survive. What other choice did she have?

That didn't mean she wanted to. Hadn't she faced enough heartache? Just once in her life, couldn't things work out the way she wanted?

Fighting back a sob, she moved to the sink and poured a glass of water so she could convince herself she hadn't completely prevaricated to Easton.

She thought of her advice to her friend a few moments earlier.

Don't sour the joy you can find in today by stewing about what might be coming tomorrow.

She couldn't ruin these last few hours with him by anticipating the pain she knew waited for her around the corner.

SOMETHING WAS WRONG.

He never claimed to be the most perceptive of men when it came to the opposite sex, but even *he* could tell Tess was distracted and troubled after dinner when he drove her back from the ranch to town.

She said little, mostly gazed out the window at the lights flickering in the darkness, few and far between in Cold Creek Canyon and becoming more concentrated as he approached the town limits.

He glanced over at her profile, thinking how serenely lovely she was. He supposed her pensiveness was rubbing off on him because he still couldn't quite process the surreal twist his life had taken these past few days.

If Brant or Cisco—or Easton, even—had told him before he came back to town that he would wrap up his visit to Pine Gulch in Tess Jamison Claybourne's bed, he would have thought it was some kind of a strange, twisted joke.

Until he showed up at the ranch a few weeks ago, he honestly hadn't thought of her much in years. He was too busy working his tail off building his business to waste much time or energy on such an unimportant—though undeniably aggravating—part of his past.

On the rare occasions when thoughts of her did filter through his mind for whatever reason, they were usually tainted with acrimony and disdain.

In these past weeks, she had become so much more to him.

Quinn let out a breath. He had tried to avoid examining those fragile, tender feelings too carefully. He appreciated her care for Jo, admired the strength she had demonstrated through her own personal tragedy, found her incredibly sexy.

He didn't want to poke and prod more deeply than that, afraid to unravel the tangled mess of his feelings.

He did know he didn't want to leave her or the haven he had found in her arms.

His hands tightened on the steering wheel as he turned down the street toward her house. For two weeks, his associates had taken the helm of Southerland Shipping. Quinn ought to be ecstatic at the idea of jumping right back into the middle of the action. Strategizing, making decisions, negotiating contracts. It was all in his blood, the one thing he found he was good at, and he had certainly missed the work while he had been at Winder Ranch.

But every time he thought about saying goodbye to Tess, he started to feel restless and uneasy and he had no idea why.

He pulled into the driveway and turned off the engine to his rented SUV.

"You probably want to be with the others," she said, her voice low. "I don't mind if we say goodbye now."

Something remarkably like panic fluttered through him. "Are you that anxious to be rid of me?"

She turned wide green eyes toward him. "No. Nothing like that! I just… I assumed you would want to spend your last few hours in town with your friends," she said, a vulnerable note to her voice that shocked him.

Though he had already said his farewells to the others when he left the house, with lots of hugs and back-slapping, he considered taking the out she was offering him. Maybe he ought to just gather his few belongings from her house and head back to bunk at the ranch for the night. That made perfect sense and would help him begin the process of rebuilding all those protective walls around his emotions.

But he had a few more hours in Pine Gulch and he couldn't bear the thought of leaving her yet.

"I'd like to stay."

He said the words as more of a question than a statement. After an endless moment when he was quite certain she was going to tell him to hit the road, she nodded, much to his vast relief, and reached for his hand.

A soft, terrifying sweetness unfurled inside him at the touch of her hand in his.

How was he going to walk away in a few hours from this woman who had in a few short weeks become so vitally important to him? He didn't have the first idea.

CHAPTER FOURTEEN

SHE DIDN'T RELEASE his hand, even as she unlocked her door to let them both inside. When he closed the door behind him, she kissed him with a fierce, almost desperate, hunger.

They didn't even make it past her living room, clawing at clothes, ripping at buttons, tangling mouths with a fiery passion that stunned him.

They had made love in a dozen different ways over the past few days—easy, teasing, urgent, soft.

But never with this explosive heat that threatened to consume them both. She climaxed the instant he entered her and he groaned as her body pulsed around him and followed her just seconds later.

He kissed her, trying to memorize every taste and texture as she clutched him tightly to her. To his amazement, after just a few moments, his body started to stir again inside her and he could feel by her response that she was becoming aroused again.

He carried her to the bedroom and took enough time to undress both of them, wondering if he would ever get enough of her silky curves and the warm, sweet welcome of her body.

This time was slow, tender, with an edge of poignancy to it that made his chest ache. Did she sense it, too? he wondered.

They tasted and touched for a long time, until both of them were breathless, boneless. She cried out his name when she climaxed and he thought she said something else against his shoulder but he couldn't understand the words.

When he could breathe again and manage to string together two semicoherent thoughts, he pulled her close under the crook of his arm, memorizing the feel of her—the curves and hollows, the soft delight of her skin.

"I wish I didn't have to go," he murmured again.

Instead of smiling or perhaps expressing the same regret, she froze in his arms and then pulled away.

Though her bedroom was well-heated against the October chill, he was instantly cold, as he watched her slip her slender arms through the sleeves of her silky green robe that matched her eyes.

"Are you lying for my sake or to appease your own guilt?" she finally asked him.

He blinked, disoriented at the rapid-fire shift from tender and passionate to this unexpected attack that instantly set him on the defensive.

"Why do I have to be lying?"

"Come on, Quinn," she said, her voice almost sad. "We both know you're not sorry. Not really."

He bristled. "When did you become such an expert on what's going on inside my head?"

"I could never claim such omnipotent power. Nor would I want it."

Okay. He absolutely did not understand how a woman's mind worked. How could she pick a fight with him after the incredible intensity they just shared? Was she just trying to make their inevitable parting easier?

"If you could see inside my head," he answered carefully, "you would see I meant every word. I *do* wish I didn't have so many obligations waiting for me back in Seattle. These past few days have been…peaceful and I don't have much of that in my life."

She gazed at him, her features tight with an expression he didn't recognize. After a moment, her prickly mood seemed to slide away and she smiled, though it didn't quite push away that strange, almost bereft look in her eyes.

"I'm happy for that, Quinn. You deserve a little peace in your life and I'm glad you found it here."

She paused and looked away from him. "But we both knew from the beginning that this would never be anything but temporary."

Whenever he let himself think beyond the wonder of the moment, the shared laughter and unexpected joy he found with her, he had assumed exactly that—this was supposed to be a short-term relationship that wouldn't extend beyond these few magical days.

Hearing the words from her somehow made the reality seem more bluntly desolate.

"Does it have to be?"

"Of course," she answered briskly. "What other option is there?"

He told himself that wasn't hurt churning through him at her dismissal of all they had shared and at the potential for them to share more.

"Portland is only a few hours from Seattle. We could certainly still see each other on the weekends."

She tightened the sash on her robe with fingers that seemed to tremble slightly. From the cold? he wondered. Or from something else?

"To what end?" she asked. "Great sex and amusing conversation?"

Despite his turmoil, he couldn't resist arching an eyebrow. "Something wrong with either of those?"

Her laugh sounded rough. "Not at all. Believe me, I've become a big fan of both these past few days."

She shoved her hands in the pockets of her robe and drew in a deep breath, as if steeling herself for unpleasantness. "But I'm afraid neither is enough for me."

That edgy disquiet from earlier returned in full force and he was aware of a pitiful impulse to beg her not to push him from her life.

He wouldn't, though. He had a sudden, ugly flashback of his mother at the dinner table trying desperately to catch his father's attention any way she could. New earrings, new silverware, a difficult new recipe. Only until she managed to push one of his father's hot buttons would he even notice her, and then only to rant and rail and sometimes worse.

He pushed it away. He certainly wasn't his mother trying desperately in her own sick way to make someone care who wasn't really capable of it. Tess was not like his father. She had a deep capacity for love. He had seen it with Jo, even Easton and Brant and Cisco.

Why else would she have stayed with an invalid husband for so long?

But maybe she couldn't care for *him*. Maybe he didn't deserve someone like her....

"I want more," she said quietly, interrupting the grim direction of his thoughts. "All I wanted when I was a girl was a home and a family and a husband who cherished me. I wanted what my parents had. They held hands in the movies and whispered secrets to each other in restaurants and hid love notes for each other all around the house. My mom's still finding them, years after Dad died. That's what I wanted."

He was silent. If not for the years he spent with Jo and Guff seeing just that sort of relationship, he would have had absolutely no frame of reference to understand what she was talking about, but the Winders had shared a love like that, deep and rich and genuine.

"I thought I found that with Scott," Tess went on, "but fate had other plans and things didn't turn out quite the way I dreamed."

"I'm sorry." He meant the words. He hated thinking of her enduring such loss and pain as a young bride.

"I'm sorry, too," she said quietly. "But that time in my life is over. I'm ready to move forward now."

"I can understand that. But why can't you move forward with me? We have something good here. You know we do."

She was silent for a long time and he thought perhaps he was making progress on getting her to see his point of view. But when she spoke, her voice was low and sad.

"Easton told me tonight that when you were younger, you vowed you were never getting married."

"What a guy says when he's fifteen and what he says when he's thirty-four are two very different things," he said, though he had said that very same sentiment to Jo in the garden at Winder Ranch just a few weeks ago.

She sat on the bed and he didn't miss the way she was careful to keep plenty of space between them. "Okay, tell me the truth. Say we continue to see each other for those weekends you were talking about. Look ahead several months, maybe a year, with a few days a month of more of that great sex and amusing conversation."

"I can do that," he said, and spent several very pleasant seconds imagining kissing her on the dock of his house on Mercer Island, of taking her up in his boat for a quick run to Victoria, of standing beside the ocean on the Oregon Coast at a wonderfully romantic boutique hotel he knew in Cannon Beach.

"So here it is a year in the future," she said, dousing his hazy fantasies like a cold surf. "Say we've seen each other exclusively for that time and have come to... to care about each other. Where do you see things going from there?"

"I don't know. What do you want me to see?"

"Marriage. Family. Can you ever even imagine yourself contemplating a forever sort of relationship with me or anyone else?"

Marriage. Kids. A dog. Panic spurted through him. Though Jo and Guff had shared a good marriage and he had spent a few years watching their example, for most of his childhood, marriage had meant cold silences alternated with screaming fights and tantrums, culminating in terrible violence that had changed his world forever.

"Maybe," he managed to say after a moment. "Who's to say? That would be a long way in the future. Why do we have to jump from here to there in an instant?"

Her sigh was heavy, almost sad. "I saw that panic in your eyes, Quinn. You can't even consider the idea of it in some long-distant future without being spooked."

"That could change. I don't see why we have to ruin this. Why can't we just enjoy what we have in the moment?"

She didn't answer him right away. "You know, brain injuries are peculiar, unpredictable things," she finally said, baffling him with the seemingly random shift in topic.

"Are they?"

"The same injury in the same spot can affect two people in completely different ways. For the first two or three years after Scott's accident, all the doctors and specialists kept telling me not to give up hope, that things would get better. He could still improve and start regaining function some day."

Through his confusion, Quinn's heart always ached when he thought of Tess facing all that on her own.

"I waited and hoped and prayed," she went on. "Through all those years and promises, I felt as if I were frozen in the moment, that the world went on while I was stuck in place, waiting for something that never happened."

She paused. "He did improve, in minuscule ways. I don't want you to think he didn't. Near the end, he could hold his head up for long periods of time and even started laughing at my silly jokes again. But it was not nearly the recovery I dreamed about in those early days."

"Tess, I'm very sorry you went through that. But I don't understand your point."

She swallowed and didn't meet his gaze. "My point is that I spent years waiting for reality to match up to my expectations, waiting for him to change. Even being angry when those expectations weren't met, when in truth, he simply wasn't capable of it. It wasn't his fault. Just the way things were."

He stared. "So you're comparing me to someone who was critically brain-injured in a car accident?"

She sighed. "Not at all, Quinn. I'm talking about myself. One of the greatest lessons Scott's accident taught me was pragmatism. I can't hang on to unrealistic dreams and hopes anymore. I want marriage and children and you don't. It's as simple as that."

"Does it have to be?"

"For me, yes. Your views might change. I hope for your sake they do. Caring for Scott all those years taught me that the only way we can really find purpose and meaning in life is if we somehow manage to move outside ourselves to embrace the chances we're offered to care for someone else."

She lifted moist eyes to his. "I hope you change your mind, Quinn. But what if you don't? Say we see each other for six months or a year and then you decide you're still no closer to shifting your perspective about home and family. I would have spent another year moving further away from my dreams. I can't do that to myself or to you."

That panic from before churned through him, icy and sharp. He didn't want to lose what they had shared these past few days.

Or maybe it didn't mean as much to her. Why else would she be so willing to throw it all away? Maybe he *was* just like his mother, trying desperately to keep her from pushing him away.

No. This wasn't about that. The fear and panic warring inside him took on an edge of anger.

"This is it, then?" His voice turned hard, ugly. "I was here to scratch an itch for you and now you're shoving me out the door."

Her lovely features paled. "Not fair."

"Fair? Don't talk to me about fair." He jumped out of the bed and reached for his Levis, still in a heap on the floor. He couldn't seem to stop the ugly words from spilling out like toxic effluent.

"You know what I just realized? You haven't changed a bit since your days as Queen Bee at Pine Gulch High. You're still the spoiled, manipulative girl you were in high school. You want what you want and to hell with anybody else and whatever they might need."

"This has nothing to do with high school or the person I was back then."

"Wrong. This has *everything* to do with Tess Jamison, Homecoming Queen. You can't have what you want, your little fantasy happily-ever-after, and so kicking me out of your life completely is your version of throwing a pissy little temper tantrum."

His gazed narrowed as another repugnant thought occurred to him.

"Or wait. Maybe that's not it at all. Maybe this is all some manipulative trick, the kind you used to be so very good at. Don't forget, I had years of experience watching you bat your eyes at some poor idiot, all the while you're tightening the noose around his neck without him having the first clue what you're doing. Maybe you think if you push me out now, in a few weeks I'll come running back with tears and apologies, ready to give you anything you want. Even that all-important wedding ring that's apparently the only thing you think matters."

"You're being ridiculous."

"You forget, I was the chief recipient of all those dirty tricks you perfected in high school. The lies. The rumors you spread. This is just one more trick, isn't it? Well, guess what? I'm not playing your games now, any more than I was willing to do it back then."

She stood on the other side of the room now, her arms folded across her chest and hurt and anger radiating from her.

"You can't get past it, can you?" She shook her head. "I have apologized and tried to show you I'm a different person than I was then. But you refuse to even consider the possibility that I might have changed."

He had considered it. He had even believed it for a while.

"Only one of us is stuck in the past, Quinn. Life has changed me and given me a new perspective. But somewhere deep inside you, you're still a boy stuck in the ugliness of his parents' marriage."

He stared at her, angry that she would turn this all back around on him when she was the one being a manipulative bitch.

"You're crazy."

"Am I? I think the reason you won't let yourself have more than casual relationships with women is because you're so determined not to turn into either one of your parents. You're not about to become your powerless, emotionally needy mother or your workaholic, abusive father. So you've decided somewhere deep in your psyche that your best bet is to just keep everyone else at arm's length so you don't have to risk either option."

He was so furious, he couldn't think straight. Her assessment was brutal and harsh and he refused to admit that it might also be true.

"Now you're some kind of armchair psychiatrist?"

"No. Just a woman who…cares about you, Quinn."

"You've got a hell of a way of showing it by pushing me away."

"I'm not pushing you away." Her voice shook and he saw tears in her eyes. Either she was a much better actress than he could possibly imagine or that was genuine regret in her eyes. He didn't know which to believe.

"You have no idea how hard this is for me," she said and one of those tears trickled down the side of her nose. "I've come to care about you these past few weeks.

Maybe I always did, a little. But as much as I have loved these past few days and part of me wants nothing more than to continue seeing you after I move to Portland, it wouldn't be fair to either of us. You can't be the kind of man I want and I'm afraid I would eventually come to hate you for that."

His arms ached from the effort it took not to reach for her but he kept his hands fisted at his sides. "So that's it. See you later, thanks for the good time in the sack and all that."

"If you want to be crude about it."

He didn't. He wanted to grab her and hang on tight and tell her he would be whatever kind of man she wanted him to be. He had discovered a safety, a serenity, with her he hadn't found anywhere else and the idea of leaving it behind left him hollow and achy.

But she was right. He couldn't offer her the things she needed. He could lie and tell her otherwise but both of them would see through it and end up even more unhappy.

"I suppose there's nothing left to say, then, is there?"

She released a shuddering kind of breath and he supposed he should be somewhat mollified that her eyes reflected the same kind of pain shredding his insides.

"I'm sorry."

"So am I, Tess."

He grabbed his things and walked out the door, hoping despite himself that she would call him back, tell him she didn't mean anything she'd said.

But the only sound as he climbed into his rental car was the mournful October wind in the trees and the distant howl of a coyote.

TESS STOOD AT the window of her bedroom watching Quinn's taillights disappear into the night.

She couldn't seem to catch her breath and she felt as if she'd just been bucked off one of the Winder Ranch horses, then kicked in the chest for good measure.

Had she been wrong? Maybe she should have just taken whatever crumbs Quinn could offer, to hell with the inevitable pain she knew waited for her in some murky future.

At least then she wouldn't have this raw, devastating feeling that she had just made a terrible mistake.

With great effort, she forced herself to draw in a deep breath and then another and another, willing her common sense to override the visceral pain and vast emptiness gaping inside her.

No. She hadn't been wrong, as much as she might wish otherwise. In the deep corners of her heart, she knew it.

She wanted a home and a family. Not today, maybe not even next year, but someday, certainly. She was ready to move forward with her life and go on to the next stage.

She had already fallen in love with him, just from these few days. If she spent a year of those weekend encounters he was talking about, she wasn't sure she would ever be able to climb back out.

Better to break things off now, when she at least had half a chance of repairing the shattered pieces of her heart.

She would survive. She had been through worse. Scott's death and the long, difficult years preceding it had taught her she had hidden reservoirs of strength.

She supposed that was a good thing. She had a feeling she was going to need all the strength she could find in the coming months as she tried to go on without Quinn.

CHAPTER FIFTEEN

"TESS? EVERYTHING OKAY?"

Three months after Jo Winder's death, Tess stood at the nurses' station, a chart in her hand and her mind a million miles away.

Or at least several hundred.

She jerked her mind away from Pine Gulch and the tangled mess she had made of things and looked up to find her friend and charge nurse watching her with concern in her brown eyes.

"I'm fine," she answered Vicki Ballantine.

"Are you sure? You look white as a sheet and you've been standing there for at least five minutes without moving a muscle. Come sit down, honey, and have a sip of water."

The older woman tugged her toward one of the chairs behind the long blue desk. Since Vicki was not only her friend but technically her boss, Tess didn't feel as if she had a great deal of choice.

She sipped at the water and crushed ice Vicki brought her in a foam cup. It did seem to quell the nausea a little, though it didn't do much for the panic that seemed to pound a steady drumbeat through her.

"You want to tell me what's bothering you?" Vicki asked.

She drew in a breath then let it out slowly, still reeling from confirmation of what she had begun to suspect for a few weeks but had only just confirmed an hour ago on her lunch break.

This sudden upheaval all seemed so surreal, the last possible development she had expected to disrupt everything.

"I don't… I haven't been sleeping well."

Vicki leaned on the edge of the deck, her plump features set into a frown. "You're settling in okay, aren't you? The house you rented is nice enough, right? It's in a quiet neighborhood."

"Yes. Everything's fine. I love Portland, you know I do. The house is great and everyone here at the hospital has been wonderful."

"But you're still not happy."

At the gentle concern in her friend's eyes and the warm touch of her hand squeezing Tess's arms, tears welled up in her eyes.

"I am," she lied. "I'm just…"

She couldn't finish the sentence as those tears spilled over. She pressed her hands to her eyes, mortified that she was breaking down at work.

Only the hormones, she assured herself, but she knew it was much, much more. Her tears stemmed from fear and longing and the emptiness in her heart that kept her tossing and turning all night.

Vicki took one look at her emotional reaction and pulled Tess back to her feet, this time ushering her into the privacy of the empty nurses' lounge.

"All right. Out with it. Tell Auntie Vick what's wrong. This is about some man, isn't it?"

Through her tears, Tess managed a watery laugh. "You could say that."

Oh, she had made such a snarled mess of everything. That panic pulsed through her again, harsh and unforgiving, and her thoughts pulsed with it.

"It always is," Vicki said with a knowing look. "Funny thing is, I didn't even know you were dating anybody."

"I'm not. We're…" Her voice trailed off and she drew in a heavy breath. Though she wanted to protect her own privacy and give herself time to sort things out, she was also desperate to share the information with *someone*.

She couldn't call her mother. Oh, mercy, there was another reason for panic. What would Maura say?

Her mother wasn't here and she wasn't anywhere close to ready to tell any of her friends in Pine Gulch. Vicki had become her closest friend since moving to Portland and on impulse, she decided she could trust her.

"I'm pregnant," she blurted out.

Vicki's eyes widened in shock and her mouth made a perfect little *O* for a moment before she shut it with a snap. She said nothing for several long moments.

Just when Tess was kicking herself for even mentioning it in the first place, Vicki gave her a careful look. "And how do you feel about that?"

"You're the one who said I'm pale as a sheet, right? That's probably a pretty good indication."

"Your color's coming back but you still look upset."

"I don't know how I feel yet, to tell you the truth," she admitted. "I just went to the doctor on my lunch hour to verify my suspicions. I…guess I'm still in shock. I've wanted a child—children—for so long. Scott and I talked about having several and then, well, things didn't quite work out."

Though she didn't broadcast her past around, she had confided in Vicki after her first few weeks in Portland about the challenging years of her marriage and her husband's death.

"And the proud papa? What's his reaction?"

Tess closed her eyes, her stomach roiling just thinking about how on earth she would tell Quinn.

"I haven't told him yet. Actually, I…haven't talked to him in three months."

"If my math is right, this must be someone from Idaho since you've only been here for two months."

She sighed. "His foster mother was my last patient."

"Did you two have a big fight or something?"

She thought of all the accusations they had flung at each other that night. *You can't have what you want, your little fantasy happily-ever-after, and so kicking me out of your life completely is your version of throwing a pissy little temper tantrum.*

Now she was pregnant—*pregnant!*—and she didn't have the first idea what to do about it. She cringed, just imagining his reaction. He would probably accuse her of manipulating the entire thing as some Machiavellian plot to snare him into marriage.

Maybe you think if you push me out now, in a few weeks I'll come running back with tears and apologies, ready to give you anything you want. Even that all-important wedding ring that's apparently the only thing you think matters.

She pushed away the bitter memory, trying to drag her attention back to the problem at hand, this pregnancy that had completely knocked the pins out from under her.

She didn't even know how it had happened. Since hearing the news from her doctor, she had been wracking her brain about their time together and she could swear he used protection every single time. The only possibility was one time when they were in the shower and both became a little too carried away to think about the consequences.

She had been a nurse for ten years and she knew perfectly well that once was all it took but she never expected this to happen to her.

"You could say we had a fight," she finally answered Vicki. "We didn't part on exactly amiable terms."

"If you need to take a little time, I can cover your shift. Why don't you take the rest of the day off?"

"No. I'm okay. I just need a moment to collect my thoughts. I promise, I can put it out of my head and focus on my patients."

"At least take a quick break and go on out to the roof for some fresh air. I think the rain's finally stopped and it might help you clear your head."

She wanted to be tough and insist she was fine. But the hard truth was she felt as if an atomic bomb had just been dropped in her life.

"Clearing my head would be good. Thanks."

When she rose, Vicki gathered her against her ample breast for a tight hug. "It will be okay, sweetheart. If this is what you want, I'm thrilled for you. I know if anyone can handle single motherhood, you can."

She had serious doubts right now about her ability to handle even the next five minutes, but she still appreciated the other woman's faith in her.

As she walked outside into the wet and cold January afternoon, she gazed out at the city sprawled out below her. So much for the best-laid plans. When she left Pine Gulch, she had been certain that she had everything figured out. Her life would be different but she had relished the excitement of making changes and facing new challenges.

In her wildest dreams, she never anticipated this particular challenge.

She pressed a hand to her abdomen, to the tiny life growing at a rapid pace there.

A child.

Quinn's child.

Emotions choked her throat, both joy and fear.

This pregnancy might not have been in her plans, but no matter what happened, she would love this child. She already did, even though she had only known of its existence for a short time.

She pressed her hand to her abdomen again. She had to tell Quinn. Even if he was bitter and angry and believed she had somehow manipulated circumstances to this end, she had to tell him. Withholding the knowledge of his child from him would be wrong, no matter how he reacted.

She only hoped she could somehow find the courage.

Two weeks later, she was still searching desperately for that strength. With each day that passed, it seemed more elusive than sunshine in a Portland winter.

Every morning since learning she was pregnant, she awoke with the full intention of calling him that day. But the hours slipped away and she made excuse after excuse to herself.

He was busy. She was working. She would wait until evening. She didn't have his number.

All of them were only pitiful justification for her to give in to her fears. That was the hard truth. She was afraid, pure and simple. Imagining his response kept her up at night and she was quite certain was contributing to the nausea she faced every morning.

That she continued to cater to that fear filled her with shame. She wasn't a weak woman and she hated that she was acting like it.

The night before, she had resolved that she couldn't put it off any longer. It was past time for her to act as the pregnancy seemed more real each day. Already, she was beginning to bump out and she was grateful her work scrubs had drawstring waists, since all her other slacks were starting to feel a little snug.

No more excuses. The next day was Saturday and she knew she had to tell him. Though she wanted nothing more than to take the coward's way out and communicate via phone—or, even better, email—she had decided a man deserved to know he was going to become a father in person.

But figuring out how to find the man in Seattle was turning into more of a challenge than she expected.

She sat once more on the rooftop garden of the hospital on her lunch break, her cell phone in her hand as she punched in Easton Springhill's phone number as a last resort.

Easton's voice rose in surprise when she answered. "Tess! I was just thinking about you!"

"Oh?"

"I've been meaning to check in and see how life in the big city is treating you."

She gazed out through the gray mist at the buildings and neighborhoods that had become familiar friends to her during her frequent rooftop breaks. "Good. I like it here. I suppose Pine Gulch will always be home but I'm settling in."

"I'm so glad to hear that. You deserve some happiness."

And she would have it, she vowed. No matter what Quinn Southerland had to say about their child.

"How are you?" she stalled. "I mean really."

Easton was silent for a moment. "All right, I guess. I'm trying to stay busy. It's calving time so I'm on the run all the time, which I suppose is a blessing."

"I'm sorry I haven't called to check on you before now. I've thought of you often."

"No problem. You've been busy starting a new life. By the way," Easton went on, "I checked in on your morning coffee klatch crowd the other day and they all miss you like crazy. I never realized old Sal Martinez had such a thing for you."

She laughed, thinking of the dearly familiar old-timers who could always be counted on to lift her spirits. "What can I say? I'm pretty popular with eighty-year-old men who have cataracts."

Maybe she was making a mistake in her decision to stay in Portland and raise her baby. Moving back to Pine Gulch would give her child structure, community. Instant family. She had time to make that particular decision, she told herself. First things first.

"Listen, I'm sorry to bother you but I'm trying to reach Quinn and I can't find his personal contact information."

"You can't?" Easton's shock filtered clearly through

the phone and Tess winced. She had never told her friend that she and Quinn had parted on difficult terms. She supposed she had assumed Quinn would have told her.

"No. I tried to call his company and ended up having to go through various gatekeepers who weren't inclined to be cooperative."

"He can be harder to reach than the Oval Office sometimes. I've got his cell number programmed on mine so I don't have it memorized but hang on while I look it up."

She returned in a moment and recited the number and Tess scribbled it down.

"Can you tell me his home address?" she said, feeling awkward and uncomfortable that she had to ask.

Easton paused for a long moment. "Is something wrong, Tess?"

If you only knew the half of it, she thought.

"Not at all," she lied. "I just… I wanted to mail him something," she improvised quickly.

She could tell her friend didn't quite buy her explanation but to her vast relief, Easton recited the address.

"You'll have to find the zip code. I don't know that off the top of my head."

"I can look it up. Thanks."

"Are you sure nothing's wrong? You sound distracted."

"Just busy. Listen, I'm on a break at the hospital and really need to get back to my patients. It was great talking to you. I'll call you next week sometime when we both have more time to chat."

"You do that."

They said their goodbyes, though she could still hear

the questions in Easton's voice. She was happy to hang up the phone. Another moment and she would be blurting it all out. Easton was too darned perceptive and Tess had always been a lousy liar.

She certainly couldn't tell Easton about her pregnancy until she'd had a chance to share the news with Quinn first.

She gazed at the address in her hand, her stomach tangled in knots at the encounter that loomed just over the horizon.

Whatever happened, her baby would still have her.

TALK ABOUT ACTING on the spur of the moment.

Quinn cruised down the winding, thickly forested street in Portland, wondering what the hell he was doing there.

He wasn't one for spontaneity and impulsive acts of insanity, but here he was, trying to follow his GPS directions through an unfamiliar neighborhood in the dark and the rain.

She might not even be home. For all he knew, she could be working nights or even, heaven forbid, on a date.

At the thought, he was tempted to just turn his car around and drive back to Seattle. He was crazy to just show up at her place out of the blue like this. But then, when it came to Tess and his behavior toward her, sanity hadn't exactly been in plentiful supply.

He felt edgy and off balance, as if he didn't even know himself anymore and the man he always thought he'd been. He was supposed to be a careful businessman, known for his forethought and savvy strategizing.

He certainly *wasn't* a man who drove a hundred and

fifty miles on a whim, all because of a simple phone call from Easton.

When she called him he had just been wrapping up an important meeting. The moment she said Tess had called her looking for his address and phone number, his brain turned to mush and he hadn't been able to focus on anything else. Not the other executives still in the room with him or the contract Southerland Shipping had just signed or the route reconfiguration they were negotiating.

All he could think about was Tess.

His conversation with Easton played through his mind now as he followed the GPS directions.

"Something seemed off, you know?" she had said. "I couldn't put my finger on it but she sounded upset. I just wanted to give you a heads-up that she might be trying to reach you."

As it had then, his mind raced in a hundred different directions. What could be wrong? After three months of empty, deafening silence between them, why was she suddenly trying to make contact?

He only had the patience to wait an hour for her call before he couldn't stand the uncertainty another moment.

In that instant, as he made the call to excuse himself from a fundraiser he'd been obligated to attend for the evening, he had realized with stark clarity how very self-deceptive he had been for the past three months.

He had spent twelve weeks trying to convince himself he was over Tess Claybourne, that their brief relationship had been a mistake but one that he was quite certain had left no lasting scars on his heart.

The moment he heard her name, a wild rush of emotion had surged through him, like water gushing from a dam break, and he realized just how much effort it had taken him to shove everything back to the edges of his subconscious.

Only in his dreams did he let himself remember those magical days he and Tess had shared, the peace and comfort he found in her arms.

He had definitely been fooling himself. Their time together had had a profound impact on his world. Since then, he found himself looking at everything from a different perspective. All the things he used to find so fulfilling—his business pursuits, his fundraising engagements, boating on the Sound—now seemed colorless and dull. Tedious, even.

Southerland was expanding at a rapid pace and he should have been thrilled to watch this company he had created begin at last to attain some of the goals he had set for it. Instead, he found himself most evenings sitting on his deck on Mercer Island, staring out at the lights reflecting on the water and wondering why all the successes felt so empty.

No doubt some of the funk he seemed to have slipped into was due to the grieving process he was still undergoing for Jo.

But he had a somber suspicion that a large portion of that emptiness inside him was due to Tess and the hole she had carved out in his life.

He sighed. Might as well be completely frank—with himself, at least. Tess hadn't done any carving. He had been the one wielding the butcher knife by pushing her away the first chance he had.

He couldn't blame her for that last ugly scene between them. At least not completely. At the first obstacle in their growing relationship, he had jumped on the defensive and had been far too quick to shove her away.

In his business life, he tried to focus most on the future by positioning his company to take advantage of market trends and growth areas. He didn't like looking back, except to examine his mistakes in an effort to figure out what he could fix.

And he had made plenty of mistakes where Tess was concerned. As he examined what had happened three months earlier in Pine Gulch, he had to admit that he had been scared, pure and simple.

He needed to see her again. He owed her an apology, a proper goodbye without the anger and unfounded accusations he had hurled at her.

That's why he was here, trying to find her house in the pale, watery moonlight.

His GPS announced her address a moment later and he pulled into the driveway of a small pale rose brick house, a strange mix of dread and anticipation twisting around his gut as he gazed through the rain-splattered windshield.

Her house reminded him very much of the one in Pine Gulch on a slightly smaller scale. Both were older homes with established trees and gardens. The white shutters and gable gave it a charming seaside cottage appeal. It was surrounded by shrubs and what looked like an extensive flower garden, bare now except for a few clumps of dead growth.

He imagined that in the springtime, it would explode with color but just now, in early February, it only looked cold and barren in the rain.

He refused to think about how he could use that same metaphor for his life the past three months.

Smoke curled from the chimney and lights gleamed from several windows. As he parked in the driveway, he thought he saw a shadow move past the window inside and his breathing quickened.

For one cowardly moment, he was tempted again to put the car in Reverse and head back to Seattle. Maybe Easton had her signals crossed and Tess wasn't really looking for him. Maybe she only wanted his address to send him a kiss-off letter telling him how happy she was without him.

Even if that was the case, he had come this far. He couldn't back out now.

The rain had slowed to a cold mist as he walked up the curving sidewalk to her front door. He rang the doorbell, his insides a corkscrew of nerves.

A moment later, the door opened and the weeks and distance and pain between them seemed to fall away.

She looked fresh and bright, her loose auburn curls framing those lovely features that wore an expectant look—for perhaps half a second, anyway, until she registered who was at her doorstep.

"Quinn!" she gasped, the color leaching from her face like old photographs left in the desert.

"Hello, Tess."

She said nothing, just continued to stare at him for a good thirty seconds. He couldn't tell if she was aghast to find him on her doorstep or merely surprised.

Wishing he had never given in to this crazy impulse to drive two and a half hours, he finally spoke. "May I come in?"

She gazed at him for another long moment. When he was certain she would slam the door in his face, she held it open farther and stepped back so he had room to get through. "I... Yes. Of course."

He followed her inside and had a quick impression of a warm space dominated by a pale rose brick fireplace, blazing away against the rainy night. The living room looked comfortable and bright, with plump furniture and colorful pillows and her upright piano in one corner, still covered with photographs.

"Can I get you something to drink?" she asked. "I'll confess, I don't have many options but I do have some wine I was given as a housewarming gift when I moved here."

"I'm fine. Thanks."

The silence stretched out between them, taut and awkward. He had a sudden vivid memory of lying in her bed with her, bodies entwined as they talked for hours.

His chest ached suddenly with a deep hunger to taste that closeness again.

"You're pale," he said, thrusting his hands in the pockets of his jacket and curling them into fists where she couldn't see. "Are you ill? Easton said you called her and she was worried."

She frowned slightly, as if still trying to make sense of his sudden appearance. "You're here because Easton asked you to check on me?"

For a moment, he thought about answering yes. That would be the easy out for both of them, but he couldn't do it.

Though he had suspected it, he suddenly knew with relentless clarity that *she* was the reason for the emptiness of the past three months.

He had never felt so very solitary as he had without Tess in his world to share his accomplishments and his worries. To laugh with, to maybe cry with. To share hopes for the future and help him heal from the past.

He wanted all those things she had talked about, exactly what she had created for herself here.

He wanted a home. He wanted to live in a house with carefully tended gardens that burst with color in the springtime, a place that provided a warm haven against the elements on a bitter winter night.

And he wanted to share that with Tess.

He wanted love.

Like a junkie jonesing for his next fix, he craved the peace he had found only with Tess.

"No," he finally admitted hoarsely. "I'm here because I missed you."

CHAPTER SIXTEEN

SHE STARED AT HIM, her eyes wide and the same color as a storm-tossed sea. "You...what?"

He sighed, cursing the unruly slip of his tongue. "Forget I said that. Yeah, I'm here because Easton asked me to check on you."

"You're lying." Though the words alone might have sounded arrogant, he saw the vulnerability in her eyes and something else, something that almost looked like a tiny flicker of hope.

He gazed at her, his blood pulsing loudly in his ears. He had come this far. He might as well take a step further, until he was completely out on the proverbial limb hanging over the bottomless crevasse.

"All right. Yes. I missed you. Are you happy now?"

She was quiet for a long moment, the only sound in the house the quiet murmuring of the fire.

"No," she finally whispered. "Not at all. I've been so miserable, Quinn."

Her voice sounded small and watery and completely genuine. He gave a low groan and couldn't take this distance between them another second. He yanked his hands out of his pockets and reached for her and she wrapped her arms fiercely around his neck, holding on for dear life.

Emotions choked in his throat and he buried his face in the crook of her shoulder.

Here. This was what he had missed. Having her in his arms again was like coming home, like heaven, like everything good he had ever been afraid to wish for.

How had he ever been stupid enough to push away the best thing that had ever happened to him?

He kissed her and a wild flood of emotions welled up in his throat at the intense sweetness of having her in his arms once more.

"I'm sorry," he murmured against her mouth. "So damn sorry. I've been a pathetic wreck for three lousy months."

"I have, too," she said. "You ruined *everything*."

He gave a short, rough laugh. "Did I?"

"I had this great new job, this new life I was trying to create for myself. It was supposed to be so perfect. Instead, I've been completely desolate. All I've been able to think about is you and how much I…" Her voice trailed off and he caught his breath, waiting for her to finish the sentence.

"How much you what?" he said when she remained stubbornly silent.

"How much I missed you," she answered and he was aware of a flicker of disappointment thrumming through him as he sensed that wasn't what she had intended to say at all.

He kissed her again and she sighed against his mouth, her arms tight around him.

Despite the cold February rain, he felt as if spring was finally blooming in his heart.

"Everything you said to me that last night was exactly right, Tess. I've given the past too much power in my life."

"Oh, Quinn. I had no right to say those things to you. I've been sorry every since."

He shook his head. "You were right."

"Everyone handles their pain differently. The only thing I know is that everyone has some in his or her life. It's as inevitable as…as breathing and dying."

"Well, you taught me I didn't have to let it control everything I do. Look at you. Your dreams of a happily-ever-after came crashing down around you with Scott's accident. But you didn't become bitter or angry at the world."

"I had my moments of despair, believe me."

His chest ached for her all over again and he cringed at the memory of how he had lashed out at her their last night together in Pine Gulch, accusing her of being the same spoiled girl he had known in high school.

He hadn't meant any of those ugly words. Even as he had said them, he had known she was a far different woman.

He had been in love with her that night, had been probably since that first moment she had sat beside him on the floor of her spare room and listened to him pour out all the ugly memories he kept carefully bottled up inside.

No. Earlier, he admitted.

He had probably been a little in love with her in high school, when he had thought he hated her. He had just been too afraid to admit the truth to himself.

"But despite everything you went through, you didn't let your trials destroy you or make you cynical or hard," he said gently, holding her close. "You still open your heart so easily. It's one of the things I love the most about you."

TESS STARED AT HIM, her heart pulsing a crazy rhythm in her chest. He couldn't have just said what she thought he did. Quinn didn't believe in love. But the echo of his words resounded in her head.

Still, she needed a little confirmation that she wasn't completely hearing things.

"You...what?"

His mouth quirked into that half grin she had adored since junior high school.

"You're going to make me say it, aren't you? All right. That's one of the millions of things I love about you. Right up there at the top of the list is your big, generous, unbreakable heart."

"Not unbreakable," she corrected, still not daring to believe his words. "It has felt pretty shattered the past three months."

He let out a sound of regret just before he kissed her again, his mouth warm and gentle. At the devastating tenderness in his kiss, emotions rose in her throat and her eyes felt scratchy with unshed tears.

"I'm sorry," he murmured between kisses. "So damn sorry. Can you forgive me? I've been a stupid, scared idiot."

He paused, his eyes intense. "You have to cut me a little slack, though."

"Do I?"

Her arch tone drew a smile. "It's only fair. I'm a man who's never been in love before. If you want the truth, it scares the hell out of me."

I'm a man who's never been in love before.

The words soaked through all the pain and loneliness and fear of the past three months.

He loved her. This wasn't some crazy dream where

she would wake up once more with a tear-soaked pillow wrapped in her arms. Quinn was standing here in her living room, holding her tightly and saying things she never would have believed if she didn't feel the strength of his arms around her.

He loved her.

She pulled his mouth to hers and kissed him hard, pouring all the heat and joy and wonder spinning around inside her into her kiss. When she at last drew away, they were both breathing raggedly and his eyes looked dazed.

"I love you, Quinn. I love you so much. I wanted to make a new life for myself here in Portland, a new start. But all I've been able to think about is how much I miss you."

"Tess—" He groaned her name and leaned down to kiss her again but she gathered what tiny spark of strength remained and stepped slightly away from him, desperate for a little space to gather her thoughts.

"I love you. But I have to tell you something…"

"Me first." He squeezed her fingers. "I know you think we want two different things out of life. I'll admit, it would probably be a bit of a stretch to say I've had some sudden miraculous change of heart and I'm now completely ready to rush right off to find a wedding chapel."

Well, that would certainly make what she had to tell him a little more difficult. Some of her apprehension must have showed in her eyes because he brought their clasped fingers to his mouth and pressed a kiss to the back of her hand.

"But the thought of being without you scares me a hell of a lot more than the idea of hearts and flowers and wedding cake. I want everything with you. I know I can get there with your help. It just might take me a few months."

"We have a few months."

"I hope we have a lot longer than that. I want forever, Tess."

She gazed at him, dark and gorgeous and male, with clear sincerity in his stunning eyes. He meant what he said. He wasn't going to use his past as an excuse anymore.

She couldn't quite adjust to this sudden shift. Only an hour ago, she had been sitting at her solitary dining table with a TV dinner in front of her, lonely and achy and frightened at the prospect of having to face his reaction the next day to the news of the child they had created together.

And here he was using words like *forever* with her.

She still hadn't told him the truth, she reminded herself. Everything might change with a few simple words. And though she wanted to hang on to this lovely feeling for the rest of her life, she knew she had to tell him.

Though it was piercingly difficult, she pulled her hands away from his and crossed her arms in front of her.

"I need to tell you something first. It may...change your perspective."

He looked confused and even a little apprehensive, as if bracing himself for bad news. "What's wrong?"

"Nothing. At least I don't think so. I hope you don't, either."

She twisted her fingers together, trying to gather her nerves.

"Tell me," he said after a long pause.

With a deep breath, she plunged forward. "I don't know how this happened. Well, I know how it happened. I'm a nurse, after all. But not *how* it happened, if you know what I mean. I mean, we took precautions but even the best precautions sometimes fail…" Her voice trailed off.

"Tess. Just tell me."

"I'm pregnant."

The words hung between them, heavy, dense. He said nothing for a long time, just continued to stare at her.

She searched his gaze but she couldn't read anything in his expression. Was he happy, terrified, angry? She didn't have the first idea.

She pressed her lips together. "I know. I was shocked, too. I only found out a few weeks ago and I've been trying to figure out how to tell you. That's why I called Easton for your address. I was going to drive to Seattle tomorrow. I've been so scared."

That evoked a reaction from him—surprise.

"Scared? Why?"

She sighed. "I didn't want you to think it was all part of some grand, manipulative plan. I swear, I didn't expect this, Quinn. You have to believe me. We were careful. I know we were. The only thing I can think is that…that time in the shower, remember?"

Something flickered across his features then, something that sent heat scorching through her.

"I remember," he said, his voice gruff.

He didn't say anything more and after a moment, she wrapped her arms more tightly around herself, cold suddenly despite the fire blazing merrily in her hearth.

"I know this changes everything. You said yourself you're not ready quite yet for all of that. I completely understand. I don't want you to feel pressured, Quinn. But I... I love her already. The baby and I will be fine on our own if you decide you're not ready. I'll wait as long as it takes. I have savings. I won't ask anything of you, I swear."

Again, something sparked in his gaze. "I thought you said you love me."

"I did. I do."

"Then how can you think I would possibly walk away now?"

His eyes glittered with a fierce emotion that suddenly took her breath away. Hope began to pulse through her and she curled her fingers into fists, afraid to let it explode inside her.

"A baby." He breathed out the word like a prayer or a curse, she couldn't quite tell. "When?"

"Sometime in early July."

"An Independence Day baby. We can name her Liberty."

Her laugh was a half sob and she reached blindly for him. He swept her into his arms and pulled her close as that joy burst out like fireworks in the Pine Gulch night sky.

"Liberty Jo," she insisted.

His eyes softened and he kissed her with more of that heart-shaking tenderness. "A baby," he murmured after a long while. His eyes were dazed as he placed a hand over her tiny bump and she covered his hand with hers.

"You're not upset?" she asked.

"*Numb* is a better word. But underneath the shock is...joy. I don't know how to explain it but it feels right."

"Oh, Quinn. That was my reaction, too. I was scared to death to find out I was pregnant. But the idea of a child—*your* child—filled me with so much happiness and peace. That's a perfect word. It feels *right*."

"I love you, Tess." He pressed his mouth to hers again. "You took a man who was hard and cynical, who tried to convince himself he was happy being alone, and showed him everything good and right that was missing in his world."

He pressed his mouth to hers and in his kiss she tasted joy and healing and the promise of a brilliant future.

* * * * *

A COLD CREEK
REUNION

To romance readers who, like me,
love happily-ever-afters.

CHAPTER ONE

HE LOVED THESE guys like his own brothers, but sometimes Taft Bowman wanted to take a fire hose to his whole blasted volunteer fire department.

This was their second swift-water rescue training in a month—not to mention that he had been holding these regularly since he became battalion chief five years earlier—and they still struggled to toss a throw bag anywhere close to one of the three "victims" floating down Cold Creek in wet suits and helmets.

"You've got to keep in mind the flow of the water and toss it downstream enough that they ride the current to the rope," he instructed for about the six-hundredth time. One by one, the floaters—in reality, other volunteer firefighters on his thirty-person crew—stopped at the catch line strung across the creek and began working their way hand over hand to the bank.

Fortunately, even though the waters were plenty frigid this time of year, they were about a month away from the real intensity of spring runoff, which was why he was training his firefighters for water rescues now.

With its twists and turns and spectacular surroundings on the west slope of the Tetons, Cold Creek had started gaining popularity with kayakers. He enjoyed floating the river himself. But between the sometimes-inexperienced outdoor-fun seekers and the occasional

Pine Gulch citizen who strayed too close to the edge of the fast-moving water, his department was called out on at least a handful of rescues each season and he wanted them to be ready.

"Okay, let's try it one more time. Terry, Charlie, Bates, you three take turns with the throw bag. Luke, Cody, Tom, stagger your jumps by about five minutes this time around to give us enough time on this end to rescue whoever is ahead of you."

He set the team in position and watched upstream as Luke Orosco, his second in command, took a running leap into the water, angling his body feetfirst into the current. "Okay, Terry. He's coming. Are you ready? Time it just right. One, two, three. Now!"

This time, the rope sailed into the water just downstream of the diver and Taft grinned. "That's it, that's it. Perfect. Now instruct him to attach the rope."

For once, the rescue went smoothly. He was watching for Cody Shepherd to jump in when the radio clipped to his belt suddenly crackled with static.

"Chief Bowman, copy."

The dispatcher sounded unusually flustered and Taft's instincts borne of fifteen years of firefighting and paramedic work instantly kicked in. "Yeah, I copy. What's up, Kelly?"

"I've got a report of a small structure fire at the inn, 320 Cold Creek Road."

He stared as the second rescue went off without a hitch. "Come again?" he couldn't help asking, adrenaline pulsing through him. Structure fires were a rarity in the quiet town of Pine Gulch. Really a rarity. The last time had been a creosote chimney fire four months ago that a single ladder-truck unit had put out in about five minutes.

"Yes, sir. The hotel is evacuating at this time."

He muttered an oath. Half his crew was currently in wet suits, but at least they were only a few hundred yards away from the station house, with the engines and the turnout gear.

"Shut it down," he roared through his megaphone. "We've got a structure fire at the Cold Creek Inn. Grab your gear. This is not a drill."

To their credit, his crew immediately caught the gravity of the situation. The last floater was quickly grabbed out of the water and everybody else rushed to the new fire station the town had finally voted to bond for two years earlier.

Less than four minutes later—still too long in his book but not bad for volunteers—he had a full crew headed toward the Cold Creek Inn on a ladder truck and more trained volunteers pouring in to hurriedly don their turnout gear.

The inn, a rambling wood structure with two single-story wings leading off a main two-story building, was on the edge of Pine Gulch's small downtown, about a mile away from the station. He quickly assessed the situation as they approached. He couldn't see flames yet, but he did see a thin plume of black smoke coming from a window on the far end of the building's east wing.

He noted a few guests milling around on the lawn and had just an instant to feel a pang of sympathy for the owner. Poor Mrs. Pendleton had enough trouble finding guests for her gracefully historic but undeniably run-down inn.

A fire and forced evacuation probably wouldn't do much to increase the appeal of the place.

"Luke, you take Pete and make sure everybody's out. Shep, come with me for the assessment. You all know the drill."

He and Cody Shepherd, a young guy in the last stages of his fire and paramedic training, headed into the door closest to where he had seen the smoke.

Somebody had already been in here with a fire extinguisher, he saw. The fire was mostly out but the charred curtains were still smoking, sending out that inky-black plume.

The room looked to be under renovation. It didn't have a bed and the carpet had been pulled up. Everything was wet and he realized the ancient sprinkler system must have come on and finished the job the fire extinguisher had started.

"Is that it?" Shep asked with a disgruntled look.

"Sorry, should have let you have the honors." He held the fire extinguisher out to the trainee. "Want a turn?"

Shep snorted but grabbed the fire extinguisher and sprayed another layer of completely unnecessary foam on the curtains.

"Not much excitement—but at least nobody was hurt. It's a wonder this place didn't go up years ago. We'll have to get the curtains out of here and have Engine Twenty come inside and check for hot spots."

He called in over his radio that the fire had been contained to one room and ordered in the team whose specialty was making sure the flames hadn't traveled inside the walls to silently spread to other rooms.

When he walked back outside, Luke headed over

to him. "Not much going on, huh? Guess some of us should have stayed in the water."

"We'll do more swift-water work next week during training," he said. "Everybody else but Engine Twenty can go back to the station."

As he spoke to Luke, he spotted Jan Pendleton standing some distance away from the building. Even from here, he could see the distress on her plump, wrinkled features. She was holding a little dark-haired girl in her arms, probably a traumatized guest. Poor thing.

A younger woman stood beside her and from this distance he had only a strange impression, as if she was somehow standing on an island of calm amid the chaos of the scene, the flashing lights of the emergency vehicles, shouts between his crew members, the excited buzz of the crowd.

And then the woman turned and he just about tripped over a snaking fire hose somebody shouldn't have left there.

Laura.

He froze and for the first time in fifteen years as a firefighter, he forgot about the incident, his mission, just what the hell he was doing here.

Laura.

Ten years. He hadn't seen her in all that time, since the week before their wedding when she had given him back his ring and left town. Not just town. She had left the whole damn country, as if she couldn't run far enough to get away from him.

Some part of him desperately wanted to think he had made some kind of mistake. It couldn't be her. That was just some other slender woman with a long sweep of honey-blond hair and big blue, unforgettable eyes. But no, it was definitely Laura, standing next to her mother. Sweet and lovely.

Not his.

"Chief, we're not finding any hot spots." Luke approached him. Just like somebody turned back up the volume on his flat-screen, he jerked away from memories of pain and loss and aching regret.

"You're certain?"

"So far. The sprinkler system took a while to kick in and somebody with a fire extinguisher took care of the rest. Tom and Nate are still checking the integrity of the internal walls."

"Good. That's good. Excellent work."

His assistant chief gave him a wary look. "You okay, Chief? You look upset."

He huffed out a breath. "It's a fire, Luke. It could have been potentially disastrous. With the ancient wiring in this old building, it's a wonder the whole thing didn't go up."

"I was thinking the same thing," Luke said.

He was going to have to go over there and talk to Mrs. Pendleton—and by default, Laura. He didn't want to. He wanted to stand here and pretend he hadn't seen her. But he was the fire chief. He couldn't hide out just because he had a painful history with the daughter of the property owner.

Sometimes he hated his job.

He made his way toward the women, grimly aware of his heart pounding in his chest as if he had been the one diving into Cold Creek for training.

Laura stiffened as he approached but she didn't meet his gaze. Her mother looked at him out of wide, frightened eyes and her arms tightened around the girl in her arms.

Despite everything, his most important job was calming her fears. "Mrs. Pendleton, you'll be happy to know the fire is under control."

"Of course it's under control." Laura finally faced him, her lovely features cool and impassive. "It was under control before your trucks ever showed up—ten minutes after we called the fire in, by the way."

Despite all the things he might have wanted to say to her, he had to first bristle at any implication that their response time might be less than adequate. "Seven, by my calculations. Would have been half that except we were in the middle of water rescue training when the call from dispatch came in."

"I guess you would have been ready, then, if any of our guests had decided to jump into Cold Creek to avoid the flames."

Funny, he didn't remember her being this tart when they had been engaged. He remembered sweetness and joy and light. Until he had destroyed all that.

"Chief Bowman, when will we be able to allow our guests to return to their rooms?" Jan Pendleton spoke up, her voice wobbling a little. The little girl in her arms—who shared Laura's eye color, he realized now, along with the distinctive features of someone born with Down syndrome—patted her cheek.

"Gram, don't cry."

Jan visibly collected herself and gave the girl a tired smile.

"They can return to get their belongings as long as they're not staying in the rooms adjacent to where the fire started. I'll have my guys stick around about an hour or so to keep an eye on some hot spots." He paused, wishing he didn't have to be the bearer of this particular bad news. "I'm going to leave the final decision up to you about your guests staying here overnight, but to be honest, I'm not sure it's completely safe for guests to stay here tonight. No matter how careful we are, sometimes embers can flare up again hours later."

"We have a dozen guests right now." Laura looked at him directly and he was almost sure he saw a hint of hostility there. Annoyance crawled under his skin. *She* dumped him, a week before their wedding. If anybody here had the right to be hostile, he ought to be the first one in line. "What are we supposed to do with them?"

Their past didn't matter right now, not when people in his town needed his help. "We can talk to the Red Cross about setting up a shelter, or we can check with some of the other lodgings in town, maybe the Cavazos' guest cabins, and see if they might have room to take a few."

Mrs. Pendleton closed her eyes. "This is a disaster."

"But a fixable one, Mom. We'll figure something out." She squeezed her mother's arm.

"Any idea what might have started the fire?" He had to ask.

Laura frowned and something that looked oddly like guilt shifted across her lovely features. "Not the *what* exactly, but most likely the *who*."

"Oh?"

"Alexandro Santiago. Come here, young man."

He followed her gaze and for the first time, he noticed a young dark-haired boy of about six or seven sitting on the curb, watching the activity at the scene with a sort of avid fascination in his huge dark brown eyes. The boy didn't have her blond, blue-eyed coloring, but he shared her wide, mobile mouth, slender nose and high cheekbones, and was undoubtedly her child.

The kid didn't budge from the curb for a long, drawn-out moment, but he finally rose slowly to his feet and headed toward them as if he were on his way to bury his dog in the backyard.

"Alex, tell the fireman what started the fire."

The boy shifted his stance, avoiding the gazes of both his mother and Taft. "Do I have to?"

"Yes," Laura said sternly.

The kid fidgeted a little more and finally sighed. "Okay. I found a lighter in one of the empty rooms. The ones being fixed up." He spoke with a very slight, barely discernible accent. "I never saw one before and I only wanted to see how it worked. I didn't mean to start a fire, *es la verdad.* But the curtains caught fire and I yelled and then *mi madre* came in with the fire extinguisher."

Under other circumstances he might have been amused at the no-nonsense way the kid told the story and how he manipulated events to make it seem as if everything had just sort of happened without any direct involvement on his part.

But this could have been a potentially serious situation, a crumbling old fire hazard like the inn.

He hated to come off hard-nosed and mean, but he had to make the kid understand the gravity. Education was a huge part of his job and a responsibility he took very seriously. "That was a very dangerous thing to do. People could have been seriously hurt. If your mother hadn't been able to get to the room fast enough with the fire extinguisher, the flames could have spread from room to room and burned down the whole hotel and everything in it."

To his credit, the boy met his gaze. Embarrassment and shame warred on his features. "I know. It was stupid. I'm really, really sorry."

"The worst part of it is, I have told you again and again not to play with matches or lighters or anything else that can cause a fire. We've talked about the dangers." Laura glowered at her son, who squirmed.

"I just wanted to see how it worked," he said, his voice small.

"You won't do it again, will you?" Taft said.

"Never. Never, ever."

"Good, because we're pretty strict about this kind of thing around here. Next time you'll have to go to jail."

The boy gave him a wide-eyed look, but then sighed with relief when he noticed Taft's half grin. "I won't do it again, I swear. Pinky promise."

"Excellent."

"Hey, Chief," Lee Randall called from the engine. "We're having a little trouble with the hose retractor again. Can you give us a hand?"

"Yeah. Be there in a sec," he called back, grateful for any excuse to escape the awkwardness of seeing her again.

"Excuse me, won't you?" he said to the Pendleton women and the children.

"Of course." Jan Pendleton gave him an earnest look. "Please tell your firefighters how very much we appreciate them, don't we, Laura?"

"Absolutely," she answered with a dutiful tone, but he noticed she pointedly avoided meeting his gaze.

"Bye, Chief." The darling little girl in Jan's arm

gave him a generous smile. Oh, she was a charmer, he thought.

"See you later."

The girl beamed at him and waved as he headed away, feeling as if somebody had wrapped a fire hose around his neck for the past ten minutes.

She was here. Really here. Blue eyes, cute kids and all.

Laura Pendleton, Santiago now. He had loved her with every bit of his young heart and she had walked away from him without a second glance.

Now she was here and he had no way to avoid her, not living in a small town like Pine Gulch that had only one grocery store, a couple of gas stations and a fire station only a few blocks from her family's hotel.

He was swamped with memories suddenly, memories he didn't want and didn't know what to do with.

She was back. And here he had been thinking lately how lucky he was to be fire chief of a small town with only six thousand people that rarely saw any disasters.

Taft Bowman.

Laura watched him head back into the action—which, really, wasn't much action at all, given that the fire had been extinguished before any of them arrived. He paused here and there in the parking lot to talk to his crew, snap out orders, adjust some kind of mechanical thing on the sleek red fire truck.

Seeing him in action was nothing new. When they had been dating, she sometimes went on ride-alongs, mostly because she couldn't bear to be separated from him. She remembered now how Taft had always seemed comfortable and in control of any situation, whether responding to a medical emergency or dealing with a grass fire.

Apparently that hadn't changed in the decade since she had seen him. He also still had that very sexy, lean-hipped walk, even under the layers of turnout gear. She watched him for just a moment, then forced herself to look away. This little tingle of remembered desire inside her was wrong on so many levels, completely twisted and messed up.

After all these years and all the pain, all those shards of crushed dreams she finally had to sweep up and throw away, how could he still have the power to affect her at all? She should be cool and impervious to him, completely untouched.

When she finally made the decision to come home after Javier's death, she had known she would inevitably run into Taft. Pine Gulch was a small town after all. No matter how much a person might wish to, it was generally tough to avoid someone forever.

When she thought about it—and she would be lying to herself if she said she *hadn't* thought about it—she had foolishly imagined she could greet him with only a polite smile and a *Nice to see you again*, remaining completely impervious to the man.

Their shared history was a long time ago. Another lifetime, it seemed. She had made the only possible choice back then and had completely moved on with her life, had married someone else, given birth to two children and put Pine Gulch far in her past.

As much as she had loved him once, Taft was really just a small chapter in her life. Or so she told herself anyway. She had been naively certain she had dealt with the hurt and betrayal and the deep sense of loss long ago.

Maybe she should have put a little more energy and effort into making certain of all that before she packed up her children and moved thousands of miles from the only home they had ever known.

If she'd had a little energy to spare, she might have given it more thought, but the past six months seemed like a whirlwind, first trying to deal with Javier's estate and the vast debts he had left behind, then that desperate scramble to juggle her dwindling bank account and two hungry children in expensive Madrid, and finally the grim realization that she couldn't do it by herself and had no choice but to move her little family across the world and back to her mother.

She had been focused on survival, on doing what she thought was right for her children. She supposed she really hadn't wanted to face the reality that moving back also meant dealing with Taft again— until it smacked her upside the head, thanks to her rascal of a son and his predilection for finding trouble wherever he could.

"What are we going to do?" Her mother fretted beside her. She set Maya down on the concrete sidewalk, and the girl immediately scampered beside Alex and stood holding her brother's hand while they watched the firefighters now cleaning up the scene and driving away. "This is going to ruin us!"

Laura put an arm around her mother's plump shoulders, guilt slicing through her. She should have been watching her son more carefully; she certainly knew better than to give him any free rein. She had allowed herself to become distracted checking in some guests—the young married couple on spring break from graduate school in Washington who had found more excitement than they had probably anticipated when their hotel caught fire before they had even seen their room.

While she was busy with them, Alex must have slipped out of the office and wandered to the wing of the hotel they were currently renovating. She still couldn't believe he had found a lighter somewhere. Maybe a previous guest had left it or one of the subcontractors who had been coming in and out the past week or so.

It really *was* a miracle her son hadn't been injured or burned the whole place down.

"You heard Chief Bowman. The fire and smoke damage was contained to only one room, so that's good news."

"How is any of this good news?" In the flash of the emergency vehicles as they pulled away, her mother's features looked older somehow and her hands shook as she pushed a stray lock of carefully colored hair away.

Despite Taft and all the memories that had suddenly been dredged up simply by exchanging a few words with the man, she didn't regret coming back to Pine Gulch. The irony was, she thought she was coming home because she needed her mother's help only to discover how very much Jan needed hers.

Care and upkeep on this crumbling twenty-room inn were obviously wearing on her mother. Jan had been deeply grateful to turn some of those responsibilities over to her only daughter.

"It could be much worse, Mom. We have to focus on that. No one was hurt. That's the important thing. And outdated as it is, the sprinkler system worked better than we might have expected. That's another plus.

Besides, look at it this way—now insurance will cover some of the repairs we already planned."

"I suppose. But what are we going to do with the guests?" Her mother seemed defeated, overwhelmed, all but wringing her hands.

Laura hugged her again. "Don't worry about anything. In fact, why don't you take the children back to the house? I think they've had enough excitement for one afternoon."

"Do you think Chief Bowman will consider it safe?"

Laura glanced over at the three-bedroom cottage behind the inn where she had spent her childhood. "It's far enough from the action. I can't see why it would be a problem. Meantime, I'll start making phone calls. We'll find places for everyone and for our reservations for the next few nights while the smoke damage clears out. We'll get through this just like everything else."

"I'm so glad you're here, my dear. I don't know what I would do without you."

If she *hadn't* been here—along with her daughter and her little firebug of a son—none of this would have happened.

"So am I, Mom," she answered. It was the truth, despite having to confront a certain very sexy fire chief with whom she shared a tangled history.

"Oh, I should go talk to poor Mr. Baktiri. He probably doesn't quite understand what's going on."

One of their long-term guests stood in the middle of the lawn, looking at the hectic scene with confusion. She remembered Mr. Baktiri from when she was a girl. He and his wife used to run the drive-in on the outskirts of town. Mrs. Baktiri had passed away and Mr. Baktiri had moved with his son to Idaho Falls, but he apparently hated it there. Once a month or so, he would escape back to Pine Gulch to visit his wife's graveside.

Her mother gave him substantially reduced rates on their smallest room, where he stayed for a week or two at a time until his son would come down from Idaho Falls to take him back home. It wasn't a very economically feasible operating procedure, but she couldn't fault her mother for her kindness.

She had the impression Mr. Baktiri might be suffering from mild dementia and she supposed familiar surroundings were a comfort to him.

"Mommy. Lights." Maya hugged her legs and looked up, the flashing emergency lights reflecting in her thick glasses.

"I know, sweetie. They're bright, aren't they?"

"Pretty."

"I suppose they are, in a way."

Trust Maya to find joy in any situation. It was her child's particular skill and she was deeply grateful for it.

She had a million things to do, most pressing to find somewhere for their guests to spend the night, but for now she gathered this precious child in her arms.

Out of the corner of her gaze, she saw Alex edge toward them somewhat warily.

"Come here, *niño*," she murmured.

He sank into her embrace and she held both children close. This was the important thing. As she had told her mother, they would get through this minor setback. She was a survivor. She had survived a broken heart and broken engagement and then a disaster of a marriage.

She could get through a little thing like a minor fire with no problem.

CHAPTER TWO

"Guess who I saw in town the other day."

Taft grabbed one of his sister's delicious dinner rolls from the basket being passed around his family's dining-room table and winked at Caidy. "Me, doing something awesome and heroic, probably. Fighting a fire. Saving someone's life. I don't know. Could be anything."

His niece, Destry, and Gabrielle Parsons, whose older sister was marrying Taft's twin brother, Trace, in a few months, both giggled—just as he had intended—but Caidy only rolled her eyes. "News flash. Not everything is about you, Taft. But oddly, in a way, this is."

"Who did you see?" he asked, though he was aware of a glimmer of uneasy trepidation, already expecting what was coming next.

"I didn't have a chance to talk to her. I just happened to see her while I was driving," Caidy said.

"Who?" he asked again, teetering on the brink of annoyance.

"Laura Pendleton," Caidy announced.

"Not Pendleton anymore," Ridge, their older brother and Destry's father, corrected.

"That's right," Trace chimed in from the other side of the table, where he was holding hands with Becca.

How the heck did they manage to eat when they couldn't seem to keep their hands off each other? Taft wondered.

"She got married to some guy while she was living in Spain and they had a couple of kids," Trace went on. "I hear one of them was involved in all the excitement the other day at the inn."

Taft pictured her kid solemnly promising he wouldn't play with matches again. He'd picked up the definite vibe that the kid was a mischievous little rascal, but for all that, his sincerity had rung true.

"Yeah. Apparently her older kid, Alex, was a little too curious about a lighter he found in an empty room and caught some curtains on fire."

"And you had to ride to her rescue?" Caidy gave him a wide-eyed look. "Gosh, that must have been awkward for both of you."

Taft reached for more mashed potatoes, hoping the heat on his face could be attributed to the steaming bowl.

"Why would it be? Everything was fine," he muttered.

Okay, that was a lie, but his family didn't necessarily need to know he hadn't been able to stop thinking about Laura for the past few days. Every time he had a quiet moment, her blue eyes and delicate features would pop into his head and some other half-forgotten memory of their time together would emerge like the Tetons rising out of a low fog bank.

That he couldn't seem to stop them annoyed him. He had worked damn hard to forget her after she walked away. What was he supposed to do now that she was back in town and he couldn't escape her or her kids or the weight of all his mistakes?

"You'll have to catch me up here." Becca, Trace's fiancée, looked confused as she reached for her glass. "Who's Laura Pendleton? I'm taking a wild guess here that she must be related to Mrs. Pendleton at the inn somehow—a client of mine, by the way—but why would it be awkward to have Taft put out a fire at the inn?"

"No reason really." Caidy flashed him a quick look. "Just that Taft and Laura were engaged once."

He fidgeted with his mashed potatoes, drawing his fork in a neat little firebreak to keep the gravy from spreading while he avoided the collective gaze of his beloved family. Why, again, had he once enjoyed these Sunday dinners?

"Engaged? Taft?" He didn't need to look at his future sister-in-law to hear the surprise in her voice.

"I know," his twin brother said. "Hard to believe, right?"

He looked up just in time to see Becca quickly try to hide her shocked gaze. She was too kindhearted to let him see how stunning she found the news, which somehow bothered him even more.

Okay, maybe he had a bit of a reputation in town—most of it greatly exaggerated—as a bit of a player. Becca knew him by now. She should know how silly it all was.

"When was this?" she asked with interest. "Recently?"

"Years ago," Ridge said. "He and Laura dated just out of high school—"

"College," he muttered. "She was in college." Okay, she had been a freshman in college. But she wasn't in high school, damn it. That point seemed important somehow.

"They were inseparable," Trace interjected.

Ridge picked up where he'd left off. "And Taft proposed right around the time Laura graduated from the Montana State."

"What happened?" Becca asked.

He really didn't want to talk about this. What he wouldn't give for a good emergency call right now. Nothing big. No serious personal injury or major property damage. How about a shed fire or a kid stuck in a well or something?

"We called things off."

"The week before the wedding," Caidy added.

Oh, yes. Don't forget to add that little salacious detail.

"It was a mutual decision," he lied, repeating the blatant fiction that Laura had begged him to uphold. Mutual decision. Right. If by *mutual* he meant *Laura* and if by *decision* he meant *crush-the-life-out-of-a-guy blow.*

Laura had dumped him. That was the cold, hard truth. A week before their wedding, after all the plans and deposits and dress fittings, she had given him back his ring and told him she couldn't marry him.

"Why are we talking about ancient history?" he asked.

"Not so ancient anymore," Trace said. "Not if Laura's back in town."

He was very much afraid his brother was right. Whether he liked it or not, with her once more residing in Pine Gulch, their past together would be dredged up again—and not by just his family.

Questions would swirl around them. Everybody had to remember that they had been just a few days away from walking down the aisle of the little church in town when things ended and Laura and her mother sent out those regrets and made phone calls announcing the big celebration wasn't happening —while he had gone down to the Bandito and gotten drunk and stayed that way until about a month or two after the wedding day that didn't happen.

She was back now, which meant that, like it or not, he would have to deal with everything he had shoved down ten years ago, all the emotions he had pretended weren't important in order to get through the deep, aching loss of her.

He couldn't blame his family for their curiosity—not even Trace, his twin and best friend, knew the full story about everything that had happened between him and Laura. He had always considered it his private business.

His family had loved her. Who didn't? Laura had a knack for drawing people toward her, finding commonalities. She and his mother used to love discussing the art world and painting techniques. His mother had been an artist, only becoming renowned around the time of her murder. While Laura hadn't any particular skill in that direction, she had shared a genuine appreciation for his parents' extensive art collection.

His father had adored her, too, and had often told Taft that Laura was the best thing that would ever happen to him.

He looked up from the memory to find Becca's eyes filled with a compassion that made him squirm and lose whatever appetite he might have had left.

"I'm sorry," she murmured in that kind way she had. "Mutual decision or not, it still must have been painful. Is it hard for you to see her again?"

He faked a nonchalant look. "Hard? Why would it be hard? It was all a decade ago. She's moved on. I've moved on. No big deal."

Ridge gave what sounded like a fake cough and Trace had the same skeptical expression on his face he always wore when Taft was trying to talk him into living a little, doing something wild and adventurous for a change.

How was it possible to love his siblings and at the same time want to throw a few punches around the table, just on general principles?

Becca eyed him and then his brothers warily as if sensing his discomfort, then she quickly changed the subject. "How's the house coming?" she asked.

His brother wasn't nearly good enough for her, he decided, seizing the diversion. "Good. I've got only a couple more rooms to drywall. Should be done soon. After six months, the place is starting to look like a real house inside now."

"I stopped by the other day and peeked in the windows," Caidy confessed. "It's looking great."

"Give me a call next time and I can swing by and give you the tour, even if I'm at the fire station. You haven't been by in a month or so. You'll be surprised at how far along it is these days."

After years of renting a convenient but small apartment near the fire station, he had finally decided it was time to build a real house. The two-story log house was set on five acres near the mouth of Cold Creek Canyon.

"How about the barn and the pasture?" Ridge asked, rather predictably. Over the years, Taft had bred a couple mares to a stallion with excellent lines he had picked up for a steal from a rancher down on his luck up near

Wood River. He had traded and sold the colts until he now had about six horses he'd been keeping at his family's ranch.

"The fence is in. I'd like to get the barn up before I move the horses over, if you don't mind keeping them a little longer."

"That's not what I meant. You know we've got plenty of room here. You can keep them here forever if you want."

Maybe if he had his horses closer he might actually ride them once in a while instead of only stopping by to visit when he came for these Sunday dinners.

"When do you think all the work will be done?" Becca asked.

"I'm hoping by mid-May. Depends on how much free time I can find to finish things up inside."

"If you need a hand, let me know," Ridge offered quietly.

"Same goes," Trace added.

Both of them had crazy-busy lives: Ridge running the ranch and raising Destry on his own and Trace as the overworked chief of police for an understaffed small-town force—in addition to planning his future together with Becca and Gabi. Their sincere offers to help touched him.

"I should be okay," he answered. "The hard work is done now and I only have the fun stuff to finish."

"I always thought there was something just a little crazy about you." Caidy shook her head. "I must be right, especially if you think finish work and painting are fun."

"I like to paint stuff," Destry said. "I can help you, Uncle Taft."

"Me, too!" Gabrielle exclaimed. "Oh, can we?"

Trouble followed the two of these girls around like one of Caidy's rescue dogs. He had visions of paint spread all over the woodwork he had been slaving over the past month. "Thanks, girls. That's really sweet of you. I'm sure Ridge can find something for you to touch up around here. That fence down by the creek was looking like it needed a new coat."

"There's always something that needs painting around here," Ridge answered. "As soon as the weather warms up a little at night, I can put you both to work."

"Will you pay us?" Gabrielle asked, always the opportunist.

Ridge chuckled. "We can negotiate terms with your attorney."

Caidy asked Becca—said attorney—a question about their upcoming June wedding and attention shifted away from Taft, much to his relief. He listened to the conversation of his family, aware of this low simmer of restlessness that had become a familiar companion.

Ever since Trace and Becca found each other and fell in love, he had been filled with this vague unease, as if something about his world had shifted a little. He loved his brother. More than that, he respected him. Trace was his best friend and Taft could never begrudge him the happiness he had found with Becca and Gabi, but ever since they announced their engagement, he felt weird and more than a little off-balance.

Seeing Laura and her kids the other day had only intensified that odd feeling.

He had never been a saint—he would be the first to admit that and his family would probably stand in line right behind him—but he tried to live a decent life. His general philosophy about the world ran parallel to the premier motto of every emergency medical worker as well as others in the medical field: Primum Non Nocere. First, Do No Harm.

He did his best. He was a firefighter and paramedic and he enjoyed helping people of his community and protecting property. If he didn't find great satisfaction in it, he would find something else to do. Maybe pounding nails for a living because he enjoyed that, too.

Despite his best efforts in the whole *do no harm* arena, he remembered each and every failure.

He had two big regrets in his life, and Laura Pendleton was involved in both of them.

He had hurt her. Those months leading up to her ultimate decision to break things off had been filled with one wound after another. He knew it. Hell, he had known it at the time, but that dark, angry man he had become after his parents' murder seemed like another creature who had emerged out of his skin to destroy everything good and right in his life.

He couldn't blame Laura for calling off their wedding. Not really. Even though it had hurt like the devil.

She had warned him she couldn't marry him unless he made serious changes, and he had stubbornly refused, giving her no choice but to stay true to her word. She had moved on, taken some exotic job in hotel management in Spain somewhere and a few years later married a man she met there.

The reminder of her marriage left him feeling petty and small. Yeah, he had hurt her, but his betrayal probably didn't hold a candle to everything else she had lost—her husband and the father of her children, whom he'd heard had drowned about six months earlier.

"Are you planning on eating any of that or just pushing it around your plate?"

He glanced up and, much to his shock, discovered Ridge was the only one left at the table. Everybody else had cleared off while he had been lost in thought, and he hadn't even noticed.

"Sorry. Been a long couple of days." He hoped his brother didn't notice the heat he could feel crawling over his features.

Ridge gave him a long look and Taft sighed, waiting for the inevitable words of advice from his brother.

As the oldest Bowman sibling left after their parents died, Ridge had taken custody of Caidy, who had been a teenager at the time. Even though Taft and Trace had both been in their early twenties, Ridge still tried to take over the role of father figure to them, too, whether they liked it or not—which they usually didn't.

Instead of a lecture, Ridge only sipped at his drink. "I was thinking about taking the girls for a ride up to check the fence line on the high pasture. Want to come along? A little mountain air might help clear your head."

He did love being on the back of a horse amid the pine and sage of the mountains overlooking the ranch, but he wasn't in the mood for more questions or sympathy from his family about Laura.

"To tell you the truth, I'm itching to get my hands dirty. I think I'll head over to the house and put in a window frame or something."

Ridge nodded. "I know you've got plenty to do on your own place, but I figured this was worth mentioning, too. I heard the other day at the hardware store that Jan Pendleton is looking to hire somebody to help her with some renovations to the inn."

He snorted. As if Laura would ever let her mother hire him. He figured Ridge was joking but he didn't see any hint of humor in his brother's expression.

"Just saying. I thought you might be interested in helping Laura and her mother out a little."

Ah. Without actually offering a lecture, this must be Ridge's way of reminding Taft he owed Laura something. None of the rest of the family knew what had happened all those years ago, but he was pretty sure all of them blamed him.

And they were right.

Without answering, he shoved away from the table and grabbed his plate to carry it into the kitchen. First, do no harm. But once the harm had been done, a stand-up guy found some way to make it right. No matter how difficult.

CHAPTER THREE

Laura stared at her mother, shock buzzing through her as if she had just bent down and licked an electrical outlet.

"Sorry, say that again. You did *what*?"

"I didn't think you'd mind, darling," her mother said, with a vague sort of smile as she continued stirring the chicken she was cooking for their dinner.

Are you completely mental? she wanted to yell. *How could you possibly think I wouldn't mind?*

She drew a deep, cleansing breath, clamping down on the words she wanted to blurt out. The children were, for once, staying out of trouble, driving cars around the floor of the living room and she watched them interact for a moment to calm herself.

Her mother was under a great deal of strain right now, financially and otherwise. She had to keep that in mind—not that stress alone could explain her mother making such an incomprehensible decision.

"Really, it was all your idea," Jan said calmly.

"*My* idea?" Impossible. Even in her most tangled nightmare, she never would have come up with this possible scenario.

"Yes. Weren't you just saying the other day how much it would help to have a carpenter on the staff to help with the repairs, especially now that we totally have to start from the ground up in the fire-damaged room?"

"I say a lot of things, Mom." *That doesn't mean I want you to rush out and enter into a deal with a particular devil named Taft Bowman.*

"I just thought you would appreciate the help, that's all. I know how much the fire has complicated your timeline for the renovation."

"Not really. Only one room was damaged and it was already on my schedule for renovations."

"Well, when Chief Bowman stopped by this morning to check on things after the excitement we had the other day—which I thought was a perfectly lovely gesture, by the way—he mentioned he could lend us a hand with any repairs in his free time. Honestly, darling, it seemed like the perfect solution."

Really? Having her daughter's ex-fiancé take an empty room at the inn for the next two weeks in exchange for a little skill with a miter saw was *perfect* in what possible alternative universe?

Her mother was as sharp as the proverbial tack. Jan Pendleton had been running the inn on her own since Laura's father died five years ago. While she didn't always agree with her mother's methods and might have run things differently if she had been home, Laura knew Jan had tried hard to keep the inn functioning all those years she had been living in Madrid.

But she still couldn't wrap her head around this one. "In theory, it is a good idea. A resident carpenter would come in very handy. But not Taft, for heaven's sake, Mom!"

Jan frowned in what appeared to be genuine confusion. "You mean because of your history together?"

"For a start. Seeing him again after all these years is more than a little awkward," she admitted.

Her mother continued to frown. "I'm sorry but I don't understand. What am I missing? You always insisted your breakup was a mutual decision. I distinctly remember you telling me over and over again you had both decided you were better off as friends."

Had she said that? She didn't remember much about that dark time other than her deep despair.

"You were so cool and calm after your engagement ended, making all those terrible phone calls, returning all those wedding presents. You acted like you didn't care at all. Honey, I honestly thought you wouldn't mind having Taft here now or I never would have taken him up on his suggestion."

Ah. Her lying little chickens were now coming home to roost. Laura fought the urge to bang her head on the old pine kitchen table a few dozen times.

Ten years ago, she had worked so hard to convince everyone involved that nobody's heart had been shattered by the implosion of their engagement. To her parents, she had put on a bright, happy face and pretended to be excited about the adventures awaiting her, knowing how crushed they would have been if they caught even a tiny glimmer of the truth—that inside her heart felt like a vast, empty wasteland.

How could she blame her mother for not seeing through her carefully constructed act to the stark and painful reality, especially when only a few years later, Laura was married to someone else and expecting Jan's first grandchild? It was unfair to be hurt, to wish Jan had somehow glimpsed the depth of her hidden heartache.

This, then, was her own fault. Well, hers and a certain opportunistic male who had always been very good at charming her mother—and every other female within a dozen miles of Pine Gulch.

"Okay, the carpentry work. I get that. Yes, we certainly need the help and Taft is very good with his hands." She refused to remember just *how* good those hands could be. "But did you have to offer him a room?"

Jan shrugged, adding a lemony sauce to the chicken that instantly started to burble, filling the kitchen with a delicious aroma. "That was his idea."

Oh, Laura was quite sure it *was* Taft's idea. The bigger question was *why*? What possible reason could he have for this sudden wish to stay at the inn? By the stunned look he had worn when he spotted her at the fire scene, she would have assumed he wanted to stay as far away from her as possible.

He had to find this whole situation as awkward and, yes, painful as she did.

Maybe it was all some twisted revenge plot. She had spurned him after all. Maybe he wanted to somehow punish her all these years later with shoddy carpentry work that would end up costing an arm and a leg to repair....

She sighed at her own ridiculous imaginings. Taft didn't work that way. Whatever his motive for making this arrangement with her mother, she had no doubt he would put his best effort into the job.

"Apparently his lease was up on the apartment where he's been living," Jan went on. "He's building a house in Cold Creek Canyon—which I've heard is perfectly lovely, by the way—but it won't be finished for a few more weeks. Think of how much you can save on paying for a carpenter, all in exchange only for letting him stay in a room that was likely to be empty anyway, the way our vacancy rate will be during the shoulder season until the summer tourist activity heats up. I honestly thought you would be happy about this. When Taft suggested it, the whole thing seemed like a good solution all the way around."

A good solution for everyone except *her*! How would she survive having him underfoot all the time, smiling at her out of those green eyes she had once adored so much, talking to her out of that delicious mouth she had tasted so many times?

She gave a tiny sigh and her mother sent her a careful look. "I can still tell him no. He was planning on bringing some of his things over in the morning, but I'll just give him a ring and tell him never mind. We can find someone else, honey, if having Taft here will make you too uncomfortable."

Her mother was completely sincere, she knew. Jan would call him in immediately if she had any idea how much Laura had grieved for the dreams they had once spun together.

For an instant, she was tempted to have her mother do exactly that, call and tell him the deal was off.

How could she, though? She knew just what Taft would think. He would guess, quite accurately, that she was the one who didn't want him here and would know she had dissuaded her mother from the plan.

Her shoulder blades itched at the thought. She didn't want him thinking she was uncomfortable having him around. Better that he continue to believe she was completely indifferent to the ramifications of being back in Pine Gulch with him.

She had done her very best to strike the proper tone

the day of the fire, polite but cool, as if they were distant acquaintances instead of once having shared everything.

If she told her mother she didn't want to have Taft here, he would know her demeanor was all an act.

She was trapped. Well and truly trussed, just like one of the calves he used to rope in the high-school rodeo. It was a helpless, miserable feeling, one that felt all too familiar. She had lived with it every day of the past seven years, since her marriage to Javier Santiago. But unlike those calves in the rodeo ring, she had wandered willingly into the ropes that bound her to a man she didn't love.

Well, she hadn't been completely willing, she supposed. From the beginning she had known marrying him was a mistake and had tried every way she could think short of jilting him also to escape the ties binding them together. But unlike with Taft, this time she'd had a third life to consider. She had been four months pregnant with Alexandro. Javier—strangely old-fashioned about this, at least—wouldn't consider any other option but marriage.

She had tried hard to convince herself she was in love with him. He was handsome and seductively charming and made her laugh with his extravagant pursuit of her, which had been the reason she had finally given in and begun to date him while she was working at the small, exclusive boutique hotel he owned in Madrid.

She had tried to be a good wife and had worked hard to convince herself she loved him, but it hadn't been enough. Not for him and not for her—but by then she had been thoroughly entangled in the piggin' rope, so to speak, by Alex and then by Maya, her sweet-natured and vulnerable daughter.

This, though, with Taft. She couldn't control what her mother had done, but she could certainly control her own response to it. She wouldn't allow herself to care if the man had suddenly invaded every inch of her personal space by moving into the hotel. It was only temporary and then he would be out of her life again.

"Do you want me to call him?" her mother asked again.

She forced herself to smile. "Not at all, Mama. I'm sorry. I was just…surprised, that's all. Everything should be fine. You're right—it's probably a great idea. Free labor is always a good thing, and like you said, the only thing we're giving up is a room that probably wouldn't have been booked anyway."

Maya wandered into the kitchen, apparently tired of playing, and gave her mother one of those generous hugs Laura had come to depend upon like oxygen and water. "Hungry, Mama."

"Gram is fixing us something delicious for dinner. Aren't we lucky to have her?"

Maya nodded with a broad smile to her grandmother. "Love you, Gram."

"I love you, too, sweetheart." Jan beamed back at her.

This—her daughter and Alex—was more important than her discomfort about Taft. She was trying her best to turn the hotel into something that could actually turn a profit instead of just provide a subsistence for her mother and now her and her children.

She had her chance to live her lifelong dream now and make the Cold Creek Inn into the warm and gracious facility she had always imagined, a place where families could feel comfortable to gather, where couples could find or rekindle romance, where the occasional business traveler could find a home away from home.

This was her moment to seize control of her life and make a new future for herself and her children. She couldn't let Taft ruin that for her.

All she had to do was remind herself that she hadn't loved him for ten years and she should be able to handle his presence here at the inn with calm aplomb.

No big deal whatsoever. Right?

IF SOME PART of him had hoped Laura might fall all over him with gratitude for stepping up to help with the inn renovations, Taft would have been doomed to disappointment.

Over the next few days, as he settled into his surprisingly comfortable room in the wing overlooking the creek, a few doors down from the fire-damaged room, he helped Mrs. Pendleton with the occasional carpentry job. A bathroom cabinet repair here, a countertop fix there. In that time, he barely saw Laura. Somehow she was always mysteriously absent whenever he stopped at the front desk.

The few times he did come close enough to talk to her, she would exchange a quick, stiff word with him and then manufacture some excuse to take off at the earliest opportunity, as if she didn't want to risk some kind of contagion.

She had dumped *him*, not the other way around, but she was acting as if he was the biggest heel in the county. Still, he found her prickly, standoffish attitude more a challenge than an annoyance.

Truth was, he wasn't used to women ignoring him—

and he certainly wasn't accustomed to *Laura* ignoring him.

They had been friends forever, even before that momentous summer after her freshman year of college when he finally woke up and realized how much he had come to care about her as much more than simply a friend. After she left, he had missed the woman he loved with a hollow ache he had never quite been able to fill, but he sometimes thought he missed his best friend just as much.

After three nights at the hotel with these frustrating, fleeting encounters, he was finally able to run her to ground early one morning. He had an early meeting at the fire station, and when he walked out of the side entrance near where he parked the vehicle he drove as fire chief—which was as much a mobile office as a mode of transportation—he spotted someone working in the scraggly flower beds that surrounded the inn.

The beds were mostly just a few tulips and some stubbly, rough-looking shrubs but it looked as if somebody was trying to make it more. Several flats of colorful blooms had been spaced with careful efficiency along the curvy sidewalk, ready to be transplanted into the flower beds.

At first, he assumed the gardener under the straw hat was someone from a landscaping service until he caught a glimpse of honey-blond hair.

He instantly switched direction. "Good morning," he called as he approached. She jumped and whirled around. When she spotted him, her instinctive look of surprise twisted into something that looked like dismay before she tucked it away and instead gave him a polite, impersonal smile.

"Oh. Hello."

If it didn't sting somewhere deep inside, he might have been amused at her cool tone.

"You do remember this is eastern Idaho, not Madrid, right? It's only April. We could have snow for another six weeks yet, easy."

"I remember," she answered stiffly. "These are all hardy early bloomers. They should be fine."

What he knew about gardening was, well, *nothing*, except how much he used to hate it when his mom would wake him and his brothers and Caidy up early to go out and weed her vegetable patch on summer mornings.

"If you say so. I would just hate to see you spend all this money on flowers and then wake up one morning to find a hard freeze has wiped them out overnight."

"I appreciate your concern for my wallet, but I've learned in thirty-one years on the earth that if you want to beautify the world around you a little bit, sometimes you have to take a few risks."

He could appreciate the wisdom in that, whether he was a gardener or not.

"I'm only working on the east-and south-facing beds for now, where there's less chance of frost kill. I might have been gone a few years, but I haven't quite forgotten the capricious weather we can see here in the Rockies."

What *had* she forgotten? She didn't seem to have too many warm memories of their time together, not if she could continue treating him with this annoyingly polite indifference.

He knew he needed to be heading to the station house for his meeting, but he couldn't resist lingering a moment with her to see if he could poke and prod more of a reaction out of her than this.

He looked around and had to point out the obvious. "No kids with you this morning?"

"They're inside fixing breakfast with my mother." She gestured to the small Craftsman-style cottage behind the inn where she had been raised. "I figured this was a good time to get something done before they come outside and my time will be spent trying to keep Alex from deciding he could dig a hole to China in the garden and Maya from picking every one of the pretty flowers."

He couldn't help smiling. Her kids were pretty darn cute—besides that, there was something so *right* about standing here with her while the morning sunlight glimmered in her hair and the cottonwood trees along the river sent out a few exploratory puffs on the sweet-smelling breeze.

"They're adorable kids."

She gave him a sidelong glance as if trying to gauge his sincerity. "When they're not starting fires, you mean?"

He laughed. "I'm going on the assumption that that was a fluke."

There. He saw it. The edges of her mouth quirked up and she almost smiled, but she turned her face away and he missed it.

He still considered it a huge victory. He always used to love making her smile.

Something stirred inside him as he watched her pick up a cheerful yellow flower and set it in the small hole she had just dug. Attraction, yes. Most definitely. He had forgotten how much he liked the way she looked, fresh and bright and as pretty as those flowers. Somehow he had also forgotten over the years that air of quiet grace and sweetness.

She was just as lovely as ever. No, that wasn't quite true. She was even more beautiful than she had been a decade ago. While he wasn't so sure how life in general had treated her, the years had been physically kind to her. With those big eyes and her high cheekbones and that silky hair he used to love burying his hands in, she was still beautiful. Actually, when he considered it, her beauty had more depth now than it did when she had been a young woman, and he found it even more appealing.

Yeah, he was every bit as attracted to her as he'd been in those days when thoughts of her had consumed him like the wildfires he used to fight every summer. But he'd been attracted to plenty of women in the past decade. What he felt right now, standing in the morning sunshine with Laura, ran much more deeply through him.

Unsettled and more than a little rattled by the sudden hot ache in his gut, he took the coward's way out and opted for the one topic he knew she wouldn't want to discuss. "What happened to the kids' father?"

She dumped a trowel full of dirt on the seedling with enough force to make him wince. "Remind me again why that's any of your business," she bit out.

"It's not. Only idle curiosity. You married him just a few years after you were going to marry me. You can't blame me for wondering about him."

She raised an eyebrow as if she didn't agree with that particular statement. "I'm sure you've heard the gory details," she answered, her voice terse. "Javier died six months ago. A boating accident off the coast of Barcelona. He and his mistress du jour were both killed. It was a great tragedy for everyone concerned."

Ah, hell. He knew her husband had died, but he hadn't heard the rest of it. He doubted anyone else in Pine Gulch had or the rumor would have certainly slithered its way toward him, given their history together.

She studiously refused to look at him. He knew her well enough to be certain she regretted saying anything and he couldn't help wondering why she had.

He also couldn't think of a proper response. How much pain did those simple words conceal?

"I'm sorry," he finally said, although it sounded lame and trite.

"About what? His death or the mistress?"

"Both."

Still avoiding his gaze, she picked up another flower start from the colorful flat. "He was a good father. Whatever else I could say about Javier, he loved his children. They both miss him very much."

"You don't?"

"Again, why is this your business?"

He sighed. "It's not. You're right. But we were best friends once, even before, well, everything, and I would still like to know about your life after you left here. I never stopped caring about you just because you dumped me."

Again, she refused to look at him. "Don't go there, Taft. We both know I only broke our engagement because you didn't have the guts to do it."

Oh. Ouch. Direct hit. He almost took a step back, but he managed to catch himself just in time. "Jeez, Laura, why don't you say what you really mean?" he managed to get out past the guilt and pain.

She rose to her feet, spots of color on her high cheekbones. "Oh, don't pretend you don't know what I'm talking about. You completely checked out of our relationship after your parents were murdered. Every time I tried to talk to you, you brushed me off, told me you were fine, then merrily headed to the Bandito for another drink and to flirt with some hot young thing there. I suppose it shouldn't have come as a surprise to anyone that I married a man who was unfaithful. You know what they say about old patterns being hard to break."

Well, she was talking to him. *Be careful what you wish for, Bowman.*

"I was *never* unfaithful to you."

She made a disbelieving sound. "Maybe you didn't actually go that far with another woman, but you sure seemed to enjoy being with all the Bandito bar babes much more than you did me."

This wasn't going at all the way he had planned when he stopped to talk to her. Moving into the inn and taking the temporary carpenter job had been one of his crazier ideas. Really, he had only wanted to test the waters and see if there was any chance of finding their way past the ugliness and anger to regain the friendship they had once shared, the friendship that had once meant everything to him.

Those waters were still pretty damn frigid.

She let out a long breath and looked as if she regretted bringing up the past. "I knew you wanted out, Taft. *Everyone* knew you wanted out. You just didn't want to hurt me. I understand and appreciate that."

"That's not how it happened."

"I was there. I remember it well. You were grieving and angry about your parents' murder. Anyone would be. It's completely understandable, which is why, if you'll remember, I wanted to postpone the wedding until you were in a better place. You wouldn't hear of it. Every time I brought it up, you literally walked away from me. How could I have married you under those circumstances? We both would have ended up hating each other."

"You're right. This way is much better, with only you hating me."

Un-freaking-believable. She actually looked hurt at that. "Who said I hated you?"

"*Hate* might be too big a word. *Despise* might be a little more appropriate."

She drew in a sharp breath. "I don't feel either of those things. The truth is, Taft, what we had together was a long time ago. I don't feel anything at all for you other than maybe a little fond nostalgia for what we once shared."

Oh. Double ouch. Pain sliced through him, raw and sharp. That was certainly clear enough. He was very much afraid it wouldn't take long for him to discover he was just as crazy about her as he had always been and all she felt in return was "fond nostalgia."

Or so she said anyway.

He couldn't help searching her expression for any hint that she wasn't being completely truthful, but she only gazed back at him with that same cool look, her mouth set in that frustratingly polite smile.

Damn, but he hated that smile. He suddenly wanted to lean forward, yank her against him and kiss away that smile until it never showed up there again.

Just for the sake of fond nostalgia.

Instead, he forced himself to give her a polite smile of his own and took a step in the direction of his truck. He had a meeting and didn't want to be later than he already was.

"Good to know," he murmured. "I guess I had better let you get back to your gardening. My shift ends tonight at six and then I'm only on call for the next few days, so I should have a little more time to work on the rooms you're renovating. Leave me a list of jobs you would like me to do at the front desk. I'll try my best to stay out of your way."

There. That sounded cool and uninvolved.

If he slammed his truck door a little harder than strictly necessary, well, so what?

CHAPTER FOUR

WHEN WOULD SHE ever learn to keep her big mouth shut?

Long after Taft climbed into his pickup truck and drove away, Laura continued to yank weeds out of the sadly neglected garden beds with hands that shook while silently castigating herself for saying anything.

The moment she turned and found him walking toward her, she should have thrown down her trowel and headed back to the cottage.

Their conversation replayed over and over in her head. If her gardening gloves hadn't been covered in dirt, she would have groaned and buried her face in her hands.

First of all, why on earth had she told him about Javier and his infidelities? Taft was the *last* person in Pine Gulch with whom she should have shared that particular tidbit of juicy information.

Even her mother didn't know how difficult the last few years of her marriage had become, how she would have left in an instant if not for the children and their adoration for Javier. Yet she had blurted the gory details right out to Taft, gushing her private heartache like a leaky sprinkler pipe.

So much for wanting him to think she had moved onward and upward after she left Pine Gulch. All she had accomplished was to make herself an object of pity in his eyes—as if she hadn't done that a decade ago by throwing all her love at someone who wasn't willing or capable at the time of catching it.

And then she had been stupid enough to dredge up the past, something she vowed she wouldn't do. Talking about it again had to have made him wonder if she were *thinking* about it, which basically sabotaged her whole plan to appear cool and uninterested in Taft.

He could always manage to get her to confide things she shouldn't. She had often thought he should have been the police officer, not his twin brother, Trace.

When she was younger, she used to tell him everything. They had talked about the pressure her parents placed on her to excel in school. About a few of the mean girls in her grade who had excluded her from their social circle because of those grades, about her first crush—on a boy other than him, of course. She didn't tell him that until much later.

They had probably known each other clear back in grade school, but she didn't remember much about him other than maybe seeing him around in the lunchroom, this big, kind of tough-looking kid who had an identical twin and who always smiled at everyone. He had been two whole grades ahead of her after all, in an entirely different social stratosphere.

Her first real memory of him was middle school, which in Pine Gulch encompassed seventh through ninth grades. She had been in seventh grade, Taft in ninth. He had been an athletic kid and well-liked, always able to make anyone laugh. She, on the other hand, had been quiet and shy, much happier with a book in her hand than standing by her locker with her friends between classes, giggling over the cute boys.

She and Taft had ended up both taking a Spanish

elective and had been seated next to each other on Senora Baker's incomprehensible seating chart.

Typically, guys that age—especially jocks—didn't want to have much to do with younger girls. Gawky, insecure, bookish girls might as well just forget it. But somehow while struggling over past participles and conjugating verbs, they had become friends. She had loved his sense of humor and he seemed to appreciate how easily she picked up Spanish.

They had arranged study groups together for every test, often before school because Taft couldn't do it afterward most of the time due to practice sessions for whatever school sport he was currently playing.

She could remember exactly the first moment she knew she was in love with him. She had been in the library waiting for him early one morning. Because she lived in town and could easily walk to school, she was often there first. He and his twin brother usually caught a ride with their older brother, Ridge, who was a senior in high school at the time and had a very cool pickup truck with big tires and a roll bar.

While she waited for him, she had been fine-tuning a history paper due in a few weeks when Ronnie Lowery showed up. Ronnie was a jerk and a bully in her grade who had seemed to have it in for her for the past few years.

She didn't understand it but thought his dislike might have something to do with the fact that Ronnie's single mother worked as a housekeeper at the inn. Why that should bother Ronnie, she had no idea. His mom wasn't a very good maid and often missed work because of her drinking, but she had overheard her mom and dad talking once in the office. Her mom had wanted to fire Mrs. Lowery, but her dad wouldn't allow it.

"She's got a kid at home. She needs the job," her dad had said, which was exactly what she would have expected her dad to say. He had a soft spot for people down on their luck and often opened the inn to people he knew could never pay their tab.

She suspected Ronnie's mom must have complained about her job at home, which was likely the reason Ronnie didn't like her. He had tripped her a couple of times going up the stairs at school and once he had cornered her in the girls' bathroom and tried to kiss her and touch her chest—what little chest she had—until she had smacked him upside the head with her heavy advanced-algebra textbook and told him to keep his filthy hands off her, with melodramatic but firm effectiveness.

She usually did her best to avoid him whenever she could, but that particular morning in seventh grade, she had been the only one in the school library. Even Mrs. Pitt, the plump and kind librarian who introduced her to Georgette Heyer books, seemed to have disappeared, she saw with great alarm.

Ronnie sat down. "Hey, Laura the whore-a."

"Shut up," she had said, very maturely, no doubt.

"Who's gonna make me?" he asked, looking around with exaggerated care. "I don't see anybody here at all."

"Leave me alone, Ronnie. I'm trying to study."

"Yeah, I don't think I will. Is that your history paper? You've got Mr. Olsen, right? Isn't that a coin-ki-dink? So do I. I bet we have the same assignment. I haven't started mine. Good thing, too, because now I don't have to."

He grabbed her paper, the one she had been working on every night for two weeks, and held it over his head.

"Give it back." She did her best not to cry.

"Forget it. You owe me for this. I had a bruise for two weeks after you hit me last month. I had to tell my mom I ran into the bleachers going after a foul ball in PE."

"Want me to do it again?" she asked with much more bravado than true courage.

His beady gaze narrowed. "Try it, you little bitch, and I'll take more from you than just your freaking history paper."

"This history paper?"

At Taft's hard voice, all the tension coiled in her stomach like a rattlesnake immediately disappeared. Ronnie was big for a seventh grader, but compared to Taft, big and tough and menacing, he looked like just what he was—a punk who enjoyed preying on people smaller than he was.

"Yes, it's mine," she blurted out. "I would like it back."

Taft had smiled at her, plucked the paper out of Ronnie's greasy fingers and handed it back to Laura.

"Thanks," she had mumbled.

"You're Lowery, right?" he said to Ronnie. "I think you've got PE with my twin brother, Trace."

"Yeah," the kid had muttered, though with a tinge of defiance in his voice.

"I'm sorry, Lowery, but you're going to have to move. We're studying for a Spanish test here. Laura is my tutor and I don't know what I would do if something happened to her. All I can say is, I would *not* be happy. I doubt my brother would be, either."

Faced with the possibility of the combined wrath of the formidable Bowman brothers, Ronnie had slunk away like the coward he was, and in that moment, Laura had known she would love Taft for the rest of her life.

He had moved on to high school the next year, of

course, while she had been left behind in middle school to pine for him. Over the next two years, she remembered going to JV football games at the high school to watch him, sitting on the sidelines and keeping her fingers crossed that he would see her and smile.

Oh, yes. She had been plenty stupid when it came to Taft Bowman.

Finally, she had been in tenth grade and they would once more be in the same school as he finished his senior year. She couldn't wait, that endless summer. To her eternal delight, when she showed up at her first hour, Spanish again, she had found Taft seated across the room.

She would never forget walking into the room and watching Taft's broad smile take over his face and how he had pulled his backpack off the chair next to him, as if he had been waiting just for her.

They hadn't dated that year. She had been too young and still in her awkward phase, and anyway, he had senior girls flocking around him all the time, but their friendship had picked up where it left off two years earlier.

He had confided his girl troubles to her and how he was trying to figure out whether to join the military like his brother planned to do, or go to college. Even though she had ached inside to tell him how she felt about him, she hadn't dared. Instead, she had listened and offered advice whenever he needed it.

He had ended up doing both, enrolling in college and joining the Army Reserve, and in the summers, he had left Pine Gulch to fight woodland fires. They maintained an email correspondence through it all and every time he came home, they would head to The Gulch to share a meal and catch up and it was as if they had never been apart.

And then everything changed.

Although a painfully late bloomer, she had finally developed breasts somewhere around the time she turned sixteen, and by the time she went to college, she had forced herself to reach outside her instinctive shyness. The summer after her freshman year of college when she had finally decided to go into hotel management, Taft had been fighting a fire in Oregon when he had been caught in a flare-up.

Everyone in town had been talking about it, how he had barely escaped with his life and had saved two other firefighters from certain death. The whole time, she had been consumed with worry for him.

Finally, he came back for a few weeks to catch up with his twin, who was back in Pine Gulch between military assignments, and she and Taft had gone for a late-evening horseback ride at the River Bow Ranch and he finally spilled out the story of the flare-up and how it was a miracle he was alive.

One minute he was talking to her about the fire, something she was quite certain he hadn't done with anyone else. The next—she still wasn't sure how it happened— he was kissing her like a starving man and she was a giant frosted cupcake.

They kissed for maybe ten minutes. She wasn't sure exactly how long, but she only knew they were the most glorious moments of her life. When he finally eased away from her, he had looked as horrified as if he had just accidentally stomped on a couple of kittens.

"I'm sorry, Laura. That was… Wow. I'm so sorry."

She remembered shaking her head, smiling at him,

her heart aching with love. "What took you so blasted long, Taft Bowman?" she had murmured and reached out to kiss him again.

From that point on, they had been inseparable. She had been there to celebrate with him when he passed his EMT training, then paramedic training. He had visited her at school in Bozeman and made all her roommates swoon. When she came home for summers, they would spend every possible moment together.

On her twenty-first birthday, he proposed to her. Even though they were both crazy-young, she couldn't have imagined a future without him and had finally agreed. She missed those times, that wild flutter in her stomach every time he kissed her.

She sighed now and realized with a little start of surprise that while she had been woolgathering, she had weeded all the way around to the front of the building that lined Main Street.

Her mom would probably be more than ready for her to come back and take care of the children. She stood and stretched, rubbing her cramped back, when she heard the rumble of a pickup truck pulling alongside her.

Oh, she hoped it wasn't Taft coming back. She was already off-balance enough from their encounter earlier and from remembering all those things she had purposely kept buried for years. When she turned, she saw a woman climbing out of the pickup and realized it was indeed a Bowman— his younger sister, Caidy.

"Hi, Laura! Remember me? Caidy Bowman."

"Of course I remember you," she exclaimed. Caidy rushed toward her, arms outstretched, and Laura just had time to shuck off her gardening gloves before she returned the other woman's embrace.

"How are you?" she asked.

Despite the six-year difference in their ages, they had been close friends and she had loved the idea of having Caidy for a sister when she married Taft.

Until their parents died, Caidy had been a fun, bright, openly loving teenager, secure in her position as the adored younger sister of the three older Bowman brothers. Everything changed after Caidy witnessed her parents' murder, Laura thought sadly.

"I'm good," Caidy finally answered. Laura hoped so. Those months after the murders had been rough on the girl. The trauma of witnessing the brutal deaths and being unable to do anything to stop them had left Caidy frightened to the point of helplessness. For several weeks, she refused to leave the ranch and had insisted on having one of her brothers present twenty-four hours a day.

Caidy and her grief had been another reason Laura had tried to convince Taft to postpone their June wedding, just six months after the murders, but he had insisted his parents wouldn't have wanted them to change their plans.

Not that any of that mattered now. Caidy had become a beautiful woman, with dark hair like her brothers' and the same Bowman green eyes.

"You look fantastic," Laura exclaimed.

Caidy made a face but hugged her again. "Same to you. Gosh, I can't believe it's been so long."

"What are you up to these days? Did you ever make it to vet school?"

Something flickered in the depths of her eyes but Caidy only shrugged. "No, I went to a couple semesters of school but decided college wasn't really for me.

Since then, I've mostly just stuck around the ranch, helping Ridge with his daughter. I do a little training on the side. Horses and dogs."

"That's terrific," she said, although some part of her felt a little sad for missed opportunities. Caidy had always adored animals and had an almost uncanny rapport with them. All she used to talk about as a teenager was becoming a veterinarian someday and coming back to Pine Gulch to work.

One pivotal moment had changed so many lives, she thought. The violent murder of the Bowmans in a daring robbery of their extensive American West art collection had shaken everyone in town really. That sort of thing just didn't happen in Pine Gulch. The last murder the town had seen prior to that had been clear back in the 1930s when two ranch hands had fought it out over a girl.

Each of the Bowman siblings had reacted in different ways, she remembered. Ridge had thrown himself into the ranch and overseeing his younger siblings. Trace had grown even more serious and solemn. Caidy had withdrawn into herself, struggling with a completely natural fear of the world.

As for Taft, his answer had been to hide away his emotions and pretend everything was fine while inside he seethed with grief and anger and pushed away any of her attempts to comfort him.

"I'm looking for Taft," Caidy said now. "I had to make a run to the feed store this morning and thought I would stop and see if he wanted to head over to The Gulch for coffee and an omelet."

Oh, she loved The Gulch, the town's favorite diner. Why hadn't she been there since she returned to town?

An image of the place formed clearly in her head—the tin-stamped ceiling, the round red swivel seats at the old-fashioned counter, the smell of frying bacon and coffee that had probably oozed into the paneling.

One of these mornings, she would have to take her children there.

"Taft isn't here. I'm sorry. He left about a half hour ago. I think he was heading to the fire station. He did say something about his shift ending at six."

"Oh. Okay. Thanks." Caidy paused a moment, tilting her head and giving Laura a long, inscrutable look very much like her brother would do. "I don't suppose you would like to go over to The Gulch with me and have breakfast, would you?"

She gazed at the other woman, as touched by the invitation as she was surprised. In all these years, Taft hadn't told his family that she had been the one to break their engagement? She knew he couldn't have. If Caidy knew, Laura had a feeling the other woman wouldn't be nearly as friendly.

The Bowmans tended to circle the wagons around their own.

That had been one of the hardest things about walking away from him. Her breakup with Taft had meant not only the loss of all her childish dreams but also the big, boisterous family she had always wanted as an only child of older parents who seemed absorbed with each other and their business.

For a moment, she was tempted to go to The Gulch with Caidy. Her mouth watered at the thought of Lou Archuleta's famous sweet rolls. Besides that, she would love the chance to catch up with Caidy. But before she could answer, her children came barreling out of the cottage, Maya in the lead for once but Alex close behind.

"Ma-ma! Gram made cakes. So good," Maya declared.

Alexandro caught up to his sister. "Pancakes, not cakes. You don't have cakes for breakfast, Maya. We're supposed to tell you to come in so you can wash up. Hurry! Grandma says I can flip the next one."

"Oh."

Caidy smiled at the children, clearly entranced by them.

"Caidy, this is my daughter, Maya, and my son, Alexandro. Children, this is my friend Caidy. She's Chief Bowman's sister."

"I like Chief Bowman," Alex declared. "He said if I start another fire, he's going to arrest me. Do you think he will?"

Caidy nodded solemnly. "Trust me, my brother never says anything he doesn't mean. You'll have to be certain not to start any more fires, then, won't you?"

"I know. I know. I already heard it about a million times. Hey, Mom, can I go so I can turn the pancakes with Grandma?"

She nodded and Alex raced back for the cottage with his sister in close pursuit.

"They're beautiful, Laura. Truly."

"I think so." She smiled and thought she saw a hint of something like envy in the other woman's eyes. Why didn't Caidy have a family of her own? she wondered. Was she still living in fear?

On impulse, she gestured toward the cottage. "Unless you have your heart set on cinnamon rolls down at The Gulch, why don't you stay and have breakfast here? I'm sure my mother wouldn't mind setting another plate for you."

Caidy blinked. "Oh, I couldn't."

"Why not? My mother's pancakes are truly delicious. In fact, a week from now, we're going to start offering breakfast at the inn to our guests. The plan is to start with some of Mom's specialties like pancakes and French toast but also to begin ordering some things from outside sources to showcase local businesses. I've already talked to the Java Hut about serving their coffee here and the Archuletas about offering some of The Gulch pastries to our guests."

"What a great idea."

"You can be our guinea pig. Come and have breakfast with us. I'm sure my mother will enjoy the company."

She would, too, she thought. She missed having a friend besides her mother. Her best friend in high school, besides Taft, had moved to Texas for her husband's job and Laura hadn't had a chance to connect with anyone else.

Even though she still emailed back and forth with her dearest friends and support system in Madrid, it wasn't the same as sharing coffee and pancakes and stories with someone who had known her for so long.

"I would love that," Caidy exclaimed. "Thank you. I'm sure Taft can find his own breakfast partner if he's so inclined."

From the rumors Laura had heard about the man in the years since their engagement, she didn't doubt that for a moment.

CHAPTER FIVE

To HER RELIEF, her children were charming and sweet with Caidy over breakfast. As soon as he found out their guest lived on a real-life cattle ranch, Alex peppered her with questions about cowboys and horses and whether she had ever seen a "real-life Indian."

Apparently she had to have a talk with her son about political correctness and how reality compared to the American Westerns he used to watch avidly with their gnarled old housekeeper in Madrid.

Maya had apparently decided Caidy was someone she could trust, which was something of a unique occurrence. She sat beside her and gifted Taft's sister with her sweet smile and half of the orange Laura peeled for her.

"Thank you, sweetheart," Caidy said, looking touched by the gesture.

Whenever someone new interacted with Maya, Laura couldn't help a little clutch in her stomach, worry at how her daughter would be accepted.

She supposed that stemmed from Javier's initial re-action after her birth when the solemn-faced doctors told them Maya showed certain markers for Down syndrome and they were running genetic testing to be sure.

Her husband had been in denial for a long time and had pretended nothing was wrong. After all, how could he possibly have a child who wasn't perfect—by the world's standards anyway? Even after the testing revealed what Laura had already known in her heart, Javier has refused to discuss Maya's condition or possible outcomes.

Denial or not, he had still loved his daughter, though. She couldn't fault him for that. He was sometimes the only one who could calm the baby's crankiness and he had been infinitely calm with her.

Maya didn't quite understand that Javier was dead. She still had days when she asked over and over again where her papa was. During those rough patches, Laura would have to fight down deep-seated fury at her late husband.

Her children needed him and he had traded his future with them for the momentary pleasure he had found with his latest honey. Mingled with the anger and hurt was no small amount of guilt. If she had tried a little harder to open her heart to him and truly love him, maybe he wouldn't have needed to seek out other women.

She was doing her best, she reminded herself. Hadn't she traveled across the world to give them a home with family and stability?

"This was fun," Caidy said, drawing her back to the conversation. "Thank you so much for inviting me, but I probably better start heading back to the ranch. I've got a buyer coming today to look at one of the border collies I've been training."

"You're going to sell your dog?" Alex, who dearly wanted a puppy, looked horrified at the very idea.

"Sue isn't really my dog," Caidy explained with a smile. "I rescued her when she was a puppy and I've been training her to help someone else at their ranch. We have plenty of dogs at the River Bow."

Alex didn't seem to quite understand the concept of breeding and training dogs. "Doesn't it make you sad to give away your dog?"

Caidy blinked a little, but after a pause she nodded. "Yes, I guess it does a little. She's a good dog and I'll miss her. But I promise I'll make sure whoever buys her will give her a really good home."

"We have a good home, don't we, Grandma?" Alex appealed to Jan, who smiled.

"Why, yes, I believe we do, son."

"We can't have a dog right now, Alex."

Laura tried to head him off before he started extolling the virtues of their family like a used-car salesman trying to close a deal. "We've talked about this. While we're settling in here in Pine Gulch and living with Grandma here at the inn, it's just not practical."

He stuck out his lower lip, looking very much like his father when he couldn't get his way. "That's what you always say. I still really, really, really want a dog."

"Not now, Alexandro. We're not getting a dog. Maybe in a year or so when things here are a little more settled."

"But I want one now!"

"I'm sorry," Caidy said quickly, "but I'm afraid Sue wouldn't be very happy here. You see, she's a working dog and her very favorite thing is telling the cattle on our ranch which way we want them to go. You don't look very much like a steer. Where are your horns?"

Alex looked as if he wanted to ramp up to a full-fledged tantrum, something new since his father died, but he allowed himself to be teased out of it. "I'm not a steer," he said, rolling his eyes. Then a moment later he asked, "What's a steer?"

Caidy laughed. "It's another name for the male version of cow."

"I thought that was a bull."

"Uh." Caidy gave Laura a helpless sort of look.

While Jan snickered, Laura shook her head. "You're right. There are two kinds of male bovines, which is another word for cow. One's a bull and one is a steer."

"What's the difference?" he asked.

"Steers sing soprano," Caidy said. "And on that lovely note, I'd better get back to the bulls *and* steers of the River Bow. Thanks for a great breakfast. Next time it's my turn."

"Alex, will you and Maya help Gram with clearing the table while I walk Caidy out? I'll do the dishes when I come back inside."

To her relief, her son allowed himself to be distracted when Jan asked him if he and Maya would like to go to the park later in the day.

"I'm sorry about the near-tantrum there," she said as they headed outside to Caidy's pickup truck. "We're working on them, but my son still likes his own way."

"Most kids do. My niece is almost ten and she still thinks she should be crowned queen of the universe. I didn't mean to start something by talking about dogs."

"We've been having this argument for about three years now. His best friend in Madrid had this mangy old mutt, but Alex adored him and wanted one so badly. My husband would never allow it and for some reason Alex got it in his head after his father died that now there was no reason we couldn't get a dog."

"You're welcome to bring your kids out to the ranch

sometime to enjoy my dogs vicariously. The kids might enjoy taking a ride, as well. We've got some pretty gentle ponies that would be perfect for them."

"That sounds fun. I'm sure they would both love it." She was quite certain this was one of those vague invitations that people said just to be polite, but to her surprise, Caidy didn't let the matter rest.

"How about next weekend?" she pressed. "I'm sure Ridge would be delighted to have you out."

Ridge was the Bowman sibling she had interacted with the least. At the time she was engaged to Taft, he and his parents weren't getting along, so he avoided the River Bow as much as possible. The few times she had met him, she had always thought him a little stern and humorless.

Still, he'd been nice enough to her—though the same couldn't have been said about his ex-wife, who had been rude and overbearing to just about everyone on the ranch.

"That's a lovely invitation, but I'm sure the last thing you need is to entertain a bunch of greenhorns."

"I would love it," Caidy assured her. "Your kids are just plain adorable and I can't tell you how thrilled I am that you're back in town. To tell you the truth, I'm a little desperate for some female conversation. At least something that doesn't revolve around cattle."

She should refuse. Her history with Taft had to make any interaction with the rest of the Bowmans more than a little awkward. But like Caidy, she welcomed any chance to resurrect their old friendship—and Alex and Maya *would* love the chance to ride horses and play with the ranch dogs.

"Yes, all right. The weekend would be lovely. Thank you."

"I'll call you Wednesday or Thursday to make some firm arrangements. This will be great!" Caidy beamed at her, looking fresh and pretty with her dark ponytail and sprinkling of freckles across the bridge of her nose.

The other woman climbed into her pickup truck and drove away with a wave and a smile and Laura watched after her for a moment, feeling much better about the morning than she had when the previous Bowman sibling had driven away from the inn.

TAFT HAD VISITORS.

The whir of the belt sander didn't quite mask the giggles and little scurrying sounds from the doorway. He made a show of focusing on the window he was framing while still maintaining a careful eye on the little creatures who would occasionally peek around the corner of the doorway and then hide out of sight again.

He didn't want to let his guard down, not with all the power equipment in here. He could just imagine Laura's diatribe if one of her kids somehow got hurt. She would probably accuse him of letting her rambunctious older kid cut off his finger on purpose.

The game of peekaboo lasted for a few more minutes until he shut off the belt sander. He ran a finger over the wood to be sure the frame was smooth before he headed over to the window to hold it up for size, keeping an eye on the door the whole time.

"Go on," he heard a whispered voice say, then giggles, and a moment later he was joined by Laura's daughter.

Maya. She was adorable, with that dusky skin,

curly dark hair in pigtails and Laura's huge blue eyes, almond-shaped on Maya.

"Hola," she whispered with a shy smile.

"Hola, senorita," he answered. Apparently he still remembered a *little* of the high-school Spanish he had struggled so hard to master.

"What doing?" she asked.

"I'm going to put some new wood up around this window. See?" He held the board into the intended place to demonstrate, then returned it to the worktable.

"Why?" she asked, scratching her ear.

He glanced at the doorway where the boy peeked around, then hid again like a shadow.

"The old wood was rotting away. This way it will look much nicer. More like the rest of the room."

That face peeked around the doorway again and this time Taft caught him with an encouraging smile. After a pause, the boy sidled into the room.

"Loud," Maya said, pointing to the belt sander with fascination.

"It can be. I've got things to block your ears if you want them."

He wasn't sure she would understand, but she nodded vigorously, so he reached for his ear protectors on top of his toolbox. The adult-size red ear guards were huge on her—the bottom of the cups hit her at about shoulder height. He reached out to work the slide adjustment on top. They were still too big but at least they covered most of her ears.

She beamed at him, pleased as punch, and he had to chuckle. "Nice. You look great."

"I see," she said, and headed unerringly for the mirror hanging on the back of the bathroom door, where she turned her head this way and that, admiring her head-gear as if he had given her a diamond tiara.

Oh, she was a heartbreaker, this one.

"Can I use some?" Alexandro asked, from about two feet away, apparently coaxed all the way into the room by what his sister was wearing.

"I'm afraid I've got only the one pair. I wasn't expecting company. Sorry. Next time I'll remember to pack a spare. I probably have regular earplugs in my toolbox."

Alex shrugged. "That's okay. I don't mind the noise. Maya freaks at loud noises, but I don't care."

"Why is that? Maya, I mean, and loud noises?"

The girl was wandering around the room, humming to herself loudly, apparently trying to hear herself through the ear protection.

The kid looked fairly protective himself, watching over his sister as she moved from window to window. "She just does. Mom says it's because she has so much going on inside her head she sometimes forgets the rest of us and loud noises startle her into remembering. Or something like that."

"You love your sister a lot, don't you?"

"She's my sister." He shrugged, looking suddenly much older than his six years. "I have to watch out for her and Mama now that our papa is gone."

Taft wanted to hug him, too, and he had to fight down a lump in his throat. He thought about his struggle when his parents had died. He had been twenty-four years old. Alex was just a kid and had already lost his father, but he seemed to be handling it with stoic grace. "I bet you do a great job, protecting them both."

The boy looked guilty. "Sometimes. I didn't on the day of the fire."

"We've decided that was an accident, right? It's over and you're not going to do it again. Take it from me, kid. Don't beat yourself up over past mistakes. Just move on and try to do better next time."

Alex didn't look as if he quite understood. Why should he? Taft rolled his eyes at himself. Philosophy and six-year-old boys didn't mix all that well.

"Want to try your hand with the sander?" he asked.

Alex's blue eyes lit up. "Really? Is it okay?"

"Sure. Why not? Every guy needs to know how to run a belt sander."

Before beginning the lesson, Taft thought it wise to move toward Maya, who was sitting on the floor some distance away, drawing her finger through the sawdust mess he hadn't had time to clear up yet. Her mom would probably love that, but because she was already covered, he decided he would clean her up when they were done.

He lifted one of the ear protectors away from her ear so he could talk to her. "Maya, we're going to turn on the sander, okay?"

"Loud."

"It won't be when you have this on. I promise."

She narrowed her gaze as if she were trying to figure out whether to believe him, then she nodded and returned to the sawdust. He gazed at the back of her head, tiny compared to the big ear guards, and was completely bowled over by her ready trust.

Now he had to live up to it.

He turned on the sander, hoping the too-big ear protectors would still do their job. Maya looked up, a look of complete astonishment on her cute little face. She pulled one ear cup away, testing to see if the sander was on, but quickly returned it to the original position. After a minute, she pulled it away again and then replaced it, a look of wonder on her face at the magic of safety wear.

He chuckled and turned back to Alex, waiting eagerly by the belt sander.

"Okay, the most important thing here is that we don't sand your fingers off. I'm not sure your mom would appreciate that."

"She wouldn't," Alex assured him with a solemn expression.

Taft had to fight his grin. "We'll have to be careful, then. Okay. Now you always start up the belt sander before you touch it to the wood so you don't leave gouges. Right here is the switch. Now keep your hands on top of mine and we can do it together. That's it."

For the next few minutes, they worked the piece of wood until he was happy with the way it looked and felt. He always preferred to finish sanding his jobs the old-fashioned way, by hand, but a belt sander was a handy tool for covering a large surface quickly and efficiently.

When they finished, he carefully turned off the belt sander and set it aside, then returned to the board and the boy. "Okay, now here's the second most important part, after not cutting your fingers off. We have to blow off the sawdust. Like this."

He demonstrated with a puff of air, then handed the board to the boy, who puckered up and blew as if he were the big, bad wolf after the three little pigs.

"Perfect," Taft said with a grin. "Feel how smooth that is now?"

The boy ran his finger along the wood grain. "Wow! I did that?"

"Absolutely. Good job. Now every time you come

into this room, you can look out through the window and remember you helped frame it up."

"Cool! Why do you have to sand the wood?"

"When the wood is smooth, it looks better and you get better results with whatever paint or varnish you want to use on it."

"How does the sander thingy work?"

"The belt is made of sandpaper. See? Because it's rough, when you rub it on the wood, it works away the uneven surface."

"Can you sand other things besides wood?" he asked.

Taft had to laugh at the third degree. "You probably can but it's made for wood. It would ruin other things. Most tools have a specific purpose and when you use them for something else, you can cause more problems."

"Me," an abnormally loud voice interrupted before Alex could ask any more questions. With the ear protectors, Maya obviously couldn't judge the decibel level of her own voice. "I go now."

"Okay, okay. You don't need to yell about it," Alex said, rolling his eyes in a conspiratorial way toward Taft.

Just like that, both of these kids slid their way under his skin, straight to his heart, partly because they were Laura's, but mostly because they were just plain adorable.

"Can I?" she asked, still speaking loudly.

He lifted one of the ear protectors so she could hear him. "Sure thing, sweetheart. I've got another board that needs sanding. Come on."

Alex looked disgruntled, but he backed away to give his sister room. Taft was even more careful with Maya, keeping his hands firmly wrapped around hers on the belt sander as they worked the wood.

When they finished, he removed her earwear completely. "Okay, now, like I told your brother, this is the most important part. I need you to blow off the sawdust."

She puckered comically and puffed for all she was worth and he helped her along. "There. Now feel what we did."

"Ooh. Soft." She smiled broadly at him and he returned her smile, just as he heard their names.

"Alex? Maya? Where are you?"

Laura's voice rang out from down the hall, sounding harried and a little hoarse, as if she had been calling for a while.

The two children exchanged looks, as if they were bracing themselves for trouble.

"That's our mama," Alex said unnecessarily.

"Yeah, I heard."

"Alex? Maya? Come out this instant."

"They're in here," he called out, although some part of him really didn't want to take on more trouble. He thought of their encounter a few days earlier when she had looked so fresh and pretty while she worked on the inn's flower gardens—and had cut into his heart more effectively than if she had used her trowel.

She charged into the room, every inch the concerned mother. "What's going on? Why didn't you two answer me? I've been calling through the whole hotel."

Taft decided to take one for the team. "I'm afraid that's my fault. We had the sander going. We couldn't hear much up here."

"Look, Mama. Soft." Maya held up the piece of wood she had helped him sand. "Feel!"

Laura stepped closer, reluctance in her gaze. He was immediately assailed by the scent of her, of flowers and springtime.

She ran a hand along the wood, much as her daughter had. "Wow. That's great."

"I did it," Maya declared.

Laura arched an eyebrow. She managed to look huffy and disapproving at him for just a moment before turning back to her daughter with what she quickly transformed into an interested expression. "Did you, now? With the power sander and everything?"

"I figured I would let them run the circular saw next," he said. "Really, what's the worst that can happen?"

She narrowed her gaze at him as if trying to figure out if he was teasing. Whatever happened to her sense of humor? he wondered. Had he robbed her of that or had it been her philandering jackass of a husband?

"I'm kidding," he said. "I was helping them the whole way. Maya even wore ear protection, didn't you? Show your mom."

The girl put on her headgear and started singing some made-up song loudly, pulling the ear guards away at random intervals.

"Oh, that looks like great fun," Laura said, taking the ear protectors off her daughter and handing them to Taft. Their hands brushed as he took them from her and a little charge of electricity arced between them, sizzling right to his gut.

She pulled her hands away quickly and didn't meet

his gaze. "You shouldn't be up here bothering Chief Bowman. I told you to stay away when he's working."

And why would she think she had to do that? he wondered, annoyed. Did she think he couldn't be trusted with her kids? He was the Pine Gulch fire chief, for heaven's sake, and a trained paramedic to boot. Public safety was sort of his thing.

"It was fun," Alex declared. "I got to use the sander first. Feel my board now, Mama."

She appeared to have no choice but to comply. "Nice job. But next time you need to listen to me and not bother Chief Bowman while he's working."

"I didn't mind," Taft said. "They're fun company."

"You're busy. I wouldn't want them to be a bother."

"What if they're not?"

She didn't look convinced. "Come on, you two. Tell Chief Bowman thank-you for letting you try out the dangerous power tools, after you promise him you'll never touch any of them on your own."

"We promise," Alex said dutifully.

"Promise," his sister echoed.

"Thanks for showing me how to use a sander," Alex said. "I need one of those."

Now *there* was a disaster in the making. But because the kid wasn't his responsibility, as his mother had made quite clear, he would let Laura deal with it.

"Thanks for helping me," he said. "I couldn't have finished without you two lending a hand."

"Can I help you again sometime?" the boy asked eagerly.

Laura tensed beside him and he knew she wanted him to say no. It annoyed the heck out of him and he wanted to agree, just to be contrary, but he couldn't bring himself to blatantly go against her wishes.

Instead, he offered the standard adult cop-out even though it grated. "We'll have to see, kiddo," he answered.

"Okay, now that you've had a chance with the power tools, take your sister and go straight down to the front desk to your grandmother. No detours, Alex. Got it?"

His stubborn little chin jutted out. "But we were having fun."

"Chief Bowman is trying to get some work done. He's not here to babysit."

"I'm not a baby," Alex grumbled.

Laura bit back what Taft was almost certain was a smile. "I know you're not. It's just a word, *mi hijo*. Either way, you need to take your sister straight down to the lobby to find your grandmother."

With extreme reluctance in every step, Alex took his little sister's hand and led her out the door and down the hall, leaving Laura alone with him.

Even though he could tell she wasn't thrilled to have found her children there with him and some part of him braced himself to deal with her displeasure, another, louder part of him was just so damn happy to see her again.

Ridiculous, he knew, but he couldn't seem to help it.

How had he forgotten that little spark of happiness that always seemed to jump in his chest when he saw her after an absence of just about any duration?

Even with her hair in a ponytail and an oversize shirt and faded jeans, she was beautiful, and he wanted to stand here amid the sawdust and clutter and just savor the sight of her.

As he might have expected, she didn't give him much of a chance. "Sorry about the children," she said stiffly. "I thought they were watching *SpongeBob* in the bedroom of Room Twelve while I cleaned the bathroom grout. I came out of the bathroom and they were gone, which is, unfortunately, not all that uncommon with my particular kids."

"Next time maybe you should use the security chain to keep them contained," he suggested, only half-serious.

Even as he spoke, he was aware of a completely inappropriate urge to wrap her in his arms and absorb all her cares and worries about wandering children and tile grout and anything else weighing on her.

"A great idea, but unfortunately I've already tried that. Within about a half hour, Alex figured out how to lift his sister up and have her work the chain free. They figured out the dead bolt in about half that time. I just have to remember I can't take my eyes off them for a second. I'll try to do a better job of keeping them out of your way."

"I told you, I don't mind them. Why would I? They're great kids." He meant the words, even though his previous experience with kids, other than the annual fire-safety lecture he gave at the elementary school, was mostly his niece, Destry, Ridge's daughter.

"I think they're pretty great," she answered.

"That Alex is a curious little guy with a million questions."

She gave a rueful sigh and tucked a strand of hair behind her delicate ear. She used to love it when he kissed her neck, just there, he remembered, then wished the memory had stayed hidden as heat suddenly surged through him.

"Yes, I'm quite familiar with my son's interrogation technique," Laura said, oblivious to his reaction, thank heavens. "He's had six years to hone them well."

"I don't mind the questions. Trace and I were both the same way when we were kids. My mom used to say that between the two of us, we didn't give her a second to even catch a breath between questions."

She trailed her fingers along the wood trim and he remembered how she used to trail them across his stomach....

"I remember some of the stories your mother used to tell me about you and Trace and the trouble you could get into. To be honest with you, I have great sympathy with your mother. I can't imagine having two of Alex."

He dragged his mind away from these unfortunate memories that suddenly crowded out rational thought. "He's a good boy, just has a lot of energy. And that Maya. She's a heartbreaker."

She pulled her hand away from the wood, her expression suddenly cold. "Don't you dare pity her."

"Why on earth would I do that?" he asked, genuinely shocked.

She frowned. "Because of her Down syndrome. Many people do."

"Then you shouldn't waste your time with them. Down syndrome or not, she's about the sweetest thing I've ever seen. You should have seen her work the belt sander, all serious and determined, chewing on her lip in concentration—just like you used to do when you were studying."

"Don't."

He blinked, startled at her low, vehement tone. "Don't what?"

"Try to charm me by acting all sweet and concerned. It might work on your average bimbo down at the Bandito, but I'm not that stupid."

Where did *that* come from? "Are you kidding? You're about the smartest person I know. I never thought you were stupid."

"That makes one of us," she muttered, then looked as if she regretted the words.

More than anything, he wanted to go back in time ten years and make things right again with her. He had hurt her by closing her out of his pain, trying to deal with the grief and guilt in his own way.

But then, she had hurt him, too. If only she had given him a little more time and trusted that he would work things through, he would have figured everything out eventually. Instead, she had gone away to Spain and met her jerk of a husband—and had two of the cutest kids he had ever met.

"Laura—" he began, not sure what he intended to say, but she shook her head briskly.

"I'm sorry my children bothered you. I won't let it happen again."

"I told you, I don't mind them."

"I mind. I don't want them getting attached to you when you'll be in their lives for only a brief moment."

He hadn't even known her kids a week ago. So why did the idea of not seeing them again make his chest ache? Uneasy with the reaction, he gave her a long look.

"For someone who claims not to hate me, you do a pretty good impression of it. You don't even want me around your kids, like I'll contaminate them somehow."

"You're exaggerating. You're virtually a stranger to me after all this time. I don't hate you. I feel nothing at all for you. Less than nothing."

He moved closer to her, inhaling the springtime scent of her shampoo. "Liar."

The single word was a low hush in the room and he saw her shiver as if he had trailed his finger down her cheek.

She started to take a step back, then checked the motion. "Oh, get over yourself," she snapped. "Yes, you broke my heart. I was young and foolish enough to think you meant what you said, that you loved me and wanted forever with me. We were supposed to take vows about being with each other in good times and bad, but you wouldn't share the bad with me. Instead, you started drinking and hanging out at the Bandito and pretending nothing was wrong. I was devastated. I won't make a secret of that. I thought I wouldn't survive the pain."

"I'm sorry," he said.

She made a dismissive gesture. "I should really thank you, Taft. If not for that heartbreak, I would have been only a weak, silly girl who would probably have become a weak, silly woman. Instead, I became stronger. I took my broken heart and turned it into a grand adventure in Europe, where I matured and experienced the world a little bit instead of just Pine Gulch, and now I have two beautiful children to show for it."

"Why did you give up on us so easily?"

Her mouth tightened with anger. "You know, you're right. I should have gone ahead with the wedding and then just waited around wringing my hands until you decided to pull your head out of whatever crevice you jammed it into. Although from the sound of it, I might still have been waiting, ten years later."

"I'm sorry for hurting you," he said, wishing again that he could go back and change everything. "More sorry than I can ever say."

"Ten years too late," she said tersely. "I told you, it doesn't matter."

"It obviously does or you wouldn't bristle like a porcupine every time you're near me."

"I don't—" she started to say, but he cut her off.

"I don't blame you. I was an ass to you. I'll be the first to admit it."

"The second," she said tartly.

If this conversation didn't seem so very pivotal, he might have smiled, but he had the feeling he had the chance to turn things around between them right here and now, and he wanted that with a fierce and powerful need.

"Probably. For what it's worth, my family would fill out the rest of the top five there, waiting in line to call me names."

She almost smiled but she hid it quickly. What would it take for him to squeeze a real smile out of her and keep it there? he wondered.

"I know we can't go back and change things," he said slowly. "But what are the chances that we can at least be civil to each other? We were good friends once, before we became more. I miss that."

She was quiet for several moments and he was aware of the random sounds of the old inn. The shifting of old wood, the creak of a floorboard somewhere, a tree branch that needed to be pruned back rattling against the thin glass of the window.

When she spoke, her voice was low. "I miss it, too," she said, in the tone of someone confessing a rather shameful secret.

Something inside him seemed to uncoil at her words. He gazed at her so-familiar features that he had once known as well as his own.

The high cheekbones, the cute little nose, those blue eyes that always reminded him of his favorite columbines that grew above the ranch. He wanted to kiss her, with a raw ferocity that shocked him to his toes. To sink into her and not climb out again.

He managed, just barely, to restrain himself and was grateful for it when she spoke again, her voice just above a whisper.

"We can't go back, Taft."

"No, but we can go forward. That's better anyway, isn't it? The reality is, we're both living in the same small town. Right now we're living at the same address, for Pete's sake. We can't avoid each other. But that doesn't mean we need to go on with this awkwardness between us, does it? I would really like to see if together we can find some way to move past it. What do you say?"

She gazed at him for a long moment, uncertainty in those eyes he loved so much. Finally she seemed to come to some internal decision.

"Sure. We can try to be friends again." She gave him a tentative smile. A real one this time, not that polite thing he had come to hate, and his chest felt tight and achy all over again.

"I need to get back to work. I'll see you later."

"Goodbye, Laura," he said.

She gave him one more little smile before hurrying

out of the room. He watched her go, more off-balance by the encounter with Laura and her children than he wanted to admit. As he turned back to his work, he was also aware of a vague sense of melancholy that made no sense. This was progress, right? Friendship was a good place to start—hadn't their relationship begun out of friendship from the beginning?

He picked up another board from the pile. He knew the source of his discontent. He wanted more than friendship with Laura. He wanted what they used to have, laughter and joy and that contentment that seemed to seep through him every time he was with her.

Baby steps, he told himself. He could start with friendship and then gradually build on that, see how things progressed. Nothing wrong with a little patience once in a while.

HER HANDS WERE still shaking as Laura walked out of the room and down the hall. She headed for the lobby, with the curving old stairs and the classic light fixtures that had probably been installed when Pine Gulch finally hit the electrical grid.

Only when she was certain she was completely out of sight of Taft did she lean against the delicately flowered wallpaper and press a hand to her stomach.

What an idiot she was, as weak as a baby lamb around him. She always had been. Even if she had hours of other more urgent homework, if Taft called her and needed help with Spanish, she would drop everything to rush to his aid.

It didn't help matters that the man was positively dangerous when he decided to throw out the charm.

Oh, it would be so easy to give in, to let all that seductive charm slide around and through her until she forgot all the reasons she needed to resist him.

He asked if they could find a way to friendship again. She didn't have the first idea how to answer that. She wanted to believe her heart had scarred over from the disappointment and heartache, the loss of those dreams for the future, but she was more than a little afraid to peek past the scars to see if it had truly healed.

She was tough and resilient. Hadn't she survived a bad marriage and then losing the husband she had tried to love? She could surely carry on a civil conversation with Taft on the rare occasions they met in Pine Gulch.

What was the harm in it? For heaven's sake, reestablishing a friendly relationship with the man didn't mean she was automatically destined to tumble headlong back into love with him.

Life in Pine Gulch would be much easier all the way around if she didn't feel jumpy and off-balance every time she was around him.

She eased away from the wallpaper and straightened her shirt that had bunched up. This was all ridiculous anyway. What did it matter if she was weak around him? She likely wouldn't ever have the opportunity to test out her willpower. From the rumors she heard, Taft probably had enough young, hot bar babes at the Bandito that he probably couldn't be bothered with a thirty-two-year-old widow with two children, one of whom with a disability that would require lifelong care.

She wasn't the same woman she had been ten years ago. She had given birth to two kids and had the body to show for it. Her hair was always messy and falling out of whatever clip she had shoved it in that morning, half the time she didn't have time to put on makeup until she had been up for hours and, between the kids and the inn, she was perpetually stressed.

Why on earth would a man like Taft, gorgeous and masculine, want anything *but* friendship with her these days?

She wasn't quite sure why that thought depressed her and made her feel like that gawky seventh grader with braces crushing on a ninth-grade athlete who was nice to her.

Surely she didn't *want* to have to resist Taft Bowman. It was better all around if he saw her merely as that frumpy mother.

She knew that was probably true, even as some secret, silly little part of her wanted to at least have the *chance* to test her willpower around him.

CHAPTER SIX

"HURRY, MAMA." ALEX PRACTICALLY jumped out of his booster seat the moment she turned off the engine at the River Bow Ranch on Saturday. "I want to see the dogs!"

"Dogs!" Maya squealed after him, wiggling and tugging against the car-seat straps. The only reason she didn't rush to join her brother outside the car was her inability to undo the straps on her own, much to her constant frustration.

"Hang on, you two." Their excitement made her smile, despite the host of emotions churning through her at visiting the River Bow again for the first time in a decade. "The way you're acting, somebody might think you'd never seen a dog before."

"I have, too, seen a dog before," Alex said. "But this isn't just *one* dog. Miss Bowman said she had a *lot* of dogs. And horses, too. Can I really ride one?"

"That's the plan for now, but we'll have to see how things go." She was loath to make promises about things that were out of her control. Probably a fallback to her marriage, those frequent times when the children would be so disappointed if their father missed dinner or a school performance or some special outing.

"I hope I *can* ride a horse. Oh, I hope so." Alex practically danced around the used SUV she had purchased with the last of her savings when she arrived back in the States. She had to smile at his enthusiasm as she un-strapped Maya and lifted her out of the vehicle.

Maya threw her chubby little arms around Laura's neck before she could set her on the ground.

"Love you," her daughter said.

The spontaneously affectionate gesture turned her insides to warm mush, something her sweet Maya so often did. "Oh, I love you, too, darling. More than the moon and the stars and the sea."

"Me, too," Alex said.

She hugged him with the arm not holding Maya. "I love you both. Aren't I the luckiest mom in the world to have two wonderful kiddos to love?"

"Yes, you are," he said, with a total lack of vanity that made her smile.

She supposed she couldn't be a completely terrible mother if she was raising her children with such solid assurance of their place in her heart.

At the sound of scrabbling paws and panting breaths, she raised her head from her children. "Guess what? Here come the dogs."

Alex whirled around in time to see Caidy approaching them with three dogs shadowing her. Laura identi-fied two of them as border collies, mostly black with white patches on their faces and necks, quizzical ears and eerily intelligent expressions. The third was either a breed she didn't recognize or some kind of mutt of undetermined origin, with reddish fur and a German shepherd–like face.

Maya stiffened nervously, not at all experienced around dogs, and tightened her arms around Laura's neck. Alex, on the other hand, started to rush toward the dogs, but Laura checked him with a hand on his shoulder.

"Wait until Caidy says it's safe," she ordered her son, who would run directly into a lion's enclosure if he thought he might have a chance of petting the creature.

"Perfectly safe," Caidy assured them.

Taft's sister wore jeans and a bright yellow T-shirt along with boots and a straw cowboy hat, her dark hair braided down her back. She looked fresh and pretty as she gave them all a welcoming smile. "The only danger from my dogs is being licked to death—or maybe getting knocked over by a wagging tail."

Alex giggled and Caidy looked delighted at the sound.

"Your mother is right, though," she said. "You should never approach any strange animal without permission until you know it's safe."

"Can I pet one?"

"Sure thing. King. Forward."

One of the lean black-and-white border collies obeyed and sidled toward them, sniffing eagerly at Alex's legs. The boy giggled and began to pet the dog with sheer joy.

"This was such a great idea," Laura said, smiling as she watched her son. "Thank you so much for the invitation, Caidy."

"You're welcome. Believe me, it will be a fun break for me from normal ranch stuff. Spring is always crazy on the ranch and I've been looking forward to this all week as a great respite."

She paused. "I have to tell you, I'm really glad you're still willing to have anything to do with the Bowmans after the way things ended with Taft."

She really didn't want to talk about Taft. This was what she had worried about after Caidy extended the invitation, that things might be awkward between them because of the past.

"Why wouldn't I? Taft and I are still friendly." And that's all they ever *would* be, she reminded herself. "Just because he and I didn't end up the way we thought we would doesn't mean I should shun his family. I loved your family. I'm only sorry I haven't stayed in touch all these years. I see no reason we can't be friends now, unless you're too uncomfortable because of…everything?"

"Not at all!" Caidy exclaimed. Laura had the impression she wanted to say something else, but Alex interrupted before she could.

"He licked me. It tickles!"

Caidy grinned down at the boy's obvious enjoyment of the dogs. He now had all three dogs clustered around him and was petting them in turns.

"We've got puppies. Would you like to see them?" Caidy asked.

"Puppies!" Maya squealed, still in her arms, while Alex clasped his hands together, a reverential look on his face.

"Puppies! Oh, Mama, can we?"

She had to laugh at his flair for drama. "Sure. Why not? As long as it's all right with Caidy."

"They're in the barn. I was just checking on the little family a few minutes ago and it looks like a few of the pups are awake and might just be in the mood to play."

"Oh, yay!" Alex exclaimed and Caidy grinned at him.

They followed her into the barn. For Laura, it was like walking back in time. The barn smelled of hay and leather and animals, and the familiar scent mix seemed to trigger an avalanche of memories. They tumbled free of whatever place she'd stowed them after she walked away from Pine Gulch, jostling and shoving their way through her mind before she had a chance to block them out.

She used to come out to the ranch often to ride horses with Taft and their rides always started here, in the barn, where he would teach her about the different kinds of tack and how each was used, then patiently give her lessons on how to tack up a horse.

One wintry January afternoon, she suddenly remembered, she had helped him and his father deliver a foal. She could still vividly picture her astonishment at the gangly, awkward miracle of the creature.

Unbidden, she also remembered that the relative privacy of the barn compared to other places on the ranch had been one of their favorite places to kiss. Sultry, long, intense kisses that would leave them both hungry for more....

She absolutely did not need to remember *those* particular memories, full of heat and discovery and that all-consuming love that used to burn inside her for Taft. With great effort, she struggled to wrestle them back into the corner of her mind and slam the door to them so she could focus on her children and Caidy and new puppies.

The puppies' home was an empty stall at the end of the row. An old russet saddle blanket took up one corner and the mother dog, a lovely black-and-white heeler, was lying on her side taking a rest and watching her puppies wrestle around the straw-covered floor of the stall. She looked up when Caidy approached and her tail slapped a greeting.

"Hey, Betsy, here I am again. How's my best girl? I brought some company to entertain your pups for a while."

Laura could swear she saw understanding and even relief in the dog's brown eyes as Caidy unlatched the door of the stall and swung it out. She could relate to that look—every night when her children finally closed their eyes, she would collapse onto the sofa with probably that same sort of look.

"Are you sure it's okay?" Alex asked, standing outside the stall, barely containing his nervous energy.

"Perfectly sure," Caidy answered. "I promise, they love company."

He headed inside and—just as she might have predicted—Maya wriggled to get down. "Me, too," she insisted.

"Of course, darling," Laura said. She set her on her feet and the girl headed inside the stall to stand beside her brother.

"Here, sit down and I'll bring you a puppy each," Caidy said, gesturing to a low bench inside the stall, really just a plank stretched across a couple of overturned oats buckets.

She picked up a fat, waddling black-and-white puppy from the writhing, yipping mass and set it on Alex's lap, then reached into the pile again for a smaller one, mostly black this time.

Now she had some very different but infinitely precious memories of this barn to add to her collection, Laura thought a few moments later. The children were enthralled with the puppies. Children and puppies just seemed to go together like peanut butter and jelly. Alex and Maya giggled as the puppies squirmed around on their laps, licking and sniffing. Maya hugged hers as enthusiastically as she had hugged her mother a few minutes earlier.

"Thank you for this," she said to Caidy as the two of them smiled at the children and puppies. "You've thrilled them to their socks."

"I'm afraid the pups are a little dirty and don't smell the greatest. They're a little young for baths yet."

"I don't worry about a little dirt," Laura said. "I've always figured if my kids don't get dirty sometimes, I'm doing something wrong."

"I don't think you're doing *anything* wrong," Caidy assured her. "They seem like great kids."

"Thank you."

"It can't be easy, especially now that you're on your own."

As much as Javier had loved the children, she had always felt very much on her own in Madrid. He was always busy with the hotel and his friends and, of course, his other women. Bad enough she had shared that with Taft. She certainly wasn't about to share that information with his sister.

"I have my mother to help me now. She's been a lifesaver."

Coming home had been the right decision. As much as she had struggled with taking her children away from half of their heritage probably forever, Javier's family had never been very welcoming to her. They had become even less so after Maya was born, as if Laura were to blame somehow for the genetic abnormality.

"I'm just going to come out and say this, okay?"

Caidy said after a moment. "I really wish you had married Taft so we could have been sisters."

"Thank you," she said, touched by the words.

"I mean it. You were the best thing that ever happened to him. We all thought so. Compared to the women he... Well, compared to anybody else he's dated, you're a million times better. I still can't believe any brother of mine was stupid enough to let you slip through his fingers. Don't think I haven't told him so, too."

She didn't know quite how to answer—or why she had this sudden urge to protect him. Taft hadn't been stupid, only hurt and lost and not at all ready for marriage.

She hadn't been ready, either, although it had taken her a few years to admit that to herself. At twenty-one, she had been foolish enough to think her love should have been enough to help him heal from the pain and anger of losing his parents in such a violent way, when he hadn't even had the resolution of the murderers being caught and brought to justice.

An idealistic, romantic young woman and an angry, bitter young man would have made a terrible combination, she thought as she sat here in this quiet barn while the puppies wriggled around with her children and a horse stamped and snorted somewhere nearby.

"I also have a confession." Caidy shifted beside her at the stall door.

She raised an eyebrow. "Do I really want to hear this?"

"Please don't be mad, okay?"

For some reason, Laura was strongly reminded of Caidy as she had known her a decade ago, the lighthearted, mischievous teenager who thought she could tease and cajole her way out of any situation.

"Tell me. What did you do?" she asked, amusement fighting the sudden apprehension curling through her.

Before the other woman could answer, a male voice rang out through the barn. "Caidy? Are you in here?"

Her stomach dropped and the little flutters of apprehension became wild-winged flaps of anxiety.

Caidy winced. "Um, I may have casually mentioned to Taft that you and the children were coming out to the ranch today and that we might be going up on the Aspen Leaf Trail, if he wanted to tag along."

So much for her master plan of escaping the inn today so she could keep her children—and herself— out from underfoot while he was working on the other renovations.

"Are you mad?" Caidy asked.

She forced a smile when she really wanted to sit right down on the straw-covered floor of the stall and cry.

Yes, when she decided to return to Pine Gulch, she had known seeing him again was inevitable. She just hadn't expected to bump into the dratted man every flipping time she turned around.

"Why would I be mad? Your brother and I are friends." Or at least she was working hard at pretending they could be. Anyway, this was his family's ranch. Some part of her had known when she accepted Caidy's invitation to come out for a visit that there was a chance he might be here.

"Oh, good. I was worried things might be weird between the two of you."

But you invited him along anyway? she wanted to

ask, but decided that sounded rude. "No. It's perfectly fine," she lied.

"I thought he could lend a hand with the children. He's really patient with them. In fact, he's the one who taught Gabi to ride. Gabi is the daughter of Becca, Trace's fiancée. Anyway, it's always good to have another experienced rider on hand when you've got kids who haven't been on a horse before."

"Caidy?" he called again.

"Back here, with the puppies," she returned.

A moment later, Taft rounded the corner of a support beam. At the sight of him, everything inside her seemed to shiver.

Okay, really? This was getting ridiculous. She huffed. So far since she had been back in town, she had seen the man in full firefighter turnout gear when he and his crew responded to the inn fire, wearing a low-slung construction belt while he worked on the renovations at the inn, and now he was dressed in worn jeans, cowboy boots and a tan Stetson that made him look dark and dangerous.

Was he purposely trying to look as if he just stepped off every single page of a beefcake calendar?

Taft Bowman—doing his part to fulfill any woman's fantasy.

"Here you are," he said with that irresistible smile.

She couldn't breathe suddenly as the dust motes floating on the air inside the barn seemed to choke her lungs. This wasn't really fair. Why hadn't his hair started to thin a little in the past decade or his gut started to paunch?

He was so blasted gorgeous and she was completely weak around him.

He leaned in to kiss his sister on the cheek. After a little awkward hesitation, much to her dismay he leaned in to kiss her on the cheek, as well. She could do nothing but endure the brush of his mouth on her skin as the familiar scent of him, outdoorsy and male, filled her senses, unleashing another flood of memories.

Before she could make her brain cooperate and think of something to say, her children noticed him for the first time.

"Hi!" Maya beamed with delight.

"Hey, pumpkin. How are things?"

"Look! Puppies!"

She thrust the endlessly patient black puppy at him and Taft graciously accepted the dog. "He's a cute one. What's his name, Caid?"

"Puppy Number Five," she answered. "I don't name them when I sell them as pups without training. I let their new owners do it."

"Look at this one." Alex pushed past his sister to hold up his own chubby little canine friend.

"Nice," Taft said. He knelt right there in the straw and was soon covered in puppies and kids. Even the tired-looking mother dog came over to him for affection.

"Hey, Betsy. How are you holding up with this brood?" he asked, rubbing the dog between the ears and earning a besotted look that Laura found completely exasperating.

"Thanks for coming out," Caidy said.

"Not a problem. I can think of few things I enjoy more than going on a spring ride into the mountains."

"Not too far into the mountains," she assured Laura.

"We can't go very far this time of year anyway. Too much snow, at least for a good month or so."

"Aspen Leaf is open, though, isn't it?"

"Yes. Destry and I checked it the other day. She was disappointed to miss the ride today, by the way," Caidy told Laura. "Becca was taking her and Gabi into Idaho Falls for fittings for their flower-girl dresses."

"And you missed out on all that girly fun?" Taft asked, climbing to his feet and coming to stand beside his sister and Laura. Suddenly she felt crowded by his heat and size and...maleness.

"Are you kidding? This will be much more enjoyable. If you haven't heard, Trace is getting hitched in June," she said to Laura.

"To Pine Gulch's newest attorney, if you can believe that," Taft added.

She *had* heard and she was happy for Trace. He had always been very kind to her. Trace, the Pine Gulch police chief, had always struck her as much more serious than Taft, the kind of person who liked to think things through before he spoke.

For being identical twins, Taft and Trace had two very unique personalities, and even though they were closer than most brothers, they had also actively cultivated friendships beyond each other, probably because of their mother's wise influence.

She did find it interesting that both of them had chosen professions in the public-safety sector, although Trace had taken a route through the military to becoming a policeman while Taft had gravitated toward fire safety and becoming a paramedic.

"Why don't we give the kids another few minutes

with the puppies?" Caidy said. "I've already saddled a couple of horses I thought would be a good fit."

"Do I need to saddle Joe?"

"Nope. He's ready for you."

Taft grinned. "You mean all I had to do today was show up?"

"That's the story of your life, isn't it?" Caidy said with a disgruntled sort of affection. "If you want to, I'll let you unsaddle everybody when we're done and groom all the horses. Will that make you feel better?"

"Much. Thanks."

The puppy on Maya's lap wriggled through her fingers and waddled over to squat in the straw.

"Look," she exclaimed with an inordinate degree of delight. "Puppy pee!"

Taft chuckled at that. "I think all the puppies are ready for a snack and a nap. Why don't we go see if the horses are ready for us?"

"Yes!" Maya beamed and scampered eagerly toward Taft, where she reached up to grab his hand. After a stunned sort of moment, he smiled at her and folded her hand more securely in his much bigger one.

Alex rose reluctantly and set the puppy he had been playing with down in the straw. "Bye," he whispered, a look of naked longing clear for all to see.

"I hear the kid wants a dog. You know you're going to have to cave, don't you?" Taft spoke in a low voice.

Laura sighed through her own dismay. "You don't think I'm tough enough to resist a six-year-old?"

"I'm not sure a hardened criminal could resist *that* particular six-year-old."

He was right, darn it. She was pretty sure she would have to give in and let her son have a dog. Not a border collie, certainly, because they were active dogs and needed work to do, but she would find something.

As they walked outside the barn toward the horse pasture, she saw Alex's eyes light up at the sight of four horses saddled and waiting. Great. Now he would probably start begging her for a horse, too.

She had to admit, a little burst of excitement kicked through her, too, as they approached the animals. She loved horses and she actually had Taft to thank for that. Unlike many of her schoolmates in the sprawling Pine Gulch school district, which encompassed miles of ranch land, she was a city girl who walked or rode her bike to school instead of taking the bus. Even though she had loved horses from the time she was young—didn't most girls?—her parents had patiently explained they didn't have room for one of their own at their home adjacent to the inn.

She had enjoyed riding with friends who lived outside of town, but had very much considered herself a greenhorn until she became friends with Taft. Even before they started dating, she would often come out to the ranch and ride with him and sometimes Caidy into the mountains.

This would be rather like old times—which, come to think of it, wasn't necessarily a good thing.

Since moving away from Pine Gulch, she hadn't been on a horse one single time, she realized with shock. Even more reason for this little thrum of anticipation.

"Wow, they're really big," Alex said in a soft voice. Maya seemed nervous as well, clinging tightly to Taft's hand.

"Big doesn't have to mean scary," Taft assured him. "These are really gentle horses. None of them will hurt you. I promise. Old Pete, the horse you're going to ride, is so lazy, you'll be lucky to make it around the barn before he decides to stop and take a nap."

Alex giggled but it had a nervous edge to it and Taft gave him a closer look.

"Do you want to meet him?"

Her son toed the dirt with the shiny new cowboy boots she had picked up at the farm-implement store before they drove out to the ranch. "I guess. You sure they don't bite?"

"Some horses do. Not any of the River Bow horses. I swear it."

He picked Maya up in his arms and reached for Alex's hand, leading them both over to the smallest of the horses, a gray with a calm, rather sweet face.

"This is Pete," Taft said. "He's just about the gentlest horse we've ever had here at River Bow. He'll treat you right, kid."

As she watched from the sidelines, the horse bent his head down and lipped Alex's shoulder. Alex froze, eyes wide and slightly terrified, but Taft set a reassuring hand on his other shoulder. "Don't worry. He's just looking for a treat."

"I don't have a treat." Alex's voice quavered a bit. These uncharacteristic moments of fear from her usually bold, mischievous son always seemed to take her by surprise, although she knew they were perfectly normal from a developmental standpoint.

Taft reached into his pocket and pulled out a handful of small red apples. "You're in luck. I always carry a supply of crab apples for old Pete. They're his favorite, probably because I can let him have only a few at a time. It's probably like you eating pizza. A little is great, but too much would make you sick. Same for Pete and crab apples."

"Where on earth do you find crab apples in April?" Laura couldn't resist asking.

"That's my secret."

Caidy snorted. "Not much of a secret," she said. "Every year, my crazy brother gathers up two or three bushels from the tree on the side of the house and stores them down in the root cellar. Nobody else will touch the things—they're too bitter even for pies unless you pour in cup after cup of sugar—but old Pete loves them. Every year Taft puts up a supply so he's got something to bring the old codger."

She shouldn't find it so endearing to imagine him picking crab apples to give to an old, worn-out horse— or to watch his ears turn as red as the apples under his cowboy hat.

He handed one of the pieces of sour fruit to her son and showed him the correct way to feed the horse. Alex held his hand out flat and old Pete lapped it up.

"It tickles like the dog," Alex exclaimed.

"But it doesn't hurt, right?" Taft asked.

The boy shook his head with a grin. "Nope. Just tickles. Hi, Pete."

The horse seemed quite pleased to make his acquaintance, especially after he produced a few more crab apples for the horse, handed to him by Taft.

"Ready to hop up there now?" Taft asked. When the boy nodded, Caidy stepped up with a pair of riding helmets waiting on the fence.

"We're going to swap that fancy cowboy hat for a helmet, okay?"

"I like my cowboy hat, though. I just got it."

"And you can wear it again when we get back. But when you're just learning to ride, wearing a helmet is safer."

"Just like at home when you have to wear your bicycle helmet," Laura told him.

"No helmet, no horse," Taft said sternly.

Her son gave them all a grudging look, but he removed his cowboy hat and handed it to his mother, then allowed Caidy to fasten on the safety helmet. Caidy took Maya from Taft and put one on her, as well, which eased Laura's safety worries considerably.

Finally Taft picked up Alex and hefted him easily into the saddle. The glee on her son's face filled her with a funny mix of happiness and apprehension. He was growing up, embracing risks, and she wasn't sure she was ready for that.

Caidy stepped up to adjust the stirrups to the boy's height. "There you go, cowboy. That should be better."

"What do I do now?" Alex asked with an eager look up into the mountains as if he were ready to go join a posse and hunt for outlaws right this minute.

"Well, the great thing about Pete is how easygoing he is," Taft assured him. "He's happy to just follow along behind the other horses. That's kind of his specialty and what makes him a perfect horse for somebody just beginning. I'll hold his lead line so you won't even have to worry about turning him or making him slow down or anything. Next time you come out to the ranch we'll work on those other things, but this time is just for fun."

Next time? She frowned, annoyed that he would give Alex the impression there would be another time—and that Taft would be part of it, if she ever did bring the kids out to River Bow again. Children didn't forget things like that. Alex would hold him to it and be gravely disappointed if a return trip never materialized.

This was not going at all like she'd planned. She and Caidy were supposed to be taking the children for an easy ride. Instead Taft seemed to have taken over, in typical fashion, while Caidy answered her cell phone a short distance away from the group.

After a moment, Maya grew impatient and tugged on his jeans. "My horse?" she asked, looking around at the animals. She looked so earnest and adorable that it was tough for Laura to stay annoyed at anything.

He smiled down at her with such gentleness that her chest ached. "I was thinking you could just ride with me on my old friend Joe. What do you say, pumpkin? We'll try a pony for you another day, okay?"

She appeared to consider this, looking first at the big black gelding he pointed at, then back at Taft. Finally she gave him that brilliant, wide heartbreaker of a smile. "Okay."

Taft Bowman may have met his match for sheer charm, she thought.

"I guess that just leaves me," she said, eyeing the two remaining horses. Something told her the dappled gray-and-black mare was Caidy's, which left the bay for her.

"Do you need a crab apple to break the ice, too?" Taft asked with a teasing smile so appealing she had to turn away.

"I think I'll manage," she said more tersely than she intended. She modified her tone to be a little warmer. "What's her name?"

"Lacey," he answered.

"Hi, Lacey." She stroked the horse's neck and was

rewarded with an equine raspberry sound that made Alex laugh.

"That sounded like her mouth farted!" he exclaimed.

"That's just her way of saying hi." Taft's gaze met hers, laughter brimming in his green eyes, and Laura wanted to sink into those eyes.

Darn the man.

She stiffened her shoulders and resolve and shoved her boot in the stirrup, then swung into the saddle and tried not to groan at the pull of muscles she hadn't used in a long time.

Taft pulled the horse's reins off the tether and handed them to her. Their hands brushed again, a slight touch of skin against skin, and she quickly pulled the reins to the other side and jerked her attention away from her reaction to Taft and back to the thousand-pound animal beneath her.

Oh, she had missed this, she thought, loosely holding the reins and reacquainting herself to the unique feel of being on a horse. She had missed all of it. The stretch of her muscles, the heat of the sun on her bare head, the vast peaks of the Tetons in the distance.

"You ready, sweetie?" he asked Maya, who nodded, although the girl suddenly looked a little shy.

"Everything will be just fine," he assured her. "I won't let go. I promise."

He loosed his horse's reins from the hitch as well as the lead line for old Pete before setting Maya in the saddle. Her daughter looked small and vulnerable at such a height, even under her safety helmet, but she had to trust that Taft would take care of her.

"While I mount up, you hold on right there. It's called the saddle horn. Got it?"

"Got it," she mimicked. "Horn."

"Excellent. Hang on, now. I'll keep one hand on you."

Laura watched anxiously, afraid Maya would slide off at the inevitable jostling of the saddle, but she needn't have worried. He swung effortlessly into the saddle, then scooped an arm around the girl.

"Caid? You coming?" Taft called.

She glanced over and saw Caidy finish her phone conversation and tuck her cell into her pocket, then walk toward them, her features tight with concern. "We've got a problem."

"What's wrong?"

"That was Ridge. A speeder just hit a dog a quarter mile or so from the front ranch gates. Ridge was right behind the idiot and saw the whole thing happen."

"One of yours?" Taft asked.

Her braid swung as she shook her head. "No. I think it's a little stray I've seen around the last few weeks. I've been trying to coax him to come closer to the house but he's pretty skittish. Looks like he's got a broken leg and Ridge isn't sure what to do with him."

"Can't he take him to the vet?"

"He can't reach Doc Harris. I guess he's been trying to find the backup vet but he's in the middle of equine surgery up at Cold Creek Ranch. I should go help. Poor guy."

"Ridge or the stray?"

"Both. Ridge is a little out of his element with dogs. He can handle horses and cattle, but anything smaller than a calf throws him off his game." She paused and sent a guilty look toward Laura. "I'm sorry to do this after I invited you out and all, but do you think you'll be okay with only my brother as a guide while I go help with this injured dog?"

If not for the look in Caidy's eyes, Laura might have thought she had manufactured the whole thing as an elaborate ruse to throw her and Taft together. But either Caidy was an excellent actress or her distress was genuine.

"Of course. Don't worry about a thing. Do you need our help?"

The other woman shook her head again. "I doubt it. To be honest, I'm not sure there's anything *I* can do, but I have to try, right? I'm just sorry to invite you out here and then ditch you."

"No worries. We should be fine. We're not going far, are we?"

Taft shook his head. "Up the hill about a mile. There's a nice place to stop and have the picnic Caidy packed."

She did *not* feel like having a picnic with him but could think of no graceful way to extricate herself and her children from it, especially when Alex and Maya appeared to be having the time of their lives.

"Thanks for being understanding," Caidy said, with a harried look, unsaddling the other horse at lightning speed. "I'll make it up to you."

"No need," Laura said as her horse took a step or two sideways, anxious to go. "Take care of the stray for us."

"I'll do my best. Maybe I'll try to catch up with you. If I don't make it, though, I'll probably see you later after you come back down."

She glanced up at the sky. "Looks like a few clouds gathering up on the mountain peaks. I hope it doesn't rain on you."

"They're pretty high. We should be fine for a few hours," Taft said. "Good luck with the dog. Shall we, guys?"

Leaving Caidy behind to deal with a crisis felt rude and selfish, but Laura didn't know what else to do. The children would be terribly disappointed if she backed out of the ride, and Caidy was right. What could they do to help her with the injured dog?

She sighed. And of course this also meant she and the children would have to be alone with Taft.

She supposed it was a very good thing Taft had no reason to be romantically interested in her anymore. She had a feeling she would be even more weak than normal on a horseback ride with him into the mountains, especially when she had so many memories of other times and other rides that usually ended with them making out somewhere on the ranch.

"Yes," she finally said. "Let's go."

The sooner they could be on their way, the quicker they could return and she and her children could go back to the way things were before Taft burst so insistently back into her life.

CHAPTER SEVEN

WITH MAYA PERCHED in front of him, Taft led the way and held the lead line for Alex's horse while Laura brought up the rear. A light breeze danced in her hair as they traveled through verdant pastureland on their way to a trailhead just above the ranch.

The afternoon seemed eerily familiar, a definite déjà vu moment. It took her a moment to realize why—she used to fantasize about a day exactly like this when she had been young and full of dreams. She used to imagine the two of them spending a lovely spring afternoon together on horseback along with their children, laughing and talking, pausing here and there for some of those kisses she had once been so addicted to.

Okay, they had the horses and the kids here and definitely the lovely spring afternoon, but the rest of it wasn't going to happen. Not on her watch.

She focused on the trail, listening to Alex jabber a mile a minute about everything he saw, from the double-trunked pine tree alongside the trail, to one of Caidy's dogs that had come along with them, to about how much he loved old Pete. The gist, as she fully expected, was that he now wanted a horse *and* a dog of his own.

The air here smelled delicious: sharp, citrusy pine, the tart, evocative scent of sagebrush, woodsy earth and new growth.

She had missed the scent of the mountains. Madrid had its own distinctive smells, flowers and spices and baking bread, but this, this was home.

They rode for perhaps forty minutes until Alex's chatter started to die away. It was hard work staying atop a horse. Even if the rest of him wasn't sore, she imagined his jaw muscles must be aching.

The deceptively easy grade led one to think they weren't gaining much in altitude, but finally they reached a clearing where the pines and aspens opened up and she could look down on the ranch and see its eponymous river bow, a spot where the river's course made a horseshoe bend, almost folding in on itself. The water glimmered in the afternoon sunlight, reflecting the mountains and trees around it.

She admired the sight from atop her horse, grateful that Taft had stopped, then realized he was dismounting with Maya still in his arms.

"I imagine your rear end could use a little rest," he said to Alex, earning a giggle.

"Sí," he said, reverting to the Spanish he sometimes still used. "My bum hurts and I need to pee," he said.

"We can take care of that. Maya, you sit here while I help your brother." He set the girl atop a couch-size boulder, then returned to the horses and lifted Alex down, then turned to Laura again. "What about you? Need a hand?"

"I've got it," she answered, quite certain it wouldn't be a good idea for him to help her dismount.

Her muscles were stiff, even after such a short time on the horse, and she welcomed the chance to stretch her legs a little. "Come on, Alex. I'll take you over to the bushes. Maya, do you need to go?"

She shook her head, busy picking flowers.

"I'll keep an eye on her," Taft said. "Unless you need me on tree duty?"

She shook her head, amused despite herself, at the term. "I've got it."

As she walked away, she didn't want to think about what a good team they made or how very similar this was to those fantasies she used to weave.

Alex thought it was quite a novel thing to take care of his business against a tree and didn't even complain when she whipped the hand sanitizer out of her pocket and made him use it afterward.

The moment they returned to the others, Caidy's dog King brought a stick over and dropped it at Alex's feet, apparently knowing an easy mark when he saw one. Alex picked up the stick and chucked it for the dog as far as his little arm could go and the dog bounded after it while Maya clapped her hands with excitement.

"Me next," she said.

The two were perfectly content to play with the dog and Laura was just as content to lean against a sun-warmed granite boulder and watch them while she listened to a meadowlark's familiar song.

Idaho is a pretty little place. That's what her mother always used to say the birds were trilling. The memory made her smile.

"I can picture you just like that when you were younger. Your hair was longer, but you haven't changed much at all."

He had leaned his hip against the boulder where she sat and her body responded instantly to his proximity, to the familiar scent of him. She edged away so their shoulders wouldn't brush and wondered if he noticed.

"I'm afraid that's where you're wrong. I'm a very different person. Who doesn't change in ten years?"

"Yeah, you're right. I'm not the same man I was a decade ago. I like to think I'm smarter these days about holding on to what's important."

"Do you ride often?" she asked.

A glint in his eye told her he knew very well she didn't want to tug on that particular conversational line, but he went along with the obvious change of topic. "Not as much as I would like. My niece, Destry, loves to ride and now Gabi has caught the bug. As often as they can manage it, they do their best to persuade one of us to take them for a ride. I haven't been up for a few months, though."

He obviously loved his niece. She had already noticed that soft note in his voice when he talked about the girl. She would have expected it. The Bowmans had always been a close, loving family before their parents' brutal murder. She expected they would welcome Becca and her sister into the family's embrace, as well.

"Too busy with your social life?"

The little niggle of envy under her skin turned her tone more caustic than she intended, but he didn't seem offended.

He even chuckled. "Sure. If by *social life* you mean the house I'm building on the edge of town that's filled all my waking hours for the last six months. I haven't had much room for other things."

"You're building it yourself?"

"Most of it. I've had help here and there. Plumbing. HVAC. That sort of thing. I don't have the patience for good drywall work, so I paid somebody else to do that, too. But I've done all the carpentry and most of the electrical. I can give you some good names of sub-contractors I trust if you decide to do more on the inn."

"Why a house?"

He appeared to be giving her question serious thought as he watched the children playing with the dog, with the grand sprawl of the ranch below them. "I guess I was tired of throwing away rent money and living in a little apartment where I didn't have room to stretch out. I've had this land for a long time. I don't know. Seemed like it was time."

"You're building a house. That's pretty permanent. Does that mean you're planning to stay in Pine Gulch?"

He shrugged, and despite her efforts to keep as much distance as possible between them, his big shoulder still brushed hers. "Where else would I go? Maybe I should have taken off for somewhere exotic when I had the chance. What do they pay firefighters in Madrid?"

"I'm afraid I have no idea. I have friends I can ask, though." He would fit in well there, she thought, and the *madrileñas*—the women of Madrid—would go crazy for his green eyes and teasing smile.

Which he utilized to full effect on her now. "That eager to get rid of me?"

She had no answer to that, so she again changed the subject. "Where did you say your house was?"

"A couple of miles from here, near the mouth of Cold Creek Canyon. I've got about five acres there in the trees. Enough room to move over some of my own horses eventually."

He paused, an oddly intent look in his green eyes. "You ought to come see it sometime. I would even let Alex pound a couple of nails if he wanted."

She couldn't afford to spend more time with him,

not when he seemed already to be sneaking past all her careful defenses. "I'm sure we've got all the nails Alex could wish to pound at the inn."

"Sure. Yeah. Of course." He nodded, appearing nonchalant, but she had the impression she had hurt him somehow.

She wanted to make it right, tell him she would love to come see his house under construction anytime he wanted them to, but she caught the ridiculous words before she could blurt them out.

Taft picked up an early-spring wildflower—she thought it might be some kind of phlox—and twirled it between his fingers, his gaze on the children playing with the dog. This time he was the one who picked another subject. "How are the kids settling into Pine Gulch?"

"So far they're loving it, especially having their grandmother around."

"What about you?"

She looked out over the ranch and at the mountains in the distance. "It's good. There are a lot of things I love about being home, things I missed more than I realized while I was in Spain. Those mountains, for instance. I had forgotten how truly quiet and peaceful it could be here."

"This is one of my favorite places on the ranch."

"I remember."

Her soft words hung between them and she heartily wished she could yank them back. Tension suddenly seethed between them and she saw that he also remembered the significance of this place.

Right here in this flower-strewn meadow was where they had kissed that first time when he had returned after the dangerous flashover. She had always considered it their place, and every time she came here after that, she remembered the sheer joy bursting through her as he finally—finally!—saw her as more than just his friend.

They had come here often after that. He had proposed, right here, while they were stretched out on a blanket in the meadow grass.

She suddenly knew it was no accident he had stopped the horses here. Anger pumped through her, hot and fierce, that he would dredge up all these hopes and dreams and emotions she had buried after she left Pine Gulch.

With jerky motions, she climbed off the boulder. "We should probably be heading back."

His mouth tightened and he looked as if he wanted to say something else but he seemed to change his mind. "Yeah, you're right. That sky is looking a little ominous."

She looked up to find dark clouds smearing the sky, a perfect match to her mood, as if she had conjured them. "Where did those come from? A minute ago it was perfectly sunny."

"It's springtime in Idaho, where you can enjoy all four seasons in a single afternoon. Caidy warned us about possible rain. I should have been paying more attention. You ready, kids?" he called. "We've got to go."

Alex frowned from where he and Maya were flopped in the dirt petting the dog. "Do we have to?"

"Unless you want to get drenched and have to ride down on a mud slide all the way to the ranch."

"Can we?" Alex asked eagerly.

Taft laughed, although it sounded strained around

the edges. "Not this time. It's up to us to make sure the ladies make it back in one piece. Think you're up to it?"

If she hadn't been so annoyed with Taft, she might have laughed at the way Alex puffed out his little chest. "Yes, sir," he answered.

"Up you go, then, son." He lifted the boy up onto the saddle and adjusted his helmet before he turned back to Maya.

"What about you, Maya, my girl? Are you ready?"

Her daughter beamed and scampered toward him. Watching them all only hardened Laura's intention to fortify her defenses around Taft.

One person in her family needed to resist the man. By the looks of things, she was the only one up for the job.

Maybe.

THEY NEARLY MADE IT.

About a quarter mile from the ranch, the clouds finally let loose, unleashing a torrent of rain in one of those spring showers that come on so fast, so cold and merciless that they had no time to really prepare themselves.

By the time they reached the barn, Alex was shivering, Laura's hair was bedraggled and Taft was kicking himself for not hurrying them down the hill a little faster. At least Maya stayed warm and dry, wrapped in the spare raincoat he pulled out of his saddlebag.

He took them straight to the house instead of the barn. After he climbed quickly down from his horse, he set Laura's little girl on the porch, then quickly returned to the horses to help Alex dismount.

"Head on up to the porch with your sister," he ordered. After making sure the boy complied, he reached up without waiting for permission and lifted Laura down, as well. He winced as her slight frame trembled when he set her onto solid ground again.

"I'm sorry," he said. "I should have been paying better attention to the weather. That storm took me by surprise."

Her teeth chattered and her lips had a blue tinge to them he didn't like at all. "It's okay. My SUV has a good heater. We'll warm up soon enough."

"Forget it. You're not going home in wet clothes. Come inside and we'll find something you and the kids can change into."

"It's fine. We'll be home in fifteen minutes."

"If I let you go home cold and wet, I would never hear the end of it from Caidy. Trust me—the wrath of Caidy is a fearful thing and she would shoot me if I let you get sick. Come on. The horses can wait out here for a minute."

He scooped both kids into his arms, much to their giggly enjoyment, and carried them into the ranch house to cut off any further argument. That they could still laugh under such cold and miserable conditions touched something deep inside him.

He loved these kids already. How had that happened? Alex, with his million questions, Maya with her loving spirit and eager smile. Somehow when he wasn't looking, they had tiptoed straight into his heart and he had a powerful feeling he wasn't going to be able to shoo them out again anytime soon.

He wanted more afternoons like this one, full of fun and laughter and this sense of belonging. Hell, he wasn't picky. He would take mornings or evenings or any time he could have with Laura and her kids.

Yet Laura seemed quite determined to keep adding bricks to the wall between them. Every time he felt as if he was maybe making a little progress, she built up another layer and he didn't know what the hell to do about it.

"Here's the plan," he said when she trailed reluctantly inside after him. "You get the kids out of their wet clothes and wrapped in warm blankets. We've got a gas fireplace in the TV room that will warm you up in a second. Meanwhile, I'll see what I can do about finding something for you to wear."

"This is ridiculous. Honestly, Taft, we can be home and changed into our own clothes in the time it's going to take you to find something here."

He aimed a stern look at her. "Forget it. I'm not letting you leave this ranch until you're dry, and that's the end of it. I'm a paramedic, trained in public safety. How would it look if the Pine Gulch fire chief stood around twiddling his thumbs while his town's newest citizens got hypothermia?"

"Oh, stop exaggerating. We're not going to get hypothermia," she muttered, but she still followed him to the media room of the ranch house, a big, comfortable space with multiple sofas and recliners.

This happened to be one of his favorite rooms at River Bow Ranch, a place where he and his brothers often gathered to watch college football and NBA basketball.

He flipped the switch for the fireplace. The blower immediately came on, throwing welcome heat into the room while he grabbed a couple of blankets from behind one of the leather sofas for the kids.

"Here you go. You guys shuck your duds and wrap up in these blankets."

"Really?" Alex looked wide-eyed. "Can we, Mama?"

"Just for a few minutes, while we throw our clothes in the dryer."

"I'll be back in a second with something of Caidy's for you," he told her.

He headed into his sister's room and quickly found a pair of sweats and a hooded sweatshirt in the immaculately organized walk-in closet.

By the time he returned to the TV room, the children were bundled in blankets and cuddled up on the couch. He set the small pile of clothes on the edge of the sofa.

"Here you go. I know Caidy won't mind if you borrow them. The only thing in this situation that would make her angry would be if I *didn't* give you dry clothes."

Even though her mouth tightened as if she wanted to argue, she only nodded. The wet locks of hair hanging loosely around her face somehow made her even more beautiful to him. She seemed delicate and vulnerable here in the flickering firelight, and he wanted to tuck her up against him and keep her safe forever.

Yeah, he probably should keep that particular desire to himself for the moment.

"Give me a few minutes to take care of the horses and then I can throw your clothes in the dryer."

"I think I can probably manage to find the laundry room by myself," she murmured. "I'll just toss everything in there together after I change."

"Okay. I'll be back in a few minutes."

Caring for the horses took longer than he'd hoped. He was out of practice, he guessed, plus he had three horses to unsaddle.

When he finally finished up in the barn about half an hour later, the rain was still pouring in sheets that slanted sideways from the wind. Harsh, punishing drops cut into him as he headed back up the porch steps and into the entryway.

Caidy wouldn't be happy about him dripping all over her floor but she would probably forgive him, especially because he had done his best to take good care of the horses—and her guests. That would go a long way toward keeping him out of the doghouse.

He headed into Ridge's room to swipe a dry pair of jeans and a soft green henley. After quickly changing, he walked through the house in his bare feet to the TV room to check on Laura and her kids.

When he opened the door, she pressed a finger to her mouth and gestured to one of the sofas. He followed her gaze and found both Alex and Maya asleep, wrapped in blankets and nestled together like Caidy's puppies while a cartoon on the television murmured softly in the background.

"Wow, that was fast," he whispered. "How did *that* happen?"

She rose with a sidelong look at her sleeping children and led the way back into the hall. She had changed into Caidy's clothes, he could see, and pulled her damp hair back into a ponytail. In the too-big hoodie, she looked young and sweet and very much like the girl he had fallen in love with.

"It's been a big afternoon for them, full of much more excitement than they're used to, and Maya, at least, missed her nap. Of course, Alex insists he's too old for a nap, but every once in a while he still falls asleep in front of the TV."

"Yeah, I have that problem, too, sometimes."

"Really? With all that company I've heard you keep? That must be so disappointing for them."

He frowned. "I don't know what you've heard, but the rumors about my social life are greatly exaggerated."

"Are they?"

He didn't want to talk about this now. What he wanted to do was wrap his arms around her, press her up against that wall and kiss her for the next five or six hours. Because he couldn't do that, he figured he should at least try to set the record straight.

"After you broke things off and left for Spain, I... went a little crazy, I'll admit." He had mostly been trying to forget her and the aching emptiness she left behind, but he wasn't quite ready to confess that much to her. A few years later when he found out she had married another man in Madrid and was expecting a baby, he hadn't seen any reason for restraint.

"I did a lot more drinking and partying than I should have. I'm not particularly proud of who I was back then. The thing is, a guy gets a reputation around Pine Gulch and that's how people tend to see him forever. I haven't been that wild in a long time."

"You don't have to explain yourself to me, Taft," she said, rather stiffly.

"I don't want you to think I'm the Cold Creek Casanova people seem to think."

"What does it matter what I think?"

"It matters," he said simply and couldn't resist taking

her hand. Her fingers were still cold and he wrapped his bigger hands around hers. "Brrr. Let me warm up your hands. I'm sorry I didn't keep a better eye on the weather. I should have at least provided gloves for you."

"It's fine. I'm not really cold anymore." She met his gaze, then quickly looked away, and her fingers trembled slightly inside his. "Anyway, I don't think the children minded the rain that much. To them, it was all part of the adventure. Alex already told me he pretended he was a Texas marshal trying to track a bad guy. Rain and all, the whole day will be a cherished memory for them both."

Tenderness for this woman—and her children— washed through him just like that rain, carving rivulets and channels through all the places inside him that had been parched for far too long. "You're amazing at that."

A faint blush soaked her cheeks. "At what?"

"Finding the good in every situation. You always used to do that. Somehow I'd forgotten it. If you had a flat tire, you would say you appreciated the chance to slow down for a minute and enjoy your surroundings. If you broke a nail, you would just say you now had a good excuse to give yourself a manicure."

"Annoying, isn't it? How do people stand me?"

Her laugh sounded embarrassed and she tried to tug her hands away, but he held them fast, squeezing her fingers.

"No, I think it's wonderful. I didn't realize until right this moment how much I've missed that about you."

She gazed up at him, her eyes that lovely columbine-blue and her mouth slightly parted. Her fingers trembled again in his and he was aware of the scent of her, flowery and sweet, and of the sudden tension tightening between them.

He wanted to kiss her as he couldn't remember wanting anything in his life, except maybe the first time he had kissed her on the mountainside so many years ago.

If he followed through on the fierce hunger curling through him, she would just think he was being the player the whole town seemed to think he was, taking advantage of a situation just because he could.

Right now she didn't even like him very much. Better to just bide his time, give her a chance to come to know him again and trust him.

Yeah, that would be the wise, cautious thing to do. But as her hands trembled in his, he knew with a grim sort of resignation that he couldn't be wise or cautious. Not when it came to Laura.

As everything inside him tightened with anticipation, he tugged her toward him and lowered his mouth to hers.

Magic. Simply delicious. She had the softest, sweetest mouth and he couldn't believe he had forgotten how perfectly she fit against him.

Oh, he had missed her, missed this.

For about ten seconds, she didn't move anything except her fingers, now curled in his, while his mouth touched and tasted hers. For those ten seconds, he waited for her to push him away. She remained still except for her hands, and then, as if she had come to some internal decision—or maybe just resisted as long as she could—she returned the kiss, her mouth warm and soft and willing.

That was all the signal he needed to deepen the kiss. In an instant, need thundered through him and he released her hands and wrapped his arms around her, pulling her closer, intoxicated by her body pressed against him.

She felt wonderfully familiar but not quite the same, perhaps a little curvier than she'd been back when she had been his. He supposed two children and a decade could do that. He tightened his arms around her, very much appreciating the difference as her curves brushed against his chest.

She made a low sound in her throat and her arms slipped around his neck and he did what he had imagined earlier, pressed her back against the wall.

She kissed him back and he knew he didn't imagine the hitch in her breathing, the rapid heartbeat he could feel beneath his fingers.

This. This was what he wanted. Laura, right here.

All the aimless wandering of the past ten years had finally found a purpose, here in the arms of this woman. He wanted her and her children in his life. No, it was more than just a whim. He *needed* them. He pictured laughter and joy, rides into the mountains, winter nights spent cuddling by the fireplace of the log home he was building.

For her. He was building it for her and he had never realized it until this moment. Every fixture, every detail had been aimed at creating the home they had always talked about building together.

That didn't make sense. It was completely crazy. Yeah, he'd heard her husband died some months back and had grieved for the pain she must have been feeling, but he hadn't even known she was coming home until he showed up to fight the fire at the inn and found her there.

He had thought he was just building the house he wanted, but now he could see just how perfectly she and her children would fit there.

Okay, slow down, Bowman, he told himself. One kiss did not equal happy ever after. He had hurt her deeply by pushing her away so readily after his parents died and it was going take more than just a few heated embraces to work past that.

He didn't care. He had always craved a challenge, whether that was climbing a mountain, kayaking rapids or conquering an out-of-control wildfire. He had been stupid enough to let her go once. He damn well wasn't going to do it again.

She made another low sound in her throat and he remembered how very sexy he used to find those little noises she made. Her tongue slid along his, erotic and inviting, and heat scorched through him, raw and hungry.

He was just trying to figure out how to move this somewhere a little more comfortable than against the wall of the hallway when the sound of the door opening suddenly pierced his subconscious.

A moment later, he heard his sister's voice from the entry at the other side of the house.

"We've got to go look for them." Caidy sounded stressed and almost frantic. "I can't believe Taft didn't make it back before the rain hit. What if something's happened to them?"

"He'll take care of them. Don't worry about it," Ridge replied in that calm way of his.

They would be here any second, he realized. Even though it was just about the toughest thing he'd ever done—besides standing by and letting her walk out of his life ten years ago—he eased away from her.

She looked flustered, pink, aroused. Beautiful.

He cleared his throat. "Laura," he started to say, but whatever thoughts jumbled around in his head didn't make it to words before his siblings walked down the hall and the moment was gone.

"Oh!" Caidy pedaled to a stop when she saw them. Her gaze swiveled between him and Laura and then back to him. Her eyes narrowed and he squirmed at the accusatory look in them, as if he was some sort of feudal lord having his way with the prettiest peasant. Yeah, he had kissed her, but she hadn't exactly put up any objections.

"You made it back safely."

"Yes."

Laura's voice came out husky, thready. She cleared it. Her cheeks were rosy and she refused to meet his gaze. "Yes. Safe but not quite dry. On our way down, we were caught in the first few minutes of the rainstorm. Taft loaned me some of your clothes. I hope you don't mind."

"Oh, of course! You can keep them, for heaven's sake. What about the kids? Are they okay?"

"More than okay." Her smile seemed strained, but he wasn't sure anyone but him could tell. "This was the most exciting thing that has happened to them since we've been back in Pine Gulch—and that's saying something, considering Alex started a fire that had four ladder trucks responding. They were so thrilled by the whole day that they were both exhausted and fell asleep watching cartoons while we have been waiting for our clothes to run through the dryer—which is silly, by the way. We could have been home in fifteen minutes, but Taft wouldn't let us leave in our wet gear."

"Wise man." Ridge spoke up for the first time. His brother gave him a searching look very much like Caidy's before turning back to her. "Great to see you again, Laura."

Ridge stepped forward and pulled her into a hug, and she responded with a warm smile she still hadn't given *Taft*.

"Welcome back to Pine Gulch. How are you settling in?"

"Good. Being home again is…an adventure."

"How's the dog?" Taft asked.

"Lucky. Looks like only a broken leg," Caidy said. "Doc Harris hurried back from a meeting in Pocatello so he could set it. He's keeping him overnight for observation."

"Good man, that Doc Harris."

"I know. I don't know what we're all going to do when he finally retires."

"You'll have to find another vet to keep on speed dial," Taft teased.

Caidy made a face at him, then turned back to Laura. "You and the kids will stay for dinner, won't you? I can throw soup and biscuits on and have it ready in half an hour."

As much as he wanted her to agree, he knew—even before she said the words—exactly how she would answer.

"Thank you for the invitation, but I'm afraid I'm covering the front-desk shift this evening. I'm sorry. In fact, I should really be going. I'm sure our clothes are dry by now. Perhaps another time?"

"Yes, definitely. Let me go check on your clothes."

"I can do it," Laura protested, but Caidy was faster, probably because she had grown up in a family of boys where you had to move quick if you wanted the last piece of pie or a second helping of potato salad.

Ridge and Laura talked about the inn and her plans for renovating it for the few moments it took for Caidy to return from the laundry room off the kitchen with her arms full of clothing.

"Here you go. Nice and dry."

"Great. I'll go wake up my kids and then we can get out of your way."

"You're not in our way. I promise. I'm so glad you could come out to the ranch. I'm only sorry I wasn't here for the ride, since I was the one who invited you. I'm not usually so rude."

"It wasn't rude," Laura protested. "You were helping a wounded dog. That's more important than a little ride we could have done anytime."

Caidy opened the door to the media room. Laura gave him one more emotion-charged look before following his sister, leaving Taft alone with Ridge.

His brother studied him for a long moment, reminding Taft uncomfortably of their father when he and Trace found themselves in some scrape or other.

"Be careful there, brother," Ridge finally said.

He was thirty-four years old and wasn't at all in the mood for a lecture from an older brother who tended to think he was the boss of the world. "About?"

"I've got eyes. I can tell when a woman's just been kissed."

He was *really* not in the mood to talk about Laura with Ridge. As much as he respected his brother for stepping up and taking care of both Caidy and the ranch after their parents died, Ridge was *not* their father and he didn't have to answer to the man.

"What's your point?" he asked, more belligerently than he probably should have.

Ridge frowned. "You sure you know what you're doing, dredging everything up again with Laura?"

If I figure that out, I'll be sure to let you know. "All I did was take her and her kids for a horseback ride."

Ridge was silent for a long moment. "I don't know what happened between the two of you all those years ago, why you didn't end up walking down the aisle when everybody could tell the two of you were crazy in love."

"Does it matter? It's ancient history."

"Not that ancient. Ten years. And take it from an expert, the choices we make in the past can haunt us for the rest of our lives."

Ridge should definitely know that. He had married a woman completely unsuitable for ranch life who had ended up making everybody around her miserable, too.

"Given your track record with women in the years since," Ridge went on, "I'm willing to bet you're the one who ended things. You didn't waste much time being heartbroken over the end of your engagement."

That shows what you know, he thought. "It was a mutual decision," he lied for the umpteenth time.

"If I remember right, you picked up with that Turner woman just a week or two after Laura left town. And then Sonia Gallegos a few weeks after that."

Yeah, he remembered those bleak days after she left, the gaping emptiness he had tried—and failed—to fill, when he had wanted nothing but to chase after her, drag her home and keep her where she belonged, with him.

"What's your point, Ridge?"

"This goes without saying—"

"Yet you're going to say it anyway."

"Damn straight. Laura isn't one of your Bandito bimbos. She's a decent person with a couple of kids, including one with challenges. Keep in mind she lost her husband recently. The last thing she probably needs is you messing with her head and heart again when she's trying to build a life here."

Like his favorite fishing knife, his brother's words seemed to slice right to the bone.

He wanted her fiercely—but just because he wanted something didn't mean he automatically deserved it. He'd learned that lesson young when his mother used to make him and Trace take out the garbage or change out a load of laundry if they wanted an extra cookie before dinner.

If he wanted another chance with her after the way he had treated her—and damn it, he *did*—he was going to have to earn his way back. He didn't know how yet. He only knew he planned to work like hell to become the kind of man he should have been ten years ago.

CHAPTER EIGHT

LAURA WAS GOING to kill him. Severely.

Five days after going riding with her and her kids above River Bow, Taft set down the big bag of supplies his sister had given him onto the concrete, then shifted the bundle into his left arm so he could use his right arm to wield his key card, the only way after hours to enter the side door of the inn closest to his room.

"Almost there, buddy," he said when the bundle whimpered.

He swiped the card, waiting for the little light to turn green, but it stayed stubbornly red. Too fast? Too slow? He hated these things. He tried it again, but the blasted light still didn't budge off red.

Apparently either the key code wasn't working anymore or his card had somehow become demagnetized.

Shoot. Of all the nights to have trouble, when he literally had his hands full.

"Sorry, buddy. Hang on a bit more and we'll get you settled inside. I promise."

The little brown-and-black corgi-beagle mix perked his ginormous ears at him and gave him a quizzical look.

He tried a couple more times in the vain hope that five or six times was the charm, then gave up, accepting the inevitable trip to the lobby. He glanced at his watch. Eleven thirty-five. The front desk closed at midnight. Barring an unforeseen catastrophe between here and the front door, he should be okay.

He shoved the dog food and mat away from the door in case somebody else had better luck with their key card and needed to get through, then carried the dog around the side of the darkened inn.

The night was cool, as spring nights tended to be in the mountains, and he tucked the little dog under his jacket. The air was sweet with the scent of the flowers Laura had planted and new growth on the trees that lined the Cold Creek here.

On the way, he passed the sign he had noticed before that said Pets Welcome.

Yeah. He really, really hoped they meant it.

The property was quiet, as he might have expected. Judging by the few cars behind him in the parking lot, only about half the rooms at the inn were occupied. He hadn't seen any other guests for a couple of days in his wing of the hotel, which he could only consider a good thing, given the circumstances—though he doubted Laura would agree.

At least his room was close to the side door in case he had to make any emergency trips outside with the injured dog his sister had somehow conned him into babysitting. He had to consider that another thing to add to the win column.

Was Laura working the front desk? She did sometimes, probably after her children were asleep. In the few weeks he'd been living at the inn, most of the time one of the college students Mrs. Pendleton hired was working the front desk on the late shift, usually a flirtatious coed he tried really hard to discourage.

He wasn't sure whether he hoped to find Laura working or would prefer to avoid her a little longer. Not that he'd been avoiding her on purpose. He had been working crazy hours the past few days and hadn't been around the inn much.

He hadn't seen her since the other afternoon, when she had melted in his arms, although she hadn't been far from his mind. Discovering he wanted her back in his life had been more than a little unsettling.

The lobby of the inn had seen major changes in the few weeks since Laura arrived. Through the front windows he could see that the froufrou couches and chairs that used to form a conversation pit of sorts had been replaced by a half-dozen tables and chairs, probably for the breakfast service he'd been hearing about.

Fresh flower arrangements gave a bright, springlike feeling to the place—probably Laura's doing, as well.

When he opened the front door, he immediately spotted a honey-blond head bent over a computer and warmth seeped through him. He had missed her. Silly, when it had been only four days, but there it was.

The dog in his arms whimpered a little. Deciding discretion was the better part of valor and all that, he wrapped his coat a little more snugly around the dog. No sense riling her before she needed to be riled.

He wasn't technically doing anything wrong—pets *were* welcome after all, at least according to the sign, but somehow he had a feeling normal inn rules didn't apply to him.

He warily approached her and as she sensed him, she looked up from the computer with a ready smile. At the sight of him, her smile slid away and he felt a pang in his gut.

"Oh. Hi."

He shifted Lucky Lou a little lower in his arm. "Uh, hi. Sorry to bug you, but either my key card isn't working or the side door lock is having trouble. I tried to come in that way, but I couldn't get the green light."

"No problem. I can reprogram your card."

Her voice was stiff, formal. Had that stunning kiss ruined even the friendship he had been trying to rekindle?

"I like the furniture," he said.

"Thanks. It was just delivered today. I'm pleased with the colors. We should be ready to start serving breakfast by early next week."

"That will be a nice touch for your guests."

"I think so."

He hated that they had reverted back to polite small talk. They used to share everything with each other and he missed it.

The bundle under his jacket squirmed a little and she eyed him with curiosity.

"Uh, here's my key," he said, handing it over.

She slid it across the little doohickey card reader and handed it back to him. "That should work now, but let me know if you have more trouble."

"Okay. Thanks. Good night."

"Same to you," she answered. He started to turn and leave just as Lou gave a small, polite yip and peeked his head out of the jacket, his mega-size ears cocked with interest.

She blinked, clearly startled. "Is that…"

"Oh, this? Oh. Yeah. You probably need to add him to your list of guests. This is Lucky Lou."

At his newly christened name, the dog peeked all

the way out. With those big corgi ears, he looked like a cross between a lemur and some kind of alien creature.

"Oh, he's adorable."

He blinked. Okay, she wasn't yelling. That was a good sign. "Yeah, pretty cute, I guess. Not exactly the most manly of dogs, but he's okay."

"Is this the dog that was hit by a car the other day?"

"This is the one."

To his great surprise, she walked around the side of the lobby desk for a closer look. He obliged by unwrapping the blanket, revealing the cast on the dog's leg.

"Oh, he's darling," she exclaimed and reached out to run a hand down the animal's fur. The dog responded just as Taft wanted to do, by nudging his head closer to her hand. So far, so good. Maybe she wasn't going to kill him after all.

"How is he?" she asked.

"Lucky. Hence the name."

She laughed softly and the sound curled through him, sweet and appealing.

He cleared his throat. "Somehow he came through with just a broken leg. It should heal up in a few weeks, but he needs to be watched closely during that time to make sure he doesn't reinjure himself. He especially can't be around the other dogs at the ranch because they tend to play rough, which poses a bit of a problem."

"What kind of problem?"

"It's a crazy-busy time at the ranch, with spring planting and all, not to mention Trace's wedding. Caidy was looking for somebody who could keep an eye on Lou here and I sort of got roped into it."

He didn't add that his sister basically blackmailed him to take on the responsibility, claiming he owed her this because she told him about the planned horseback ride with Laura and her children in the first place.

"I guess I should ask whether you mind if I keep him here at the inn with me. Most of the time he'll be at the station house or in my truck with me, but he'll be here on the nights I'm not working there."

She cupped the dog's face in her hand. "I would have to be the most hardhearted woman on the planet to say no to that face."

Okay, now he owed his sister big-time. Who knew the way to reach Laura's heart was through an injured mongrel?

As if she suddenly realized how close she was standing, Laura eased away from him. The dog whimpered a little and Taft wanted to join him.

"Our policy does allow for pets," she said. "Usually we charge a hundred-dollar deposit in case of damages, but given the circumstances I'm sure we can waive that."

"I'll try to keep him quiet. He seems to be a well-behaved little guy. Makes me wonder what happened. How he ended up homeless."

"Maybe he ran away."

"Yeah, that's the logical explanation, but he didn't have a collar. Caidy checked with animal control and the vet and everybody else she could think of. Nobody in the county has reported a lost pet matching his description. I wonder if somebody just dropped him off and abandoned him."

"What's going to happen to him? Eventually, I mean, after he heals?" she asked.

"Caidy has a reputation for taking in strays. Her plan is to nurse him back to health and then look for a good placement somewhere for the little guy. Meantime I'm just the dogsitter for a few days."

"And you can take him to the fire station with you?"

"I'm the fire chief, remember? Who's going to tell me I can't?"

She raised an eyebrow. "Oh, I don't know. Maybe the mayor or the city council."

He laughed, trying to imagine any of the local politicians making a big deal about a dog at the fire station. "This is Pine Gulch," he answered. "We're pretty casual about things like that. Anyway, it's only for a few days. We can always call him our unofficial mascot. Lucky Lou, Fire Dog."

The dog's big ears perked forward, as if eager to take on the new challenge.

"You like the sound of that, do you?" He scratched the dog's ears and earned an adoring look from his new best friend. He looked up to find Laura watching him, an arrested look in her eyes. When his gaze collided with hers, she turned a delicate shade of pink and looked away from him.

"Like I said, he doesn't seem to be much of a barker. I'll try to keep him quiet when I'm here so he doesn't disturb the other guests."

"Thank you, I appreciate that. Not that you have that many guests around you to be disturbed."

The discouragement in her voice made him want to hold her close, dog and all, and take away her worries. "Things will pick up come summer," he assured her.

"I hope so. The inn hasn't had the greatest reputation over the years. My mom did her best after my dad died, but I'm afraid things went downhill."

He knew this to be an unfortunate fact. Most people in town steered their relatives and friends to other establishments. A couple new B and Bs had sprung up recently and there were some nice guest ranches in the canyon. None had the advantage of Cold Creek Inn's location and beautiful setting, though, and with Laura spearheading changes, he didn't doubt the inn would be back on track in no time.

"Give it time. You've been home only a few weeks."

She sighed. "I know. But when I think about all the work it's going to require to counteract that reputation, I just want to cry."

He could certainly relate to that. He knew just how tough it was to convince people to look beyond the past. "If anybody can do it, you're perfect for the job. A degree in hotel management, all those years of international hotel experience. This will be a snap for you."

She gave him a rueful smile—but a smile nonetheless. He drew in a breath, wishing he could set the dog down and pull Laura into his arms instead. He might have considered it, but Lucky made a sound as if warning him against that particular course of action.

"What you need is a dog," he said suddenly. "A *lucky* dog."

"Oh, no, you don't," she exclaimed on a laugh. "Forget that right now, Taft Bowman. I'm too smart to let myself be swayed by an adorable face."

"Mine or the dog's?" he teased.

This smile looked definitely genuine, but she shook her head. "Go to bed, Taft. And take your lucky dog with you."

I'd rather take you.

The words simmered between them, unsaid, but she blushed anyway, as if she sensed the thoughts in his head.

"Good night, then," he said with great reluctance. "I really don't mind paying the security deposit for the dog."

"No need. Consider it my way of helping in Lucky Lou's recovery."

"Thanks, then. I'll try to be sure you don't regret it."

He hitched the dog into a better position, picked up the key card from the counter and headed down the hall.

He had enough regrets for the both of them.

HER CHILDREN WERE in love.

"He's the cutest dog *ever*," Alex gushed, his dark eyes bright with excitement. "And so nice, too. I petted him and petted him and all he did was lick me."

"Lou tickles," Maya added, her face earnest and sweet.

"Lucky Lou. That's his name, Chief Bowman says."

Alex was perched on the counter, pulling items out of grocery bags, theoretically "helping" her put them away, but mostly just jumbling them up on the counter. Still, she wasn't about to discourage any act of spontaneous help from her children.

"And where was your grandmother while Chief Bowman was letting you play with his dog?" she asked.

The plan had been for Jan to watch the children while Laura went to the grocery store for her mother, but it sounded very much as if they had been wandering through the hotel, bothering Taft.

"She had a phone call in the office. We were coloring at a new table in the lobby, just like Grandma told us to. I promise we didn't go anywhere like upstairs. I was coloring a picture of a horse and Maya was just scribbling. She's not a very good colorer."

"She's working on it, aren't you, *mi hija*?"

Maya giggled at the favorite words and the everyday tension and stress of grocery shopping and counting coupons and loading bags into her car in a rainstorm seemed to fade away.

She was working hard to give her family a good life here. Maybe it wasn't perfect yet, but it was definitely better than what they would have known if she'd stayed in Madrid.

"So you were coloring and…" she prompted.

"And Chief Bowman came in and he was carrying the dog. He has great big ears. They're like donkey ears!"

She had to smile at the exaggeration. The dog had big ears but nothing that unusual for a corgi.

"Really?" she teased. "I've never noticed that about Chief Bowman."

Alex giggled. "The dog, silly! The *dog* has big ears. His name is Lucky Lou and he has a broken leg. Did you know that? He got hit by a car! That's sad, huh?"

"Terribly sad," she agreed.

"Chief Bowman says he has to wear a cast for another week and he can't run around with the other dogs."

"That's too bad."

"I know, huh? He can only sit quiet and be petted, but Chief Bowman says I can do it anytime I want to."

"That's very kind of Chief Bowman," she answered, quite sure her six-year-old probably wouldn't notice the caustic edge to her tone. She knew just what Taft was after—a sucker who would take the dog off his hands.

"He's super nice."

"The dog?"

"No! Chief Bowman! He says I can come visit Lou

whenever I want, and when his cast comes off, I can maybe take him for a walk."

The decided note of hero-worship she heard in Alex's voice greatly worried her. Her son was desperate for a strong male influence in his life. She understood that.

But Taft wasn't going to be staying at the inn forever. Eventually his house would be finished and he would move out, taking his little dog with him.

The thought depressed her, although she knew darn well it was dangerous to allow herself to care what Taft Bowman did.

"And guess what else?" Alex pressed, his tone suddenly cagey.

"What?"

"Chief Bowman said Lucky Lou is going to need a new home once he recovers!"

Oh, here we go, she thought. It didn't take a child-behavior specialist to guess what would be coming next.

Sure enough, Alex tilted his head and gave her a deceptively casual look. "So I was thinking maybe *we* could give him a new home."

You're always thinking, aren't you, kiddo? she thought with resignation, gearing up for the arguments she could sense would follow that declaration.

"He's a super-nice dog and he didn't bark one single time. I know I could take care of him, Mama. I just *know* it."

"I know it," Maya said in stout agreement, although Laura had doubts as to whether her daughter had even been paying attention to the conversation as she played with a stack of plastic cups at the kitchen table.

How was she going to get out of this one without seeming like the meanest mom in the world? The dog *was* adorable. She couldn't deny it. With those big ears and the beagle coloring and his inquisitive little face, he was a definite charmer.

Maybe in a few months she would be in a better position to get a pet, but she was barely holding on here, working eighteen-hour days around caring for her children so she could help her mother rehabilitate this crumbling old inn and bring it back to the graceful accommodations it once had been.

She had to make the inn a success no matter how hard she had to work to do it. She couldn't stomach another failure. First her engagement to Taft, then her marriage. Seeing the inn deteriorate further would be the last straw.

A dog, especially a somewhat fragile one, would complicate *everything*.

"I would really, really love a dog," Alex persisted.

"Dog. Me, too," Maya said.

Drat Taft for placing her in this position. He had to have known her children would come back brimming over with enthusiasm for the dog, pressing her to add him to her family.

Movement outside the kitchen window caught her gaze and through the rain she saw Taft walking toward the little grassy area set aside for dogs. He was wearing a hooded raincoat and carrying an umbrella. At the dog-walking area, he set Lucky Lou down onto the grass and she saw the dog's cast had been wrapped in plastic.

She watched as Taft held the umbrella over the little corgi-beagle mix while the dog took care of business.

The sight of this big, tough firefighter showing such care for a little injured dog touched something deep inside her. Tenderness rippled and swelled inside her and she drew in a sharp breath. She didn't want to let him inside her heart again. She couldn't do it.

This was Taft Bowman. He was a womanizer, just as Javier had been. The more the merrier. That was apparently his mantra when it came to women. She had been through this before and she refused to do it again.

From his vantage point on top of the counter, Alex had a clear view out the window. "See?" he said with a pleading look. "Isn't he a great dog? Chief Bowman says he doesn't even poop in the house or anything."

She sighed and took her son's small hand in hers, trying to soften the difficulty of her words. "Honey, I don't know if this is the best time for us to get a dog. I'm sorry. I can't tell you yes or no right now. I'm going to have to think hard about this before I can make any decision. Don't get your hopes up, okay?"

Even as she said the words, she knew they were useless. By the adoration on his face as he looked out the rain-streaked window at the little dog, she could plainly tell Alex already had his heart set on making a home for Lou.

She supposed things could be worse. The dog was apparently potty-trained, friendly and not likely to grow much bigger. It wasn't as if he was an English sheepdog, the kind of pet who shed enough fur it could be knitted into a sweater.

But then, this was Taft Bowman's specialty, convincing people to do things they otherwise wouldn't even consider.

She was too smart to fall for it all over again. Or at least that's what she told herself.

CHAPTER NINE

NEARLY A WEEK LATER, Laura spread the new duvet across the bed in the once-fire-damaged room, then stepped back to survey her work.

Not bad, if she did say so herself. She was especially proud of the new walls, which she had painted herself, glazing with a darker earth tone over the tan to create a textured, layered effect, almost like a Tuscan farmhouse.

Hiring someone else to paint would have saved a great deal of time and trouble, of course. The idea of all the rooms yet to paint daunted her, made her back ache just thinking about it. On the other hand, this renovation had been *her* idea to breathe life into the old hotel, and the budget was sparse, even with the in-kind labor Taft had done for them over the past few weeks.

It might take her a month to finish all the other rooms, but she would still save several thousand dollars that could be put into upgrading the amenities offered by the inn.

She intended to make each room at the inn charming and unique. This was a brilliant start. The room looked warm and inviting and she couldn't wait to start renting it out. She smoothed a hand over the wood trim around the windows, noting the tightness of the joints and the fine grain that showed beautifully through the finish.

"Wow, it looks fantastic in here."

She turned at the voice from the open doorway and found Taft leaning against the doorjamb. He looked tired, she thought, with a day's growth of whiskers on his cheeks and new smudges under his eyes. Not tired, precisely. Weary and worn, as if he had stopped here because he couldn't move another step down the hall toward his own room.

"Amazing the difference a coat of paint and a little love can do, isn't it?" she answered, worried for him.

"Absolutely. I would stay here in a heartbeat."

"You *are* staying here. Okay, not *here* precisely, in this particular room, but at the inn."

"If this room is any indication, the rest of this place will be beautiful by the time you're finished. People will be fighting over themselves to get a room."

"I hope so," she answered with a smile. This was what she wanted. The chance to make this historic property come to life.

"Do you ever sleep?" he asked.

"I could ask the same question. You look tired."

"Yeah, it's been a rough one."

She found the weary darkness in his gaze disconcerting. Taft was teasing and fun, with a smile and a lighthearted comment for everyone. She rarely saw him serious and quiet. "What's happened?"

He sank down onto the new sofa, messing up the throw pillows she had only just arranged. She didn't mind. He looked like a man who needed somewhere comfortable to rest for a moment.

"Car accident on High Creek Road. Idiot tourist took one of those sharp turns up there too fast. The car went off the road and rolled about thirty feet down the slope."

"Is he okay?"

"The driver just had scrapes and bruises and a broken arm." He scratched at a spot at the knee of his jeans. "His ten-year-old kid wasn't so lucky. We did CPR for about twenty minutes while we waited for the medevac helicopter and were able to bring him back. Last I heard, he survived the flight to the children's hospital in Salt Lake City, but he's in for a long, hard fight."

Her heart ached for the child and for his parents. "Oh, no."

"I hate incidents with kids involved." His mouth was tight. "Makes me want to tell every parent I know to hug their children and not let go. You just never know what could happen on any given day. If I didn't know Ridge would shoot me for it, I'd drive over to the ranch and wake up Destry right now, just so I could give her a big hug and tell her I love her."

His love for his niece warmed her heart. He was a man with a huge capacity to love and he must have deep compassion if he could be so upset by the day's events. Hadn't he learned how to keep a safe distance between his emotions and the emergency calls he had to respond to as a firefighter and paramedic?

"I'm sorry you had to go through that today."

He shrugged. "It's part of the job description, I guess. Sometimes I think my life would have been a hell of a lot easier if I'd stuck to raising cattle with Ridge."

These moments always took her by surprise when she realized anew that Taft was more than just the light-hearted, laughing guy he pretended to be. He felt things deeply. She had always known that, she supposed, but it was sometimes easy to forget when he worked so hard to be a charming flirt.

After weighing the wisdom of being in too close proximity to him against her need to offer comfort, she finally sank onto the sofa beside him.

"I'm sure you did everything you could."

"That's what we tell ourselves to help us sleep at night. Yet we always wonder."

He had been driving back to the ranch after being with her that terrible December night his parents were killed, when a terrified Caidy had called 9-1-1, she remembered now. Taft had heard the report go out on the radio in his truck just as he'd been turning into the gates of the ranch and had rushed inside to find his father shot dead and his mother bleeding out on the floor.

Not that he ever talked about this with her, but one of the responding paramedics had told her about finding a blood-covered Taft desperately trying to do CPR on his mother. He wouldn't stop, even after the rescue crews arrived.

His failure to revive his mother had eaten away at him, she was quite certain. If he had arrived five minutes earlier, he might have been able to save her.

She suspected, though of course he blocked this part of his life from her, that some part of him had even blamed Caidy for not calling for rescue earlier. Caidy had been home, as well, and had hidden in a closet in terror for several moments after her parents were shot, not sure whether the thieves—who had come to what they thought was an empty ranch to steal the Bowmans' art collection and been surprised into murder—might still actually be in the house.

After Laura left Pine Gulch, she had wondered if he blocked out his emotions after the murders in an effort to protect himself from that guilt at not being able to do enough to save his parents.

Even though he pretended he was fine, the grief and loss had simmered inside him. If only he had agreed to postpone the wedding, perhaps time would have helped him reach a better place so they could have married without that cloud over them.

None of that mattered now. He was hurting and she was compelled by her very nature to help ease that pain if she could. "What you do is important, Taft, no matter how hard it sometimes must feel. Think of it this way— if not for you and the other rescuers, that boy wouldn't have any chance at all. He wouldn't have made it long enough for the medical helicopter. And he's only one of hundreds, maybe thousands, of people you've helped. You make a real difference here in Pine Gulch. How many people can say that about their vocation?"

He didn't say anything for a long time and she couldn't read the emotion in his gaze. "There you go again. Always looking for the good in a situation."

"It seems better than focusing on all the misery and despair around me."

"Yeah, but sometimes life sucks and you can't gloss over the smoke damage with a coat of paint and a couple new pictures on the wall."

His words stung more than they should have, piercing unerringly under an old, half-healed scar.

Javier used to call her *dulce y inocente*. Sweet and innocent. He treated her like a silly girl, keeping away all their financial troubles, his difficulties with the hotel, the other women he slept with, as if she were too fragile to deal with the harsh realities of life.

"I'm not a child, Taft. Believe me, I know just how

harsh and ugly the world can be. I don't think it makes
me silly or naive simply because I prefer to focus on the
hope that with a little effort, people can make a difference in each other's lives. We can always make tomorrow a little better than today, can't we? What's the point
of life if you focus only on the negative, on what's dark
or difficult instead of all the joy waiting to be embraced
with each new day?"

She probably sounded like a soppy greeting card,
but at that moment she didn't care.

"I never said you were silly." He gave her a probing
look that made her flush. "Who did?"

She wanted to ignore the question. What business
was it of his? But the old inn was quiet around them
and there was an odd sort of intimacy in this pretty,
comfortable room.

"My husband. He treated me like I was too delicate
to cope with the realities of life. It was one of the many
points of contention between us. He wanted to put a
nice shiny gloss over everything, pretend all was fine."

He studied her for a long moment, then sighed. "I
suppose that's not so different from what I did to you
after my parents died."

"Yes," she answered through her surprise that he
would actually bring up this subject and admit to his
behavior. "If not for our…history, I guess you could say,
it might not have bothered me so much when Javier insisted on that shiny gloss. But I had been through it all
before. I didn't want to be that fragile child."

Before she realized what he intended, he covered her
hand with his there on the sofa between them. His hand
was large and warm, his fingers rough from years of
both working on the ranch and putting his life on the line

to help the residents of Pine Gulch, and for one crazy
moment, she wanted to turn her hand over, grab tightly
to his strength and never let go.

"I'm so sorry I hurt you, Laura. It was selfish and
wrong of me. I should have postponed the wedding until
I was in a better place."

"Why didn't you? A few months—that might have
made all the difference, Taft."

"Then I would have had to admit I was still struggling to cope, six months later, when I thought I should
have been fine and over things. I was a tough firefighter,
Laura. I faced wildfires. I ran into burning buildings.
I did whatever I had to. I guess I didn't want to show
any signs of weakness. It was…tough for me to accept
that my parents' murders threw me for a loop, so I pretended I was fine, too selfish and immature a decade
ago to consider that you might have been right, that I
needed more time."

She closed her eyes, wondering how her life might
have been different if she had gone ahead with the wedding, despite all her misgivings. If she had been a little more certain he would come through his anger and
grief, if she had married him anyway, perhaps they
could have worked through it.

On the other hand, even though she had loved him
with all her heart, she would have been miserable in a
marriage where he refused to share important pieces of
himself with her. They probably would have ended up
divorced, hating each other, with a couple of messed-
up kids trapped in the middle.

He squeezed her fingers and his gaze met hers.
Something glimmered in the depths of those green

eyes, emotions she couldn't identify and wasn't sure she wanted to see.

"For the record," he murmured, "nothing was right after you left. It hasn't been right all this time. I've missed you, Laura."

She stared at him, blood suddenly pulsing through her. She didn't want to hear this. All her protective instincts were urging her to jump up from this sofa and escape, but she couldn't seem to make herself move.

"I should have come after you," he said. "But by the time I straightened out my head enough to do it, you were married and expecting a baby and I figured I had lost my chance."

"Taft—" Her voice sounded husky and low and she couldn't seem to collect her thoughts enough to add anything more. It wouldn't have mattered if she had. He didn't give her a chance to say a word before he leaned in, his eyes an intense, rich green, and lowered his mouth to hers.

His mouth was warm and tasted of coffee and something else she couldn't identify. Some part of her knew she should move now, while she still had the will, but she couldn't seem to make any of her limbs cooperate, too lost in the sheer, familiar joy of being in his arms again.

He kissed her softly, not demanding anything, only tasting, savoring, as if her mouth were some sort of rare and precious wine. She was helpless to do anything but try to remember to breathe while her insides twisted and curled with longing.

"I missed you, Laura," he murmured once more, this time against her mouth.

I missed you, too. So much.

The words echoed through her mind but she couldn't say them. Not now. Not yet.

She could do nothing now but soak in the stunning tenderness of his kiss and let it drift around and through her, resurrecting all those feelings she had shoved so deeply down inside her psyche.

Finally, when she couldn't think or feel past the thick flow of emotions, he deepened the kiss. Now. Now was the time she should pull away, before things progressed too far. Her mind knew it, but again, the rest of her was weak and she responded instinctively, as she had done to him so many times before, and pressed her mouth to his.

For long moments, nothing else existed but his strength and his heat, his mouth firm and determined on hers, his arms holding her tightly, his muscles surrounding her. She wasn't sure exactly how he managed it without her realizing, but he shifted and turned her so she was resting back against the armrest of the sofa while he half covered her with his body until she was lost in memories of making love with him, tangled bodies and hearts.

She was still in love with him.

The realization slowly seeped through her consciousness, like water finding a weakness in a seam and dripping through.

She was still in love with Taft and probably had been all this time.

The discovery left her reeling, disoriented. She had loved her husband. *Of course* she had. She never would have married him if she hadn't believed they could make a happy life together. Yes, she had discovered she was unexpectedly pregnant after their brief affair, but she hadn't married him for that, despite the intense pressure he applied to make their relationship legal.

Her love for Javier hadn't been the deep, rich, consuming love she had known with Taft, but she had cared deeply for the man—at first anyway, until his repeated betrayals and his casual attitude about them had eaten away most of her affection for him.

Even so, she realized now, throughout the seven years of her marriage, some part of her heart had always belonged to Taft.

"We were always so good together. Do you remember?"

The low words thrummed through her and images of exactly how things had been between them flashing through her head. From the very first, they had been perfectly compatible. He had always known just how to kiss, just where to touch.

"Yes, I remember," she said hoarsely. All the passion, all the heat, all the heartbreak. She remembered all of it. The memories of her despair and abject loneliness after leaving Pine Gulch washed over her like a cold surf, dousing her hunger with cruel effectiveness.

She couldn't do this. Not again. Not with Taft.

She might still love him, but that was even more reason she shouldn't be here on this sofa with him with their mouths entwined. She froze, needing distance and space to breathe and think, to remind herself of all the many reasons she couldn't go through this all over again.

"I remember everything," she said coldly. "I'm not the one whose memory might have been blurred by the scores of other people I've been with in the meantime."

He jerked his head back as if she had just slapped him. "I told you, reputation isn't necessarily the truth."

"But it has some basis in truth. You can't deny that."

Even as she snapped the words, she knew this wasn't the core of the problem. She was afraid. That was the bare truth.

She still loved him as much as she ever had, maybe more now that she was coming to know the man he had become over the past decade, but she had given her heart to him once and he had chosen his grief and anger over all she had wanted to give him.

If she only had herself to consider, she might be willing to take the risk. But she had two children to think about. Alex and Maya were already coming to care for Taft. What if he decided he preferred his partying life again and chose that over her and the children? He had done it once before.

Her late husband had done the same thing, chosen his own selfish pursuits over his family, time and again, and she had to remember she wouldn't be the only one devastated if Taft decided he didn't want a family. Her children had already been through the pain of losing their father. At all costs, she had to protect them and the life she was trying to create for them.

"I don't want this. I don't want *you*," she said firmly, sliding away from him. Despite her resolve, her hands trembled and she shoved them into the pocket of her sweater and drew a deep breath for strength as she stood.

"Like apparently half the women in town, I'm weak when it comes to you, so I'm appealing to your better nature. Don't kiss me again. I mean it, Taft. Leave me and my children alone. We can be polite and friendly when we see each other in town, but I can't go through this again. I won't. The children and I are finally in a good place, somewhere we can be happy and build a future. I can't bear it if you bounce in and out again and break our hearts all over again. Please, Taft, don't make me beg. Go back to the life you had before and leave us alone."

HER WORDS SEEMED to gouge and claw at his heart.

I don't want this. I don't want you.

That was clear enough. He couldn't possibly mis-understand.

The children and I are finally in a good place, some-where we can be happy and build a future. I can't bear it if you bounce in and out again and break our hearts all over again.

As she had done mere days before their wedding, she had looked at him and found him somehow want-ing. Again.

He sucked in a ragged breath, everything inside him achy and sore. This was too much after the misery of the day he had just been through, and left him feeling as battered as if he'd free-floated down several miles of level-five rapids.

In that moment, as he gazed at her standing slim and lovely in this graceful, comfortable room, he realized the truth. He loved her. Laura and her family were his life, his heart. He wanted forever with them—while *she* only wanted him gone.

The loss raced over him like a firestorm, like the sud-den flashover he had once experienced as a wildlands firefighter in his early twenties. The pain was just like that fire, hot and raw and wild. He couldn't outrun it;

he could only hunker down in his shelter and wait for it to pass over.

He wanted to yell at her—to argue and curse and tell her she was being completely unreasonable. He wasn't the same man he'd been a decade ago. Couldn't she see that? He had been twenty-four years old, just a stupid kid, when she left.

Yeah, it might have taken ten years to figure things out, but now he finally knew what he wanted out of life. He was ready to commit everything to her and her children. He wanted what Trace had found with Becca. Once he had held exactly that gift in his hands and he had let it slip away and the loss of it had never hurt as keenly as it did right in this moment.

What did it matter that he might have changed? She didn't want to risk being hurt again by him and he didn't know how to argue with that.

She was right, he had turned away from the warmth of her love at a time in his life when he had needed it most. He couldn't argue with that and he couldn't change things.

He didn't know how to demonstrate to her that *he* had changed, though, that he needed her now to help him become the kind of man he wanted to be. He would be willing to sacrifice anything to take care of her and her children now, and he had no idea how to prove that to her.

"Laura—" he began, but she shook her head.

"I'm sorry. I'm just… I'm not strong enough to go through this all over again."

The misery in her features broke his heart, especially because he knew he had put it there—now and ten years ago.

She gave him one last searching look, then rushed out of this bright, cheerily decorated room, leaving him alone.

He stood there for a long time in the middle of the floor, trying to absorb the loss of her all over again in this room that now seemed cold and lifeless.

What now? He couldn't stay here at the inn anymore. She obviously didn't want him here and he wasn't sure he could linger on the edges of her life, having to content himself with polite greetings at the front desk and the occasional wave in the hallway.

He had finished the carpentry work Jan asked of him in this room and the other six in this wing that had needed the most repair. Because his house was ready for occupancy, with only a few minor things left to finish, he had no real excuse for hanging around.

She hadn't wanted him here in the first place, had only tolerated his presence because her mother had arranged things. He would give her what she wanted. He needed to move out, although the thought of leaving her and Alex and Maya left him feeling grimly empty.

Losing her ten years ago had devastated him. He had a very strong suspicion the pain of their broken engagement would pale compared to the loss of her now.

CHAPTER TEN

"So how's the house?"

Taft barely heard his brother's question, too busy watching a little kid about Alex's age eating one of The Gulch's famous hamburgers and chattering away a mile a minute while his parents listened with slightly glazed expressions on their faces.

Tourists, he figured, because he didn't recognize them and he knew most of the people in his town, at least by sight. It was a little early for the full tourism season to hit—still only mid-May, with springtime in full bloom—but maybe they were visiting family for the Mother's Day weekend.

Where were they staying? he wondered. Would it be weird if he dropped over at their booth and casually mentioned Cold Creek Inn and the new breakfast service people were raving about? Yeah, probably. Trace, at least, would never let him hear the end of it.

Anyway, if they asked him about the quality of the food, he would have to admit he had no idea. He had moved out of his room at the inn and into his new house the day before Laura started the breakfast service.

But then, he wasn't going to think about Laura right now. He had already met his self-imposed daily limit about ten minutes after midnight while he had been answering a call for a minor fender bender, a couple of kids who wouldn't be borrowing their dad's new sedan again anytime soon.

And then exceeded his thinking-about-Laura quota about 1:00 a.m. and 2:00 a.m. and 3:00 a.m. And so on and so on.

He was a cute kid, Taft thought now as he watched the kid take a sip of his soda. Not as adorable as Alex, of course, but then, he was a little biased.

"The house?" Trace asked again and Taft had to jerk his attention back to his brother.

"It's been okay," he answered.

"Just okay? Can't you drum up a little more excitement than that? You've been working on this all winter long."

"I'm happy to be done," he answered, not in the mood for an interrogation.

If his brother kept this up, he was going to think twice next time about inviting Trace for a late lunch after a long shift. It had been a crazy idea anyway. He and his twin used to get together often for meals at The Gulch, but since Trace's engagement, his brother's free time away from Becca and Gabi had become sparse, as it should be.

He hadn't been quite ready to go home for a solitary TV dinner after work, so had persuaded Trace to take a break and meet him. They could usually manage to talk enough about the general public safety of Pine Gulch for it to technically be considered a working lunch.

Except now, when the police chief appeared to have other things on his mind.

"I can tell when somebody's lying to me," Trace said with a solemn look. "I'm a trained officer of the law, remember? Besides that, I'm your brother. I know you pretty well after sharing this world for thirty-four years. You're not happy and you haven't been for a couple of weeks now. Even Becca commented on it. What's going on?"

He couldn't very well tell his brother he felt as if Laura had made beef jerky out of his heart. He ached with loneliness for her and for Maya and Alex. Right now, he would give anything to be sitting across the table from them while Maya grinned at him and Alex jabbered his ear off. Even if he could find the words to explain away his lousy mood, he wasn't sure he was ready to share all of that with Trace.

"Maybe I'm tired of the same-old, same-old," he finally said, when Trace continued to give him the Bowman interrogation look: *Talk or you* will *be sorry*.

"I've been doing the same job for nearly six years, with years fighting wildland fires and doing EMT work before I made chief. Maybe it's time for me to think about taking a job somewhere else."

"Where?"

He shrugged. "Don't know. I've had offers here and there. Nevada. Oregon. Alaska, even. A change could be good. Get out of Pine Gulch, you know?"

Trace lifted an eyebrow and looked at him skeptically. "You just finished your new house a week ago. And now you're thinking about leaving it? After all that work you put into it?"

He had come to the grim realization some nights ago during another sleepless episode that it would be torture continuing to live here in Pine Gulch, knowing she was so close but forever out of reach. He missed her. A hundred times a day he wanted to run over to the hotel claiming fire-code enforcement checks or something ridiculous like that just for the chance to see her and the children again.

Being without her had been far easier when she was half a world away in Spain. He was afraid the idea of weeks and months—and possibly *years*—of having her this close but always just out of his reach was more than he could endure.

Maybe it was his turn to leave this time.

"It's just an idea. Something I'm kicking around. I haven't actually *done* anything about it."

Before Trace could answer, Donna Archuleta, who owned The Gulch with her husband, brought over their order.

"Here you go, Chief Bowman." She set down Trace's plate, his favorite roast-beef sandwich with green peppers and onions. "And for the other Chief Bowman," she said in her gravelly ex-smoker voice, delivering Taft's lunch of meat loaf and mashed potatoes, a particular specialty of Lou's.

"Thanks, Donna."

"You're welcome. How are the wedding plans coming along?" she asked Trace.

His brother scratched his cheek. "Well, I'll admit I'm mostly staying out of it. You'll have to ask Becca that one."

"I would if she would ever come around. I guess now she's opened that fancy attorney-at-law office and doesn't have to wait tables anymore, she must be too busy for us these days."

Trace shook his head with a smile at the cantankerous old woman. "I'll bring her and Gabi in for breakfast over the weekend. How would that be?"

"I guess that'll do. You two enjoy your lunch."

She headed away amid the familiar diner sounds of rattling plates and conversation.

He had hoped the distraction would derail Trace's train of thought but apparently not. "If you think taking a job somewhere and moving away from Pine Gulch is what you want and need right now, I say go for it," his brother said, picking up right where he had left off. "You know the family will support you in whatever you decide. We'll miss you but we will all understand."

"Thank you, I appreciate that."

He considered it one of his life's greatest blessings that he had three siblings who loved him and would back him up whenever he needed it.

"We'll understand," Trace repeated. "As long as you leave for the right reasons. Be damn careful you're running *to* something and not just running away."

Lou must be having an off day. The meat loaf suddenly tasted like fire-extinguisher chemicals. "Running away from *what*?"

Trace took a bite of his sandwich and chewed and swallowed before he answered, leaving Taft plenty of time to squirm under the sympathy in his gaze. "Maybe a certain innkeeper and her kids, who shall remain nameless."

How did his brother do that? He hadn't said a single word to him about Laura, but Trace had guessed the depth of his feelings anyway, maybe before he did. It was one of those weird twin things, he supposed. He had known the first time he met Becca, here in this diner, that Trace was already crazy about her.

The only thing he could do was fake his way out of it. "What? Laura? We were done with each other ten years ago."

"You sure about that?"

He forced a laugh. "Yeah, pretty darn sure. You might have noticed we didn't actually get married a decade ago."

"Yeah, I did pick up on that. I'm a fairly observant guy." Trace gave him a probing look. "And speaking of observant, I've also got an active network of confidential informants. Word is you haven't been to the Bandito for the greater part of a month, which coincidentally happens to be right around the time Laura Santiago showed up back in town with her kids."

"Checking up on me?"

"Nope. More like vetting questions from certain segments of the female society in Pine Gulch about where the hell you've been lately. Inquiring minds and all that."

He took a forkful of mashed potatoes, but found them every bit as unappealing as the meat loaf. "I've been busy."

"So I hear. Working on renovations at the inn, from what I understand."

"Not anymore. That's done now."

He had no more excuses to hang around Cold Creek Inn. No more reason to help Alex learn how to use power tools, to listen to Maya jabber at him, half in a language he didn't understand, or to watch Laura make the inn blossom as she had dreamed about doing most of her life.

Yeah, he wasn't sure he could stick around town and watch as Laura settled happily into Pine Gulch, working on the inn, making friends, moving on.

All without him.

"When I heard from Caidy that you'd moved into the

inn and were helping Laura and her mother with some carpentry work, I thought for sure you and she were starting something up again. Guess I was wrong, huh?"

Another reason he should leave town. His family and half the town were probably watching and waiting for just that, to see if the two of them would pick up where they left off a decade and an almost-wedding later.

"Laura isn't interested in rekindling anything. Give her a break, Trace. I mean, it hasn't even been a year since she lost her husband. She and the kids are trying to settle into Pine Gulch again. She's got big plans for the inn, and right now that and her children are where her focus needs to be."

Some of his despair, the things he thought he had been so careful not to say, must have filtered through his voice anyway. His brother studied him for a long moment, compassion in his green eyes Taft didn't want to see.

He opened his mouth to deflect that terrible sympathy with some kind of stupid joke, but before he could come up with one, his radio and Trace's both squawked at the same moment.

"All officers in the vicinity. I've got a report of a Ten Fifty-Seven. Two missing juveniles in the area of Cold Creek Inn. Possible drowning."

Everything inside him froze to ice, crackly and fragile.

Missing juveniles. Cold Creek Inn. Possible drowning.

Alex and Maya.

He didn't know how he knew so completely, but his heart cramped with agony and bile rose in his throat for a split second before he shoved everything aside.

Not now. There would be time later, but right now he needed to focus on what was important.

He and Trace didn't even look at each other. They both raced out of the restaurant to their vehicles parked beside each other and squealed out of the parking lot.

He picked up his radio. "Maria, this is Fire Chief Bowman. I want every single damn man on the fire department to start combing the river."

"Yes, sir," she answered.

His heart pounding in his chest, he sped through the short three blocks to Cold Creek Inn, every light flashing and every siren blaring away as he drove with a cold ball of dread in his gut. He couldn't go through this. Not with her. Everything inside him wanted to run away from what he knew would be deep, wrenching pain, but he forced himself to push it all out of his head.

He beat Trace to the scene by a heartbeat and didn't even bother to turn off his truck, just raced to where he saw a group of people standing beside the fast-moving creek.

Laura was being restrained by two people, her mother and a stranger, he realized. She was crying and fighting them in a wild effort to jump into the water herself.

"Laura, what's happened?"

She gazed blankly at him for a moment, her eyes wide and shocky, then her features collapsed with raw relief.

"Taft, my children," she sobbed and it was the most heartrending sound he had ever heard. "I have to go after them. Why won't anyone let me go after them?"

Jan, still holding her, was also in tears and appeared even more hysterical, her face blotchy and red.

He wouldn't be able to get much information out of either of them.

Beyond them, he could see the water running fast and high and Lucky Lou running back and forth along the bank, barking frantically.

"Laura, honey, I need you to calm down for just a moment." While everything inside him was screaming urgency, he forced himself to use a soothing, measured tone, aware it might be his only chance to get through to her.

"Please, sweetheart, this is important. Why do you think they're in the river? What happened?"

She inhaled a ragged breath, visibly struggling to calm herself down to answer his question—and he had never loved her more than in that single moment of stark courage.

"They were just here. Right here. Playing with Lucky. They know they're not to go near the creek. I've told them a hundred times. I was out here with them, planting flowers, and kept my eye on them the whole time. I walked around the corner of the inn for another flat and was gone maybe thirty seconds. That's all. When I came back Lucky was running along the bank and they were g-gone." She said the last word on a wailing sob that made everything inside him ache.

"How long ago?"

The stranger, who must have restrained her from jumping in after them, spoke. "Three minutes. Maybe four. Not long. I pulled into the parking lot just in time to see her running down the bank screaming something about her kids. I stopped her from jumping in after them and called 9-1-1. I don't know if that was right."

He would shake the guy's hand later and pay for his

whole damn stay, but right now he didn't have even a second to spare.

"You did exactly right. Laura, stay here. Promise me," he ordered. "You won't find them by jumping in and you'll just complicate everything. The water is moving too fast for you to catch up. Stay here and I will bring them back to you. Promise me."

Her eyes were filled with a terrified anguish. He wanted to comfort her, but damn it, he didn't have time.

"Promise me," he ordered again.

She sagged against the stranger and Jan and nodded, then collapsed to her knees in the dirt, holding on to her mother.

He raced back to his truck, shouting orders into his radio the whole time as he set up a search perimeter and called in the technical rescue team. Even as one part of his mind was busy dealing with the logistics of the search and setting up his second in command to run the grid, the other part was gauging the depth of the water, velocity of the current, the creek's route.

Given that the incident happened five minutes ago now, he tried to calculate how far the children might have floated. It was all guesswork without a meter to give him exact stream flow, but he had lived along Cold Creek all his life and knew its moods and its whims. He and Trace and their friends used to spend summers fishing for native rainbows, and as he grew older, he had kayaked the waters innumerable times, even during high runoff.

Something urged him to head toward Saddleback Road. Inspiration? Some kind of guardian angel? Just a semi-educated guess? He didn't know, but a picture formed itself clearly in his head, of a certain spot where the creek slowed slightly at another natural bow and split into two channels before rejoining. Somehow he knew *that* was the spot where he needed to be right now.

He could be totally off the mark but he could only hope and pray he wasn't.

"Battalion Twenty, what's your status?" he heard over the radio. Trace.

"Almost to Saddleback," he said, his voice hoarse. "I'm starting here. Send a team to the road a quarter mile past that. What is that? Barrelwood?"

"Copy. Don't be stupid, Chief."

One of the hazards of working with his brother—but he didn't care about that now, when he had reached the spot that seemed imprinted in his mind, for all those reasons he couldn't have logically explained.

He jerked the wheel to the side of the road and jumped out, stopping only long enough to grab the water-rescue line in its throw bag in one of the compartments in the back of his truck. He raced to the water's edge, scanning up and down for any sign of movement. This time of year, mid-May, the runoff was fast and cold coming out of the mountains, but he thanked God the peak flow, when it was a churning, furious mess, was still another few weeks away as the weather warmed further.

Had he overshot them or had they already moved past him? Damn it, he had no way of knowing. Go down or up? He screwed his eyes shut and again that picture formed in his head of the side channel that was upstream about twenty yards. He was crazy to follow such a vague impression but it was all he had right now.

He raced up the bank, listening to the reports of the search on his radio as he ran.

Finally he saw the marshy island in the middle of the two channels. A couple of sturdy pine trees grew there, blocking a good part of his view, but he strained his eyes.

There!

Was that a flash of pink?

He moved a little farther upstream for a different vantage point. The instant he could see around the pines, everything inside him turned to that crackly ice again.

Two small dark heads bobbed and jerked, snagged in the deadfall of a tree that was half-submerged in the water. The tree was caught between two boulders in the side channel. From here, he couldn't tell if the kids were actually actively holding on or had just been caught there by the current.

He grabbed his radio, talking as he moved as close as he could. "Battalion Twenty. I've got a sighting twenty yards east of where my truck is parked on Saddleback Road. I need the tech team and Ambulance Thirty-Six here now."

He knew, even as he issued the order, that no way in hell was he going to stand here and do nothing during the ten minutes or so it might take to assemble the team and get them here. Ten minutes was the difference between life and death. Anything could happen in those ten minutes. He didn't know if the children were breathing—and didn't even want to think about any other alternative—but if they weren't, ten minutes could be critical to starting CPR.

Besides that, the water could be a capricious, vengeful thing. The relentless current could tug them farther downstream and away from him. He wasn't about to take that chance.

This was totally against protocol, everything he had trained his own people *not* to do. Single-man water rescues were potentially fatal and significantly increased the dangers for everybody concerned.

Screw protocol.

He needed to reach Laura's children. Now.

This would be much more comfortable in a wet suit but he wasn't about to take the time to pull his on. He raced upstream another ten yards to a small bridge formed by another fallen tree. On the other side of the creek, the children were only a dozen feet away. He called out and thought he saw one of the dark heads move.

"Alex! Maya! Can you hear me?"

He thought he saw the head move again but he couldn't be sure. No way could they catch the throw bag. He was going to have to go after them, which he had known from the moment he spotted that flash of pink.

If he calculated just right and entered at the correct place upstream, the current would float him right to them, but he would have to aim just right so the first boulder blocked his movement and his weight didn't dislodge the logjam, sending the children farther downstream.

He knew the swift-water safety algorithm. Talk. Reach. Wade. Throw. Helo. Go. Row. Tow. The only thing he could do here was reach them and get them the hell out.

He tied the rescue rope around the sturdy trunk of a cottonwood, then around his waist, then plunged into the water that came up to his chest. The icy water was agony and he felt his muscles cramp instantly, but he waded his way toward the deadfall, fighting the current as hard as he could. It was useless. After only a few steps, the rushing water swept his feet out from under him, as he expected.

It took every ounce of strength he could muster to keep his feet pointed downstream so they could take the brunt of any impact with any boulders or snags in the water. The last thing he needed here was a head injury.

He must have misjudged the current because he ended up slightly to the left of the boulder. He jammed his numb feet on the second boulder to stop his momentum. A branch of the dead tree gouged the skin of his forehead like a bony claw, but he ignored it, fighting his way hand over hand toward the children, praying the whole time he wouldn't dislodge the trunk.

"Alex, Maya. It's Chief Bowman. Come on, you guys." He kept up a nonstop dialogue with them but was grimly aware that only Alex stirred. The boy opened one eye as Taft approached, then closed it again, looking as if he were utterly exhausted.

The boy's arm was around his sister, but Maya was facedown in the water. He used all his strength to fight the current as he turned her and his gut clenched when he saw her eyes staring blankly and her sweet features still and lifeless.

He gave her a quick rescue breath. She didn't respond, but he kept up the rescue breaths to her and Alex while he worked as quickly as he could, tying them both to him with hands that he could barely feel, wondering as he worked and breathed for all three of them how much time had passed and what the hell was taking his tech rescue crew so long.

This was going to be the toughest part, getting them all out of the water safely, but with sheer muscle, determination—and probably some help from those guardian angels he was quite certain had to be looking after these two kids—he fought the current and began pulling himself hand over hand along the tree trunk, wet and slippery with moss and algae, pausing every ten seconds to give them both rudimentary rescue breaths.

Just as he reached the bank, completely exhausted by the effort of fighting the current, he heard shouts and cries and felt arms lifting him out and untying the kids.

"Chief! How the hell did you find them clear over here?" Luke Orosco, his second in command, looked stunned as he took in the scene.

He had no idea how to explain the process that had led him here. Miracle or intuition, it didn't matter, not when both children were now unresponsive, although it appeared Alex was at least breathing on his own.

Satisfied that his crew was working with Alex, he immediately turned to the boy's sister and took command. He was the only trained paramedic in this group, though everyone else had basic EMT training. "Maya? Come on, Maya, honey. You've got to breathe, sweetheart."

He bent over the girl and turned her into recovery position, on her side, nearly on her stomach, her knee up to drain as much water from her lungs as he could. He could hear Alex coughing up water, but Maya remained still.

"Come on, Maya."

He turned her and started doing CPR, forcing himself to lock away his emotions, the knowledge that Laura would be destroyed if he couldn't bring back her daughter. He continued, shaking off other crew members who wanted to take over.

Some part of him was afraid all this work was for nothing—she had been in the water too long— but then, when despair began to grip him colder than the water, he felt something change. A stirring, a movement, a heartbeat. And then she gave a choking cough and he turned her to her side just in time as she vomited what seemed like gallons of Cold Creek all over the place.

Pink color began to spread through her, another miracle, then she gave a hoarse, raspy cry. He turned her again to let more water drain, then wrapped her in a blanket one of his crew handed over.

"Oxygen," he called. Maya continued to cry softly and he couldn't bring himself to let her go.

"Good job, Chief!"

He was vaguely aware of the guys clapping him and themselves on the back and the air of exultation that always followed a successful rescue, but right now he couldn't focus on anything but Maya.

"You ready for us to load her up?" Ron asked.

He didn't want to let her go, but he knew she needed more than the triage treatment they could offer here. There was still a chance she had been without oxygen long enough for brain damage, but he had to hope the cold water might help ease that possibility.

"Yeah, we'd better get her into the ambulance," he answered. When the EMTs loaded her onto the stretcher, he finally turned to find Alex being loaded onto another stretcher nearby. The boy was conscious and watching the activity around him. When Taft approached, his mouth twisted into a weary smile.

"Chief." The kid's voice sounded hoarse, raw. "You saved us. I knew you would."

He gripped the boy's hand, humbled and overwhelmed at that steady trust. "What happened, Alex? You know you're not supposed to be near the water."

"I know. We always stay away from it. *Always.* But Lucky ran that way and Maya followed him. I chased after her to take her back to Mama and she thought it was a game. She laughed and ran and then slipped and went in the creek. I didn't know what to do. I thought... I thought I could get her. I had swimming lessons last year. But the water was so *fast.*"

The boy started to cry and he gathered him up there on the stretcher as he had done Maya. What a great kid he was, desperately trying to protect his little sister. Taft felt tears threaten, too, from emotion or delayed reaction, he didn't know, but he was deeply grateful for any guardian angels who had been on his rescue squad for this one.

"You're safe now. You'll be okay."

"Is Maya gonna be okay?" Alex asked.

He still wasn't sure he knew the answer to that. "My best guys are just about to put her in the ambulance. You get to take a ride, too."

Before Alex could respond to that, Taft saw a Pine Gulch PD SUV pull up to the scene. His brother's vehicle. The thought barely registered before the passenger door was shoved open and a figure climbed out.

Laura.

She stood outside the patrol vehicle for just a moment as if not quite believing this could be real and then she rushed toward them. In a second she scooped Alex into her arms and hugged him.

"Oh, baby. Sweetheart," she sobbed. "You're okay. You're really okay? And Maya?" Still carrying Alex, she rushed over to Maya and pulled her into her other arm.

"I'm sorry, ma'am, but we need to transport both of the children to the clinic in town." Ron looked compassionate but determined. "They're in shock and need to be treated for possible hypothermia."

"Oh. Of course." Her strained features paled a little at this further evidence that while the children were out of the water, they still required treatment.

"They're going to be okay, Laura," Taft said. He hoped anyway, though he knew Maya wasn't out of the woods.

She glanced over at him and seemed to have noticed him for the first time. "You're bleeding."

Was he? Probably from that branch that had caught him just as he was reaching the children. He hadn't even noticed it in the rush of adrenaline but now he could feel the sting. "Just a little cut. No big deal."

"And you're soaking wet."

"Chief Bowman pulled us out of the water, Mama," Alex announced, his voice still hoarse. "He tied a rope to a tree and jumped in and got us both. That's what *I* should have done to get Maya."

She gazed at her son and then at Taft, then at the roaring current and the rope still tied to the tree.

"You saved them."

"I told you I would find them."

"You did."

He flushed, embarrassed by the shock and gratitude

in her eyes. Did she really think he would let the kids drown? He loved them. He would have gone after them no matter what the circumstances.

"And broke about a dozen rules for safe rescue in the process," Luke Orosco chimed in, and he wanted to pound the guy for opening his big mouth.

"I don't care," she said. "Oh, thank you. Taft, thank you!"

She grabbed him and hugged him, Alex still in her arms, and his arms came around her with a deep shudder. He couldn't bear thinking about what might have happened. If he had overshot the river and missed them. If he hadn't been so close, just at The Gulch, when the call came in. A hundred small tender mercies had combined to make this moment possible.

Finally Luke cleared his throat. "Uh, Doc Dalton is waiting for us at the clinic."

She stepped away from him and he saw her eyes were bright with tears, her cheeks flushed. "Yes, we should go."

"We should be able to take you and both kids all in one ambulance," Luke offered.

"Perfect. Thank you so much."

She didn't look at him again as the crews loaded the two kids into their biggest ambulance. There wasn't room for him in there, although he supposed as battalion chief he could have pulled rank and insisted he wanted to be one of the EMTs assisting them on the way to the hospital.

But Laura and her children were a family unit that didn't have room for him. She had made that plain enough. He would have to remain forever on the outside of their lives. That was the way Laura wanted things and he didn't know how to change her mind.

He watched the doors close on the ambulance with finality, then Cody Shepherd climb behind the wheel and pull away from the scene. As he watched them drive away, he was vaguely aware of Trace moving to stand beside him. His brother placed a hand on his shoulder, offering understanding without words.

Another one of those twin things, he supposed. Trace must have picked up on his yearning as he watched the family he wanted drive away from him.

"Good save," Trace said quietly. "But it's a damn miracle all three of you didn't go under."

"I know." The adrenaline rush of the rescue was fading fast, leaving him battered and embarrassingly weak-kneed.

"For the record, you ever pull a stunt like that again, trying a single-man water rescue, Ridge and I will drag what's left of you behind one of the River Bow horses."

"What choice did I have? I knew the deadfall wasn't going to hold them for long, the way the current was pushing at them. Any minute, they were going to break free and float downstream and I wouldn't have had a second chance. Think if it was Destry or Gabi out there. You would have done the same thing."

Taft was silent for a moment. "Yeah, probably. That still doesn't make it right."

Terry McNeil, one of his more seasoned EMTs, approached the two of them with his emergency kit. "Chief, your turn."

He probably needed a stitch or two, judging by the amount of blood, but he wasn't in the mood to go to the clinic and face Laura again, to be reminded once more of everything he couldn't have. "I'll take care of it myself."

"You sure? That cut looks deep."

He gave Terry a long look, not saying anything, and the guy finally shrugged. "Your call. You'll need to clean it well. Who knows what kind of bacteria is floating in that water."

"I'm heading home to change anyway. I'll clean it up there."

He knew he should be jubilant after a successful rescue. Some part of him was, of course. The alternative didn't bear thinking about, but he was also crashing now after an all-nighter at the fire station combined with exhaustion from the rescue. Right now, all he wanted to do was go home and sleep.

"Don't be an idiot," Terry advised him, an echo of what his brother had said earlier.

He wanted to tell both of them it was too late for that. He had been nothing short of an idiot ten years ago when he let Laura walk away from him. Once, he had held happiness in his hands and had blown it away just like those cottonwood puffs floating on the breeze.

She might be back but she wouldn't ever be his, and the pain of that hurt far worse than being battered by the boulders and snags and raging current of Cold Creek.

CHAPTER ELEVEN

So close. She had been a heartbeat away from losing everything.

Hours after the miracle of her children's rescue, Laura still felt jittery, her insides achy and tight with reaction. She couldn't bear to contemplate what might have been.

If not for Taft and his insane heroics, she might have been preparing for two funerals right now instead of sitting at the side of her bed, watching her children sleep. Maya was sucking her thumb, something she hadn't done in a long time, while Alex slept with his arm around his beloved dog, who slept on his side with his short little legs sticking straight out.

So much for her one hard-and-fast rule when she had given in to Alex's determined campaign and allowed the adoption of Lucky Lou.

No dogs on the bed, she had told her son firmly, again and again, but she decided this was a night that warranted exceptions.

She hadn't wanted to let either of them out of her sight, even at bedtime. Because she couldn't watch them both in their separate beds, she had decided to lump everyone together in here, just this once. She wasn't sure where she would sleep, perhaps stretched across the foot of the bed, but she knew sleep would be a long time coming anyway.

She should be exhausted. The day had been draining. Even after the rescue, they had spent several hours at the clinic, until Dr. Dalton and his wife, Maggie, had been confident the children appeared healthy enough to return home.

Dr. Dalton had actually wanted to send them to the hospital in Idaho Falls for overnight observation, but after a few hours, Maya was bouncing around the bed in her room like a wild monkey and Alex had been jabbering a mile a minute with his still-raspy voice.

"You can take them home," Dr. Dalton had reluctantly agreed, his handsome features concerned but kind, "as long as they remain under strict observation. Call me at once if you notice any change in breathing pattern or behavior."

She was so grateful to have her children with her safe and sound that she would have agreed to anything by that point. Every time she thought about what might have happened if Taft hadn't been able to find the children, her stomach rolled with remembered fear and she had to fold her arms around it and huddle for a few moments until she regained control.

She would never forget that moment she climbed out of his brother's patrol vehicle and had seen Taft there, bloodied and soaking wet, holding her son close. Something significant had shifted inside her in that moment, something so profound and vital that she shied away from examining it yet.

She was almost relieved when a crack of light through the doorway heralded her mother's approach. Jan pushed the door open and joined her beside the bed. Her mother looked older than she had that morning, Laura reflected. The lines fanning out from her eyes and bracketing her mouth seemed to have been etched a little deeper by the events of the day.

"They look so peaceful when they're sleeping, don't they?" Jan murmured, gazing down at her only grandchildren.

Laura was suddenly awash with love for her mother, as well. Jan had been a source of steady support during her marriage. Even though Laura hadn't revealed any of the tumult of living with Javier—she still couldn't—she had always known she could call or email her mother and her spirits would lift.

Her mother hadn't had an easy life. She had suffered three miscarriages before Laura was born and two after. When Laura was a teenager, she had often felt the pressure of that keenly, knowing she was the only one of six potential siblings who had survived. She could only hope she was the kind of daughter her mother wanted.

"They do look peaceful," she finally answered, pitching her voice low so she didn't wake the children, although she had a feeling even the high-school marching band would have a tough time rousing them after their exhausting day. "Hard to believe, looking at them now, what kind of trouble they can get into during daylight hours, isn't it?"

"I should have fenced off the river a long time ago." Weary guilt dragged down the edges of her mother's mouth.

Laura shook her head. "Mom, none of this was your fault. I should have remembered not to take my eyes off them for a second. They're just too good at finding their way to trouble."

"If Taft hadn't been there…"

She reached out and squeezed her mother's hand, still strong and capable at seventy. "I know. But he *was* there." And showed incredible bravery to climb into the water by himself instead of waiting for a support team. The EMTs couldn't seem to stop talking about the rescue during the ambulance ride to the clinic.

"Everyone is okay," she went on. "No lasting effects, Dr. Dalton said, except possibly intestinal bugs from swallowing all that creek water. We'll have to keep an eye out for stomachaches, that sort of thing."

"That's a small thing. They're here. That's all that matters." Her mother gazed at the children for a long moment, then back at Laura, her eyes troubled. "You're probably wondering why you ever came home. With all the trouble we've had since you arrived—fires and near-drownings and everything—I bet you're thinking you would have been better off to have stayed in Madrid."

"I wouldn't want to be anywhere else right now, Mom. I still think coming home was the right thing for us."

"Even though it's meant you've had to deal with Taft again?"

She squirmed under her mother's probing look. "Why should that bother me?"

"I don't know. Your history together, I guess."

"That history didn't seem to stop you from inviting the man to live at the inn for weeks!"

"Don't think I didn't notice during that time how you went out of your way to avoid him whenever you could. You told me things ended amicably between you, but I'm not so sure about that. You still have feelings for him, don't you?"

She started to give her standard answer. *The past was a long time ago. We're different people now and have both moved on.*

Perhaps because the day had been so very monumental, so very profound, she couldn't bring herself to lie to her mother.

"Yes," she murmured. "I've loved him since I was a silly girl. It's hard to shut that off."

"Why do you need to? That man still cares about you, my dear. I could tell that first day when he came to talk to me about helping with the inn renovations. He jumped into the river and risked his life to save your children. That ought to tell you something about the depth of his feelings."

She thought of the dozens of reasons she had employed to convince herself not to let Taft into her life again. None of them seemed very important right now—or anything she wanted to share with her mother. "It's complicated."

"Life is complicated, honey, and hard and stressful and exhausting. And *wonderful*. More so if you have a good man to share it with."

Laura thought of her father, one of the best men she had ever known. He had been kind and compassionate, funny and generous. The kind of man who often opened the doors of his inn for a pittance—or sometimes nothing—to people who had nowhere else to go.

In that moment, she would have given anything if he could be there with them, watching over her children with them.

Perhaps he had been, she thought with a little shiver. By rights, her children should have died today in the swollen waters of Cold Creek. That they survived was nothing short of a miracle and she had to think they had help somehow.

She missed her father deeply in that moment. He had loved Taft and had considered him the son he had always wanted. Both of her parents had been crushed by the end of her engagement, but her father had never pressed her to know the reasons.

"While you were busy at the clinic this afternoon," Jan said after a moment, "I was feeling restless and at loose ends and needed to stay busy while I waited for you. I had to do something so I made a caramel-apple pie. You might not remember but that was always Taft's favorite."

He did have a sweet tooth for pastries, she remembered.

"It's small enough payment for giving me back my grandchildren, but it will have to do for now, until I can think of something better. I was just about to take it to him…unless you would like to."

Laura gazed at her sleeping children and then at her mother, who was trying her best to be casual and nonchalant instead of eagerly coy. She knew just what Jan was trying to do—push her and Taft back together, which was probably exactly the reason she agreed to let him move into the inn under the guise of trading carpentry work for a room.

Jan was sneaky that way. Laura couldn't guess at her motives—perhaps her mother was looking for any way she could to bind Laura and her children to Pine Gulch. Or perhaps she was matchmaking simply because she had guessed, despite Laura's attempts to put on a bright facade, that her marriage had not been a happy one and she wanted to see a different future for her daughter.

Or perhaps Jan simply adored Taft, because most mothers did.

Whatever the reason, Laura had a pivotal decision to make: Take the pie to him herself as a small token of their vast gratitude or thwart her mother's matchmaking plans and insist on staying here with the children?

Her instincts urged her to avoid seeing him again just now. With these heavy emotions churning inside her, she was afraid seeing him now would be too dangerous. Her defenses were probably at the lowest point they had been since coming home to Pine Gulch. If he kissed her again, she wasn't at all certain she would have the strength to resist him.

But that was cowardly. She needed to see him again, if for no other reason than to express, now that she was more calm and rational than she had been on that riverbank, her deep and endless gratitude to him for giving her back these two dear children.

"I'll go, Mom."

"Are you sure? I don't mind."

"I need to do this. You're right. Will you watch the children for me?"

"I won't budge," her mother promised. "I'll sit right here and work on my crocheting the entire time. I promise."

"You don't have to literally watch them. You may certainly sit in the living room and check on them at various intervals."

"I'm not moving from this spot," Jan said. "Between Lou and me, we should be able to keep them safe."

THE EVENING WAS LOVELY, unusually warm for mid-May. She drove through town with her window down, savoring the sights and sounds of Pine Gulch settling down for the night. Because it was Friday, the drive-in on the edge of the business district was crowded with cars. Teenagers hanging out, anxious for the end of the school year, young families grabbing a burger on payday, senior citizens treating their grandchildren to an ice-cream cone.

The flowers were beginning to bloom in some of the sidewalk planters along Main Street and everything was greening up beautifully. May was a beautiful time of year in eastern Idaho after the inevitable harshness of winter, brimming with life, rebirth, hope.

As she was right now.

She had heard about people suffering near-death encounters who claimed the experience gave them a new respect and appreciation for their life and the beauty of the world around them. That's how she felt right now. Even though it was her children who had nearly died, Laura knew she would have died right along with them if they hadn't been rescued.

She had Alex and Maya back now, along with a new appreciation for those flowers in carefully tended gardens, the mountains looming strong and steady over the town, the sense of home that permeated this place.

She drove toward those mountains now, to Cold Creek Canyon, where the creek flowed out of the high country and down through the valley. Her mother had given her directions to Taft's new house and she followed them, turning onto Cold Creek Road.

She found it no surprise that Jan knew Taft's address. Jan and her wide circle of friends somehow managed to keep their collective finger on the pulse of everything going on in town.

The area here along the creek was heavily wooded with Douglas fir and aspen trees and it took her a moment to find the mailbox with his house number. She peered through the trees but couldn't see anything of his house except a dark green metal roof that just about matched the trees in the fading light.

A bridge spanned the creek here and as she drove

over it, she couldn't resist looking down at the silvery ribbon of water, darting over boulders and around fallen logs. Her children had been in that icy water, she thought, chilled all over again at how close she had come to losing everything.

She couldn't let it paralyze her. When the runoff eased a little, she needed to take Alex and Maya fishing in the river to help all of them overcome their fear of the water.

She stayed on the bridge for several moments, watching lightning-fast dippers crisscross the water for insects and a belted kingfisher perching on a branch without moving for long moments before he swooped into the water and nabbed a hapless hatchling trout.

As much as she enjoyed the serenity of the place, she finally gathered her strength and started her SUV again, following the winding driveway through the pines. She had to admit, she was curious to see his house. He had asked her to come see it, she suddenly remembered, and she had deflected the question and changed the subject, not wanting to intertwine their lives any further. She was sorry now that she hadn't come out while it was under construction.

The trees finally opened up into a small clearing and she caught her breath. His house was gorgeous: two stories of honey-colored pine logs and river rock with windows dominating the front and a porch that wrapped around the entire house so that he could enjoy the view of mountains and creek in every direction.

She loved it instantly, from the river-rock chimney rising out of the center to the single Adirondack chair on the porch, angled to look out at the mountains. She couldn't have explained it but she sensed warmth and welcome here.

Her heart pounded strangely in her ears as she parked the SUV and climbed out. She saw a light inside the house but she also heard a rhythmic hammering coming from somewhere behind the structure.

That would be Taft. Somehow she knew it. She reached in for the pie her mother had made—why hadn't she thought of doing something like this for him?—and headed in the direction of the sound.

She found him in another clearing behind the house, framing up a building she assumed would be an outbuilding for the horses he had talked about. He had taken off his shirt to work the nail gun, and that leather tool belt he had used while he was working at the inn— not that she had noticed or anything—hung low over his hips. Muscles rippled in the gathering darkness and her stomach shivered.

Here was yet another image that could go in her own mental Taft Bowman beefcake calendar.

She huffed out a little breath, sternly reminding herself that standing and salivating over the man was *not* why she was here, and forced herself to move forward. Even though she wasn't trying to use stealth, he must not have heard her approach over the sound of the nail gun and the compressor used to power it, even when she was almost on top of him. He didn't turn around or respond in any way and she finally realized why when she saw white earbuds dangling down, tethered to a player in the back pocket of his jeans.

She had no idea what finally tipped him off to her presence, but the steady motion of the nail gun stopped, he paused for just a heartbeat and then he jerked his head around. In that instant, she saw myriad emotions cross his features—surprise, delight, resignation and something that looked very much like yearning before he shuttered his expression.

"Laura, hi."

"Hello."

"Just a second."

He pulled the earbuds out and tucked them away, then crossed to the compressor and turned off the low churning sound. The only sound to break the abrupt silence was the moaning of the wind in the treetops. Taft quickly grabbed a T-shirt slung over a nearby sawhorse and pulled it over his head, and she couldn't help the little pang of disappointment.

"I brought you a pie. My mother made it for you." She held out it, suddenly feeling slightly ridiculous at the meagerness of the offering.

"A pie?"

"I know, it's a small thing. Not at all commensurate with everything you did, but…well, it's something."

"Thank you. I love pie. And I haven't had anything to eat yet, so this should be great. I might just have pie for dinner."

He had a square bandage just under his hairline that made him look rather rakish, a startling white contrast to his dark hair and sun-warmed features.

"Your head. You were hurt during the rescue, weren't you?"

He shrugged. "No big deal. Just a little cut."

Out of nowhere, she felt the hot sting of tears threaten. "I'm sorry."

"Are you kidding? This is nothing. I would have

gladly broken every limb, as long as it meant I could still get to the kids."

She stared at him there in the twilight, looking big and solid and dearly familiar, and a huge wave of love washed over her. This was Taft. Her best friend. The man she had loved forever, who could always make her laugh, who made her feel strong and powerful and able to accomplish anything she wanted.

Everything she had been trying to block out since she arrived back in Pine Gulch seemed to break through some invisible dam and she was filled, consumed, by her love for him.

Those tears burned harder and she knew she had to leave or she would completely embarrass herself by losing her slippery hold on control and sobbing all over him.

She drew in a shuddering breath. "I... I just wanted to say thank-you. Again, I mean. It's not enough. It will never be enough, but thank you. I owe you...everything."

"No, you don't. You owe me nothing. I was only doing my job."

"Only your job? Really?"

He gazed at her for a long moment and she prayed he couldn't see the emotions she could feel nearly choking her. "Okay, no," he finally said. "If I had been doing my job and following procedure, I would have waited for the swift-water tech team to come help me extricate them. I would have done everything by the book. I spend seventy percent of my time training my volunteers in the fire department *not* to do what I did today. This wasn't a job. It was much, much more."

A tear slipped free but she ignored it. She could barely make out his expression now in the twilight and had to hope the reverse was also true. She had to leave. Now, before she made a complete fool of herself.

"Well... I'm in your debt. You've got a room anytime you want at the inn."

"Thanks, I appreciate that."

She released a breath and nodded. "Well, thank you again. Enjoy the pie. I'll, uh, see you later."

She turned so swiftly that she nearly stumbled but caught herself and began to hurry back to her SUV while the tears she had struggled to contain broke free and trickled down her cheeks. She didn't know exactly why she was crying. Probably not a single reason. The stress of nearly losing her children, the joy of having them returned to her. And the sudden knowledge that she loved Taft Bowman far more than she ever had as a silly twenty-one-year-old girl.

"Laura, wait."

She shook her head, unable to turn around and reveal so much of her heart to him. As she should have expected, she only made it a few more steps before he caught up with her and turned her to face him.

He gazed down at her and she knew she must look horrible, blotchy-faced and red, with tears dripping everywhere.

"Laura," he murmured. Just that. And then with a groan he folded her into his arms, wrapping her in his heat and his strength. She shuddered again and could no longer stop the deluge. He held her as she sobbed out everything that suddenly seemed too huge and heavy for her to contain.

"I could have lost them."

"I know. I know." His arms tightened and his cheek rested on her hair, and she realized this was exactly where she belonged. Nothing else mattered. She loved Taft Bowman, had always loved him, and more than that, she trusted him.

He was her hero in every possible way.

"And you." She sniffled. "You risked your life to go after them. You could have been carried away just as easily."

"I wasn't, though. All three of us made it through."

She tightened her arms around him and they stood that way for a long time with the creek rumbling over rocks nearby while the wind sighed in the trees and an owl hooted softly somewhere close and the crickets chirped for their mates.

Something changed between them in those moments. It reminded her very much of the first time he had kissed her, on that boulder overlooking River Bow Ranch, when she somehow knew that the world had shifted in some fundamental way and nothing would ever be the same.

After several moments, he moved his hands from around her and framed her face, his eyes reflecting the stars, then he kissed her with a tenderness that made her want to weep all over again.

It was a perfect moment, standing here with him as night descended, and she never wanted it to end. She wanted to savor everything—the soft cotton of his shirt, the leashed muscles beneath, his mouth, so firm and determined on hers.

She spread her palms on his back, pressing him closer, and he made a low sound in his throat, tightening his arms around her and deepening the kiss. She opened her mouth for him and slid her tongue out to dance with his while she pressed against those solid muscles, needing more.

His hand slipped beneath her shirt to the bare skin at her waist and she remembered just how he had always known how to touch her and taste her until she was crazy with need. She shivered, just a slight motion, but it was enough that he pulled his mouth away from hers, his breathing ragged and his eyes dazed.

He gazed down at her and she watched awareness return to his features like storm clouds crossing the moon, then he slid his hands away and took a step back.

"You asked me not to kiss you again. I'm sorry, Laura. I tried. I swear I tried."

She blinked, trying to force her brain to work. After a moment, she remembered the last time he had kissed her, in the room she had just finished decorating. She remembered her confusion and fear, remembered being so certain he would hurt her all over again if she let him.

That all seemed another lifetime ago. Had she really let her fears rule her common sense?

This was Taft, the man she had loved since she was twelve years old. He loved her and he loved her children. When she had climbed out of his brother's police vehicle and seen him there by the stretcher with his arms around Alex—and more, when she had seen that rope still tied to the tree and the churning, dangerous waters he had risked to save both of her children—she had known he was a man she could count on. He had been willing to break any rule, to give up everything to save her children.

I would have gladly broken every limb, as long as it meant I could still get to the kids.

He had risked his life. How much was she willing to risk?

Everything.

She gave him a solemn look, her heart jumping inside her chest, feeling very much as if *she* was the one about to leap into Cold Creek. "Technically, *I* could still kiss you, though, right?"

He stared at her and she saw his eyes darken with confusion and a wary sort of hope. That little glimmer was all she needed to step forward into the space between them and grab his strong, wonderful hands. She tugged him toward her and stood on tiptoe and pressed her mouth to the corner of his mouth.

He didn't seem to know how to respond for a moment and then he angled his mouth and she kissed him fully, with all the joy and love in her heart.

Much to her shock, he eased away again, his expression raw and almost despairing. "I can't do this back-and-forth thing, Laura. You have to decide. I love you. I never stopped, all this time. I think some part of me has just been biding my time, waiting for you to come home."

He pulled his hands away. "I know I hurt you ten years ago. I can't change that. If I could figure out how, I would in a heartbeat."

At that, she had to shake her head. "I wouldn't change anything," she said. "If things had been different, I wouldn't have Alex and Maya."

He released a breath. "I can tell you, I realized right after you left what a fool I had been, too stubborn and proud to admit I was hurting and not dealing with it well. And then I compounded my stupidity by not coming after you like I wanted to."

"I waited for you. I didn't date anyone for two years, even though I heard all the stories about...well, the Bandito and everything. If you had called or emailed or anything, I would have come home in an instant."

"I'm a different man than I was then. I want to think I've become a *better* man, but I've still probably picked up a few more nicks and bruises than I had then."

"Haven't we all?" she murmured.

"I need to tell you, I want everything, Laura. I want a home, family. I want those things with you, the same things I wanted a decade ago."

Joy burst through her. When he reached for her hand, she curled her fingers inside his, wondering how it was possible to go from the depths of hell to this brilliant happiness in the course of one day.

"I hope you know I love your children, too. Alex is such a great kid. I can think of a hundred things I would love to show him. How to ride a two-wheeler, how to throw a spitball, how to saddle his own horse. I think I could be a good father to him."

He brought their intertwined fingers to his heart. "And Maya. She's a priceless gift, Laura. I don't know exactly what she's going to need out of life, but I can promise you, right now, that I would spend the rest of my life doing whatever it takes to give it to her. I swear to you, I would watch over her, keep her safe, give her every chance she has to stretch her wings as far as she can. I want to give her a place she can grow. A place where she knows, every single minute, that she's loved."

If she hadn't already been crazy in love with this man, his words alone and his love for her fragile, vulnerable daughter would have done the trick. She gazed up at him and felt tears of joy trickle out.

"I didn't mean to make you cry," he murmured, his own eyes wet. The significance of that did not escape her. The old Taft never would have allowed that sign of emotion.

"I love you, Taft. I love you so very much."

Words seemed wholly inadequate, like offering a caramel-apple pie in exchange for saving two precious lives, so she did the only thing she could. She kissed him again, holding him tightly to her. Could he feel the joy pulsing through her, powerful, strong, delicious?

After long, wonderful moments, he eased away again and she saw that he had been as moved as she by the embrace.

"Will you come see the house now?" he asked.

Was this his subtle way of taking her inside to make love? She wasn't quite sure she was ready to add one more earthshaking experience on this most tumultuous of days, but she did want to see his house. Besides that, she trusted him completely. If she asked him to wait, he would do it without question.

"Yes," she answered. He grinned and grabbed her hand and together they walked through the trees toward his house. He guided her up the stairs at the side of the house that led first to the wide uncovered porch and then inside to the great room with the huge windows.

She saw some similarities to the River Bow ranch house in the size of the two-story great room and the wall of windows, but there were differences, too. A balcony ringed the great room and she could see rooms leading off it.

How many bedrooms were in this place? she wondered. And why would a bachelor build this house that seemed made for a family?

The layout seemed oddly familiar to her and some of the details, as well. The smooth river-rock fireplace, the open floor plan, the random use of knobby, bulging, uniquely shaped logs as accents.

Only after he took her into the kitchen and she looked around at the gleaming appliances did all the details come together in her head.

"This is my house," she exclaimed.

"Our house," he corrected. "Remember how you used to buy log-home books and magazines and pore over them? I started building this house six months ago. It wasn't until you came back to Pine Gulch that I realized how I must have absorbed all those dreams inside me. I guess when I was planning the house, some of them must have soaked through my subconscious and onto the blueprints. I didn't even think about it until I saw you again."

It was a house that seemed built for love, for laughter, for children to climb over the furniture and dangle toys off the balcony.

"Do you like it?" he asked, and she saw that wariness in his eyes again that never failed to charm her far more than a teasing grin and lighthearted comment.

"I love everything about it, Taft. It's perfect. Beyond perfect."

He pulled her close again and as he held her there in the house he had built, she realized that love wasn't always a linear journey. Sometimes it took unexpected dips and curves and occasional sheer dropoffs. Yet somehow, despite the pain of their past, she and Taft had found their way together again.

This time, she knew, they were here to stay.

EPILOGUE

HIS BRIDE WAS LATE.

Taft stood in the entryway of the little Pine Gulch chapel under one of the many archways decorated with ribbons and flowers of red and bronze and deep green, greeting a few latecomers and trying his best not to fidget. He glanced at his watch. Ten minutes and counting when he was supposed to be tying the knot, and so far Laura was a no-show.

"She'll go through with it this time. The woman is crazy about you. Relax."

He glanced over at Trace, dressed in his best-man's Western-cut tuxedo. His brother looked disgustingly calm and Taft wanted to punch him.

"I know," he answered. For all his nerves, he didn't doubt that for a moment. Over the past six months, their love had only deepened, become more rich and beautiful like the autumn colors around them. He had no worries about her pulling out of the wedding at the last minute.

He glanced through the doors of the chapel as if he could make her appear there. "I'm just hoping she's not having trouble somewhere. You don't have your radio on you, do you?"

Trace raised an eyebrow. "Uh, no. It's a wedding, in case you forgot. I don't need to have my radio squawking in the middle of the ceremony. I figured I could do without it for a few hours."

"Probably a good idea. You don't think she's been in an accident or something?"

Trace gave him a compassionate look. One of the hazards of working in public safety was this constant awareness of all the things that could go wrong in a person's life, but usually didn't. He was sure Trace worried about Becca and Gabi just as much as he fretted for Laura and the children.

"No. I'm sure there's a reasonable explanation. Why don't we check in with Caidy?"

That would probably be the logical course of action before he went off in a panic, since as maid of honor, she should be with Laura. "Yeah. Right. Good idea. Give me your phone."

"I can do it. That's what a best man is for, right?"

"Just give me your phone. Please?" he added, when Trace looked reluctant.

Trace reached into the inside pocket of his black suit jacket for his phone. "Hold on. I'll have to turn it back on. Wouldn't want any phones going off as you're taking your vows, either."

He waited impatiently, and after an eternity, his brother handed the activated phone over. Before he could find Caidy's number in the address book, the phone buzzed.

"Where are you?" he answered when he saw her name on the display.

"Taft? Why do you have Trace's phone?"

"I was just about to call you. What's wrong? Is Laura okay?"

"We're just pulling up to the church. I was calling to

give you the heads-up that we might need a few more minutes. Maya woke up with a stomachache, apparently. She threw up before we left the cottage and then again on our way, all over her dress. We had to run back to the inn to find something else for her to wear."

"Is she all right now?"

"Eh. Okay, but not great. She's still pretty fretful. Laura's trying to soothe her. Have the organist keep playing, and as soon as we get there, we'll try to fix Maya up and calm her down a little more, then we can get this show on the road. Here we are now."

He saw the limo he had hired from Jackson Hole pulling up to the side door of the church, near the room set aside for the bridal party. "I see you. Thanks for calling."

He hung up the phone and handed it back to Trace. Ridge had joined them, he saw, and wore a little furrow of concern between his eyes.

"The girls okay?" Ridge asked.

"Maya's got a stomachache. Can you stall for a few more minutes?"

"Sure. How about a roping demonstration or something? I think I've got a lasso in the pickup."

He had to look closely at his older brother to see that Ridge was teasing, probably trying to ease the tension. Yeah, it wasn't really working. "I think a few more songs should be sufficient. I'm going to go check on Maya."

"What about the whole superstition about not seeing the bride before the wedding?" Trace asked. "As I recall, you and Ridge practically hog-tied me to keep me away from Becca before ours."

"These are special circumstances. You want to try

to stop me, you're more than welcome. Good luck with that."

Neither brother seemed inclined to interfere, so Taft made his way through the church to the bridal-party room. Outside the door, he could hear the low hush of women's voices and then a little whimper. That tiny sound took away any remaining hesitation and he pushed open the door.

His gaze instinctively went to Laura. She was stunning in a cream-colored mid-length lace confection, her silky golden hair pulled up in an intricate style that made her look elegant and vulnerable at the same time. Maya huddled in her lap, wearing only a white slip. Caidy and Jan stood by, looking helpless.

When Maya spotted him, she sniffed loudly. "Chief," she whimpered.

He headed over to the two females he loved with everything inside him and picked her up, heedless of his rented tux.

"What's the matter, little bug?"

"Tummy hurts."

She didn't seem to have a fever, from what he could tell.

"Do you think it's the giardiasis?" Jan asked.

He thought of the girl's abdominal troubles after her near-drowning, the parasite she had picked up from swallowing half the Cold Creek. "I wouldn't think so. She's been healthy for three months. Doc Dalton said she didn't need any more medicine."

His knees still felt weak whenever he thought of the miraculous rescue of the children. He knew he had been guided to them somehow. He found it equally miraculous that Alex had emerged unscathed from the ordeal and Maya's only lingering effect was the giardia bug she'd picked up.

She sure didn't look very happy right now, though. He wondered if he ought to call in Jake Dalton from the congregation to check on her, when he suddenly remembered a little tidbit of information that had slipped his mind in the joy-filled chaos leading up to the wedding.

"Maya, how many pieces of cake did you have last night at the rehearsal dinner?"

Two separate times he'd seen her with a plate of dessert but hadn't thought much about it until right now.

She shrugged, though he thought she looked a little guilty as she held up two fingers.

"Are you sure?"

She looked at her mother, then back at him, then used her other hand to lift up two more fingers.

Laura groaned. "No wonder she's sick this morning. I should have thought of that. We were all so distracted, I guess we must not have realized she made so many trips to the dessert table."

"I like cake," Maya announced.

He had to smile. "I do too, bug, but you should probably go easy on the wedding cake at the reception later."

"Okay."

He hugged her. "Feel better now?"

She nodded and wiped a fist at a few stray tears on her cheeks. She was completely adorable, and he still couldn't believe he had been handed this other miraculous gift, the chance to step in and be the father figure to this precious child and her equally precious brother.

"My dress is icky."

"You won't be able to wear your flower-girl dress with the fluffy skirt," Jan agreed. "We're going to have to wash it. It will probably be dry by the reception tonight, though. And look! I bought this red one for you for Christmas. We'll use that one at the wedding now and you'll look beautiful."

"You're a genius, Mom," Laura murmured.

"I have my moments," Jan said. She took her granddaughter from his arms to help her into the dress and fix her hair again.

"Crisis averted?" he asked Laura while Jan and Caidy fussed around Maya.

"I think so." She gave him a grateful smile and his heart wanted to burst with love for her, especially when she stepped closer to him and slipped her arms around his waist. "Are you sure you're ready to take on all this fun and excitement?"

He wrapped his arms around her, thinking how perfectly she fit there, how she filled up all the empty places that had been waiting all these years just for her. He kissed her forehead, careful not to mess up her pretty curls. "I've never been more sure of anything. I hope you know that."

"I do," she murmured.

He desperately wanted to kiss her, but had a feeling his sister and her mother wouldn't appreciate it in the middle of their crisis.

The door behind them opened and Alex burst through, simmering with the energy field that always seemed to surround him except when he was sleeping. "When is the wedding going to start? I'm tired of waiting."

"I know what you mean, kid," Taft said with a grin, stepping away from Laura a little so he could pull Alex over for a quick hug.

His family. He had waited more than ten years for this, and he didn't know if he had the patience to stand another minute's delay before all his half-buried dreams became reality.

"Okay. I think we're good here," Caidy said, as Jan adjusted the ribbon in the girl's brown hair.

"Doesn't she look great?"

"Stunning," he claimed.

Maya beamed at him and slipped her hand in his. "Marry now."

"That's a great idea, sweetheart." He turned to Laura. "Are you ready?"

She smiled at him, and as he gazed at this woman he had known for half his life and loved for most of that time, he saw the rest of their lives ahead of them, bright and beautiful, and filled with joy and laughter and love.

"I finally am," she said, reaching for his hand, and together they walked toward their future.

* * * * *

If you loved this story by New York Times
bestselling author

RAEANNE THAYNE

be sure to check out her fan-favorite
miniseries

THE COWBOYS OF
COLD CREEK!

THE RANCHER'S CHRISTMAS SONG
THE HOLIDAY GIFT
A COLD CREEK CHRISTMAS STORY
THE CHRISTMAS RANCH
A COLD CREEK CHRISTMAS SURPRISE
A COLD CREEK NOEL
A COLD CREEK SECRET
A COLD CREEK HOLIDAY
THE COWBOY'S CHRISTMAS MIRACLE

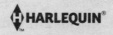

HARLEQUIN®

SPECIAL EDITION
Life, Love and Family

HARLEQUIN®

SPECIAL EDITION

Life, Love & Family

Save **$1.00**
on the purchase of ANY
Harlequin® Special Edition book.

Available wherever books are sold, including most bookstores, supermarkets, drugstores and discount stores.

Save **$1.00**

on the purchase of any Harlequin® Special Edition book.

Coupon valid until April 30, 2018.
Redeemable at participating outlets in the U.S. and Canada only.
Not redeemable at Barnes & Noble stores. Limit one coupon per customer.

52615535

5 65373 00076 2   (8100)0 12344

® and ™ are trademarks owned and used by the trademark owner and/or its licensee.
© 2018 Harlequin Enterprises Limited

HSEMMCOUPBPA0118

Get 2 Free Books,
Plus 2 Free Gifts -
just for
trying the
*Reader
Service!*

Get 2 Free Books,
Plus 2 Free Gifts —
just for trying the Reader Service!

Get 2 Free Books,
Plus 2 Free Gifts—
just for trying the Reader Service!

 HARLEQUIN *Presents*